PRAISE FOR "MY DEAR RAPIST"

"This memoir is about being raised in a high demand religion, the aftermath of a traumatic event, and how the effects are woven into every faucet of your life and how they can last a lifetime."

- CHANTEL BENDER

"This book is honest. It shares personal stories and emotions that people can relate to, even though their experiences of life are not the same. The author tells us that our experiences shape us, they give us knowledge that we can learn from, yet they don't define us. Something overwhelming throughout was hope. Even in the darkest moments, where it seemed redemption was impossible, there was an underlying hope."

- KATHRYN SMUTEK

"This book is much more than a manuscript, it's difficult to define because it brings so many conflicts with institutions and women's societal, religious expectations and toxic ideals into play. It is very easy to see my own struggles within the book and the ability to reflect honestly that many of these struggles shaped us as women. The way it is written is compelling, the way that there is a lesson that is learned and then the direct or indirect correlation with the lesson in her confronting her abuser. There is power in each message."

- MICHELLE JENSEN TALLEY, KANSAS DEPT OF HEALTH AND ENVIRONMENT

"The story of a woman who confronts her rapist by writing him letters showcasing her childhood and young adulthood growing up in the Mormon Church." This is who I am. This is what you did to me."

"I would describe this book as a gut-wrenching, raw, reflective, and insightful narrative written as a memoir. It is bold and courageous. She is so descriptive; she pulls you in. She paints pictures here, a beautiful, striking picture-painting artist of words. I love her closing to each letter; the foreword takes its only departure from the rapist as the recipient. It provides a bookend to protecting the hearts and minds of family and friends with China wrapping and giving them permission to not travel on this bumpy ride with her. The introduction takes the reader to the deepest, darkest place she fought so hard to get too. It was the space in her soul that was the most violently destroyed, and she brought it out somehow in all its terrifying, dangerous form."

"Like a red pill for those disenchanted with Mormonism; a wakeup call to the abuse we're groomed for as young girls in the church."

"Ginger is telling her story from childhood church life, which is so very true. Her experience with her rapist devastated her and her dreams. He stole something sacred, pure, and sweet from her. It is Witty! Funny! Truthful! SAD! A story absolutely worth telling!"

"This is a story about a brave woman who was raped physically, mentally, emotionally, and spiritually by another person and a religion claiming to be her only saving grace. It is a story about recovery and the need to tell and write so she could process what happened. As a recovering Jehovah's Witness, so many things in the name of the one true religion resonated with me."

MY DEAR RAPIST

NEVER YOURS,

Ginger Price

MY

DEAR

RAPIST

NEVER YOURS,

Ginger Price

The contents of this book include graphic
descriptions of the following and may be
emotionally or mentally challenging for some.

Reader discretion is advised. If you are struggling
with any of these, please discuss with your
healthcare provider and take time for self-care.

Physical abuse
Sexual abuse
Suicide idealization
Mental and Emotional manipulation
Eating disorders
Body dysmorphia
Mental illness
Racism and racial slurs
Homophobia
Sexism
Misogyny

DISCLAIMER:

Most names in this book have been changed
to protect the privacy of the those involved.

TABLE OF CONTENTS

The Dairyman's Daughter
22 - 38

Sexually Ignorant Circus Freak
39 - 48

Chosen
49 - 63

Atypically Loved
64 - 75

Haunted in Jackson
76 - 88

Hostage
89 - 133

Called to Serve
134 - 158

Detroit
159 - 190

Adventures in Levi-Loving
191 - 201

Celestial Porn Star

202 - 216

A Jersey Atheist

217 - 251

Zion's Heartbeat

252 - 272

You

273 - 315

My Mormon Prince

316 - 343

I Am No Eve

344 - 361

An Apostate Traitress

362 - 393

Afterword

394 - 398

Acknowledgements

399 - 400

Author Bio

401

FORWARD

My Dearest Family and Friends,

My Dear Rapist will be a tough and heavy book to read. My story is about rape, it is about abuse, it is about the silence of patriarchal institutions, and at times it contains very strong and explicit language. It is about the discovery of sex, masturbation, and pornography addictions in my former Mormon world, and about the control structures that create and shelter monsters. In stating this, I must take time to acknowledge that I have many Mormon family members and friends who do not struggle with these things and I know that they, as well as their husbands, fathers, brothers, and sons, also do not struggle with these things. I would also like to state that there are many Mormon men who do respect and honor women and who do not treat them disparagingly or in abusive ways.

However, it is through my dating experiences, the countless number of stories I have personally heard, and confirmations by several bishops that I do believe there is a rampant problem of sex addictions within the Mormon church. I also believe there is an unspoken layer of women who are experiencing "betrayal trauma" and grief over their husbands' use of pornography. Something needs to change in Mormonism. Healthy sex-education does not exist in the church, and language pertaining to shame, worthiness, and the continuous, doctrinal pursuit of obtaining a perfect body is only adding to the problem.

At times, expressions of both love and angst toward being raised in the Mormon church will be felt. For some, this may be confusing; for others, there will be an understanding that these opposing truths can exist in the same space. I hold no anger or resentment toward my parents and former community. What I do hold is frustration and contempt toward any institution that does not create safe places to discuss sex in open, honest, and comfortable ways. From my experience, the two institutions that need a transformation on this issue are Mormonism and the USA Olympics. As the first tends to shield its members from thriving sexual conversations, the latter tends to promote rampant and promiscuous sex while handing out hundreds of thousands of free condoms during the Olympic Games.

With this in mind, the National Olympic Committee should be doing more to protect the general public from their aggressive, narcissistic athletes—athletes whom the world puts on pedestals, whom the world cheers on, and whom our very children look up to. These athletes hang up their gold medals, take off their Olympic attire, but then continue to prey on women around the world with the same levels of testosterone and aggression they held throughout the Olympic Village. Surely, I am not the only one in this world who has endured gender-based violence from an Olympic athlete.

I go further into depth on this topic in my second book.

In these pages is my perspective that a church claiming to have God's sole power on earth, through male-centered authority, should not be having such a significant and rampant problem with porn and sex-addicted men. If we are going to strive to better protect women and children from abuse, rape, and betrayal trauma, we must create more balanced and raw conversations surrounding sex. And it starts with education. After all, should we not follow the counsel of Brigham Young, second prophet of the Mormon Church when he said, "When you educate a man; you educate a man. When you educate a woman; you educate a generation."

At the end of the day, if you are able to read the pages of this book and can still continue being my friend, I thank you. Perception is our own reality, and for those who are capable of holding space for my reality and not allow it to affect your love of the church, I thank you even more. I do love and honor my family and friends who are still a part of the Mormon faith. Though I no longer choose to align with its teachings, I do acknowledge their choice to continue on in the faith and understand their reasons for staying.

I can only hope that I will be given the same respect that I am extending toward others as I open up about my experiences and reflections. My purpose is not to make the Mormon church look bad; my purpose is simply to share my story. My story is unfortunately filled with harmful and abusive experiences, as well as doctrines that fueled intense feelings of shame that thrived uninterrupted beneath the surface.

It is my hope that this book empowers those who feel silenced and help victims know that healing transforms when our pain and trauma is articulated into the air. It is now time. Time for my healing to transfigure as I spit out eighteen years of silence through the pages of my published work.

With much love,

Ginger

INTRODUCTION

"Who can find a virtuous woman?
For her price is far above rubies."

It was fall of 2021. I stood at the bathroom sink trembling, struggling to feel the warmth of the water trickle through the palms of my hands. Looking into the mirror, I could not take my eyes off the horrified stranger staring back. My eye sockets were deep and hollow, skin ashen and flat, mascara smeared and ruined. I was a decrepit corpse with a heartbeat, and I was seeing the truth for the first time.

I had spent three years peeling away the layers of my Mormon identity, and I had now been brought to the bare bones. This was a new identity to confront—one I was never fully conscious of. I was a victim and I knew, without a shadow of a doubt, that my soul was approaching its last breath.

To those who know and love me most, the woman in the mirror is Ginger. I am the friend, the sister, the daughter, the mother, and the wife. I am a woman filled with compassion, grace, love, and humor, a country girl with a bit of spice and the farmer's daughter who is everything nice. I am a gregarious, identical twin with an unassuming, adventurous soul.

But none of them really know. They have no idea who I am under this facade, not even my own husband, I thought to myself. *How can I blame them? This part of me has been buried into the furthest corners of my toes for sixteen exhausting years. My God, psilocybin has unearthed a past that was never confronted. What the hell have I done? Is the corpse in the mirror a warning? A prophecy? Does the medicine or the facilitator know something I don't?*

My thoughts were interrupted by a soft knock on the bathroom door. "Ginger, are you okay?" Sariah, the facilitator asked.

Looking down at my wrinkled, cold hands, I responded in an almost silent whisper, "I'm not sure. I'll be out in a moment."

Lifting my head, I cautiously looked back into the mirror and took a long, final look at myself. I was downright scared. The skeletal form was so haunting, so eerie. I could feel the marrow in my bones quivering in dismay.

You're anorexic. You've been abusing laxatives. If you stay on this course and continue to starve yourself, you're going to die. It's time you accept you have an eating disorder. It's time you stop shrinking. It's time to get help.

I dried my hands on the towel and opened the door. Sariah was leaning against the wall, her long, auburn hair laying tenderly upon her shoulders. A nervous smile peeked through her anxious eyes, dark brown and questioning.

"How are you feeling?" she asked.

I went to open my mouth, but paused. I was having trouble articulating the words into the sacred air between us. After a few moments, the only words I could put together were, "I am terrified."

I had just spent seven and a half hours on Sariah's couch, and though my body had been frozen in a psychedelic state, my tongue was loosened for the second time since I left him. In sheer despair and fear, I had shared with the facilitator the details of his rape, abuse, and neverending sentiments of committing suicide and murder. Like a haunted ghost from my past, visions of him resurrected from within, forcing me to stare him in the face and feel his darkened presence once more. Worms slithered in and out of every orifice of his body, hissing into my ear that after being his victim for almost a year, his rot had infiltrated me to my core.

"Nobody has ever said that to me before, Ginger," she said, interrupting my thoughts again. I studied Sariah's face; my mind was completely numb to her statement. One thing was certain, she was feeling my terror and she wasn't quite sure how to process it.

We hugged goodbye, and as I reached for the doorknob, I barely heard Sariah ask, "Are you okay to drive home?"

I solemnly moved my way through the front door, never offering a response to her question.

No, I'm not okay. I shouldn't be doing anything right now. I don't feel my body. I want to sleep. What the hell just happened? Why did the mushrooms bring this forward? I wasn't prepared for this. I don't have a single person I can talk to. He's an Olympian, an actor in Hollywood. He will kill me if I speak out.

I need to get home. I need a therapist. Where is the

nearest mental hospital?

It was dark outside and the fall air was brisk and chilly. I climbed into my white Toyota RAV and started the engine, but could not put the gear into drive. I sat there for what felt like hours, stunned. Contemplating what I should do, I looked up toward Sariah's condo and could see her peeking through the blinds, watching me. Just as the white, rectangular blind moved back into place, my phone buzzed. I looked down and saw Sariah's name blinking brightly in the dark.

"Ginger, why are you just sitting there? Are you okay?" she inquired.

"I don't know. I think I need food. I'm craving fried mushrooms and Dr. Pepper." I hung up the phone, put the car in gear, and drove three miles to the nearest Crown Burger. Within a mile, I passed by my old apartment complex, the place where it had all happened. God, what were the chances. *My first psilocybin ceremony, less than a mile from where he raped and abused me. What the actual. . . .*

After ordering my food, I sat in my car and watched a few homeless men wandering the parking lot, begging for food. Dumping copious amounts of salt onto my battered, deep-fried mushrooms, I attempted to wrap my head around the sheer terror of what two and a half grams of psilocybin had brought forth. Stuck in an unexplainable, out-of-body time warp, I eventually made a reckless decision and drove home.

I spent the next six weeks in a dissociated state, groveling and begging for a divine, invisible power to relieve me from my body. I had craved death before, but this time, it was different. In the past, my identity and self-worth lied in being a precious ruby that was set into a golden, Mormon spirit. Before, I had Jesus and his murderous cross to throw my grief and pain toward. Now I had none of these.

I no longer had a Savior to give this uprooting to, or a tribe of Mormons to share my burdens with. There was no safety in opening up to family or friends. Being vulnerable with my loved ones would make me a living testimony of what happens to those who deny the faith and leave the Mormon Garden of Eden. Who would believe me? I had just paid a Shaman to sit with me safely through a psilocybin ceremony, a drug none of them would understand, and a Shaman, who in their eyes, would be doing devil's work.

Together, they would all confirm with one another that life outside our ancestral "one true religion" had taken me down a path of self and familial destruction, leading me to a barren road filled with alcoholism, infidelity, drug addiction, and sheer misery. I was worthless, and the skeleton in the mirror was evidence that my soul had turned to ash, with no virtuous ruby existing anywhere in its pile.

The Divine never caved to my pleas, never did relieve me from this earthly life. Instead, an unseen power guided me into the hands of licensed medical professionals who understood the healing powers of plant medicine and somatic therapy. These forms of therapy became the merciful savior I needed to help me work through my buried, compacted trauma.

Several weeks into therapy, I was home alone when an omniscient, internal voice stopped me dead in my tracks. My children were in school, my husband was working 3,000 miles away in Alaska, and I could not deny that something beautiful and divine was speaking to me. I had just stepped out of the shower and girded a plush, navy-blue towel around my body. Moving through the bathroom door, I bent over and began wrapping a second, matching towel around my hair. The sunlight pushed its rays through the hall window, and as I straightened myself upward, my feet froze to the faux-weathered Formica floor.

It's time to write. You will write a book and you will call it, My Dear Rapist. *You will write him letters. You will tell him of significant events, in all stages of your life, that have made you human. Your letters will help him see why you were never meant to be an insignificant object, kept hidden behind closed doors. It is time he knows who you are, and that you were so much more than a feminine piece of art to use and abuse with his muscular, savage hands. He never knew you then, but he* **MUST** *know you now.*

So, write, Ginger. This is what you must do. You must write him letters. You own the narrative of him. You own how to heal from him. You own how to let go of him. These letters will be the safe place to **FINALLY** *tell your story.*

And so, I did. I gave in to my Joseph Smith experience and I answered the heavenly message. In the past two years, I have taken 5,840 days of silence, formed a language for my open, bleeding wounds, and transferred 200,000 words into letters.

These epistles were composed from a place of deep authenticity, reflection, and integrity. They were drafted from my two-story, cedar Alaskan home that is tucked away in snow-covered birch, spruce, and cottonwood trees. Snugged deep into the Chugach Mountain Range, it is a home made up of four beautiful children, a twelve-pound Maltipoo, and a handsome, protective, loving husband.

I have no big accolades to boast about. I have no Olympic medals, no bragging rights to Hollywood films and entertainers, no formal education, and no aspiring career. I am not a published author, like him, where he describes disturbing, predatory behavior and shares how to manipulate women into having sex. I have none of these, absolutely nothing of what he has.

What I do have are three simple achievements that will be placed upon my life's resume. They are Mother, Wife, and Survivor. If all goes right, I may now have the opportunity to add the title of author to my resume. I have risen from my own ashes and no longer ache for death. I see it now, that writing these letters were never really meant for him—they were solely meant for me. They have saved me, they have healed me, and they have helped me to discover that my priceless, precious ruby never did burn to the ground. It was there all along, just hidden beside the silence of my own voice.

My virtuous ruby sparkled vibrant and clear on the day I finally confronted him. With the help of the Divine, I was given something most women never receive: a chance to lay sixteen years of buried trauma at the feet of my rapist. I am finally free. I no longer bear the weight of his animalistic, inhumane actions. The burden is now for him to own. And while he now sits with the heavy weight of his actions, I get to move on and revel in his response of, "I believe you. You were always more honest than I ever was. I believe you."

In the beginning I wrote as a **Victim**.
Today, I write as a **Survivor**.

CHAPTER 1

THE DAIRYMAN'S DAUGHTER

"The family is ordained of God. Marriage between man and woman is essential to His eternal plan... Happiness in family life is most likely to be achieved when founded upon the teachings of Jesus Christ... By divine design, fathers are to preside over their families in love and righteousness and are responsible to provide the necessities of life and protection for their families. Mothers are primarily responsible for the nurture of their children."

(The Family: A Proclamation to the World (1995, November) Ensign, 25, p. 102)

My Dear Rapist,

I grew up in a tiny Mormon community on the Utah-Idaho border, a farming town of roughly two hundred and fifty people. The majority of families in town were Caucasian, with perhaps three Hispanic families scattered throughout its 4.8-square-mile radius. My father and mother began their lives together in 1973, on a half-acre property in between the town's main stop sign and the old industrial railroad tracks, which run north-south through fields of hay and desert brush.

A half-mile north of my parents' home lay the family farm, which was my father's childhood home. The farm consisted of a small, light tan, two-bedroom home, a milking barn, 150 cows, a dozen baby calves, two large hay sheds, and about 300 acres of land to harvest. Next to Grandma and Grandpa's house was Great-Grandma Christofferson's house: a tiny, red-bricked, one-bedroom home where she resided alone until her death.

To this day, my hometown has no grocery store, no gas station, and no stoplight. The fifteen-minute drive through town often alternates between a lovely smell of manure and a summer scent of fresh-cut hay. After living seventeen years and nine months in this town, these two fragrances have seared a home within my nose and will forever remind me of my pleasant, country upbringing.

On July 6, 1978, my father made a surprising phone call to a handful of family members and friends. "We are bringing home twins," he exclaimed. Phone call after phone call was made to loved ones about the birth of two new babies and yet, nobody believed him. My mother had gone into the hospital fully expecting to give birth to one baby. Ultrasounds had not always been used at my mother's prenatal check-ups and when the doctor had listened for the heartbeat, all he'd ever heard was one. At 10:05 p.m., my mother gave birth to a healthy, happy baby girl. Three minutes later, the doctor informed her another was on its way, and before my mother and father knew it, I showed up feet-first.

I like to believe my sister was taking up too much space and I felt some embryonic need to kick her out of my mother's womb. Also, I'm quite positive I planned all along to keep myself unknown to both the doctors and my mother. I had no idea that this incessant need to hide and shrink, even as a fetus, would end up being a constant theme well into my forties.

It would take several days for my parents to come up with a name for me. My mother could not decide between the names Virginia or Ginger and in the end, I thank God they went with the porn star name over the old lady name.

Prior to the birth of my twin and I, my mother had my two brothers, who are roughly two years apart. With four children all under the age of four, this sudden level of madness likely factored into why my parents waited another twelve years before they would have another: their final baby boy.

I had the perfect childhood. My upbringing was filled with family, adventure, friendships, community, sports, and a simplicity and freedom that only a child of the '80s would understand. Summer days were sweaty, dirty, and long. My sister, friends, and I explored the Bear River Bottoms to the East, filled with lots of brush, shrubbery, and trees to hide beneath. We climbed the rolling hills to the west, having picnics in mud-covered clothes and shoes. We went swimming in the local canal, never noticing or minding the cow shit aimlessly floating by our black inner tubes. We ran through and played games within fields of barley, wheat, and corn.

We played hide and go seek on the entirety of the farm, hiding in tractors, combines, and cow stalls. We loved allowing the baby calves to suck on our fingers as we waited for our father to deliver the extra-large, plastic bottles filled with their momma's milk. A most favorite pastime was tormenting the momma cows by grabbing onto their tails, slapping their beefy, hardened rumps, and forcing them to pull us angrily through the shit-filled pen as if we were water skiing on a large, open lake.

We spent many summers days and nights swimming in Hansen's Pond. While we acted like the Little Mermaid with our girlfriends from church, cute boys moved across the zip line and dropped ten feet below into the water. Our fathers ran the BBQ grill and our mothers were in charge of organizing random dishes of potluck-style food.

During the winter, we would ice-skate on the pond with a Styrofoam cup filled with homemade, hot chocolate in our hands. We were always willing and ready to find some sort of excuse to be outdoors with our friends. We constantly played on and underneath the railroad tracks, ever on the lookout for homeless men in abandoned railroad carts or peeing off the slow-moving locomotive as it went by.

We loved to put pennies on the tracks just prior to

the train coming through, and then see if we could find the flattened coin in the rocks or weeds close by. A metal tunnel runs east and west underneath the tracks, one of our most favorite places to climb through and explore. We would often use our imaginations and wonder what kind of monsters we would stumble upon, both in insect and human form. When the movie *It* by Steven King hit the theaters, I was certain the terrifying clown lived inside this tunnel, which was fifty feet away from my home.

If we weren't exploring the country, we were making up skits, songs, and dances, and begging for entrance fees from the adults to watch our prized, yet less-than-perfect performances.

We played basketball in the farm shed, softball at the town park, and volleyball at the local Mormon church. We rode horses, bikes, and made pathetic attempts at skateboarding. We had church girl's camp, sleepovers, lemonade stands, and we even walked or rode our bicycles to the small gas station three miles away. There we would buy penny candy, pixie sticks, candy cigarettes, Big League Chew bubble gum, and soda for 50 cents. We stayed up late on the weekends, my girlfriends and I, eagerly awaiting the chance to toilet paper our favorite bishop's home. In the Mormon Church, a bishop is considered to be the father or head pastor of the congregation.

In Mormonism, Saturdays were our special day, a day to get ready for Sunday. After a good day of being with friends, the evening was spent bathing and prepping for church the next day. Every Saturday evening after our bath, my twin sister and I would pull out the wooden cutting board, grab our favorite Pac-Man puzzle, and spend hours on our tummies, seeing how fast we could put together the 100 pieces. The words from the Mormon primary school song "Saturday" best describes our family's weekend routine:

> *Saturday is a special day.*
> *It's the day we get ready for Sunday:*
> *We clean the house, and we shop at the store,*
> *So, we won't have to work until Monday.*
> *We brush our clothes, and we shine our shoes,*
> *And we call it our get-the-work-done day.*
> *Then we trim our nails, and we shampoo our hair,*
> *So, we can be ready for Sunday.*

(Words & Music: Robinson, Rita S. "Saturday." Children's Songbook Church of Jesus Christ of Latter Day Saints, 1989, p.196.)

I loved this song. No, I didn't just love it, I adored it and I memorized it. Whenever we sang this song at church, I felt so much pride in it, because our mother truly did wonders when it came to getting four kids ready for the most special day of the week. Along with getting cleaned up on Saturday evenings, my mother would make sure to stick a beef roast in the Crock-Pot with a Lipton Onion Soup mix. We were fortunate to smell the succulent, savory cow cooking all night long and into the following morning.

Once Sunday morning came, my twin and I would spend hours getting ready for the three-hour block of church. I desperately wanted my hair and dress to be perfect—not so much for myself, but because I believed that one day, I would potentially marry one of the young boys from church. I wanted to be perfect, and I wanted everyone in my community to know I was devoted to our faith, even as a young Primary girl.

Oh, how I deeply loved and cherished my community and church growing up. Everything revolved around this tiny, farming town. It offered up the best of friends and the best of times. Church was not just a Sunday thing; church was an everyday thing. It wove itself into every single aspect of our lives. Services on Sunday were long, but felt especially lengthy and tiresome on the Sundays in which we were required to fast.

I do not know if you recall this, but you did come to church with me one time. It was the congregation for single members in South Salt Lake, specifically the Millcreek ward. Looking back, I recall how often you vocalized your disdain for Mormonism. It leaves me to wonder why you chose to come with me to church, even if it was just once. Although you had a one-time church experience with me, I do feel the need to explain the dynamics and structure of our church to you. Certainly, this single experience would not have given insight into the uniqueness and devotion that Mormonism requires of its members.

The first hour of church is when families sit together and listen to either clergy or members from the congregation give self-prepared sermons concurrent to Mormonism. We also watch musical performances put on by other children, families, or church members. During this hour, the most important part of church takes place: the Sacrament. Young boys between the ages of twelve and eighteen break bread and fill little cups with water to pass to the congregation.

Boys who pass the sacrament are generally required to wear white shirts, ties, and dress pants. The expectation is to generally look like tiny little businessmen with clean, crisp, perfected haircuts and no indication of facial hair. Before passing the emblems to the congregation, a separate prayer is recited over both the bread and the water.

The prayers are expected to be recited to perfection, and if any mistake is made, the prayer must be started over. The fragments of bread represent the broken body of Christ and the water represents the blood of Christ that he shed for the world.

This part of the service is *the* reason we are meant to be at church. If you let the sacrament tray pass by you and you do not partake of it, others may notice. The bishop and his counselors sit on the stand facing the members of the congregation and watch the members each partake of, or dismiss, the serving tray that passes by. Being unworthy to take the sacrament can be a very shameful and humiliating experience.

Mormon scriptures teach serious consequences of partaking of the bread and water unworthily. One such scripture in the Book of Mormon states, "Ye shall not suffer any one knowingly to partake of my flesh and blood unworthily, when ye shall minister it; For whoso eateth and drinketh my flesh and blood unworthily eateth and drinketh damnation to his soul" *(The Book of Mormon, 3 Nephi 18:28-29)*.

I let that little plastic sacrament tray pass by many

times when we were together. I felt incredibly unworthy and was filled with immense guilt over what I allowed you to do to me. Now is not the time to go into detail about why I believed God was disgusted with me. I simply need you to know that I deemed myself unworthy of God's love and avoided reaching out to those trays because of you, and that would someday lead me to allow the Mormon God to completely disintegrate from my life. Thankfully, this dissolution of the Mormon God would allow me to one day heal and hold you accountable for your abuse.

However, during the time I was with you, my nonparticipation of the sacrament eroded my self-esteem and self-love just as much as your offenses toward me did. This information may be irrelevant to you, but to me, it was a toll on my mental health, and a factor in why I continued to stay with you.

When we were together, I could not wait for this portion of the church service to come to an end. I hated being reminded each week that I was not worthy of this symbolism of Christ's flesh and blood. I would suffer through this first hour ridden with ugly tears and pray that the next hour would arrive quickly.

The second hour was broken up according to age and is called Sunday School. Nursery children under the age of three gathered into a room designed just for infants and toddlers. Primary children between three years old and eleven years old would be divided up and meet in tiny rooms with individualized lessons.

Once the individualized lesson was given, the Primary would come together for the last half of the hour and sing Mormon-composed children's songs. Young Men's and Young Women's Group, those between the ages of twelve and eighteen years old, would follow the same pattern as the primary, but they would gather separately and among their own sex. The Relief Society and the Priesthood embraced anyone over the age of eighteen, but they also followed suit and gathered as separate sexes.

Sunday School consisted of one hour discussing and dissecting the different doctrines and scriptures of the church. Each year, Sunday School rotates between studying the Book of Mormon, the Old Testament, the New Testament, and the Doctrine and Covenants. The Doctrine and Covenants is considered holy scripture revealed to Joseph Smith, founder of the Church of Jesus Christ of Latter-Day Saints, by the voice of God.

During the third hour, women over the age of eighteen gather together to discuss the gospel and church teachings strictly from the female perspective, all the while loving and supporting each other within their assigned, eternal roles as a divinely appointed mother and wife. The men gather together with the same intent, also discussing the importance of their role as fathers and as Priesthood leaders who hold God's authority on earth, with sole permission to act in his name.

Every Sunday is laid out in this pattern, except for one. The one exemption is a signature day called Fast Sunday. On the fourth Sunday of each month, the last two hours remain the same, but it is the hour with the sacrament that is changed. On this day, members come in a state of fasting and prayer. Adults and children over the age of eight are required to go without food and water for a twenty-four-hour period.

As members gather together in Sacrament meeting in fasting and in prayer, the microphone is left open for anyone to share their testimony of principles such as: the truth of The Book of Mormon, eternal families, Joseph Smith's role as a prophet, Jesus, Temples, tithing, and any faith-promoting story that could inspire someone sitting in the congregation to be better or to believe more strongly.

These faith-promoting stories can be anything from a miracle of finding their keys, to a travel log of road rage, to the dream of spending eternity with a dead cat. Sometimes, you would leave testimony meeting feeling invigorated and full of faith, and other times you would leave wondering why the hell Brother or Sister So-and-So had felt inspired to share a discombobulated story of nothing.

In all reality, this is one of the things that makes Mormonism unique. Mormons are really wonderful at finding a faith-promoting story in anything and everything they come across. I did this often, even while being with you. The fact you showed up to church with me was faith-promoting. I thought for sure my prayers were being answered and that I was on the road to converting you. My arrogance was so stout, so vigorous, that of course you showed up in that Mormon pew as a result of my faith. It was all me, or so I thought.

We both know that I was wrong. We both know the only reason you came to church with me was because it was one step closer for you to get into my pants. Your chiseled, Olympic body sitting next to me in church was never faith-promoting, it was sex-promoting. I had no idea that a decade later, I would attempt to use your abuse as a faith-promoting story over a Mormon pulpit. I ignorantly shamed myself, claiming I deserved your abuse due to my inability to follow the promptings of the Holy Ghost. I shared your atrocities for the first time, in the hopes that it would create faith in others. Perhaps it did, but for me, it halted my own healing to blame myself in front of the congregation.

Mormonism spills over into our daily lives, it is not just a Sunday service. Moment by moment, day by day, we are to always stand as a witness of Christ, which essentially means we are to stand as perfect examples and representatives of the Mormon Church. It is vital to our existence that we not only save ourselves but that we seek to save others.

Weeks are filled with youth activities under the long arm of the church. Sporting events on top of weekly lessons and activities keep us very busy and involved with our local ward community and our tribe. If we are not spending time with our church tribe, we are spending time with family and friends, who are all members of the church.

For me, as much as I loved church and community gatherings, it was the weekly tradition after church that I looked forward to most. After the final prayer was given and church was officially declared over, my family would rush back home and strip out of our church clothes as fast as possible.

The duty of the kids was to set the table, while our mother pulled out the pot roast, mashed the potatoes, made the gravy, and steamed the corn. It only took a matter of minutes for my siblings and I to inhale our mama's delectable food. As we lay on the couch in a food coma with bloated bellies, our father would still be sitting at the table, dipping his homemade roll into the gravy and slowly slurping the last of its drippings into his mouth. I always knew when I heard my father's slurp that he was not only almost finished, but that I could walk back into the kitchen and find evidence of the juicy, beefy gravy slowly sliding down his thick, bushy beard.

When the dishes were cleaned and we had recovered from the overindulgence of our mother's home-cooked, country meal, it was time to go to Grandma and Grandpa's farm. It wasn't just our family that would make their way to the farm after church, it was the *entire* McKnight Family. This included four uncles, four aunts, twelve cousins, and my immediate family, totaling twenty-eight children and ten adults congregating into Grandma and Grandpa's tiny, two-bedroom home.

Sundays at Grandma and Grandpa's house was pure bliss, an archetype of the Mormon Celestial Kingdom. The Sabbath day was spent playing a family game of kickball or maybe Grandma teaching us how to pull old-fashioned taffy. If it wasn't taffy, it would be homemade popcorn balls and homemade fudge, my favorite being her white fudge recipe.

Toward the evening, we would all gather into the small living room and watch old-school Disney movies and *America's Funniest Home Videos* on the vintage, boxed television set. Grandpa wandered around the house in his blue coveralls, swatting at flies with his plastic, dollar store fly swatter. Sometimes he would tease one of us grandkids by smacking us on the head, hoping to convince us with his mischievous smile that a fly had landed on us, and it was his duty to kill it wherever it landed.

The farm was truly one big country playground that included space to saddle up the horses and go for long rides through the fields and into the hills. We always made sure to stop by the farmhouse and say hi to Grandma and Grandpa on the way home.

Christmas on the farm was even more magical and empyrean. Families began to show up by 9:00 a.m. for Christmas breakfast. Grandma always had sausage, eggs, and bacon cooking, while Grandpa would do his one and only job: butter the toast. As each family gathered inside and nibbled on breakfast, the grandkids converged into the large back room to show off the one or two toys we were each allowed to bring. By afternoon, we were playing bingo, grazing on snacks, or nibbling on a light lunch until the entire clan assembled together to exchange gifts.

There was never a bad memory or a bad time when it came to Grandma and Grandpa McKnight and the farm. There were, however, a few unfortunate events that happened on the homestead.

The first tragedy I can recall was the discovery of our Great Grandmother's dead body in Grandma Ella's bathroom. My twin and I were the first to enter the bathroom, and my mother was not able to push us out the door fast enough. My mother had tried to shield our eight-year-old innocent eyes from the lifeless form lying between the toilet and the counter, but it was too late. As frightening as it should have been to a child, it wasn't. Even at that age, I knew she really wasn't dead. I knew I would get to see her again because her spirit was floating toward Heaven to be with Jesus.

The second tragedy on Grandma and Grandpa's farm involved the big pool behind the milking barn. This was not a swimming pool, but a large pool filled with shit from 150 cows. Every Monday, my father, my grandfather, and my uncle would scrape the cow corral and push all manure into this pit. As a child, I was petrified to walk by it, knowing that if I fell in, I would die a lonely, stinky death. So, when I heard the story of my aunt jumping in it to save her dog, she suddenly became a superhero to me. I must admit, I do wonder at times why I never shared this as a faith-promoting story over the church pulpit.

The third tragedy took place when I was a bit older. The boys learned the harder parts of running a farm while the girls were given the job of feeding the baby calves and washing the barn after each milking. During the summers, we moved hand pipes in the fields, cleaned out the cattle stalls, and refilled them with fresh hay.

At one point, my twin and I were taught how to drive the farm's antique tractor. One afternoon, we had our chunky, rubber milk boots on, and for some unknown reason, my sister tried to move the tractor and accidentally started it out in high gear. I was standing right in her path of destruction, and my middle school brain didn't think to run to the left or right, rather it told me to run in a straight line. As she came up quickly behind me, I tripped in my clunky boots. I was confident I was going to be squashed by the very egg that had split from me in my mother's womb. But out of nowhere, a neighbor hopped onto the tractor and pulled it to a halt, saving me from an untimely death.

My dear rapist, my farm girl childhood was a gift, and I had no plans to ever take you near the family farm. I knew that your presence would have left a stain on an era that was filled with innocence, adventure, friendships, and an abundance of love. I knew that marrying you would have damaged my relationship with this wonderful family of mine, which was nothing but heaven on earth. You were the complete opposite of my father who protected, provided, and lived up to the high expectations of an honorable, Mormon man. You didn't nurture me like my humble, quiet mother.

If Mormonism is right and the family unit is indeed eternalized, then I hope every human being will have the chance to experience something like the McKnight family experience. Sharing my upbringing with you brings to surface some major questions I have for you.

I cannot help but wonder, what kind of family life did you experience as a child? Did you have aunts, uncles, cousins, and grandparents that loved you unconditionally? What was it like growing up in an inner city with several millions of people? Was your father a gentle man or was he abusive? Who were your examples? What led you to live a life of deceit? How did you justify yourself playing mental games with the many women who walked into your life and into your bed? What happened to disintegrate your conscience and discolor your soul?

I am inclined to believe that you did not have the same wonderful upbringing that I had been gifted. Occasionally, I am asked if I am grateful for my upbringing in Mormonism and its correlation to such a positive childhood. What I have come to realize is that my gratitude lies toward having a strong support system, filled with loving family and friends.

I am grateful that not just my parents, but my friend's parents, were available to mentor, be an example to me, and help raise me. Growing up, I believed the only way to achieve this happy, balanced, and thriving support system was through the Mormon Church. I now know that positive communities of support exist in and outside of the one, true church.

So, I ask you, my dear rapist, was it a lack of family love and structure that led you to becoming someone who would victimize women around the world? If there is any validity to my question, I pity you. As I consider this as an option, it moves me to want to go back in time and ask you just one question when we were together. Perhaps if I had asked this then, my hatred for you today would be a little more softened.

My dear rapist, as a child, did you feel loved by your family?

Never Yours,
The Dairyman's Daughter

CHAPTER 2

SEXUALLY IGNORANT CIRCUS FREAK

"Among the most common sexual sins our young people commit are necking and petting. Not only do these improper relations often lead to fornication, pregnancy, and abortions --- all ugly sins --- but in and of themselves they are pernicious evils..."

(Kimball, Spencer, The Miracle of Forgiveness, p. 65)

My Dear Rapist,

When I met you at the age of twenty-seven, I was a gullible and uneducated woman, especially when it came to sex. My innocence does not only shine through in the following example of a conversation that took place just months before we exchanged numbers, but I am fairly certain I glistened naivety the first time you laid eyes on me.

I had just begun employment at the job where you and I had met. My new boss and I were sitting in the company van at a Target parking lot. She was in the driver's seat; I was in the passenger seat. The sun was bearing down on us and there were a handful of people walking by. Some seemed to notice the two of us engaged in lighthearted conversation, while others gave us no attention.

She was just a few years older than I, but she was my superior at work. I had only been working under her supervision for several months, and we had hit it off well. At times, it felt like a friendship was forming, and this was one of those times. Her long blonde hair, big brown eyes, slim figure, and nice perky breasts made her California personality and physical appearance fit in easily within the Mormon bubble. Though she was not a native to Utah, she looked like a typical Utah Barbie Doll.

I found her beautiful, confident, and unrestrained. There was a level of maturity and experience about her that I deeply longed for. I knew I could ask her anything, and so I was not surprised when my out-of-the-blue, risqué question brought an amused smile to her face, followed by uncontrollable laughter.

"Hey, Lonnie," I said. "When someone is having sex,

how does the penis find the hole? Is it similar to a worm and it just kind of slithers its way in?"

Yes, I was twenty-seven years old and I did not quite understand how the penis actually entered the vagina. With tears in her eyes and laughter booming out of her mouth, my new boss-friend proceeded to show me, in the driver's scat of a Target parking lot, just how the slithering creature should be guided into its proper place. At this point, I was no longer paying attention to anyone outside of our work van, rather I was fixated on my new boss and her willingness to provide me with a bit of sex education.

I do not know if it was just me that was this sexually illiterate, or if the majority of my friends and family were also this naïve when it came to the mechanics of sex, but I do not remember ever having "the talk" from my parents. I do not blame them for this, nor do I resent them. For one, as a child of the '80s, I was never home. Second, these conversations just did not happen in the culture I was raised in.

I do recall learning most sex definitions from Sean, a boy I went to elementary school with. Sean also taught me that if you're going to make out in the back of the movie theater with your girlfriend, you should probably figure out how to put her shirt back on correctly before you leave the darkness of the theater. We may not have had access to porn magazines in those days, but what we did have access to was watching the semi-innocent shenanigans of Sean with his girlfriends.

For the most part, the discussion of sex in any form was taboo and naughty while growing up in the Mormon church. Sex was "sacred," an act only between a husband and wife. Masturbation was such a foreign concept that anytime the word was even mentioned, it somehow felt murderous. I don't remember reading any particular scripture or manual suggesting masturbation somehow could lead to murder, but culturally, this was a common perception. I knew it was considered a problem among the boys, but the idea of a girl masturbating felt even more strange and ungodly.

I essentially had five basic understandings about sex as a young Mormon girl, and the lessons usually came through seminary and young women's lessons. I do not recall the word sex actually being used often, but usually referred to in words like *chastity, worthiness,* and *procreation.*

Each lesson and discussion always led to the same conclusions: one, you don't go near it unless you're married. Two, sex is meant for procreation. Three, if you think about it, you'll end up having it, so don't ever think about it. Four, sex before marriage is the second greatest sin; murder is the first. Five, don't ever think about it, it is bad and it is sacred.

A male Seminary teacher gave me one of my most prominent lessons in high school. During one such lecture on chastity, the instructor drew a triangle on the white board and on each point wrote, *husband, wife,* and *God,* with *God* being positioned at the top. He proceeded to explain that the base of the triangle was when the husband and wife came together in marriage.

Pausing briefly, he moved his marker from each base point and drew an arrow up toward God on both sides of the triangle. Further expounding on his drawing, he said, "When a husband and wife come together in consummating their holy marriage, it is in the orgasm that they become one with God." This was my first and only education on the Big O.

Most of my friends would be surprised that I knew so little about sex, as my behavior at get-togethers portrayed otherwise. I was the girl spewing out sex jokes at slumber parties, grabbing my crotch like Michael Jackson, and lip singing while trying to jump off the couch with my hands between my legs. I had no idea what I was saying or doing. I just knew my sexually-charged words triggered a reaction, and I liked the shock factor it created as the erotic words came flying off of my uncultivated tongue.

Once, when I was twelve, I instigated a conversation with my grandmother about "limp dick." "Grandma," I said when no one else was around, "Is it true? I hear sex after sixty is like shooting pool with a rope." I fully expected my grandmother to spit her set of false teeth at me, but I got a response I did not expect to hear.

"Oh, honey," she said. "Your grandfather and I sure have a lot of fun…"

WTF. No, Grandma, No. I was trying to be funny and spark a reaction, I most certainly was not searching for information on my grandparents' sex life. Though in all honesty, this is one of the reasons why I deeply loved this grandmother. As I aged, I discovered she was an open book when it came to intimacy. The witty jokes that she was able to throw out were not normal for Mormon women, and this is something that I came to find endearing about her.

I do not know what sparked my obsession with sex at such a young age, because in all reality, I was deeply afraid and uneducated about it. Early on, my fear of sex was more about crossing sacred boundaries and upsetting God. Making light of sex was one thing—acting on it was a completely different story.

My fears surrounding marriage, on the other hand, had little to do with sex and more to do with my physical looks and not feeling attractive enough for any boy to want to marry me. Ironically, this fear began as young as eight years old, which also happens to be the age of accountability as a Mormon child—the age you are mature enough and intellectually ready to make the decision to be baptized.

I don't know if it was just a coincidence that this is when the fear set in, but I do remember it was at this age I began to be afraid. I can pinpoint the exact location and moment it surfaced.

I often sat alone on the big yellow school bus and hid myself by scrunching down low with my knees pressed against the back of the seat in front of me. In my hands, I held tightly to a mirror I had stolen from my mother's bathroom drawer. I stared at myself for the entire one-and-a-half-hour ride to school. I could not leave the house without the mirror; it was an extension of myself. I was in the third grade, and I was obsessed and disgusted by my face. Repeatedly, I would look in the mirror and ask myself, "How could anyone ever love or want to marry this?"

There was a new girl on the bus that year, and she would sneer at me and roll her eyes. "Oh my gosh, you are so vain," she'd say. I'd feel sudden tears and sadness at her unwillingness to simply ask what I was doing.

I knew, even then as an eight-year-old girl, that my sole purpose in life was to get married and have babies.

Nothing was more important in life than to be a mom. So, if this was my purpose, how would I ever find anyone to love my freckled, exceptionally long-nosed face? I couldn't look at a boy without wondering, "Is this my soulmate? Is this the boy that I will marry and have children with someday? Is this the boy that will take me to the Temple? The boy that will be by my side for eternity? The boy with whom I will create worlds with after I die?"

The doctrine and teachings in the Mormon Church focus greatly on families. The family unit is a core belief in Mormonism, and like a sponge, my little feminine spirit soaked up the beautiful messages on what one must do to be with your family for eternity. I had no idea that it was even possible a child could grow up with a "bad family."

In my head, every single girl would have the exact same dreams that I had in regard to being a wife and mother someday. With such words from our revered leaders, how could any girl turn away from such an eternal, sacred role? For example, Apostle M. Russell Ballard, a high-ranking member of church leadership, once said: "There is no role in life more essential and more eternal than that of motherhood." *General Conference Talk and Ensign Article (Ballard, 2008, par 8).*

"Motherhood is more than bearing children. It is the essence of who we are as women. Motherhood defines our very identity, our divine stature and nature, and the unique traits, talents and tendencies our father gave us," says Sister Sheri Dew, LDS author and speaker. *General Conference Talk and ensign Article (Dew, 2001, par 6).*

And LDS President and Prophet Harold B. Lee

(1899-1973) exclaimed, "A successful mother is one who is never too tired for her sons and daughters to come and share their joys and their sorrows with her." *Teachings of Presidents of the Church: Harold B. Lee. The Righteous Influence of Mothers (Lee, Chapter 15, par 35.)*

These types of teachings were held close to my heart as a young child, as a teenager, and as a young adult. I hoped and prayed that I would someday fulfill the role of this divine calling. I took these teachings seriously. I did not have the patience for pretend play. I did not enjoy the idea of playing house with my twin sister and neighborhood friends. For me, there was no purpose in this form of play if I was foreordained and destined for this very thing. My elementary days belonged to the immature dream of someday becoming the perfect wife and mother.

Sadly, the obsession with my face and how I portrayed myself to the world began even earlier than my baptism age. I was actually five years old when the mania started, after my mother entered my sister and I into a twin contest in Salt Lake City. My fragmented memory recalls feeling excited and nervous as we arrived at the fairgrounds, but then shocked as we started walking around. I had difficulty registering what I was seeing. I began to wonder if I was at the circus.

Everywhere I looked, I saw identical twins—tall twins, short twins, fat twins, skinny twins, old twins, and young twins. It looked and felt like a deranged, abnormal world created by Dr. Seuss. And before I knew it, we were standing on stage and receiving a plaque for first place.

What the hell just happened? My twin and I had just

been crowned the biggest anomaly of all, at this freakshow. From that moment, I knew I was different. I began to notice the stares, a complex formed, and I became obsessed with my ugly, freakish face.

My dear rapist, if I could go back to the five-year-old girl at the twin circus and the eight-year-old girl on the bus, I would warn them both about you. I would tell this scared and insecure girl that one day they would meet a man that would really hurt her. A man that would threaten to take her life. A man that would beat down her emotional and mental walls and do everything he could to shred her worth into tiny pieces that could not be seen with the naked eye.

I would tell that little eight-year-old girl to look in that mirror and exclaim she is beautiful, long nose, freckles, and all. I would tell her to feed herself with positive words every single moment of her life. I would affirm daily that she deserved to be treated with nothing but kindness, gentleness, and love, not just by those who she allowed into her world, but by herself as well.

I would teach her the importance of consent and the definitions of rape, abuse, coercion, and manipulation. I would stress the need for her to love herself at full capacity so that she could save herself from a future of negative coping mechanisms leading to depression, anxiety, two eating disorders, and debilitating silence.

Above all, I would tell her that though she will try like hell to avoid improper relations leading to fornication, pregnancy, and abortion, acts that everyone in her world deemed as ugly sins and pernicious evils, she would still end up embracing evil by allowing you into her life. I would warn her that her compassionate heart would lead to her demise, and she would end up as one of your many victims—a wounded, frightened passenger, frozen in the trunk of your "satanic vehicle, filled with loads of future residents." Did I quote you right?

Never Yours,
A Sexually Ignorant Circus Freak

CHAPTER 3

CHOSEN

"You are a chosen generation, foredetermined by God to do a remarkable work- to help prepare the people of this world for the Second Coming of the Lord."

(Church News Article, "Becoming True Millennials", 2016 Nelson, M. Russell, Prophet. Churchnews.com)

My Dear Rapist,

They told me I was chosen. For as long as I can remember, the message brewed deeply, informing me I was more righteous than anyone who wasn't of the Mormon faith. Ironically, I only knew of one non-Mormon girl before the age of eighteen. Regardless, I felt immense pressure to be an example at all times, in all things, and in all places. This pivotal message was seared into my soul, with middle school being the time it began to matter most.

It is not a coincidence that when a Mormon youth enters middle school, he or she can qualify to enter the Temple. This is the time to really determine which side of the Mormon fence you will be on, and friends are the major influence in helping you decide. There is a well-known pamphlet in Mormonism called *For the Strength of Youth*, and this pamphlet is a type of Mormon scripture designed to help teens and young adults become unscathed by Satan's power. The following quote about friendship is an excerpt from the pamphlet:

> *"Choose friends who share your values so you can strengthen and encourage each other in living high standards. Invite your friends of other faiths to your Church meetings and activities. Help them feel welcome and included. Many people have joined the Church through the example and fellowship of their friends. Also make a special effort to reach out to new converts and to those who are less active."*

(For The Strength of Youth Pamphlet, Friends, 2001, 2011 pg. 16-17. https://www.churchofjesuschrist.org/bc/content/shared/content/english/pdf/language-materials/09403_eng.pdf?lang=eng)

Even though I did not know of a single teenager with a different faith or who did not practice Mormonism to its fullest degree, I felt the need to live my life in accordance to how Jesus and Mormonism would expect me to live it.

That was tested when Jay asked me to be his girlfriend in the sixth grade, which was a first for me. Jay had beautiful olive skin, big brown eyes, and dark brown hair. I was ecstatic to finally have a boyfriend. Eagerly, I said yes. Though I didn't understand the full context of what this meant, I knew there was a possibility he could someday be my husband.

Soon after accepting his invite, he asked me to sit next to him at an upcoming school assembly, and I easily obliged. Titillation faded quickly into confusion as he placed a gift into my hands right before the school gathering. It was a lovely box of gumdrops, but the entire thing smelled strongly of cigarette smoke. To my dismay, I instantly knew I would be breaking up with him, because I refused to have a boyfriend who smoked.

This was a strong indication that neither he, nor his parents, were worthy to attend the Temple and as a twelve-year old, I *needed* temple-worthy influences in my life. Without a single question or explanation, I told Jay that I could no longer be his girlfriend. In my head, I knew Jesus was more important than Jay, and I wanted to be a good Mormon girl and choose Jesus. Before this relationship had a chance, it was over.

This was a prominent moment for me. I knew I could no longer immediately say yes to such serious questions. I knew I would need to be more careful and more diligent in screening which boys I would allow into my life. Because of my internal fear of marriage and my low self-esteem at this age, I decided to put more of a focus on developing good friendships rather than chasing after boys.

My twin sister and I started our formative years blessed in the friendship department. There was a core group of twelve that formed by the end of middle school, and included in this group were two more sets of identical twins. All twelve of us were very strong with our beliefs in Mormonism, never straying from the covenant path. We naturally helped each other make good choices, never having a desire to try and tempt each other with drugs or alcohol.

The worst thing we ever did was rebel against the dictum from the *For the Strength of Youth* pamphlet not to watch R-rated movies. Some of the most favorite tapes we snuck into the old-fashioned VCR player were *Dirty Dancing, Chucky, The Shining, Cujo,* and *Pet Cemetery.* If we weren't watching contraband at slumber parties, we were doing the complete opposite by discussing religious teachings we'd heard at church or in seminary. We were usually drawn to doctrine on Satan and prophecies of the Second Coming from past and present Mormon leaders.

The first time I felt an evil influence in my life was at a friend's seventh-grade slumber party. The twelve of us were gathered in her basement, staying up late discussing all things Jesus and his anxiously awaited return. My twin sister began speaking of a frightening experience we had together a few months before the party. We had been in our bedroom, listening to Book of Mormon scripture on cassette tape. As we were tuned in to the narration of the story, a deep, dark voice overtook the narrator's voice, changing the original, recorded wording. We immediately both looked at each other, wondering what the hell we had just heard. My twin climbed off the bed and walked over to hit Rewind on the cassette player.

She hit play again but this time there was nothing there, just the same narrative voice that should have been there all along. She hit rewind again, stopped it, and played it a third time; again, it was the same, distorted voice. We were scared and confused. We had both definitely heard an alternate voice appear out of nowhere, coming through the cassette player. Together we came up with one conclusion— Satan was trying to prevent us from listening to God's holy word.

As my sister began to share this with our friends, I started to panic and could not control the tears of fear bursting from my eyes. I didn't want to hear her words, so I bent over, put my head in between my legs, and plugged my ears. I pleaded with her to stop, and without warning, my tongue froze in place, leaving me unable to speak.

My panic worsened as the entire room of thirteen-year-old girls became hysterical. One distressed friend claimed that the eyes of the Native American Indian on a wall painting turned red. The basement was becoming pure pandemonium, and the host of the slumber party sent her little sister running up the stairs to get their mother. As her mother lay dead asleep, the little sister started shaking her roughly, "Mom, mom, he's here, he's here."

Her mother sat straight up, climbed out of bed, and knew exactly who the little girl was referring to. She ran down the stairs and found twelve terrified girls in utter chaos. With a divorced mother in the home, we had no "priesthood holder" available to cast out the evil spirit. What happened next is an ordinance and power found within Mormonism that both men and women are believed to have access to, regardless of age or gender.

Our friend's mother gathered us in a circle and asked that we each raise our right hand to the square, elbow at a right angle. Once all middle-school arms were in the air, the mother said a prayer commanding Satan to leave her home. Within minutes, we all felt a calm and assurance that this matriarch had just folded Lucifer up like a taco and sent him straight to Antarctica.

My dear rapist, I was thirteen years old when I first felt evil. This evil felt different than your evil. Satan's evil disappeared quickly, and it was replaced by the comfort of my father's hands. I felt safe talking to my father about this supernatural evil, but later in life, never did feel safe talking to him about human evil—your evil.

The thirteen-year-old girl in me was so petrified of Satan that I couldn't even take a shower by myself without crying. I also had trouble sleeping for fear that the evil spirit was going to return and haunt me or overtake me in my sleep.

Without hesitation, I knew I could go to my father and ask him for a father's blessing. In Mormonism, a priesthood blessing can only be given by one who is living worthy and abiding by all rules within the church. My father had always lived his life in a worthy way and was always ready to give a blessing when requested. A drop of consecrated oil is placed onto the crown of the head and a father, or male leader, will then place their hands on the head and seal the oil in the name of Jesus Christ. After sealing the oil, a prayer is given. It is believed that the words from the one giving the blessing are words from God himself.

Before performing this sacred ordinance, my father found a chair for me to sit upon and this quiet, gentle father of mine stood behind me and placed his hands upon my head. I don't remember the words of this blessing, but I do remember the safety I felt as my humble father spoke his prayer. There was nothing but peace and comfort radiating from him.

When he finished, I gave him a hug and thanked him. I then made my way down the stairs to my bedroom and climbed into bed. Before closing my eyes, I had one brief moment of fear but before it completely enveloped me, I felt a tingling on my head where my father's hands were. I knew that not only was I going to be safe because of my earthly father, but that my father in heaven would also keep me safe through the night. I continued to remind myself that though I was fearful of Satan, I was chosen and that everything was going to be okay.

My dear rapist, I would have given anything to have the same reassurance and calm from my father in the time when I was with you. Your behavior made me feel that I no longer deserved my own father's love, or his hands placed upon my head. The tattered effects of you in my life closed off all access to the love of the Divine. The rape, the abuse, and the threats you barked at me radically embedded a fear that lasted much longer than the fear of Satan entering a middle school slumber party.

Never Yours,
A Scared 13-Year-Old Girl

***

My Dear Rapist,

You were not the first male to bark at me in my twenty-seven years of life. As a sixth grader, I was an office aid to Mary, the school secretary. Part of my responsibility was to walk to each classroom and collect the roll call from the teachers. Most teachers, except one, slipped the piece of paper underneath their door, relieving me of having to interrupt the class to collect the attendance.

Mr. M, the art teacher, was an older man with thin graying hair and a bit of a round belly protruding from his middle. I don't know if he stayed in his seat from age or pure laziness, but every day, he forced me to walk in front of the entire class to collect the required form. I hated his room. The minute I opened the door and stepped inside, the barking began. Nathan, a chubby, brown-haired gangster boy, had some weird, pubescent need to behave like a feral dog every time he saw me.

I had come up with a plan to quiet the asshole and shared it with a friend. My friend encouraged me to stand up for myself and I decided to take his advice. The next day, I walked through the classroom and Nathan started the expected behavior. Instead of walking back toward the door, I walked toward his desk. During my slow promenade, I quietly worked some magic inside my mouth and gathered up as much spit as my twelve-year-old female body could formulate.

With a racing heart, I forced a ginormous, wet slobberknocker out of my mouth and straight into Nathan's face. As he wiped the disgusting snot off of his face, I yelled, "Don't ever bark at me again."

His face went beet red, his eyes filled with hate, and his lips formed six words: *"I'm going to get you, bitch."*

I turned around and walked toward the door with my head up and a crooked smile spread across my blotched, freckled face. The minute I shut the door behind me, I ran back to the office, fell into the office chair and broke into uncontrollable sobs. I told Mary everything that happened and to my surprise, she forced Nathan to the office and made *him* apologize to *me*.

For the first time in my life, I had stood up for myself. Some of the other kids thought I was the shit, but deep down, I felt bad and un-Christlike. I was a female, and I had resorted to spitting. This was far from proper, and it definitely wasn't something Jesus would have done. How could feeling empowered and ashamed exist in the same space?

My dear rapist, as I reflect on this, my mind wanders between his bark and yours. With *him*, I found the courage to defend myself and refused to be *his* bitch. I chose not to let *him* continue bullying me every day. *His* barking was that of an annoying kid, and it took place in the light, with thirty other individuals around. Yours was in the dark and done in private, and it began after you forced yourself on me in a state of anger. Your growling came from a grown-ass man with a desire to instill pure terror into his innocent, Mormon bitch. Your feral behavior came on in the stillness of the night, followed by the sentiment, "I feel like killing…" Admittedly, my memory struggles to remember what you said after the word *kill*.

Was it someone else you wanted to kill, or was it me?

Over and over, these words have continuously replayed in my mind for sixteen years and then, I go blank. My memory, frozen in time, cannot remember what happened next, but instead it goes mysteriously black. Did I let you sleep over or did I kick you out?

The only thing I do know for certain is that I did not search for you in the closet and spit in your face. I did not get up and leave the bedroom with my head held high in confidence. I did not immediately go anywhere safe, or collapse into tears, and tell someone what had just happened.

My dear rapist, I had always believed I was special and saved for a unique life filled with purpose. Then you came along and, like an aggressive cancer, you eroded any sense of being special. My hope that God had something solitary and beautiful in mind just for me completely dissolved when you were in my life.

With statements from our Prophets and Apostles, perhaps you will understand why I needed and craved to be spiritually and morally perfect. Any deviation from a perfect,

Mormon life brings so much pain and anguish to most Mormon souls. President Ezra Taft Benson, the thirteenth Prophet of the Mormon Church, shared these words among the youth of the church at a Brigham Young University devotional in 1979. Though these words were spoken over forty years ago, they lived on through the teachings among my Seminary teachers in 1996.

"For nearly six thousand years, God has held you in reserve to make your appearance in the final days before the Second Coming of the Lord. Every previous gospel dispensation has drifted into apostasy, but ours will not. God has saved for the final inning some of his strongest children, who will help bear off the Kingdom triumphantly. Make no mistake about it, you are a marked generation. You, the youth of the church today, were generals in the war of Heaven.

Someday when you are back in the Spirit World, you will be enthralled by other souls who will be from many other interesting time periods and who lived during the time of many great prophets. You may ask one person, "When did you live?" and hear something like, "I was with Moses when he parted the Red Sea," or "I helped build one of the great pyramids," or "I fought with Captain Moroni."

And as you are standing there amazed at the people you are with, someone will ask you during which prophets' time you lived in; when you tell them that you lived during the time of President Kimball, President Benson, President Hunter, and President Hinckley, a

> *hush will fall over every hall and corridor of Heaven and all in attendance will bow in your presence.*
>
> *There has never been more expected of the faithful in such a short period of time as there is of us. Never before on the face of this earth have the forces of evil and the forces of good been as well organized. Each day we personally make many decisions that show where our support will go. The final outcome is certain, the forces of righteousness will finally win. What remains to be seen is where each of us personally, now and in the future will stand in this fight and how tall we will stand. Will we be true to our last-days, foreordained mission?*
>
> *This is a very important stewardship we have been given. We were held back for 6000 years because we were the most righteous, most talented, most obedient servants of our Heavenly Father.*
> *ARE WE STILL?"*

(BYU Speeches, "In His Steps". Benson, Ezra T. 1979, par 3-5 https://speeches.byu.edu/talks/ezra-taft-benson/in-christs-steps/).

I memorized these words, soaking them up like I was a dry sponge. Later, I glued these exact words to the front two pages of the large set of scriptures I inherited from my grandfather, the ones I used as an LDS missionary.

Who wouldn't want to be revered and honored by prophets of old? Who wouldn't want to be saved six thousand years for the final days before Jesus's return? Who wouldn't want to be true to a foreordained mission that God set in motion long before you were ever born?

I was told I was one of the noble and great ones who lived during the time of Prophets Heber C. Kimball, Ezra Taft Benson, Howard W. Hunter, and Gordon B. Hinckley. I have lived through *all* of them. The pressure to live up to this did not feel too heavy after being taught your whole life that you were special. With teachings like this, gravitating to like-minded friends came easily. Having a tribe of girlfriends who also wanted to win the end-of-days battle made middle school and even high school easy to manage.

Because I was chosen, I wouldn't date until I was exactly sixteen years old. Because I was chosen, I held out as long as I could for my first kiss. Because I was chosen, I never let a young, horny teenage boy touch my breasts. Because I was chosen, I never looked at porn. Because I was chosen, I never saw a male penis until you smacked me in the face with yours. I was a very strict Mormon girl, a girl saved for the very last days, a girl who wanted to prove to Jesus that she loved him. I wanted God to never, ever be disappointed in me. I never wanted to let my mother and father down. I wanted to be worthy of my father's hands on my head, receiving a priesthood blessing. As a chosen girl, I always chose the safe route and stayed away from boys.

Every day, I chose my sister and I chose my girlfriends. My twin sister was, and has always been the good twin, the righteous twin. I believed that God had foreordained her to be my twin so that she could help keep me on the straight and narrow Mormon path. God gave me my twin to save me. Without her, I deeply believed I would never make it back to God again. So, my tribe included her, the twelve girls in middle school, and the girls from church.

I was special, they were special, and we were all determined to be worthy of Jesus's love and acceptance. We were all committed to the principles of Mormonism, including no coffee, no tea, no smoking, no drugs, no dating before the age of sixteen, and certainly no heavy petting or sex prior to marriage.

My dear rapist, I cannot help but compare how Mormonism made me feel special and how you made me feel special. You both set me apart by supporting and encouraging naivety, ignorance, and submissiveness. I don't say this out of disrespect for my family and friends who still believe. The Church wanted to keep me shielded and isolated from the world, and you wanted to keep me isolated from my family and friends. Mormonism fueled a high level of spiritual narcissism in me and you, at least in the beginning, also generated a high level of egocentrism in me. For forty years, I discarded myself in pleasing the church, and for ten months, I discarded any self-worth and self-love I had, all for you.

While living in this dual relationship with you and the church, I lived a life of guilt and shame, a life of isolation and fear. I was offered incentives and rewards for complying with certain desires, beliefs, and behaviors. In the same breath of being made to feel special, you both also made me feel like I would never, ever be good enough. Feeling simultaneously special and unworthy ultimately gave me a distorted view of reality.

I was a fool. Living in ignorance and seclusion did nothing but set me up to be taken advantage of. I want to scream at my teenage self and tell her that the burden to save or prepare others for Jesus was never meant to be hers. I want to shake her and inform her that no Moses, no Abraham, no Mormon Prophet, and certainly no rapist would ever fall down at her feet and worship her.

She was not chosen to be anything other than a girl of the '80s, simply destined to be an awkward middle school kid who loved bright neon colors, jelly bracelets, Roxette, Debbie Gibson, *The Goonies*, hairspray, big bangs, Cyndi Lauper, sleep overs, Steven King, *Dirty Dancing*, and Madonna.

Her fate was to explore this crazy and beautiful world; she was never destined to be afraid of it.

Never Yours,
A Chosen One

CHAPTER 4

ATYPICALLY LOVED

"Certainly, in the infinite mercy of God, those with physical and mental limitations will not remain so after the resurrection. At this time, Alma says, 'the spirit and the body shall be reunited again in its perfect form; both limb and joint shall be restored to its proper frame.' (Alma 11:43) Afflictions, like mortality, are temporary."

(General Conference Talks and Ensign Articles, Faust, James E., 1984, par 17)

My Dear Rapist,

As I moved on into high school, avoiding relationships with boys continued to be very easy. Sure, I still maintained friendships with the core group of twelve girls from middle school, as well as the girls from church, but a different kind of friendship had formed among a group of kids that was not expected. During my sophomore year of high school, I had the opportunity to become something called a peer tutor. In the late 1990s, classrooms for those with disabilities were still somewhat segregated in Utah.

As a result, neurotypical students could sign up to be a tutor in these classrooms and still gain high school credit. I decided to give this experience a try, and it didn't take long for me to realize just how much I was going to love this program.

Students in the classroom ranged from having severe to moderate disabilities. Special needs included anything from high-functioning autism, to Down syndrome, to general learning and speech delays, to cerebral palsy, to those confined in wheelchairs, and to those who were nonverbal.

A large part of my love for students in the Special Education classrooms had to do with the stories in religious doctrine surrounding their spiritual role with God, Jesus, and Satan in the pre-existence. Two doctrines I need to address before explaining the roles of those with disabilities, are the events that took place in the "pre-existence" and the ordinance of receiving a "patriarchal blessing."

Mormon theology teaches that before mankind came to Earth, we were all living in a pre-existence with God as one big family and as spirit children. It is alleged that God knew that solely living there with him would halt us from becoming more like him. Therefore, He created the mortal world for us to become as he is, a perfected God. After earth was created, a Great Council took place, with God describing an opportunity for us to come to earth, our "second estate," so we could receive a physical body and be tested. During the Great Council, two specific plans were presented. The first was by our elder brother Lucifer, and the second was by our other elder brother Jesus Christ.

Lucifer's plan included total control. He wanted us to all come to earth and to be forced to live the laws of God so that God wouldn't lose a single one of his children to an eternity of hell. Jesus stepped forward and offered the alternative. His option included free choice and the offering of himself as a sacrifice. Mormon doctrine teaches that, through Jesus' atonement, the spirit children who chose Jesus's plan, yet who also chose a sinful, imperfect path in the mortal world, still had a way to return to live with God. It is believed that choosing eternal life with God or choosing eternal life in Hell would essentially come down to personal desire.

Once these two options were declared, a "war in heaven" began and the sides between good and evil formed. Because Lucifer rebelled against God, he was cast out of heaven, taking one-third of God's spirit children with him. It is believed that anyone who has ever been born, or whoever will be born, illustrates the decision that they chose the righteous plan, the plan presented by Jesus. In addition, it is understood that the opportunity to come to earth, receive a body, and be tested was so vital and crucial to God's plan, that Satan and his minions became envious and were granted special permission to torment those who have a body. Satan's ultimate goal is to tempt and prevent God's children from returning to live with him forever.

Unfortunately, this Premortal, "Us vs. Them" narrative continues to shape Mormon theology and attitudes today. Many families and friendships are being torn apart by those whose feet are not firmly planted on the covenant path. Sadly, any form of deviance is simply chalked up to an individual being embraced by Satan and his followers. As long as these teachings exist, Mormonism will always exhibit an "Us vs. Them" mentality.

One of the tools given to baptized members of the church to help spiritually guide us through this life is a "special" blessing called a patriarchal blessing. It is not typical to receive this blessing prior to your teenage years and it is given by one who is set apart specifically to do so. This person is defined as the church Patriarch.

A description of patriarchal blessings can be found on the official church website, and it reads that a patriarchal blessing:

> *"... contains personal revelation and instructions from Heavenly Father, who knows our strengths, weaknesses, and eternal potential. Patriarchal blessings may contain promises, admonitions, and warnings. Those who follow the counsel in their patriarchal blessing will be less likely to go astray or be misled. Only by following the counsel in a patriarchal blessing can one receive the blessings contained therein. . . . Patriarchal blessings are sacred and personal. They may be shared with immediate family members but should not be read aloud or in public or read or interpreted by others. Not even the patriarch or bishop or branch president should interpret it."*

(Church of Jesus Christ of Latter Day Saints, Study Manual Gospel Topics, Patriarchal Blessing. https://www.churchofjesuschrist.org/study/manual/gospel-topics/patriarchal-blessings?lang=eng)

In simple terms, a patriarchal blessing could be compared to a fortune-telling, though this comparison would be looked down upon by members and leaders of the church. Any spiritual energy work, outside the church, is viewed as devil's work and is a type of dark arts that should be avoided at all costs.

Generally, children and adults with physical and mental disabilities are not required to receive the ordinance of baptism, nor do they typically receive patriarchal blessings. It is believed that these individuals are already perfected, vigorous spirits who will receive no final judgment other than that of inheriting eternal life with God. It is difficult to find a solid source for teachings on those with special needs, but these ideas have been spread for years via Seminary and Institute classes, Sunday School, Sacrament meeting talks, testimony meetings, and occasional Mormon gossip.

One such story frequently shared in Mormonism is that of a child with a disability who received his patriarchal blessing in his youth. In the blessing, the child was informed that while in the pre-existence, he fought on the front lines in the war in heaven, and he was one of the valiant who had physically helped usher Satan out of Heaven. Because of this unique role, God decided to give him a disabled body in this life so that Satan could not tempt him, nor have any power over him. This type of story furthered the belief that all children born with disabilities were more than likely just as stalwart in the pre-existence as this particular boy.

I have never seen evidence of this story, nor have I seen a direct source. However, it has shaped the way many Mormons think about and view individuals with special needs, including myself. Whether or not there is any veracity to this theology, from the moment I met my first special ed student, I did feel a special spirit emanating from each and every one.

I am sure you are wondering, My Dear Rapist, why I am talking extensively about individuals with special needs. I am compelled to help you understand that I feel these individuals are *the* reason I developed a compassionate and empathetic heart. It is because of these kids that I felt I was able to stay close to God. If these kids did indeed help usher Satan out of heaven, I wanted their unyielding and unwavering faith to rub off on me. Not only did they *feel* special, but they exuded a type of atypical love that I did not find in my neurotypical friends.

These kids did not seem to care about appearances, nor did they seem to care about fitting in. They were oblivious to all the stupid high school social norms that made us all feel awkward and insecure. They loved hard and they were always quick to forgive. I was shy and insecure with my neurotypical peers, and I did not dare speak out publicly or show personality. All I wanted to do was hide behind my colossal Utah hair.

But with these kids, I could have fun, I could be myself, and I could make mistakes without being judged. They didn't care if I was not wearing name-brand clothing, if I was popular, about my religion, or what I looked like. What they did care about was my heart and how I loved and treated them in return. It wasn't them who needed me; it was I who needed them.

One of my first experiences as a peer tutor was with a blind boy named David. David could not walk, nor could he speak. Though he could not communicate verbally, he did seem to understand some things and was able to communicate using simple sign language. David was fourteen years old and spent most of his days lying down in a socially appropriate crib or propped up in a slanted wheelchair. Some of my assignments with David were to feed him, read to him, or to sit next to him and throw a ball. His eyes loved to watch the ball move up and down in my hands while joy spilled out from his laughter.

After getting a bit more comfortable with David and understanding his unique personality, I decided to ask him a question. Sitting close to him so no one could hear, I stopped throwing the ball, leaned in, and whispered into his ear, "David, can you see God?" Without hesitation, David's eyes widened, and a beautiful smile spread from ear to ear. He slowly raised his right hand and signed the word, *yes*.

I sat there stunned as chills ran up and down my entire body. I paused for a moment, wondering if I had imagined him signing that he could see God. Curious, I leaned in a second time and asked him another question. "David," I whispered. "Will you tell God hi for me?" Once again, his eyes widened, a smile spread across his face, and his right hand slowly came up and he signed the word, *yes*. This experience with David only lasted a few minutes, but it impacted my entire future.

David told me he could see God and I believed him. The prickly skin and the hair standing up on my arms was my way of determining truth. I now had my testimony that this fourteen-year-old soul lying next to me was not only special, but had more spiritual grandeur than I. In these few moments, I made a promise to myself—somehow, some way, I would spend the rest of my life surrounding myself with God's most celestial spirits.

These spirits had not only ushered out a traitorous elder brother from heaven, but they were so valiant and righteous, God protected them by placing them in confined and broken bodies.

David catapulted me into a full-force friendship with my newfound community. I signed up for every special need program I could find, both in school and throughout the church. If there is one thing Mormonism does right, it is in integrating those with disabilities into society and into the Church. In my little corner of the Utah world, the church had talent shows, dances, seminary programs, Young Men's and Young Women's groups, and even sacrament meetings customized specifically for the disabled community. I dove deeply into all of them.

My senior year of high school was not the normal free-for-all of having fun, partying it up, playing sports, or going to prom and football games. It was a year full of atypical love and acceptance within the special needs world. As seniors, my twin sister and I registered to be peer tutors for the early morning Special Needs Seminary Class. When this class came to an end, we would jump into our white 1989 Sport Grand Prix and drive twenty minutes into town to finish our day at a program for adults with special needs.

This program was a pilot program started through Utah State University, and the program manager happened to be one of our most favorite people in the world, our Aunt P. This program was for adults with more severe physical and mental disabilities who needed a way to access the community, acquire social skills, gain independent living skills, and learn how to work and manage money. The center was a weekly training program where clients would spend six hours of their day learning these skills and then return home to their families on the evenings and weekends.

My twin sister and I had earned enough high-school credits that we were granted permission to earn the remaining credits to graduate through our volunteer work at the center. Aunt P graded our performance and our attendance, giving us a rare fortuity to earn a 4.0 GPA on our report cards throughout our entire senior year.

After just three months of volunteer work, Utah State University decided they would hire us as full-time employees. One of the university students within the assistive-technology department spent many hours trying to create options to help the more severe individuals adapt to new ways of working. That student nominated my twin sister and I for the JC Penney Golden Rule Award for our work as high school students at the center. We won the award, and with it came a $1,000 grant to go toward program needs. Winning this award was a definite highlight for my twin and I, as well as getting hired at Utah State University while still attending high school.

The center attracted the needs of some of the most severely challenged individuals with disabilities. Some of these included wheelchair-bound clients with cerebral palsy, those who were blind and deaf, and others who had low-functioning autism, Down syndrome, or severe learning and mental delays. Working with the majority of these disabilities came naturally to me, and taking them into the public's eye, regardless of the stares and whispers, did not seem difficult or troublesome, except for one.

I really struggled in working with those on the autism spectrum. Not only was it a constant challenge to figure out how to meet their needs, but clients with autism seemed to receive the most stares and the most judgment. The sensory overload and the fight or flight response that an individual with autism continuously lives with overwhelmed me as a young girl and I did not know how to respond. If there was one area in which I had a lack of patience and understanding, it was within this perplexing and puzzling world.

Ashamedly, my dear rapist, I am about to be raw and share my once bigoted and ignorant prayers with you. Naively, as a young girl I would pray and express my desire to God that if he ever needed to send a child with a special need to someone, that he should send one to me. The prayer did not stop here. I got much more detailed and descriptive with God in my desire and gave him stipulations. It was as if I had a Special Needs Menu in front of me, picking and choosing which disability I could handle and which disability I could not.

A child with Down syndrome was at the top of my menu and a child with autism wasn't to be found anywhere on my self-created, bigoted list. I share this prayer with you because God, in his infinite wisdom and love, later answered my prayers in a significant way. I would one day become a mother to both a Down syndrome daughter and an autistic daughter. The one I did not think I could handle brewed in my belly, and the one at the top of my list was born to another mother, in another country. The details of this will be shared with you in another letter; I don't want to get too far ahead of myself.

With a full-time job landing so easily in our laps, my twin and I were ready to graduate high school and take off running. Three months before we turned eighteen and weeks after our graduation ceremony with the Class of 1996, we moved out of our parents' home and into a three-bedroom townhouse near Utah State University. We were officially on our own. We had adventurous new roommates, we had a job that we were in love with, we were free from parental rules, and we were still very awkward around boys. The carefree, innocent days of our childhood and teenage years carried well into this unfamiliar life of responsibility and the becoming of a young adult. When the workday was done, the play time set in.

We looked forward to weekly activities with our singles church group and singles dances at the USU Institute building. Our favorite night was Thursday, a night that belonged to Retrix, Logan's most popular club for country dancing. This was a place where college-aged kids gathered in the hopes they would be asked to two-step or swing dance to the top country songs of the '90s. By day, I spent my time working with my friends in an atypical world. By night, I spent my time playing with my friends in a neurotypical world. Both worlds meshed very well together, and I loved and flourished in both of them.

My Dear Rapist, my special needs friends transformed me. They are the ones who taught me unconditional love and to focus on one's ability, rather than one's disability. They taught me to never give up on someone for being different or strange. They are the ones who gave me the heart to see the good in you. They offered me atypical love in a neurotypical world, and in a distorted way, I tried doing the same for you. I thought if I could love you hard enough and focus on your abilities, your disabled spirit would stop causing me so much pain.

As I reflect on these friends of mine sixteen years later, I see a stark difference between the two of you. They had imperfect, confined bodies, but their spirits were pure and whole. You had a perfected, chiseled body, but your spirit was broken and maimed. Unlike my friends, your dcbilitated spirit didn't care about anyone's heart—all it cared about was causing a storm of trauma to anyone with a vagina who walked into your path.

I have conceded that you walked into my life as one of Satan's minions, wrapped in an Olympic body, with the charm and charisma of a snake. You were a serpent sent to test me and to open my eyes to the difference between good and evil. Saying yes to a date was like taking a bite of the forbidden fruit, and no amount of neurotypical love I tried to offer could have stopped your atypical behavior.

Mormon doctrine teaches that one day, my special needs friends will have perfect bodies and perfect minds. If this is true, does this mean your impaired spirit will someday be perfected to match your already perfected sculpted physical form?

Never Yours,
Atypically Loved

CHAPTER 5

HAUNTED IN JACKSON

"I know very well that, whether we are active or not, the invisible spirits are active. And every person who desires and strives to be a Saint is closely watched by fallen spirits that came here when Lucifer fell, and by the spirits of wicked persons who have been here in tabernacles and departed from them, but who are still under the control of the prince of the power of the air. Those spirits are never idle, they are watching every person who wishes to do right and are continually prompting them to do wrong".

(Journal of Discourses, Young, Brigham , 2nd Prophet of the Mormon Church, 1859, vol.7, pp. 237-244)

My Dear Rapist,

After about a year of working full time, my twin and I were ready for a bit of adventure. We called up a couple of girlfriends that we had known since our elementary days and invited them to take a little weekend getaway with us to Jackson Hole, Wyoming. We had informed them of the summer employment opportunities available in this valley, which is near the Teton Mountain Range and a brief sixty-six-mile drive from Yellowstone National Park. The four of us loaded up our car with the sole intent of finding summer work in one of the most beautiful parts of the Northwest.

Our four-hour drive began on the Utah-Idaho border, and it took us through Star Valley and Alpine, Wyoming. Once we hit Alpine, we began our ascent along the Snake River and into Snake River Canyon. The hot sun blared down upon us through the twisted curves of the canyon and the four of us were feeling excitement and freedom at the tips of our fingers. We knew we were about to experience a summer filled with hard work and recreation in a stunning, mountainous playground.

Our first stop in Jackson Hole was at the 49er Inn & Suites on Pearl Avenue, just a few blocks from where the main tourist shops and restaurants resided. The four of us were lined up for interviews with a skinny, dark-haired man named Miles, the manager of the hotel's housekeeping department. Miles pretty much hired us on the spot, but wanted to show us the employee housing options before letting us go. He led us through the bottom south part of the Inn and through the back doors, then walked us thirty feet to a small, wooden cabin on a corner lot.

The cabin was a run-down, three-bedroom, two-bath home and had a smell to it that we could not quite explain. Talking faster than we could understand, Miles informed us about the summer work in Jackson Hole while he guided us throughout the house. Eventually, we found ourselves standing in the master bedroom, and our new boss seemed completely unfazed by the blood on the walls. Oblivious to the shock on our faces, the question that was begging to be answered finally hit the musty air.

"Whose blood is on the wall?" one of us spit out.

"Oh, that blood?" Miles said, suddenly present to our complete horror. "Don't worry, that will be cleaned off the walls by the time you ladies move in. The girl staying in this room thinks Satan lives inside her head. She sits and bangs her head on the wall, hoping she can get him to leave," he explained, as if it was a normal occurrence.

Like a herd of deer high on Mary Jane, the four of us locked our wide-open eyes on each other. As we struggled to articulate a response to Miles, he decided to throw one more bomb at us.

"There are two lesbians living in the other bedroom. But don't stress, all three of them will be out of here before you move in."

This was bad, like really bad. No wonder Satan was in this home—he had two women living in sin inside the walls of this shithole. My homophobic heart was more alarmed about meeting two lesbians than it was about meeting Satan himself.

Up until a few years ago, the church always taught that homosexuality was nothing more than a temptation, a lifestyle inspired by our brother Lucifer. In recent years, the church has changed its stance and has stated that the sin is found in the acting out on homosexual behavior, not in its inherent nature. Though there has been a subtle shift in this teaching, many members and leaders of the church still promote antiquated beliefs toward the LGBTQ+ community, which is sadly wreaking havoc on the mental health of those members who belong to the community.

As I think about my time in Mormonism, sometimes it feels like Satan is focused on more than Jesus. If you were to go to the main website for the Mormon church and type the words "Satan," "Adversary," or "Devil"" into the search menu, it would bring up over 8,000 references with links to all the different talks given about him. One of the things that we are taught is that Satan can mimic God and the feelings of the Spirit. It is stressed that we are to be constantly on guard and live our life to perfection so that we won't be deceived by the "Great Imitator."

My dear rapist, it is difficult not to think of you when I hear others speak of Satan or when I consider memories of Mormon teachings surrounding him. During the forty years I believed in Satan, he took up a significant amount of space in my head. Many of his characteristics are similar to yours, and perhaps this is why I was drawn to you; I seemed to naturally attract that which I feared.

At this time, I was terrified of not only these two lesbians, but anyone within the LGBTQ+ community. Though I felt unnerved by Miles's news, I believed our four Mormon spirits would return to Jackson Hole and drive the evil spirits away with our righteousness.

With summer employment and housing solidified, we returned home to Utah, gathered our belongings, and immediately turned around to start our summer of work. My twin and I didn't want to share a room together, so we split up. Stephanie and I moved into the room with blood on the wall, and Holly and my twin moved into the lesbian room.

My twin decided she did not want to wait for Holly to arrive, so she immediately went to work putting their room together. For as long as I can remember, my twin has taken great pride in decorating her bedroom. Her belongings included carousel horses that she had collected from different places over the years, and she placed them on several of the wall shelves around her room. Stephanie and I didn't care much for decorating, we just needed our large closet and a place to do our hair and makeup, and we were good to go.

The four of us had the housekeeping job as our main employment, but we each acquired part-time jobs in the evening. My twin got a job at a candy shop, Stephanie worked part-time at a name brand clothing store, and Holly and I began waitressing at a popular steakhouse. After several weeks, the four of us were informed that we would be getting a new roommate.

Suzie was a few years older than us, and she was a free-spirited hippie who had recently returned from her Mormon mission. In the front of the house, there was a tiny bedroom she had all to herself. We found ourselves getting along okay with her, and just as we did at our seventh-grade slumber party, we would often stay up late talking about Jesus and his Second Coming, specifically the signs of the times, and the prophecies of destruction. Having a returned missionary in the house made the conversations seem even more special and educational.

One particular night, we were having a religious discussion and, unlike the slumber party, everything remained calm. That is, until Holly woke up during the night to use the restroom. After doing her business, she stood up and began washing her hands. For no real reason, she casually looked up and into the mirror. She saw the face of a distorted man with dark, black hair staring back at her.

She started freaking out, stumbled out of the bathroom, and walked toward the living room. Her eyes landed on a picture of Jesus on the wall, and a black shadow with long, dark hair overtook his face. The unmitigated horror of this moment left us feeling unsettled the remainder of the night.

From that point on, it felt like we were living in an *Amityville Horror* film. Lights flickered on and off with not a single one of us near a light switch. Without any warning, bedroom doors that were closed would randomly open. We would hear unseen footsteps and random shadows often appeared out of nowhere.

One evening, I had gone to bed early for my morning waitressing shift and was lying on my side so that I faced the wall. I had a difficult time falling asleep, but I knew my twin, Holly, and Suzie were home and watching movies in the living room. I had heard my bedroom door open and a couple of light footsteps saunter into the walk-in closet. After ruffling through some clothing for a few moments, and without saying a word to me, my roommate quickly left the closet and our bedroom. I was annoyed that Stephanie had come into the bedroom, made disruptive noise, and then left without closing the door. My sleep was extremely important to me, and my annoyance pushed me to climb out of bed and confront Stephanie in the living room.

As I entered the room and greeted the other girls, Stephanie was nowhere to be found. I asked my roommates where she had gone and they all looked at me in complete bewilderment. Stephanie had not come home, and they were adamant that not a single one of them had left the living room and intruded into my sleeping space. I knew unequivocally that someone had opened my door, entered my room, wandered into the closet, and tousled through the clothing. Fear and exasperation quickly set in, and I refused to sleep in our bedroom again.

I convinced my twin and Holly to let me sleep on the floor between their beds, and the three of us attempted to get a good night's rest. Eventually, we reached our slumber, but the peace did not last long.

One night about two weeks later, I opened my eyes and saw a darkened silhouette walk into the bedroom and peer at my two roommates sleeping.

I sat up from the hard floor to watch the obscure spirit and after a few moments, I watched it walk into the closet and disappear. With a racing heart, I moved to wake up Holly and my sister. This is when I noticed my sister with her eyes wide open and tears running down her cheeks. She explained to us what she had just experienced. Unbeknownst to me, she had been frozen in fear, feeling tied down to her bed by the unseen spirit. As she was fighting to speak, she claimed the shadows from the unmoving carousels on her wall had begun to dance.

Over the coming days, lights would continue to randomly flicker, strange noises resumed out of nowhere, doors continued to open and close, and it became very evident that an unseen power did not want us in this home. But our fear by now was mixed with feelings of anger and annoyance. As five stalwart, Mormon girls, we decided we had one choice to make: it was time to fight back.

Our first line of defense was to invite the patriarch from the local Mormon church, who also happened to work at the steakhouse with Holly and I, to come over and do a Mormon exorcism on the house. It is similar to what we did at the seventh-grade slumber party, but we wanted a male leader involved, due to his priesthood power.

Within a few days, the kind old man showed up to our cabin. The moment he entered the living room, all of the color from his wrinkled face drained out of him, his appearance going entirely pallid. He expressed a feeling of something dark and sinister and urgently asked us to gather in a circle to start the prayer. We huddled close to each other and at a right angle, we raised our right arms to the square while we waited on the patriarch to cast out Satan and his minions.

Casting out devils is always done in the name of Jesus, and it is believed that the success of these exorcisms is achieved through our faith and through the power of God. It is important to show confidence and courage. If the opposite is shown, the spirits may have the power to ignore the prayer and do as they wish. It is also believed that the minute the name "Jesus Christ" is articulated into the air, the diabolical spirits will immediately depart due to their inability to stand hearing Jesus's name.

While the sweet patriarch began the customary prayer to cast out demons, my twin sister decided to open her eyes and take a peek at the sacramental ceremony. After a few moments of taking in the scene, her eyes drifted over to the window overlooking a dirt field. In the field, she witnessed a group of obscured spirits floating in a sphere, appearing to have a séance. It seemed the forces of light and the forces of dark were battling to win the space of this run-down, decrepit, haunted Jackson Hole cabin.

We were nothing but a few innocent Mormon girls who simply wanted to do our housekeeping jobs by day, our part-time job at nights, and explore the beautiful mountains of the Tetons in our spare time. We could not understand why they felt a need to torment us. We hadn't invited them in, and we certainly did not want them there. They were not living inside our minds, forcing us to bang our heads on the wall to get them to leave. We were not lesbians frolicking in sinful behavior. We were naive, inexperienced girls that just wanted to make money and have fun.

The exorcism held us over for a few days, giving us a chance to experience some peace and quiet, but unfortunately, it was short-lived. We began to be less and less afraid of these damned incubi and found ourselves becoming extremely intolerant of their eerie and constant tauntings.

Our next attempt to persuade these bastards to leave the house included gathering several Mormon friends from work and collecting as many New Era magazines as possible. This magazine is a publication by the church, targeting teenagers and young adults.

In the *New Era*, the Mormon ads were trendy and meant to keep us moving forward faithfully and honorably as members of the church. They often had images of ordinary young adults casting shadows of warriors, paired with messages like: *"The men and women who desire to obtain seats in the celestial kingdom will find that they must battle every day."*

The girls and I thought perhaps we could drive the spirits away by plastering these Mormon images all over our bedroom and living room walls. It would have been impossible to consistently utter, "In the name of Jesus Christ, we command you to leave," so we were hopeful this was the next best thing.

With Scotch tape in hand, we all went to work and placed upwards of thirty of these messages throughout our haunted house, behaving as if we were modern day, religious Ghostbusters. The smiles on our faces and the premature arrogance of triumph gave us the courage to stake claim on our summer home.

However, like every other attempt at eradicating these sons of bitches, this endeavor was also transitory and powerless. Over the course of a few days, each and every ad would subtly fall off the wall, leaving us to wonder, was it the asshole spirits removing them or did we just purchase crappy tape? We acquired more tape and made great effort at returning the ads back to the wall. Resolute in winning the war, I was insistent on blaming the lesbians and Satanic headbanger for getting us into this haunted mess. I just could not understand why our holy, religious spirits were not enough to drive them out.

After months of doing business with the Jackson Hole poltergeists, we finally caved and decided to let them have their shitty shack. We each gave our notice, found alternate housing arrangements, and moved out. We committed to finishing out the summer in Jackson Hole, but had to separate due to our differences in new employment opportunities. Several of the girls who took over our former home happened to be acquaintances from high school.

The new inhabitants of the home moved in before we could warn them, so we found it unnecessary to relate our experiences to them. Within two weeks, our former classmates were running for the bloody mountains. Wondering what the hell was going on, they found us and asked if we had encountered any of the same paranormal activity they had. After validating and confirming their fears, they had zero desire to wage war against the invisible roommates and promptly hauled their belongings and their asses out.

My dear rapist, I choose to no longer believe in Satan or give him space in my head—his abusive traits remind me too much of you. Bishop Victor Brown had this to say in the Mormon Ensign:

> *"Satan's legions are many. In their battle to enslave mankind, they use weapons such as selfishness; dishonesty; corruption; sexual impurity, be it adultery, fornication, or homosexuality; pornography; permissiveness; drugs; and many others."*

(General Conference Talks and Ensign Articles, Brown, Victor, 1973. Our Youth: Modern Sons of Helaman. par, 6)

I have discovered that believing in Satan did nothing but give me anxiety and make me a judgmental asshole. Instead of looking at another's choices and scoffing at them for caving to sin, I now contemplate the possible traumas one might have endured to take on such negative coping mechanisms and choices. There are times, when my heart is soft, that I wonder what trauma you endured to have treated me, and other women, so poorly. But to be frank, when I am angry and grieving over your abuse and its lingering effects, I lean toward believing that you were one of Satan's followers.

Unlike my days in Jackson Hole, I did not put much effort into eliminating your evil. I did not put up Mormon ads to push your corruption away. A patriarch was never called in to cast out your evil nature, and I never did raise my right arm to the square and command you to leave. Banging my head against a wall to get you out of my head never even crossed my mind. With you, all I did was freeze in fear and allow shame to overpower me, becoming too weak and too lost to know how to get away from you.

Eventually, I found a way through my weakened faith to choose God and seek a path to forgiveness. It was my fault. I deserved the things you did because I ignored a warning from God to run from you. For seven long years, I repented and begged God to forgive me, and though his redemption did come, it took an additional five more years for me to wake up and realize that I never should have felt a need to repent for your abuse in the first place.

Never Yours,
Haunted

CHAPTER 6

HOSTAGE

"Twenty years from now you will be more disappointed by the things that you didn't do than by the ones you did do. Explore. Dream. Discover."

-Mark Twain

My Dear Rapist,

After our summer in Jackson, we all returned to
Logan, Utah, and we went our separate ways. I returned
to working with those with special needs for a time, but
the yearning to travel and explore the world outside of my
tiny community once again began to stir within me. The
experience 150 miles away in Wyoming had not been far
enough. I wanted to go further and spend time on the East
Coast, specifically New York City. I had wasted away my
summer earnings and did not have the financial means to
make such a big move on my own. I had zero desire to stick
around and tie myself to the pursuit of a college education
when all I was destined for was to be a mother.

If I wanted anything before settling down, I wanted
adventure and entertainment. If getting married was truly
what God wanted for me, I was certain that marrying a
Mormon boy from Utah was not in his plan for me. I wanted
a polished and enlightened Mormon boy that was raised in a
part of the world that was far away from Utah or Idaho.

Becoming an East Coast nanny piqued my interest,
and it was an objective I seriously decided to explore. In the
late 1990s, the safest and most common route in obtaining
a position as a nanny was to apply through a nanny agency.
The agencies did background and reference checks on both
employee and employer, ensuring the safety of both parties.
I had heard that many families preferred hiring young
Mormon girls due to their experience in being around many
children, as well as the religion's strict avoidance of alcohol
and drugs. The high standards on sex among Mormon girls
was another admirable characteristic the employer was

drawn to. The wives could go to bed at night with a peace of mind, knowing that the new, perky, young nanny in the home would more than likely *not* be having forbidden sex with her husband.

I got in touch with a nanny agency based out of Salt Lake City, filled out their application, and made the two-hour drive to do an in-person interview. My references and background check processed promptly. It wasn't long before I received a phone call from the agency that a family was interested in interviewing me. I was sitting in my parents' sun-filled living room, listening to the description of the family from the agency representative, and one sentence stuck out that made me shout out loud, "Yes."

"Yes, this is the family I want, I'll take it," I told the agency.

I didn't mind that the job description would be for three girls under the age of six, one of them being a newborn baby. I didn't mind that I would be a mother's helper, not knowing this meant the mother was a stay-at-home mom who would scrutinize and watch my every move. I simply heard, "You will spend five weeks in Europe, all expenses paid," and the deal was sealed.

After a quick conversation and a job offer with the New England couple, I found myself packing my bags and preparing for a move to Norwalk, Connecticut. The only information I had on the family, outside of a summer of travel, was that both husband and wife were from England and Mr. Banks operated an eyewear business for a company based out of London. My flight was booked for a weekend in February, and I figured this gave us a good five months to get to know one another before we took off for a foreign country.

Mrs. Banks had just had the baby two weeks prior to my arrival, so the only one that showed up to the airport to pick me up was Mr. Banks. I'd had a late flight and was still somewhat mesmerized by seeing the lights of NYC from my seat on the airplane, when I walked off the plane and saw a tall, handsome man with a friendly smile holding a sign with my name on it.

A pair of sharp-looking glasses were placed perfectly on his nose, and his energetic British accent made the young thirty-three-year-old father seem very kind and comforting. My anxiety about this unknown adventure melted away as we spent the next two hours gathering my belongings, talking, and making the commute to my new home in Connecticut.

The house we pulled up to was not the type of home I had envisioned in my head. I had heard stories of nannies living in East Coast mansions, but this home was far from a mansion. It was a tiny, three-bedroom home, tucked away from the road and partially hidden by large, beautiful New England trees. I had no idea that this state was so heavily forested, and I was surprised how soothing it felt that I would be living in a small bungalow rather than a large estate. To me, a small home meant more love, more friendliness, and more togetherness.

Mr. Banks helped me out of the green Jeep Cherokee and eagerly took me inside to meet his wife. The children were asleep, but Mrs. Banks did not let that stop her from giving me a boisterous and friendly welcome. She was a thirty-six-year-old woman with blonde, '70s shag hair.

Her lovely British accent was more overpowering than her brimming alabaster buck teeth.

After several minutes of visiting, we all decided it was best to get some sleep and meet the children in the morning. They led me to my new bedroom, which was through the kitchen, past a playroom, a bathroom, and down a tiny hallway. The bedroom was a good size, with lots of windows and a considerably large closet. I was the only one with a bedroom on the main level of the house—everyone else was upstairs in the two remaining bedrooms and one more bathroom.

I decided to wait until the next day to unpack and instead pulled out my Book of Mormon. I made a commitment at this moment to be more studious and purposeful in my scripture reading. I wanted and needed God's direction more than ever and wanted to start out this new adventure right. After taking some time to read, I closed the book, knelt beside my bed, and asked God to be with me while I was living over 2,000 miles away from home. I had good feelings about this new family of mine and was looking forward to the experiences that would come to me while living on the East Coast.

I woke up the next morning and heard the girls playing and whispering in the playroom next to me. It took a few moments to wake up, rub my eyes, and say my morning prayers. After getting off my knees, I took a deep breath and opened my bedroom door. I don't know who was more bashful, me or them, but the energy in the room was pure timidity. I finally broke the ice by engaging with the girls in their playroom. The oldest girl, Chloe, was six; the middle girl, Juliet, was three; and the baby girl, Evelyn, was two weeks old.

The older girls did not want to play long—instead they wanted to show off and introduce me to their new little sister. We had a beautiful, happy morning eating breakfast and getting to know one another. After several hours of spending time together, we all gathered in the car and drove to Saturday ice-skating lessons for Chloe. She was super excited to have this new friend of hers watch her ice skate all on her own. Juliet was a bit shyer; she had a much sweeter and more introverted nature about her compared to her older sister, who was obviously louder and more extroverted. Chloe looked more like her mother, while Juliet resembled her father.

The day continued to go well, and I was feeling more comfortable with the decision to have moved across the country and live with complete strangers—strangers who also lived a religion completely different from my own. Mr. and Mrs. Banks claimed to be Jewish, but the only tradition they chose to do each week was Shabbat. Every Friday evening, they gathered their family together, lit a candle, broke bread, sipped grape juice, and said their prayers. Outside of this one ritual, they were fairly nuanced in their beliefs and rarely spoke about their faith.

The thirty-nine forbidden acts that they were expected to avoid on Shabbat were never discussed in their home, nor were they ever practiced. I was fascinated by this weekly practice and felt somewhat honored that they would invite me to partake in it. The sacramental offering was different from Mormonism. In Mormonism, you are required to be a baptized member of the church in order to take communion, but my new family did not care about my unbelief and invited me to partake regardless.

The Bankses knew I was Mormon, and the one agreement we worked out prior to my arrival was that I would be given Sundays off so that I could worship and be with my fellow Connecticut Mormons. I was thrilled to find out that a singles ward existed twenty minutes away from my new home. Singles ward simply means I had an opportunity to attend a congregation filled with only single people. Knowing there were going to be single men in the ward, I felt extra anxious and excited at the thought that my eternal companion could be in Connecticut. I spent extra time getting ready that first Sunday morning and wanted to feel extra cute and prepared.

I walked into the church building with my big, brown hair, knee-length skirt, and my set of Mormon scriptures, portraying more confidence than I truly had. Within seconds of entering the chapel, the faux composure quickly fell apart as I noticed that every church pew was filled with women. I looked around, stunned. Where in the world was my eternal companion? I counted about ten men in the room and roughly fifty women. Shit, the prospects were not looking good for me.

The most attractive man in the room was a fifty-year-old man sitting on the stand, smiling kindly at everyone entering into the chapel. I would later find out that this handsome, married man was a counselor in the bishopric (a priest), and that he was Steve Young's father. Yes, the former NFL quarterback for the San Francisco 49ers.

Though my confidence was quickly crushed by the number of women in the room, I actually left church feeling optimistic and hopeful. The other nannies were kind and friendly, and the idea of needing to find an eternal companion in Norwalk had faded within the three-hour church service. I did not leave with a best friend that day, but something told me not to worry and that it would come.

I knew in time I was going to make lifelong friends and that we were going to create many remarkable experiences together. Prior to heading home, I decided to take the Jeep Cherokee on a self-guided tour around Norwalk, Stamford, and Greenwich. I got lost a few times, but didn't have too difficult of a time finding my way home.

Mr. and Mrs. Banks were eager to see me again, and now it was my turn to explain to them a little bit about Mormonism. I was fascinated by their beliefs, and they seemed to be captivated by mine. Even though I was supposed to be a missionary at all times, I had zero intent to convert them to my one true religion.

However, I did have an underlying hope that if a conversion happened at all, it would do so organically by my Mormon example and not by any verbal instruction. When the religious conversation ended, we discussed the weekly schedule and the Bankses laid out their expectations of childcare and house cleaning.

Monday morning came quickly, and like the good little Mormon girl, I showered and got ready before they were all awake. I took this job seriously and treated it like I would any other job, wanting to be fully present to the children and my duties. My first responsibility that morning was to drive Chloe to school while Mrs. Banks stayed home and tended to the baby. Little Juliet had preschool around lunch time and so, after dropping off Chloe, I spent the morning playing with Juliet and taking care of her needs. I did get a lunch break while Juliet was at school and used this time to work out, journal, or read my scriptures.

In the afternoon, I picked up both Juliet and Chloe from school and spent the remainder of the afternoon playing with them. As time wore on and I got comfortable with this routine, Mrs. Banks started leaving me with more and more responsibilities while she would go shopping or spend time with friends.

Disappointingly, the honeymoon stage of the position wore off within the first two months. In the evenings, I went to bed stressed out and with headaches due to the constant yelling of Mrs. Banks. She was never happy—whether it was with the children, her husband, or drama with friends, the woman had a constant scream coming from her mouth. Mr. Banks usually just took it, always remaining quiet until he'd had enough and started yelling back.

The girls' true colors started shining through, especially from Chloe. Calling me names, like "you're a fat pig," in a young British accent was not endearing, adorable, or funny. Kicking me and hitting me became the norm, and the Bankses did nothing about it. When I did confront the parents, they often believed the lies from their little urchins and in an implied manner, looked at me as if I deserved it.

The original chore list began to increase and expand outside of my contractual duties, and my title of nanny began to shift as I watched myself become the Mary Poppins of this ostentatious, British family. Polishing the silverware, ironing the bed sheets and baby clothes, and vacuuming and cleaning the vehicles were just a few of the tasks that began to pile up on the list of chores I never agreed to do.

One day, Mrs. Banks decided she wanted to go out with her friends and left me with the baby, a load of laundry to iron, and some cleaning to do. I didn't mind the list—though ironing baby clothes seemed a bit ridiculous to me—and I decided to call home and talk to my mother while the baby slept and I ironed the clothes.

I was on the phone for roughly twenty minutes when Mrs. Insanity burst through the door in rage. The year 1998 was prior to cell phones, so I was standing in the kitchen ironing and talking on the landline phone, when, without any warning, she promptly walked over to the phone and ended the conversation between my mother and I. Her long, pointy, witch finger pushed down on the hang up button and she turned around, glaring at me with her beady little eyes.

Going off on an elementary tirade, she rambled incoherent nonsense about my use of the phone during work hours. While standing in her kitchen, and in complete shock, she ordered me to polish her large set of silverware. The whole encounter left me pissed off and feeling as if this nanny position was no longer for me. However, I was committed to that damned free trip to Europe, so I remained devoted to the job and continued to suffer through the madness of Mrs. Banks.

I had started getting into a groove with making friends from church, and the timing could not have been more perfect, as I had been really struggling with the high demands my employers were placing on me. One of the first girls I became friends with was a spunky, short-haired blonde who had the mouth of a sailor, smoked a few cigarettes when no one was looking, and had several small tattoos that I found myself envying.

There was something about her, something that I knew my little naïve spirit wanted but didn't have. She was unfettered and dauntless, not giving two shits about what anyone thought of her. Her loud laughter and immense smile were infectious, and I knew I had to find a way to make her my friend.

Sara didn't fit the mold I was used to in Utah; she was certainly not a cookie cutter Mormon girl. Sara was from Seattle and had converted to Mormonism when she was sixteen years old. She had wanted a different life outside of Seattle and wanted to experience the great Big Apple like the rest of the nannies in our congregation. Sara had found an incredible, kind family to work for, and I craved the relationship and respect her employers had built with her.

The more I spent time with Sara, the more I secretly wanted to be like her. We were complete opposites. I was shy, she was bold. She had a personality like Cyndi Lauper, and I had the personality of a mop. She ran toward the boys; I ran away from them. She was blonde; I was brunette. She was daring; I was apprehensive. We became magnets, always connected at the hip and ready to explore the ins and outs of NYC and New England together. Ultimately, we discovered we had one thing in common; we both considered ourselves to be big-bottomed girls with genuine, empathetic hearts. I think this is what I loved most about Sara. On the outside she appeared to be rugged and tough, but on the inside, she had a heart more like Jesus than anyone else I had ever known. The smell of smoke and the rebellious tongue was nothing but a distraction from who she really was.

Sara and I ended up becoming friends with two more girls from church, Jaryn and Caltin. The four of us had a blast wandering the streets of NYC together, taking Kodak moments of our taxi rides and tours of landmarks like Times Square, the Empire State Building, and the Statue of Liberty. We also loved trying out trendy restaurants and enjoyed random jaunts through Central Park.

We found ourselves especially enjoying the many beaches, diners, and ice cream joints Connecticut had to offer. We created many memorable moments, without a lick of alcohol, simply by relaxing and hanging out at each other's homes.

Well, homes except my own.

The irrationality and madness coming from my employers made me want to get away and escape to my friend's homes as much as possible. It was becoming more and more clear to me that I was nothing but property to Mrs. Banks. She never spoke to me by name, and in fact, whenever she introduced me to her friends, she constantly referred to me as "her nanny." Mr. Banks was always kind and acted the complete opposite of his wife. He seemed worn out by her constant complaints and negativity, and there was a gentleness in his eyes that seemed to say, "I know, she can be a bit much." He never spoke these words out loud, but his demeanor expressed exhaustion, maybe even a little bit of surrender, to her level of hysteria and unbalance. The one thing he did seem to agree on with his wife was the countless discussions regarding lawsuits and why they justified financially going after certain places or people.

Part of my contract with Mr. and Mrs. Banks was a two-week paid vacation outside of our summer travel to Europe. The month before we were to leave for England, I was invited to go on a vacation to Jamaica with two other girlfriends, Miley and Kari. Miley and her sister Courtney were not nannies from church, but were living in Connecticut with their mother and father. Miley was a flight attendant for American Airlines at the time and Courtney was attending college. Kari was from Idaho, and I had actually known her during my summer employment in Jackson Hole.

Kari was one of those friends who had helped put up the *New Era* ads in the haunted cabin to help ward off evil spirits. We had met in the singles ward in Jackson Hole, but I hadn't known Kari was going to be in my singles ward in Connecticut. When we'd seen each other at church, it was a much-welcomed, pleasant surprise, but also a confirmation on just how small the Mormon world really was.

Miley and Courtney were my very first African American girlfriends, and I was intrigued by their parents' immigration to America. I was especially impressed by Miley and Courtney's conversion to Mormonism. There were not many African American converts during this time, at least not in the circles I had been running in. These two sisters would eventually find their way to the West Coast, with Miley becoming a conservative political figure. I loved getting to know these Mormon sisters and felt it an honor that they would find me worthy to be their friend during this time of my life.

With Miley being a flight attendant, she was able to get Kari and I buddy passes for our flight, and we had each given Miley additional money to book our hotel in Jamaica. Getting the time off work was not difficult, and things really seemed to be falling into place for us to leave for our tropical vacation. My relationship with my employers was becoming more strained, and I am certain they knew I was not happy.

I was becoming increasingly withdrawn and spending less time with them when I wasn't working. I avoided them at all costs and did only what was asked of me. My outgoing and friendly persona was changing in front of them, but I hated contention and was not good at standing up for myself. Regardless, I really wanted to make things work and I did not want to go home to Utah.

The day came for us to leave on our much-anticipated vacation. Miley picked Kari and I up in her SUV and we said goodbye to our employers. We were only going to be in Jamaica for three nights and with two travel days attached to this, and we would technically be gone for just under a week. Our flight was out of Newark, so we took the New Jersey Turnpike and drove fifty miles to the airport. It was a beautiful, sunny day and Miley, Kari, and I were fired up and ready for our getaway. We followed Miley's lead on where to go and what to do for our international trip, and we finally got our luggage checked in. This was prior to 9/11, so getting through security was quick and easy.

The time came to board our flight, but because we were traveling with buddy passes, we were required to wait until all passengers were boarded and seated before we could board the plane. Miley had failed to tell Kari and I that this was how the buddy pass system worked, and before we knew it, the plane took off with all of our luggage, leaving the three of us behind. There had been no room for us. We were instructed by Miley that we could wait and catch the next flight, but by doing this, we would be getting back a day or two late and would need to request additional time off from our employers.

Miley and Kari decided to go and see what information they could find about our luggage and where exactly it would end up in Jamaica. While they spent their time seeking out further information, I decided to find a payphone and call my employers to tell them of our dilemma. I was nervous and had a feeling the call wasn't going to go well. My instincts told me they were not going to approve of the additional time off, but I didn't want to lose out on this vacation, the money put towards the hotel, the buddy pass, or ruin things for Miley and Kari.

I cannot recall if it was Mr. or Mrs. Banks that had picked up the phone, but as expected, the request for extra time off was returned with a fast and firm no. They were upset that I would even dare ask for extra time off and told me I needed to get home immediately. I pushed back on their demands, which only furthered their fury and their disgust of me. I was not turning out to be the subservient Mary Poppins that they had believed I should be, and my defiance was disrupting their fantasy of owning me as a piece of property.

Their refusal to work with me on the matter forced me to hang up the phone, leaving me with the final word and decision. I told them that I would not be losing out on the money nor would I be the one to ruin things for my friends. I did not care about the repercussions at this point and was willing to lose my job over this and, even more so, give up on the free trip to Europe.

The constant fighting from the Bankses, the nonstop demand of extra chores that I never agreed to, and the perpetual snotty behavior of the two older daughters had begun pushing me toward the edge of quitting. This reaction to requesting a few extra days off from work finally pushed me over their bloody, British edge. There was no longer any chim-chiminey, chim cher-ee coming from me, and they certainly did not expect it, or like it.

After hanging up the phone, I found a private spot to sit down and contemplate my behavior. This was not like me; I never pushed back on anyone. I was a peacemaker, a meek little Mormon girl that never said no to anyone. I put my elbows on my knees, my face in my hands, and let the tears flow down my freckled, pink cheeks. Having a backbone felt unfamiliar to me and I was not sure how to process this new spark in my personality.

Amongst the hustle and bustle of the busy airport, I heard a random but familiar voice shouting toward the crowds of people. I took a deep breath, but not yet looking up, I wondered if the chipper, bubbly voice really belonged to whom I thought it did. "Work it, baby, work it," the high-pitched, energetic voice yelled. Ever so slowly, I began looking up, and before my eyes I saw two feet in white gym shoes running in place before me. I peeked upward a bit more and saw the bony knees, the short shorts, the tank-top, and the peach fuzz. There was a tremendous amount of curly chest hair spread across the man's torso, legs, and arms.

Running in place before me, I questioned if it really could be the eccentric, flamboyant exercise guru that I used to work out with, with my special needs friends. Was this energetic sweatin' to the oldies man really jogging in front of me? Eventually, I looked up and found myself staring into one hell of a glowing and joyful face. His smile was broader than the Brooklyn Bridge and his shiny, kind eyes were peering straight into my soul. Towering over me in a very unthreatening way, Richard Simmons' eyes seared brazenly into me and said, "Work it, baby, work it."

He held my gaze and kept his smile until I was willing to let a soft, natural grin escape my face. The second I accepted his moment of kindness and thoughtfulness, he was off, jogging down the remaining corridor of the Newark, New Jersey, airport. In those few moments of interacting with Richard Simmons, a sense of peace washed over me, telling me that everything was going to be okay.

My dear rapist, Richard Simmons was the first famous person I had ever encountered, and it is difficult not to compare my brief interaction with him to my long-term interaction with you. I felt palpable kindness and regard from Mr. Simmons that hot summer day in New Jersey. In fact, I felt more solicitude in one minute from this energetic, acclaimed fitness model than I ever did in those ten months with you.

He spent his life striving to be athletic and healthy, just as you have. He was in the media and in the film industry, just as you have been. Just like you, at one point he made a big move to Hollywood. Ironically, you both now struggle with mental health issues, but as far as we know, he did not spend his career lying, cheating, or manipulating others the way you have.

The energy Richard Simmons offered in sixty seconds was enough to get me out of my funk and onto my feet. I don't recall you ever doing one thing to try and lift my spirits. In fact, the more I was with you, the less I moved and the more I became frozen by fear. Mr. Simmons not only got my ass moving, but in less than a minute his energy filled me with confidence. Because of him, I stood up and I spent the next twenty minutes looking for Miley and Kari.

Never Yours,
A Richard Simmons Fan

***

My Dear Rapist,

Once I had found Miley and Kari, I shared with them the news of possibly losing my job, meeting Richard Simmons, and my sure determination to get to Jamaica. Miley and Kari confirmed that our luggage did indeed get on the plane and would be delivered to the hotel where we had booked our stay. We had a good nine hours to kill so, with time on our hands and a desire to get out of the airport, we decided we would go spend our time playing at Six Flags, a mere one-hour drive from the airport.

We didn't have much to bring with us, only our small carry-on bags. We had no idea we would get separated from our checked luggage and had not thought clearly in our packing. We had no change of clothes, no toiletries, and absolutely nothing to help us get freshened up after a day of sweat and amusement park rides. This did not seem too big of a deal, until my girlfriends decided to play a prank on me. The girls beckoned for me to walk over to them and watch a particular water coaster ride.

I had never been to a large amusement park other than the small one in my home state, and I did not know what to expect. Kari and Miley were intent on pointing something out to me so, I walked up the stairs to the cement platform and turned to look at what they were pointing at. Just as I arrived, they ran off down the stairs away from me. As my eyes locked onto the coaster, a large wave of water fell over me, drenching me from head to toe.

Within seconds, every single strand of hair, clothing, and eyelash was sodden with water. My black mascara wept slowly down my face and my hair became matted and hard due to the sick amount of hairspray I had used that morning. My khaki pants and white t-shirt immediately changed color, and the shame and embarrassment showed up in my cheeks almost instantly. If I had a nice rack, maybe I could have been proud of being in a wet t-shirt at a family-centered theme park. I looked like a hot mess and I had absolutely no clothes to change into, no tools to fix my makeup and hair, and not even a damn Q-tip to wipe away my thick, grimy mascara.

I was cold and I was mad. My white, pale skin started to turn into thick, bumpy chicken skin and nothing I could do would warm me up. I was now as deflated as my Utah hair. After a few more rides, I finally convinced Miley and

Kari to leave Six Flags and take me somewhere to buy some new clothes. We found a Marshalls in Trenton, and though my face and hair still looked like shit, at least my sunken AA titties were once again warm.

The girls were craving sushi, something I had never tried before, but I felt in the minority on this one and decided to trust them and give it a try. We still had several hours until we needed to be back at the airport, so Miley and Kari spent the next hour driving around looking for a sushi restaurant.

Again, a reminder that this was 1998. We had no cell phones and no Google map or Wi-Fi in our hands to find something quick and reputable. When we finally found a place, our stomachs were aching too much to care how sketchy and run-down the place looked. The girls suggested something as daring as eel for my first attempt at raw fish. I wish they would have proposed something slightly softer, perhaps a California or Philadelphia roll—maybe then, I would not have retched up the elongated, snake-like fish right in the middle of the squalid Jersey restaurant.

I was becoming more lethargic and enervated as the evening wore on. My sense of adventure had been greatly diminished, and I was aching for the warmth and relaxation that the Jamaican beaches were offering. I wanted nothing more than to get on that plane and forget about this entire day. Miley and Kari finally finished their sushi and climbed into the car with full bellies, while I still felt the pains of hunger and the aftertaste of the emitted anguilliform.

I curled up in the back seat, exhausted, as my girlfriends maintained a high level of energy and excitement for our upcoming flight. We needed fuel before we made our way toward the airport, so Miley started searching for the next available gas station. Once we found one, she had to climb out of the vehicle and look through her belongings for her driver's license while she filled her car with fuel.

Miley was constantly telling us to be careful and that we needed to always be mindful of our surroundings. She seemed to forget this in the moment, as she anxiously looked for her license. Kari and I were on the lookout, and I am not sure who noticed it first, but out of nowhere a small group of young men were walking straight toward us with crowbars in their hands.

There was no sign of friendliness penned upon their faces, so we both began yelling at Miley to get back inside and lock the door. Harshly, the boys started pounding loudly and violently on our car window, not just inquiring if we needed their help, but insisting on it. Horrified, we tried pulling away from the brusque group of boys, but like dirty little cockroaches, they clung to Miley's car, screaming unfamiliar words into our unsullied, Mormon girl ears. With racing hearts and a shit ton of fear, Miley pushed harder on the gas pedal, and one by one, each homicidal little aphid let go of the car and disappeared from our sight.

We drove in silence toward the Newark airport, each of us trying to wrap our heads around what had just happened. By this time, we were all feeling pretty defeated and our sense for adventure had completely waned. Our only solace was knowing we would soon be seated on a plane and our eyes could close and sleep off the exhausting events of the day.

We followed Miley's lead again, checked back in

with the ticket agent, and waited at the terminal for the invitation to board our flight. Once again, the invitation never came. Just like earlier that morning, the flight was full and our buddy passes would not be giving us a seat on the plane.

Going to Jamaica was just not in the cards for us and we finally conceded; it was time to go home. Unlike Miley and Kari, relaxation did not kick in for me as we headed northeast to Connecticut. My angst heightened as we passed each green mile marker on I-95. The peace and calm that Richard Simmons had injected into me earlier had completely left as I now had the indignation of Mr. and Mrs. Banks to face, as well as the potential loss of my job and my European vacation.

I didn't want to face my employers after such an exhausting day and decided to stay the night with Kari. But even after a night of sleep, it took some time for me to work up the courage to go home. Late afternoon came and I finally decided to grow some big, hairy balls and deal with the consequences of my actions. Kari dropped me off, and with my tail between my testicles, I walked through the side door of the home and immediately into the kitchen where Mr. and Mrs. Banks were having a conversation.

Once the shock and then the disappointment in seeing me wore off, they raged at what a horrible employee I was and how dare I talk to them the way I did. All I could do was grovel, apologize, and cry. I didn't lose my job, but I did lose my dignity as it became more and more apparent in their arguments that I was not a human, I was something to be owned, nothing more than a piece of their contractual property.

I suppose, my dear rapist, looking back now, you were not the first in my life to look at me as something other than human. In a sordid way, I was a naïve Mormon servant to them, just as I was a naïve captive Mormon girl to you.

Like you, they used anger, fear, and threats to also manipulate me into subserviency and complacency. Their threats of lawsuits, their words of shame, their scare tactics, and their forms of abuse in adding on more and more workload, all scared me into staying. Had I carried a crystal ball with me and foreseen that their behavior would worsen in Europe, I would have caught the next plane back to Utah, rather than the plane to London with the Bankses.

Never Yours,
A Submissive Piece of Property

***

My Dear Rapist,

Being captive in Europe with the Bankses was in some ways as frightening as being held captive by you in Utah. I did not necessarily feel like they were going to end my life, but their treatment of me in Europe was severe enough that I had the hotel staff helping me out in secret when they were not around.

Prior to the Jamaican drama, Mr. and Mrs. Banks had helped me plan to visit several tourist destinations on my scheduled days off in Europe. The itinerary included the first week to be spent in London, the following two weeks in

Malaga, Spain, and then the final two weeks back in London. In 1998, I didn't have access to a debit or bank account, as it was custom to pay nannies with cash.

Therefore, Mr. Banks deducted the tourist bookings from my weekly allowance and then gave me a $1,500 cash advance for the five weeks of my future work in Europe. Most of my sightseeing was scheduled for the last two weeks in London, as they wanted to show me off as their prized, all-American nanny to their British friends and family in the first week.

We landed at Heathrow Airport on a drizzly and murky Sunday evening. The flight was dreadful—baby Evelyn cried the entire seven-hour flight, and the two older girls were miserable little shits, constantly whining and complaining about everything. Mrs. Banks was excellent at bossing me around in front of the other passengers.

She proudly displayed her lordship over me as yappy, annoying demands spewed forth from her pitiful, enormous overbite. I was mortified; this woman operated on a level that I just could not, in any plausible way, resonate with. In her world, no one else mattered other than herself. Her ridiculous, thundering voice and crazed desire to be seen were embarrassing and shameful and I wanted nothing more than to crawl under the middle row of the small airplane seat and hide.

I kissed the ground when we arrived in England, believing her insistent and unfulfilled demands were about to come to an end. My wishful thinking did not last long. Gathering our luggage and acquiring the rental car was nothing but pure disaster in Mrs. Banks's eyes.

The modest fact there was a mix-up in the rental request sent her over the bloody edge. She was the most strung-out, pessimistic, impatient woman I had ever known. Once they figured out the rental car error and placed all of our belongings into the vehicle, Mrs. Banks went on with one of her usual tirades about the need to sue the rental car company for not having things perfectly lined up for her imperial majesty's arrival.

After an hour drive from the airport, we unloaded our items into the hotel room and rushed down to the restaurant for a bite to eat. The energy and the excitement from the happy crowd temporarily relieved my headache from Mrs. Banks's constant wretchedness. Blue lights, techno music, and the freedom of alcohol swept through the halls of the hotel like a California wildfire. It was magical, and my young Mormon spirit lifted for a brief moment.

I rested against the restaurant bench, amazed with myself and how far I had traveled. I was a dairyman's daughter, a shy Mormon girl who had spent most of her life in a small farming town. I had made it to London and did so without the help of my mother, my father, and without a single drop of alcohol in my system. My impressionable Mormon mind sat there, breathing it all in, not wanting to miss a heartbeat of this fresh and foreign world. Mrs. Banks appeared to have even settled down a bit and succumbed to the vivacity and exuberance that her native home was offering her.

Following this time of relaxation, we made our way to our hotel room with full bellies and crashed onto our crisp white hotel pillows, drifting peacefully off to sleep. The following morning was the start of a cumbersome week of visits with Mr. and Mrs. Banks's family and friends.

During these visits, I was introduced to British culture and foods like tuna fish on baked potato, tea and biscuits, Cadbury chocolate, and an abundance of toast. I had never known toast could be used in so many creative ways, nor consumed for all three meals of the day.

More so than the food, I fell in love with Britain's landscape. I adored the cobbled streets and brick homes, with the surprise beautiful green gardens growing in the backyards. It turned out that Mrs. Banks's mother was a beautiful, kind soul, which left me to wonder whom Mrs. Banks had inherited her patronizing and grueling behavior from.

Toward the end of our first week, I had it lined up to tour some of the big sites known to London. These sites included the London Bridge, Big Ben, the Changing of the Guards, Buckingham Palace, the Tower of London, the Crown Jewels, and even a little day cruise on the River Thames. As a twenty-year-old who had grown up in the middle of nowhere, seeing these particular sights felt significant.

It felt empowering and in many ways freeing to be untethered and adventurous in a foreign country. I especially loved the fact that nobody knew who I was and that nobody gave a damn if I was Mormon. At this point in my life, I had done more traveling and sightseeing than my own parents, and I had a feeling I had only just begun. I considered my first week in Europe a success as we began preparing for our Friday flight to Malaga, Spain.

The small two-and-a-half-hour flight to Spain was uneventful and quite a bit less stressful than the flight from New York City to London. Malaga, a port city on Spain's southern coast, is known for its hotels and resorts jutting up from its beautiful, sandy beaches. Malaga is part of the Costa del Sol, and its rich culture and exquisite food is a popular draw for the British, making it a notorious destination for holiday vacations.

The drive along the coast to reach our villa was breathtaking. Tucked away in a community filled with palm trees, we found our small three-bedroom, two-story, bricked flat, perfectly placed with a large and inviting outdoor pool.

Mr. and Mrs. Banks had several friends join in on the holiday in Spain, so there were a handful of extra children running around, which led me to believe the Bankses children would be sure to have a much more enjoyable experience. Saturday was our first full day of vacation, and though I was meant to have this day off, I ended up swimming well into the afternoon with the children until I was told to put them down for their naps.

Later, we gathered with the other families and barbecued until the sun went down. Of course, the next day, being Sunday, I would honor it as a holy day and choose not to swim. In Mormonism, it is taught that the Devil controls the waters on Sunday, but it is also a day of rest. Choosing to swim would mean I would be breaking the holy law of rest and testing my fate with Satan.

Not wanting to do either, I chose to sunbathe, read, nap, and write letters home. While most single nineteen-year-old girls would be out searching for parties, booze, boys, and sex, I chose alone time, in a villa, in Spain. God, I was so boring.

Monday began my first official workday in Spain. I spent the morning cleaning and ironing for Mrs. Banks and wrestling with the question of why I was cleaning on top of what the villa maid was already paid to do. At first I shrugged it off, not giving it too much attention, as my main assignment was to take care of the girls and just have fun swimming with them.

This seemed easy enough, especially because I really enjoyed the company of a thirteen-year-old girl named Louise, a family friend named Pauline, and her two daughters Cassy and Nicky. Pauline was my safe haven—she reminded me of a Mormon woman back home, and I felt safe and cared for in her presence. Pauline noted the way my employers treated me and without saying so many words, told me she did not approve. She also allowed me to use her phone to call home collect. Mr. and Mrs. Banks never even had the courtesy or foresight to think that I could be experiencing some feelings of homesickness. We had been in Europe three weeks at this point, and I did not once have an opportunity to call my parents and check in until Pauline offered her phone.

Hearing my mother's voice was music to my ears, and the few minutes I had with her left me briefly feeling a little less jaded toward my employers. I had a lot of built-up resentment for this couple who looked at me as nothing more than their American servant. The longer we were in Malaga, the more cleaning became my main assignment.

The more I cleaned, the more angry I became. The

more angry I became, the more homesick I became. The more homesick I became, the more the tears fell from my eyes. I was not happy, and my only refuge when Pauline was not around was thirteen-year-old Louise.

Louise carried more maturity and sexual insight than I, a twenty-year-old American-Mormon girl, ever had. Louise was stunned that I had never experienced sex, a sip of alcohol, or a cigarette. Louise thought I was "perfect" and wanted to spend every waking moment with me. She was so lonely, living as a British girl in a Spanish world, desperately craving attention and friends.

One evening, Louise and I went to a fiesta together and I informed her I was not going to stay long. The Banks family sucked the energy out of me, and I really valued my sleep and alone time. Upon expressing my desire for a short evening out, Louise lost her temper with me and begged me to stay for a while. I'm a sucker for pleasing people and even then, I felt the need to please a thirteen-year-old girl whom I knew I would never see again.

I stayed with Louise and spent the evening listening to her unload a bunch of verbal diarrhea about how bad her life was, all the while getting hit on by a group of fourteen-year-old boys. The highlight of the night, a moment in time I shall never forget, was getting my ear licked by a young Spaniard boy on the Ferris wheel. On one hand, I felt honored that the boy could even find my ear through my enormous hair, and on the other hand, I was mortified. I had never kissed a boy, let alone allowed a random stranger to drag his tongue along my hairspray-covered ear. I was twenty, he was fourteen, and while I should have punched him in the face, I chose to remain a meek, Mormon girl who did not want to start drama. Louise, on the other hand, found it all hilarious and entertaining.

I wanted to go back to my villa, scrub my ears until they were bloody raw, and vomit in the extra-clean, porcelain toilet that I had cleaned three times that day.

I tried hard to unleash the unsettled food into the foreign toilet, but it just would not happen. Instead, I climbed into my little bed and I did what I always did best—I cried. My homesickness had reached its maximum height, and I begged God to find a way to get me out of this worldly mess and back into Zion, the place where I could fulfill my life's mission of being a mother and wife. I journaled like crazy and made stupid, silly promises to God in my journal that if he would just go ahead and bring me a husband, I would be the best mother in Zion he could ask for. My only stipulation was that he bring me a husband that would tolerate my cottage cheese and be patient with my imperfect body until the resurrection. Yes, my dear rapist, you weren't the only one that disliked my cellulite. I despised it so much I often asked God to turn my body into Pamela Anderson's when it was my time to be resurrected.

Working for the Bankses in Europe had really started to take its toll on me. I was becoming more of a servant than a nanny to them and their bratty children. I spent hours in the morning ironing clothes and cleaning the villa while Mr. Banks slept and Mrs. Banks shopped with her girlfriends. Even as our time came to an end with one last beach trip, the parents spent their time sunbathing while I built sandcastles with the irksome little girls. But the icing on the cake was the fact it was a nude beach.

I have no real memory of what a European beach looks like. I have no memory of the landscape of this beach, no memory of palm trees, sunny skies, or the beautiful horizon. My memory of the one European beach we had visited consists of two images: aggravating children and boobs. While I entertained the girls, I couldn't help being completely transfixed by all the different sizes and shapes of female breasts.

My virgin Mormon eyes could not handle the realization that the Bankses had taken us all to a topless beach. I was astonished that Mr. Banks was not sitting up on his beach chair, drooling over all the free-floating knockers with a boner bigger than the Eiffel Tower. Why wasn't Mrs. Banks screaming and slapping the snot out of her husband for sneaking a peek at all the other women? I felt so dirty looking at other female breasts and felt intense shame as I was desperately asking myself if I needed to find a bishop so I could repent. My twenty-year-old brain was struggling to comprehend this topless, foreign beach and why there were not a plethora of men watching and jacking off nearby.

Europe was meant to be fun, an experience of a lifetime, but it was turning into a sinful, Mormon nanny nightmare. I was aching to go back to my sheltered Utah world where I felt safe in the arms of naivety and innocence. I yearned to be among a mother and father who were not always fighting with each other or threatening lawsuits on anyone and anything that pissed them off.

I wanted to go back to a normal job where I felt respected and valued. I wanted to be around children I chose, not these British brats who liked to kick me, call me a pig, or stick their sassy little tongues at me. I longed for a home where people knew me as Ginger, and not *our American nanny*.

I knew that with all of the extra work they were adding on in Europe, they were breaking their contract. In the next several weeks, I had plans to fly home for my brother's wedding, so I was leaning towards making the move a permanent one. The respectful and honest thing for me to do would be to give my two-week notice.

I began contemplating when and how to give my notice the night before we left Spain. Ironically, my journal entry says, "Three weeks from today, and I'll be home, unless Mr. and Mrs. Banks kidnap me, lock me up, or kill me after I tell them I cannot handle their oldest child anymore." Little did I know, within a few days, a portion of the entry would come to pass.

The very next day, Friday, we left for London. I was anxious throughout the entire flight, but it felt good to be back in a country where the predominant language was English.

The girls were rough that day, and every little teensy, weensy thing they did grated on my nerves. We landed around 2:30 p.m., but it took us five hours to get back to the hotel. During the car ride, the pressure and the overwhelming experience of how they had treated me, along with my homesickness, had finally caught up. Huge tears began to spew from my eyeballs as my stomach started twisting up in knots.

I could not speak, could not find the much-needed

words to tell them how much I hated working for their family. Once inside the hotel, the verbiage found its way out and spilled in a discombobulated mess all over Mr. and Mrs. Banks's laps. I let them know I could no longer handle them or their children, and I wanted to go home.

Initially, their reaction was kind. Mr. Banks did bring up the money and the contract and informed me I would have to reimburse him for the agency fee, but I knew what was in the contract and how they had broken it. For the first time since being in Europe, I went to bed that night with a smile on my face and a heavy burden lifted from my shoulders.

I woke up on Saturday morning feeling refreshed and ready for my day off. On my calendar was a scheduled tour of Leeds Castle, the town of Canterbury, and the White Cliffs of Dover. I had picked this tour out prior to putting my feet on European soil, so I didn't have to worry about the finer details of getting there or getting home. My favorite part of this particular day was the Tour of Leeds Castle. Exploring the rooms and learning of its 900-year history was absolutely breathtaking for me.

Outside, there was a maze, the Knights' Stronghold Playground, and the 500 acres of gardens that were brilliant to behold. I could not get enough of the castle and envied those who lived in Britain and had access to such rich history. Knowing my great-grandfather was born in Scotland and emigrated to Utah to be among fellow Mormons, I felt just a wee bit closer to my McKnight family heritage.

Upon returning to the hotel, Mr. Banks approached me and informed me that I needed to give him the $1,500 cash-advance money back that he had paid me prior to our leaving Connecticut. I don't recall the amount I gave him back, but my committed Mormon heart knew I had worked and felt I needed to still pay my tithing to the church.

Without him seeing, I kept the commanded 10% tithe and hid it in my scriptures, something I believed the Lord would bless me for. I then gave him all the cash that I had, not even thinking or flinching at how wrong the demand was. I had put the work and the time in as his European Cinderella and I had given a respectful two-week notice.

Sunday arrived and a lovely couple from the local Mormon Church, Harry and Pat, paid me a visit at my hotel. The Bankses had left to go visit family, so I had my room all to myself. After sharing my current troubles, concerns, and fears regarding my employers, Harry gave me a beautiful priesthood blessing. He blessed the room so Satan could not enter it and gave me a promise that I would go home with no animosity between the Bankses and I. He told me that God was with me and things would work out how God intended them to be. Knowing I was completely broke, Harry handed me a twenty-dollar bill before he walked out the door to help me make it through the coming week.

During my two days off, Mr. Banks flew back to Connecticut and left his family and I behind to finish out two more weeks in London. Mrs. Banks was not happy with me, and it was obvious that I was not happy with her or her girls. We were both miserable.

Any spare chance I had, I was calling Harry, Pat, my mother, or my girlfriends in Connecticut. A few days into the new work week, Mrs. Banks found out I had been making phone calls, and I had informed her that the advice given to me from back home was to not talk about the contract until we were back on American soil. This did not sit well with her, as all she wanted to do was talk about the contract. Informing her that I had sought advice on the circumstance made her feel like I had gone behind her back and was being deceitful.

I refused to budge on this discussion, and eventually she walked away from me. She wanted to spend the afternoon with her sister and offered me the chance to stay back at the hotel. I jumped on this, wanting to avoid her and the girls as much she would allow. It did not take long before I realized why she was so generous in her offer—the British hussy had put a block on the hotel room phone, preventing me from making any phone calls.

Fortunately, the staff at the hotel had noticed from our first night how crazy Mrs. Banks was and decided to sneak me back into their office and let me make my phone calls. Unbeknownst to her, I was forging my little plan to escape behind closed doors. For all she knew, I was trapped in my room all day with no phone and no money to go anywhere.

My friend Sarah had tried going to the house in Connecticut to gather my belongings and move me out, but Mr. Banks wouldn't let her in the house. She told him she would be coming back the next night, and if he didn't let her in, she would be calling the police. Brother Young, the counselor in the Bishopric, was a lawyer, and I had the opportunity to speak with him while I was using the hotel's office phone. He assured me that the things they were doing could get them in legal trouble, and continued to advise me not to talk about the contract while in England.

The more I refused to talk, the more upset Mrs. Banks became and the less she wanted me around to help. My only requirement was to help get the girls ready in the morning and then get them ready for bed. I felt somewhat like a hostage at the hotel. Harry and Pat did the best that they could during the week, offering me a place of refuge on the weekend.

My only lifeline while stuck at the hotel were the secret phone calls to my parents, friends, the lawyer, and Harry and Pat. Sherrie, the nanny agency representative, spoke with my parents and she was livid. She could not believe the things that they were doing and assured my parents and I that the Bankses had broken the contract long before I ever did. Sara finally was able to get all of my belongings, and while they tucked me away quietly in the hotel room, without food or money for those final two weeks, I was working out a plan to get away.

The stress I was causing Mrs. Banks was becoming more and more apparent. She wanted a day to herself to do some shopping without the girls, and asked if I would swim with the girls while she spent some time alone. I gave it a try, and the girls were so naughty and cheeky that a random lady from the locker room turned to both of them and shamed them for how unruly they were behaving. Mrs. Banks called during lunch to follow up and see how the girls were doing, and I did not hesitate to tell her the truth. We were waiting in the hotel lobby when Mrs. Banks returned, and she immediately walked in causing quite an embarrassing scene.

Screaming her head off, and with no regard to any of the other guests around, she grabbed the girls' hands and started smacking them repeatedly and as hard as she possibly could. She was oblivious to all the guests in the lobby staring at her awkwardly. Dumbfounded by her willingness to harshly slap her children in public, I disassociated from the scene and thought about the cute, blonde lifeguard at the pool with the sexy British accent who had asked for my phone number earlier that day.

Thankfully, the weekend arrived, and I was able to get away to Harry and Pat's home. It was a beautiful reprieve from the lonely hotel room life. Their flat was gorgeous, but it was their alluring backyard that filled me with peace and serenity, something that I had been longing for since giving my two-week notice. The garden that arose from their backyard was magnificent. My favorite memory was sitting with them in their garden after a beautiful Sunday service soaking up the beauty of the flowers and the greenery surrounding us.

Oh, how I grew to love this couple in just a matter of weeks. We bonded quickly over Mormonism and spent many hours talking and getting to know one another. Harry shared a very personal near-death experience and how he was given the choice to either live or die. They were such a lovely couple, their affection and beauty radiated from the inside out. They were generous and kind in every way imaginable.

I had planned a day trip to Paris and paid for the Eurostar to take me from London in the same way I paid and planned for the Leeds Castle tour. This Paris trip was also booked months before we arrived in Europe. However, because I had given Mr. Banks all of my money back, I had no money to spend for the trip to Paris. I was going to just miss the planned excursion, but Harry and Pat would not hear of it. They insisted that I go and gave me the finances to make the trip possible. I promised them that when I arrived home to the States and earned some money, I would pay them back tenfold.

We all went to bed early that night, knowing I would need to get up during the middle of the night to catch a taxi for Edgware Station. I was feeling somewhat empowered until I met Leonard, a strange drunk guy that would not leave me alone. He followed me into the train, sat down next to me, and was constantly in my face, asking questions. I thought this was the perfect opportunity to do some missionary work, with the hopes that if I brought up God, he wouldn't try to kidnap, rape, or sell me into sex trafficking.

I boldly and proudly announced to him that I was Mormon and spent the next thirty-three minutes educating him on the church until we got to Waterloo Station. Though we were discussing religion the entire time, deep down, I was terrified. I silently prayed and pleaded with God to protect me. Sure enough, he answered my prayer. As soon as Leonard got off the train, the guy across from me informed me that he was a cop and that I handled Leonard just right. Up to this point, I could probably count on one hand how many drunk guys I have had interactions with. Hearing the police officer's praise in how I handled him was more evidence that I was a chosen Mormon girl being protected in Babylon.

At 6:00 a.m. I boarded the Eurostar for the two hour

and sixteen-minute train ride to Paris. I thought the twenty minutes underwater from England to France would freak me out, but traveling on the longest underwater train system in the world was electrifying. The countryside of Calais, France, reminded me a little bit of my hometown but with no mountains. I was exhausted from getting up during the middle of the night, so I slept the remainder of the ride to Paris.

The first half of the day, we toured the main attractions—the Louvre, the Eiffel Tower, Notre Dame, and a boat tour on the Seine River. I met a wonderful family from Long Island who invited me to spend the day with them shopping and trying out delicious cafes. It was a quick but edifying experience. It was so nice to be away from Mrs. Banks and the girls. The stress of their drama and hatred toward me was too much.

Experiencing Europe without them fed my soul and made me feel like a normal young adult. I did question my sanity and wondered if I was just being an American brat, but as I spent more time with complete strangers, strangers who behaved normally and didn't treat me like a piece of property, I knew I wasn't being a snob. Deep down, I knew the Bankses had never treated me right and I knew I had the right to speak up for myself and walk away from the job. Being around people who were kind and considerate of others left me feeling like things were going to be okay, that I was going to be okay. Spending time in Paris on my own was the perfect gift for the end of the European vacation.

On the Eurostar ride home, I sat next to a beautiful young woman named Ada and we ended up talking about

Mormonism. In fact, I ended up talking about the church with everyone I met in Europe, not realizing this had planted the seed to consider serving a Mormon mission. It was a quiet and exhausting ride home, but a day that I will never forget. I was twenty years old and again reveled in the realization that I had seen more of the world than my own parents, grandparents, friends, and siblings.

Pat picked me up from the Uxbridge Station at 11:30 p.m., took me back to her home, fed me dinner, and then put me to bed. We spent most of the following day at church. Church consisted of three hours in England, just as it did in the United States. The nice thing about Mormonism is that the same lesson that was taking place in my small hometown was also taking place at the Mormon churches in France, England, Russia, China, Ghana, and every other country where Mormonism existed. This made it comforting to go to church, knowing that my parents back home would be hearing the exact same sermon as I was. Being inside a Mormon Church, no matter where it is in the world, always made me feel like I was home.

Pat and Harry were my European parents, and I was deeply grateful that I could go to a Mormon church with them and find peace and acceptance. When church ended, we went back to their home, had some dinner, and decided we all needed a good nap. I was forced to say my goodbyes to this wonderful couple, and as they dropped me off at the hotel at 10:00 p.m., I remembered to ask for their address so I could repay them for all that they had done for me while in London.

The remaining few days in London were

uneventful—lots of goodbyes for Mrs. Banks and her girls, and me doing the bare minimum. I was checked out, Mrs. Banks was checked out, and we were both tired of seeing each other's faces. The seven-and-a half-hour plane ride back to New York could not come fast enough. Little did Mr. and Mrs. Banks know that waiting at the terminal would be my friend Sara. They were completely ignorant to the fact that their American servant was about leave them, never to return for a spoonful of sugar or to polish another fucking set of silverware again.

My dear rapist, I will never forget the look of shock on Mrs. Banks's face as we walked down the terminal and I told her Sara was waiting for me. For the first time since I had known her, her buck-toothed mouth went completely quiet. As I reflect on Mrs. Bank's behavior, I cannot help but wonder if she was either experiencing postpartum depression or engulfed by the stress of raising three young girls in a foreign country without the support of family and friends.

As an overwhelmed mother myself, and one who lives far away from a strong support system, I want to now extend some grace toward her. I don't know if this is good or bad, all I know is that I have behaved poorly at times and sincerely hope that others don't hold me to old, toxic versions of myself that I have tried to shed and move on from. I must admit, I do find it difficult to extend this same grace to you. I have moments of a softened heart, but at this time these moments are fleeting. In fact, they are as fleeting as Richard Simmons jogging away down a Newark, New Jersey Airport. But, I digress.

Now, back to the Banks family.

With my luggage in my hand and Sara by my side, I said a quick goodbye and turned to walk away. Mr. Banks now stood by Mrs. Banks's side, and in silent anger, glared at me through his European glasses. I turned around one last time, stuck my tongue out at the girls, and whispered, "Your fat nanny pig won't be coming back."

Yes, I wish I would've had the courage to walk away from you, like I did with the Banks family. I wish I would've had loved ones in the background assisting me in formulating a plan on how to get away from you. With them, I had help from the hotel staff, from a lawyer at church, from the nanny agency, from my family and from my friends. Most of all, I believed that God still had my back. With you? I had no one. I didn't have a single person I could trust to help me find a way to leave you—not even God could help me leave you safely. I knew that not only was it solely up to me to get out alive, but it was up to me to figure out how to get my power back.

With them, I was a contractual pig kept hidden behind a hotel door. With you, I was a desperate dog kept hidden behind apartment walls, never even worthy to receive the scraps of your McDonald's Happy Meal.

Never Yours,
A Freed Fat Pig

***

My Dear Rapist,

With one week left in Connecticut, I had one final

thing to do before I said goodbye to my East Coast Life—experiencing my first kiss. I was excited to get to church and see all of my friends, the bishop, and to thank Brother Young for his help while I was held captive in London. A new boy had moved into the ward while I was away, and Sara and my friends thought for sure I would be into him.

Parker was tall, blonde, brown-eyed, and eccentric just like Sara. They told me he was interested in me, so my girlfriends orchestrated a little one-on-one time with him. He knew I had never kissed a boy, and the girls wanted him to be my first kiss and have me leave Connecticut with a bang.

Sara arranged a party the night before I flew out, at her house, with a group of single adult friends from church. Parker showed up and right away took me into a bedroom and had me lie down on the bed. I was so nervous, I was sweating. I told him I had never done this before, and he assured me that it was all going to be okay and would be worth it. He quickly moved his lips over mine and began to kiss me hard. He was biting me and making noises, and as he climbed on top of me, I felt something bony between my legs.

I wasn't quite sure what was going on, all I knew was that my lips were hurting like hell and there was something hard, painfully pressing up against me.

I was finding nothing romantic, or cute, about our random vampire biting fest. The makeout session went on for a neverending forty-five minutes, and I was screaming in my head for it to be done. This experience with my first kiss was ambiguously similar to your violations,my dear rapist. The difference, however, was the giving of my consent and the fear surrounding him was only looking lame if I called it quits, not a fear of being killed. I'm sure, as with many girls, my "firsts" were not the only ones that were far from magical or special. No, my firsts were more about Parker's gratification and yours than it ever was about what I wanted.

I figured since Parker was experienced, he would know when to quit, but he didn't. It went on and on and on and finally, once he decided the rough kissing marathon was over, I got up from the bed and walked out to my friends. I was in a complete daze. My big hair was disheveled, my lips hurt like hell, and my pubic bone felt like it had been sawed down by a metal bat. My girlfriends took one look at me and started laughing hysterically. I'm not sure where Parker ended up, but I ended up walking painfully toward a mirror and saw a horrid gizmo doll staring back. The bastard had kissed me so damn hard, my lips had swelled up and turned purple.

I had planned to walk off the Utah-bound plane with confidence. It had been eight long months since I had seen my family and friends, but instead I would be walking down the terminal with lips the color and size of Barney the Dinosaur. I tried setting my ego aside, not wanting to give a damn, but all that mattered in the end was that I was flying home to safety. I was going home to Zion, to parents who never fought, parents who never talked about frivolous and petty lawsuits, and parents who actually enjoyed being parents.

My dear rapist, I had adventure and I had dreams. I have no regrets working eight months for or traveling to Europe with a family that looked at me as property. I had given my all to Mr. and Mrs. Banks and I truly wanted it to work out with them. Like you, they didn't treat me well, and I was nothing but an object to them.

But I was chosen and special.

I believed it to be more important to stand as a silent, passive, Mormon girl and avoid contention at all costs, than to advocate for myself.

Like you, they kept me hidden behind closed doors, stripping me of my sense of safety. Looking back, I should have learned from this experience and had it prepare me better for my time with you. But it didn't, and I allowed both of you to walk all over me. The difference between them and you is that I moved on from them. They didn't rape my mind with sixteen years of fear. Mr. and Mrs. Banks were only after my money; it was always about the money with them. But you, you were after my mind, my body, my soul.

I would love to give my twenty-year-old self a big hug and whisper into her ear the importance of opening her eyes and learning what it means to be manipulated and taken advantage of. I would tell her that as wonderful as it is to have a big heart, it would be vital to not let the heart overshadow the brain. I would tell her to stand up for herself and to never allow anyone to hide her in a corner, behind closed doors, or behind an apartment and hotel wall ever again. Nobody should ever put the Dairy Man's Daughter in a corner.

Never Yours,
Bruised & Swollen Lips

CHAPTER 7

CALLED TO SERVE

"The Lord made it clear at the very start of this last dispensation that we were to take the gospel to all the world... Whatever their age, capacity, Church calling or location, Latter-day Saints are called to the work to help take the gospel to all the world."

(General Conference Talks and Ensign Articles, Erying, Henry B., 2013, par 1)

My Dear Rapist,

I boarded that flight from New York to SLC, anxious and ready to move back to Zion to find my eternal companion. I proudly entered Utah with all the confidence of a twenty-year-old girl who had just given up her virgin lips to a boy in animalistic heat. Even so, I was ready to start my quest for the ideal husband.

I was especially eager to reconnect with Elder Henderson, whom I had met in the Connecticut ward. We had written to each other while I was in Europe, and he had been home in Utah a month by now from his mission in Connecticut.

I was anxious to see if this handsome boy—with his dark hair, natural bronze skin, and brown eyes—was going to be the one to kneel with me at the temple altar. By his looks alone, I had determined I could marry him, but because he was a missionary, we hadn't dared date or flirt in Connecticut.

Marriage constantly took up space in my head, but I was still petrified of it. As much as I daydreamed about exchanging vows and rings, making babies, and becoming a perfect Mormon wife, deep down, I wanted to run as far away from it as I possibly could. I could not imagine a Mormon man really loving me for me, when *I* didn't really even know who I was. In my head, the pressure to be a perfect Mormon wife consisted of looking like Pamela Anderson, cooking like Julia Child, performing like Jenna Jameson in the bedroom, and acting like Mother Teresa by day.

Do the right things, say yes to the inspired callings,

support your husband in his career and his church service, serve your neighbors and church members, push out lots of babies and raise them perfectly, and then give all your time and attention to the upbuilding of the Kingdom of Mormonism. This laundry list left me feeling incredibly overwhelmed and unqualified for my future. However, I *knew* that this was my purpose in life and somehow I had to fulfill all of these roles not just perfectly, but worthily, and with a righteous and humble desire.

I had moved into an apartment near the special needs center with my twin sister and two girlfriends. My wonderful Aunt P offered me a position once again, and I loved being back among these beautiful souls. Elder Henderson and I had met up several times to try and get to know each other outside of his title as Elder and my title as Nanny. With both of us being shy, communication did not flow well between us. He was certainly dreamy to look at, but outside of that, I had a difficult time holding a conversation with him.

One evening, we were together at my new apartment, making out on a small bean bag, and when it came time for him to leave, he mentioned something briefly about marriage. I freaked out and was in no way ready for this handsome returned missionary to see me naked, let alone see my plump cottage cheese legs.

Just as quickly as I ended things with my sixth-grade boyfriend, I did so with Elder Henderson. This abrupt halt ceased any exploration of a union between the two of us; my imperfect body just wouldn't allow it. Instead, I put my head down and dove back into the world of special needs, working over sixty-five hours a week and volunteering with my beloved community. As I did in high school, I felt comfortable around them and didn't feel like I had to pretend. I could be me, and I felt free.

Several months passed, and my twin sister and I wanted a new car of our own, tired of sharing the same one we'd had since high school. Our wonderful father agreed to cosign for each of us, but with one request—that we pray to find out if we were meant to serve a Mormon mission.

In the late '90s, it was becoming more common for young women from the church to serve missions. My desire to serve a mission was never strong—I had perhaps entertained the idea for a few moments, but it never lasted. My mind was always in the gutter, I liked to swear, and I liked to live on the edge of Mormonism. I believed in it, but I would try and bend the rules as often as I could.

Multiple piercings, bleach blonde hair, funky clothing, and a willingness to hang out in bars and dance clubs were just some of the things that I liked to do, even though I was committed to not drink, do drugs, have sex, or drink coffee. I liked living on the edge, so I knew the rigid rules and lifestyle of a Mormon mission would not suit me.

My twin, on the other hand, was a rule-follower. She loved all things Mormon, loved being a homemaker early on in life, and dressed like the church librarian. I used to joke with her that God made us twins so that she would keep me in line and keep me in the church, and I would add a little spice to her life so she wouldn't be so boring. Because of how different we were, I believed my father's simple request would end up with my twin receiving a yes from God, and I would get the gift of a hard and fast no.

Wanting a new car more than wanting even a new pair of sexy underwear, I committed to his request and prayed. I gathered my scriptures and sequestered myself into my bedroom. Kneeling down upon the floor with my elbows pressed on top of my bed, a sizable smirk on my face, and a comfy pair of granny panties resting comfortably on my ass, I began to pray.

I was so sure of what kind of answer I'd get, so it was a half-attempt at a prayer that was only meant to humor my father. I sloppily asked God if I was meant to serve a mission, waited a few moments, and thankfully did not receive a powerful Joseph Smith moment. I decided I'd give it a little more effort and try the ol' "flip open your scriptures and see where it lands" concept.

I don't know that this technique was ever doctrinal, but I know many times in Mormonism, members will say a prayer looking for answers, then flip open their scriptures and just start reading. Whatever answer was meant for us would somehow magically appear on the random landing of a page, leading us to believe this was God's way of communicating his answer. It so happened I landed on a section in the Doctrine and Covenants that talked about missionary work, and as I read with my mouth agape, I knew God was telling me to serve a mission. I was pissed, I couldn't believe it. God wanted me to serve a Mormon mission.

I sat on my bed, wondering what the actual hell was going on. Certainly God had to have mixed me up with my twin sister. Others got us mixed up all the time, so why was God exempt from confusion? I kept reading and I kept reading and I kept reading, and the words "missionary work" continued to appear on the pages of my scriptures. I wanted to burn the book, or at least stick a fork into the center of my eyeballs. I wanted it to stop, I did not want my eyes to see what they were reading. I did the only thing that I could think of, and I cried. Hard.

I thought for sure my sister would get the answer to go as well, but to my dismay, she got the answer that I had hoped for. She was the one to get a flat-out no. Feeling a bit bewildered and unsettled, we both approached our father and told him our answers: she was staying and I was going. She was going to get to the privilege of wearing her librarian-styled granny panties in her new cosigned vehicle. I was going to get the privilege of wearing the new, sacred, long underwear while walking door to door to spread God's everlasting word.

What was I going to do? Well, I did what I was taught not to do. I ignored the answer. I avoided my scriptures, I avoided my knees on the floor, I avoided my hands clasped in prayer, and I focused on my job at the special needs center—to no avail. The nagging, the internal nagging of *knowing*, would not stop grating on my nerves. A tiny voice inside my head continued to annoy me until my head and my heart went to war with each other. I spent weeks feeling this internal conflict, until one day, I caved and approached my father in tears.

"Why would God give me an answer to go when I have zero desire to go?" I asked him.

With nothing but kindness in his eyes and love in his heart, my father simply replied, "Maybe God knows what's best for you."

My dear rapist, this same knowing was what I experienced just hours before you asked me out on a date years later. Just as my heart and head collided with a desire to serve a mission, my heart and head collided with saying yes to you. With the mission, I *knew* I needed to go. With you, I *knew* I needed to run. However, there was one major difference in the decision-making between you and the mission, and that was the support and wisdom of my father.

My father's words sealed the deal with my missionary fate, and I began the paperwork to serve.

Never Yours,
Dazed and Confused

***

My Dear Rapist,

Soon after submitting my missionary application, the McKnight family experienced the unexpected death of our beloved patriarch, Grandpa Paul. On Tuesday, April 6, 1999, my Aunt P received the sudden and devastating news. She came out of her office in a panic, tears running down her face, and said that Grandma Ella had called and requested she meet her at the hospital. Grandpa was there with her, but he was dead. Fortunately, the special needs clients had left for the day and I was just finishing up my chart notes.

My aunt allowed me to join her on the drive to the hospital and within minutes, we found Grandma, still clothed in her temple dress and white slippers.

We learned that Grandpa had died during the middle of a temple session. It is not uncommon for retired, elderly members to spend most of their day serving at the temple, and my grandparents cherished their time volunteering in God's earthly home and did it as often as they could. Each endowment session would take about two and a half hours to work through. Grandma and Grandpa would do a session in the morning, travel to the cafeteria in the basement for lunch, then would fit one or two more sessions into the afternoon.

After eating lunch that day, Grandma and Grandpa had decided to do a second session. During the endowment, the women sit on the left side of the room and the men sit on the right side of the room. About twenty minutes into the session, the men are invited to stand and begin the process of making their covenants with God. It is not uncommon for the geriatric population to fall asleep during this part of the endowment, and so when it came time for my grandfather to stand and he didn't, the gentleman behind him tapped him on the shoulder to wake him up. My grandfather never came to, he simply bowed his head and silently passed away.

Grandma was a mess. I had never seen her so emotional, so we hugged her tightly, and together we cried. My aunt and I were both allowed to enter the room where Grandpa was, something I feel very fortunate to have experienced. When I stepped inside, he was lying on the hospital gurney dressed in his white temple clothing, looking peaceful and serene. Reverently, I walked toward him and planted a gentle kiss on his cold, dead cheek. Despite being in a rigor mortis state, Grandpa was practically glowing in his holy clothing.

Like most Christian religions, Mormons believe that baptism is necessary for eternal salvation. However, since many people have never been baptized, Mormons believe God provided a way for the dead to enter into baptism. This is done by "proxy," meaning that I, as a twelve-year-old girl, could enter the baptismal font inside the temple, stand in the water in an all-white, zip-up jumper, and be held by the arms of a man with God's authority. We are then dunked on behalf of our dead ancestors, giving them a choice to accept or reject the offering.

Once you decide to serve a mission or choose to marry within the temple, you move on from baptisms for the dead to receiving your endowments. The endowment is the most exalted and redeeming ordinance a Mormon believer can obtain in this life. It is a sacred ceremony where we are washed, anointed, instructed, endowed, and sealed with eternal promises and blessings.

It is at this first endowment ceremony when we remove our worldly underwear and replace it with the holy underwear. The sacred garment consists of two pieces, a top and a bottom. They are worn under normal street clothing and carry deep meaning and symbolic significance.

It wasn't until a month after Grandpa died that I went through the endowment for myself. I was taught that if I wore the garment appropriately, with strict obedience and integrity, I would be protected from the fiery darts of Satan and would be stronger at warding off sinful desires. The garment would be my metaphorical piece of God's armor.

Once I committed to the garments, I was meant to wear them for the rest of my life. I was instructed to never remove them except for intimacy, swimming, bathing, and showering. The bottom garment reached to my knees and the top garment covered my chest and extended to the cap of my shoulders. This design pushed for modesty, ensuring shorts were long, disqualifying tank tops, and preventing any exposure of the breasts.

My dear rapist, the garment, and other robes meant for the temple, are considered so vital to our salvation that we are buried in them when we die. If one commits a serious sin, such as adultery, it can be requested by a bishop or stake president that the transgressor remove the garment until they meet certain steps of repentance. Once removed, it is the bishop or stake president that approves the garment to be worn again.

Though I was never instructed to remove my garments while we were together, I spent many days questioning if I should just remove them myself and not wait for a bishop's admonition to do so. It was difficult to not look at my garments as a defilement, not just from me caving to certain sinful temptations, but because they did not protect me from your hands pulling them to my ankles.

I did dress modestly, I did wear them as instructed, and I did wear them with strict obedience and integrity. In the end, it did not matter. You still raped me, they did not protect me, and as a result, I knew I would never again feel a glow about them in the way my grandfather glowed on the day he died in his holy robes.

Never Yours,
A Grieving Granddaughter

***

My Dear Rapist,

I was stunned, devastated, and struggling to understand how to process my grandfather's death as I continued to wait for my mission assignment. In a very selfish way, I was incredibly angry with God that he would take him away as I was preparing to serve.

The weeks continued to drag by, and I was surprised that I had not yet received the large, white envelope, stamped in large print with *The Office of the First Presidency, The Church of Jesus Christ of Latter-Day Saints* that contained my anticipated acceptance. The application had included answering many personal questions about schooling, one's testimony of Mormonism, of Jesus, and of one's own emotional and mental health.

There had been interviews with bishops and stake presidents and visits with doctors and dentists. It had taken six weeks to obtain all the required forms, and it would be an additional month before I would receive the official envelope.

During that time—on April 20, 1999 to be exact— Littleton, Colorado, experienced what would later be known as one of the worst high school mass shootings in the history of America. Two students opened fire at Columbine High School, killing twelve classmates and one teacher, wounding twenty-one others, and then ultimately killing themselves. I am horrified to admit that the selfish twenty-one-year-old Mormon in me immediately started to worry that God would need to delay my mission call due to this act of terrorism. If I didn't think so grandiosely of myself or believe that I had a mission to fulfill and people to preach his gospel to, perhaps I would have had more compassion for what had just happened at Columbine.

Rather than sit and process what this meant for the future of our country, I wanted God's attention on me. This mass shooting was more evidence to me that we were on the verge of a religious apocalypse, and it filled me with a sense of urgency to convert the world to Mormonism.

This shooting fueled an inner oath to accept the answer I was given and commit myself to saving souls before the Second Coming of Jesus Christ. Several times throughout my growing up in Mormonism, we were asked by our leaders if we would die for our faith. I always claimed I would, and witnessing this type of mass shooting in real time took this hypothetical one step closer to reality.

I knew that if I were to go on a mission and someone pointed a gun to my head, asking me to deny my faith in Mormonism or get shot, I would rather take a bullet to my brain than deny my faith. Questions of comfort and safety stirred within me as I contemplated leaving my family and friends just to come home in a body bag, with the black missionary nametag placed proudly upon my Sunday dress.

Between the Columbine shooting and the sudden death of my grandfather, I was becoming more and more anxious about leaving home. I knew that I had my answer to go, so I continued to ignore my unease and prepare for the mission, all the while grieving the loss of my wonderful grandfather.

Eventually, through the grief and angst, the envelope came. I chose to open my letter not only in front of my family and high school friends, but with my special needs clients at work. My parents, my Aunt P, my Grandma Ella, my sister, my little brother, and several girlfriends were in attendance. It was a snug little tribe of those who I loved most, and it felt simple and perfect.

I had spent many hours up to this moment daydreaming about the exotic and unique place God would pick out for me. Deep down, I ached for a third world country, specifically somewhere in Africa. Growing up in a predominantly white community, I was drawn to the commercials on TV imploring Americans to either help feed the children in Africa or sponsor them in school.

Many times, I wanted to call the 1-800 number on our rotary phone and tell the person on the other end that I was just a child and I had no money, but request permission to be a pen pal to the children they were advertising. I never did make that call, but every time the commercials came on, I would stop dead in my tracks, transfixed by the kids who were so different from me. When it came time to serve my mission, I pleaded with God that the letter would list this part of the world as my destination.

I was nervous and excited to see if my prayers would be answered. We arranged the chairs in a large circle and I stood at the head of it. I ripped the envelope open and began to pull out its contents so I could begin the official reading of my mission call.

Dear Sister McKnight,

You are hereby called to serve as a missionary of The Church of Jesus Christ of Latter-day Saints. You are assigned to labor in the Detroit, Michigan Mission. It is anticipated that you will serve for a period of 18 or 24 months. You should report to the Provo Missionary Training Center on July 3, 1999. You will prepare to preach the gospel in the English language. Your assignment may be modified according to the needs of the mission president.

When I stood in front of my little group of loved ones and I read aloud the words, "Detroit, Michigan Mission," I immediately started to cry. These were tears of regret, not joy, and I had silently wondered if God had been drinking a bottle of vodka when he whispered to the prophet where Sister McKnight should go. WTF wasn't an acronym in 1999, but if it was, I probably would have said it aloud and shocked every adult with a special need out of their disability. I wanted to rip that white paper into shreds, shove it back into its holy envelope, and walk it back to the prophet's desk myself.

How could it possibly be safe for a white country girl with enormous Aqua Net hair to walk the streets of Detroit, the murder capital of America? I belonged in Africa with the giraffes, the elephants, and the lions. All the piles of books that I had checked out from the library highlighting Kenya, Zimbabwe, Nigeria, and Ghana had been read in vain. Perhaps God really didn't know the most intricate desires of my heart or care about what I wanted. I didn't even want to go on a mission, so why in the hell could he not at least send me somewhere exotic, or somewhere cool to talk about? Nobody ever comes right out and says it, but stateside missions are lame, especially if you are assigned to Utah or Idaho. Everyone wants to open their mission call to a foreign country, and culturally, the more bizarre the destination, the more special the missionary seems to be.

All of the mixed thoughts running through my head were interrupted by a heavy-set Down syndrome woman knocking me over with a beautiful smile and hug. Marla, sweet red-headed Marla, decided to run to me and make me feel better. The next thing I knew, I was on my back on the floor with her on top of me, embracing me and giggling like a little girl with her bottle-rimmed glasses.

This endearing act of love brought me back to reality and back to the arms of each of my loved ones hugging me and congratulating me on my mission call. I was to report in July, giving me two months to prepare for my departure to the Provo Missionary Training Center. The only arms I had missed during this moment were the bronze, strong, dairy-farming arms of my Grandpa Paul.

Regardless of my disappointment in my mission call, I pressed on like a good Mormon girl. The next step in the process would be to take out my own endowments and go to the temple. A small group of us gathered together on a beautiful May morning in the Logan, Utah Temple parking lot. My father, mother, Grandma Ella, several aunts and uncles, and my brother joined in on my Mormon milestone. My brother had already served his mission in St. Louis, Missouri, and was a great support for me at this time. I feigned happiness and excitement for my family, since I knew they were happy for me and proud of me, but deep down, I did not want this at all. To make matters worse, just prior to walking through the doors, my brother pulled me aside and whispered something a bit perplexing into my ear. "Ginger, just remember Satan makes good things look bad," he said.

I was startled and had no idea what he could possibly mean. I had taken temple prep classes at the church to help me prepare for this important event, so I wasn't quite sure how to process his warning. With my loved ones by my side, I chose to press on, spending the next four hours weighed down by confusion, embarrassment, more confusion, fear, and more confusion. Out of respect for my loved ones, I will not go into the details of the endowment rituals, but what I will say is that I wanted to run, but the cognitive dissonance kept my feet planted inside the walls of the castle on the hill.

I didn't understand the confusion and fear I was experiencing as I stared at the smiling, happy, tear-filled faces of my loved ones. This was the place that my Grandpa loved, where he spent all of his spare time, and where he had taken his last breath.

My dear rapist, I *should* have been feeling what they were all feeling, but I wasn't. I thought this could only mean one thing—something was wrong with me. I spent the time convincing myself I did not have the spirit with me, that I didn't have enough faith, and I was being punished because I lacked the sincere desire to really serve a mission. Just as Mormonism caused me to second-guess myself, so did you. All of these feelings I experienced on the day I went to the temple, I felt with you. Both scenarios made perfect sense; I was the one with the problem.

Outside of preparing to leave for Detroit and going to the temple as much as I could, I continued to work and volunteer with the special needs community. I was such an awkward twenty-one-year-old Mormon girl. I attempted a few dates, but nothing ever went anywhere. I secretly hoped I would meet my prince charming, someone who would save me from the eighteen-month sentence I just signed up for.

My pre-mission dates were never memorable, except one. I was set up with a red-headed, freckle-faced boy who was a returned missionary. He informed me of two things while eating an awkward dinner at Angie's Restaurant on Main Street. First, he had a secret fetish for lesbian porn. Second, he reinforced the cultural notion that girls who serve missions are weird, and if they are not weird before they leave, they will certainly come home weird.

In addition, he felt I should know that women who serve missions will most likely only find a husband to marry in the afterlife. Hearing this misogynistic bullshit instigated a huge complex over making sure I did not come home from Detroit weird.

Never Yours,
I am the problem

***

My Dear Rapist,

Fortunately, I had two adventures planned before my

commitment to the black nametag that declared my devotion to Jesus Christ and Mormonism. One month before I was to arrive at the Missionary Training Center in Provo, my sister and I and several friends decided to travel to Washington, DC and NYC. I was missing the energy of the East Coast and felt like I deserved one last act of freedom.

My number one goal for NYC was to come home with a tattoo. I was dying to live a little on the edge, because I knew how strict mission life was going to be. I was determined to get a tiny, feminine, CTR symbol tattooed on my ankle. CTR stands for Choose the Right, and it is a tradition in Mormonism to be gifted a CTR ring when you get baptized. I had always wanted a tattoo, but it is widely frowned upon in the church.

The doctrine declares that our bodies are a temple and choosing to ink ourselves means we are choosing to defile it. There have been hundreds of talks in the church, if not thousands, specifically addressing this very thing.

Knowing tattoos were frowned upon, but feeling like God would be cool with it because this was a symbol from his one true church, I found ways to justify and save money for my unrighteous desire. The girls and I booked our flights, planned our itinerary, and headed to the East Coast. Five gullible girls from rural Utah who didn't smoke, drink, or really know how to party like other kids our age, made our way to Washington, DC.

Our first goal was to hail a cab, take our luggage to the hotel, and freshen up before we began a tour of the city. As we were walking out of the airport with our luggage, though, we were taken off guard by a group of tall, older

Black men encircling us and our belongings. Without asking for their help, they grabbed our luggage from our hands and told us to follow them.

I'm certain we had an invisible cardboard sign declaring our naivety and an invitation to be taken advantage of. Thank goodness we had our friend Star with us. This brazen friend stood up to these DC Metro bastards, grabbed our luggage from their hands, and demanded they leave us the hell alone. If this wasn't enough to jar our sensitive souls, what we were about to discover inside our hotel room left us reeling with anxiety and fear.

With just five of us, we had booked one room with two double queen beds with the intention to request a cot. The cot was delivered quickly while we took some time to freshen up. When we finished getting dolled up, we decided to set everything up so that when we returned from our late night out, we could climb straight into bed and crash. Upon opening the cot, we found a mysterious, medium-sized crumpled paper bag shoved between the mattress and the metal frame.

Curious, we timidly opened the brown bag to see what was inside. My sister cautiously pulled her hand out of the bag and in it were three extra-large butcher knives. Our innocent minds quickly conspired to believe that we were either being framed as murder suspects or being set up to be kidnapped and sold into DC's sex trafficking ring. Were the big, scary men from the airport standing outside our door? I was the only female in the group who had gone through the temple, so my underlying layer of conceit believed my holy garments would not only protect me, but would also protect my friends from murderers and kidnappers. I had the armor of God on my body, so surely I could take down sex traffickers and serial killers.

Eventually, we called the front desk and asked them to relieve us of the murder weapons. Once the knives were turned over to the hotel staff, we left for the night both fearful and excited to explore the nightlife of Washington. After spending two days in DC, we hopped on a Greyhound bus and made our way to the Big Apple.

We did the typical tourist sites like the Statue of Liberty, Central Park, the World Trade Center, and the Empire State Building. One of the highlights of our time in NYC was waiting in line for seats at the *Sally Jesse Raphael Show*. In the late '90s and early 2000s, Sally Jesse Raphael was a well-known tabloid talk show host, predating Oprah Winfrey by just a few years.

Sally Jesse was an older, white woman, notorious for her orange-blonde hair, thick red glasses, and bright red lipstick. For reasons I cannot remember, the producers chose to give our group seats closest to the stage. Witnessing the behind-the-scenes production for daytime TV was fascinating, with the lights, the revolving lit-up signs telling the audience when to applaud, when to laugh, and when to boo. The camera crew seemed to focus a lot of time on our faces, often with Sally holding her microphone and standing right next to us in the aisle. I'm not sure why we were given special attention, but my guess is that we were young, and we looked incredibly out of place.

The highlight of the show did not come from the large cameras aimed at our faces, or from Sally standing so close to us while in the audience. The highlight was my twin sister being personally invited by a cameraman to dance on stage. He tried doing a little bumping and grinding with her, but my poor, innocent sister had never attempted such an immoral move in her life. This day was different—this day she made an attempt at being a brave, dirty dancer on live TV. Unfortunately, she failed, but I will forever be proud of her for trying.

Our East Coast vacation had started out scary, but it ended on this very humorous note. Unfortunately, the unrighteous desire of getting a CTR tattoo never happened in NYC. We had all blown through our money too quickly and waiting in line to see a tabloid talk show host was way more important, and less eternally damning than inking up my body with one of Mormonism's most popular symbols.

We arrived back in Utah happy and energized. We all went our separate ways, leaving me just a few more weeks to prepare to enter the Missionary Training Center. I was getting more and more anxious at the thought of giving up my freedom, so I planned a final weekend getaway with my sister and girlfriends. We booked a hotel in Salt Lake City, planned on doing a little shopping, some dining, and a whole lot of dancing.

One of the most popular dance clubs in Salt Lake City at the time was a place called The Bay, an historic Eagles building that was built between 1915 and 1916. It is a three-story building designed with a neo-Renaissance feel to it, including arched windows and openings, a grand staircase, and large pillars. It sits on the corner of 404 S West Temple, within walking distance of the Salt Lake City Temple, and home to the infamous Mormon Tabernacle Choir.

Our hotel had a gorgeous view of the temple, but our goal was not to sit and admire it, it was to get out and dance, have fun, be worldly, be young, and be wild. I had only ever been country dancing, so clubbing to hip hop music made me feel a bit rebellious, maybe even a little naughty.

The girls and I spent our time getting ready with that stunning view of the temple shining brightly through the window. Again, I was the only one wearing the sacred garment, forcing me to clothe myself more modestly than the other girls. It didn't really bother me until we were inside the dimly lit dance club, moving through the strobe lights and dry ice. Karma decided to be a bitch and have me experience the awkwardness of bumping and grinding. My intention was to envision a Book of Mormon taped to both my breasts and my ass so no one would be tempted to rub up against me in my navy-blue tent pants.

As I was dancing in my own little world, to my chagrin, a random guy appeared behind me and thrust his pelvis into my butt-crack. I was so shocked that I didn't even turn around to see what he looked like, I just started moving with him, pretending I knew what the hell I was doing.

Thank God it was dark and nobody could see my flushed red cheeks quickly filling with shame and guilt. I had my holy underwear on and I was letting this man defile me. The wrestling in my head involved the prophet telling me I was going to hell and Satan whispering it was completely normal to allow a stranger's penis thrust up against my backside. I suffered through the remainder of the song and then immediately walked outside to get some fresh air.

How could I have danced so dirty after only wearing my new underwear for two months? I thought for sure I had disappointed God and that he would whisper to my bishop that I had sinned and made light of the vows I had made in the temple.

I didn't enjoy any more of my time at The Bay that night and refused to return to such a worldly, tempting place. Instead, I waited outside until my girlfriends were ready to go back to the hotel. Once back there, I climbed into bed and cried, silently pleading with God to forgive me for my dirty, sexualized dancing. I groveled with a thousand apologies, feeling like complete shit for so quickly disregarding the covenants I made in the temple. I was confident that debasing my garments with such provocative dancing would deem me unworthy to wear the black nametag.

I left Salt Lake City completely defeated, wondering how someone as weak as me would be able to handle eighteen months of strict rules. I felt like an imposter and was worried that I would be caught at my mission farewell or when I was set apart with a blessing confirming me as a full-time missionary. Which priesthood leader would it be that would know I was a dirty skank and didn't fit the description of what a missionary should be?

My dear rapist, I'm happy to report that my farewell and setting apart proceeded uneventfully, and a week later, the big day finally arrived to enter the Missionary Training Center. With the hundreds of other families dropping off their missionaries, my family was yet again by my side. I was the first daughter and granddaughter on both sides of the family to have made this decision to serve the Lord. My father was the first to come to me, wrap his arms around me, and tell me how proud he was of me. I held onto my mother and my grandmother as long as I could. But it was most difficult to say goodbye to my sister. This would be the longest amount of time that we would have ever been separated, and yet we were both feeling like we wanted to switch places.

She was the one who had always wanted to be the missionary, not me. She was the righteous one, not me. But I did what any good Mormon girl would do and I kissed and hugged them all goodbye. I slowly walked out of the room and followed the signs telling me where the next phase of the MTC integration would be, having faith that God knew what he was doing to me.

My dear rapist, I was ready to be properly trained and taught in the gospel. I wanted to be prepared to be a mother of a priesthood army of boys. I wanted to be worthy of giving birth to those chosen spirits whom God intended to help usher in the Second Coming of Jesus Christ. Rather than ignore the urge to run after my family and tell my father that this wasn't for me, I did what most good Mormon girls would do—I put one foot in front of the other and moved deeper and deeper into the unknown territory of the Missionary Training Center.

From this moment on I would be known as Sister McKnight. Not Ginger, not the twin, not the roommate, not the waitress in Jackson Hole, not the nanny in Connecticut, not the respite care provider, not the day-training aide, and not the special needs advocate. I would now be Sister McKnight, a representative of the Church of Jesus Christ of

Latter-Day Saints, a Disciple of Jesus Christ.
I would be a full-time freaking missionary.

Never Yours,
Sister McKnight, A Disciple of Jesus Christ

CHAPTER 8

DETROIT

"The Standard of Truth has been erected; no unhallowed hand can stop the work from progressing; persecutions may rage, mobs may combine, armies may assemble, calumny may defame, but the truth of God will go forth boldly, nobly, and independent, till it has penetrated every continent, visited every clime, swept every country, and sounded in every ear, till the purposes of God shall be accomplished, and the Great Jehovah shall say the work is done."

(History of the Church, 4:540, Smith, Joseph Jr.)

My Dear Rapist,

My feet continued to move forward through the 1978 bricked corridors of the MTC. We were told to find our luggage and head to our dorm room to meet our missionary companions. The assignment of a companion is meant as a safety measure, but it also has biblical meaning. In the Bible, 2 Corinthians states, "In the mouth of two or three witnesses shall every word be established." From this point on in the MTC, and throughout my eighteen-month missionary service, the standard rule and expectation was that I would never be alone.

If I need to use the restroom, my companion must go with me, and under no circumstance should we be separated. A companion is also required to report any sneaky or immoral behavior to the mission president. In the missionary handbook it states that a missionary's first priority is to Jesus, his or her second priority is to the mission president, and his or her third priority is to the companion.

My companion was a sweet, shy girl from Carlsbad, California who was assigned to the Lansing mission. The other sister in the room, who would be going to Detroit with me, was Sister N, a native beauty from Hawaii. Sister N was very intimidating. She had a rough exterior and seemed to enjoy maintaining a resting bitch face. The other sister, who was also going to Lansing, was a tall, serious rule follower.

The dorm rooms were quite small, with the same yellow-bricked walls as the rest of the building we had walked through. The dorms also had ugly carpet, with gross, unflattering fluorescent lighting. The space had enough square footage for two bunk beds and two closets. There was absolutely nothing homey or comfortable about it, which strongly indicated they were meant for sleep, the changing of clothes, and nothing more. This left the sister missionaries with a communal bathroom and shower to share, which was annoying and quite embarrassing. There was literally not a single space or moment in the MTC designed for privacy and personal time.

After spending a bit of time meeting each other and unpacking our bags, we were required to meet our district. Our district included ten to twelve missionaries with whom we would spend the majority of our time. Most days consisted of an unyielding schedule jam-packed with classes, breaks for meals, time for laundry, and time for exercise. Our district had more male missionaries than female missionaries. It was amazing to discover that with such differing backgrounds, we could all become such good friends in such a quick amount of time.

For several days, we were all on a spiritual high, not truly grasping the role we were meant to play or what we were really getting ourselves into. When the honeymoon phase started to dissipate and the rigid routine and homesickness started sinking in, all the concealed anxiety, fear, and depression finally decided to make its appearance— not just for me, but for many. As the pressure to be a perfect disciple of Jesus began to rise, so did the guilt and the shame. Many missionaries began to feel unworthy to be in such a religious boot camp. Others began to question, for the first time in their lives, their testimony of the church, of Joseph Smith, and of the Book of Mormon.

Prior to entering the MTC I had never taken a serious

read of the Book of Mormon. I was learning things for the first time about the Book of Mormon that I had never paid attention to before. Up until the MTC, I had no idea that the Book of Mormon was a proposed account of Jesus and his ministry written in the Americas. I was mortified that I did not have a basic understanding of the sacred book, leaving me to be one who questioned the validity of the church's truth claims early on in my missionary training. During class, we were forced to roleplay with each other in a missionary and investigator relationship.

In this way, we were able to practice sharing our testimony and teach the church's foundational doctrines to each other. This was difficult for me. I knew I was not prepared to speak or testify about a church I wasn't sure that I believed in. How could I testify to others when I didn't know for sure if Joseph Smith really was a prophet of God, if the Book of Mormon was really scripture, or if the church really did have a prophet on the earth today?

During one particular roleplay with an elder, I broke down in tears and confided in him that I wasn't sure if I really believed in Joseph Smith. I was so upset by vocalizing this out loud, I had to get up and leave the room. The MTC instructor followed me out the door and asked me what was wrong. I had nothing to lose, so I shared the truth of my doubts. It was at this moment that I heard the phrase, "A testimony is found in the sharing of it."

I'm sure these same words had been shared in another time and in another place, but for me, it was the first time I had really listened to the words and revered their meaning. It was a phrase that I would continue to hear for the next eighteen months of my life.

The instructor successfully calmed me down, and after a few minutes of composing myself, I walked back into that classroom and decided to give it a try. I started into roleplaying again and officially began the process of faking it to make it. I was counting on this to work; I *needed* this to work. Hopefully, this process would take my lack of faith and turn it into a sure knowledge. I desperately wanted this to happen before leaving the MTC so that I could testify in Detroit, with conviction, of the truthfulness of Mormonism. I had two weeks to gain a testimony, and I prayed fervently that God would give it to me.

Moroni, an ancient prophet in the Book of Mormon, makes a promise to all who read his writings: ask God if the words in the Book of Mormon are true. If you ask with a sincere heart, with real intent, and having faith in God, he will answer you. It was time to put Moroni's challenge to the test. I knelt next to my bunk bed in my tiny dorm room, and I poured my heart out to God. I begged and I begged for him to tell me if I was meant to be in this place. I pleaded with him to answer my unanswered questions: was Joseph Smith a true Prophet of God and was the Book of Mormon valid scripture?

I perseverated on these questions for what seemed like eternity. The begging ultimately paid off, and I was rewarded handsomely with a victory. The warm tingly sensation that Mormonism identifies as "the Spirit" washed over me. My white chicken-textured skin filled with goosebumps and the hair stood straight up on my arms. This sensation, according to Mormonism, is how one receives the "truth." This is what I had been hoping for but had never really felt before when I prayed.

With cheeks soiled by tears and a nose covered in snot, I opened my eyes, rubbed my sore knees, and stood up. God answered me. God answered *me*. God *answered* me. Omg, *God answered me*! I joyfully climbed into my bunk bed feeling confident that God had just informed me that not only was the Mormon Church true, but that I was safe to continue on with my future in Detroit.

My dear rapist, the Missionary Training Center turned out to be one of the most incredible experiences of my life. As you are an athlete, I'm sure you recall the energy you felt at a high school pep rally, or the preparation for an Olympic competition. If you take that same energy and multiply it by 4,000 young men and women, you now have a thirty-nine-acre site filled with God's loudest and most boldest cheerleaders.

It was not uncommon for some missionaries to go home early out of shame and guilt, but most missionaries would press on through the scary, negative emotions and keep their eye on the target of baptism and bringing souls to Christ. The energy inside the MTC was not only spiritually tantalizing, but in some ways for my young female hormones, it was sexually tantalizing. For the first time in my life, I was not only in the minority, but I was also feeling semi-attractive.

The moment I entered its walls, I had noticed the male-to-female ratio, as it was not very common in 1999 for females to serve missions. With the missionary mantra attached to me, as well as knowing we could "look but not touch," I had found a sudden wave of self-assurance to bat my thickly mascaraed eyes at all the missionary boys. No, I did not come to find a husband, but I was certainly going to play my cards right and try to be a cute and fun sister missionary.

Never Yours,
A Cheerleader for Jesus

***

My Dear Rapist,

Many elders I had befriended requested permission to write and stay in touch while we all served in different parts of the world. My little MTC black book acquired pages and pages of elders gluing pictures of themselves and writing down their memories and thoughts of me.

This level of attention was abnormal for me, and it gave me moments of hope that maybe I could find a husband that would love me for me, regardless of my imperfect body. Due to the amount of attention I was receiving, I finally put that third-grade mirror away and no longer saw myself as ugly. I actually began to see glimpses of something beautiful looking back at me.

The MTC experience gifted me two things: one, a touch of beauty and two, a testimony of the Mormon church. With these two things as my sword and shield, I was ready to be a warrior for Christ and his church.

After living through the largest pep rally of my life, I packed up my little black book and all my belongings and said goodbye to my favorite missionaries. I headed to the SLC airport with Sister N, and along the way, we met six new elders who would be going to Detroit with us.

Before boarding the plane, I would have one final goodbye with my family. It was through some very exciting, but also sad tears, that I hugged my twin, my parents, my Grandma Ella, and a few girlfriends goodbye. I would not see them for eighteen long months, or maybe more. I held on to each of them, wondering if this was the last time we were going to hug.

What if something happened to them, or to me? What if I came home early and couldn't hack the streets of Six Mile or Eight Mile? The hugs had so much more in them than excitement and sadness. The hugs carried fear, potential shame, love, faith, acceptance, hope, and a sincere desire to come home honorably. They carried an absolute and resounding missionary power, with pure, unadulterated pride that I was the first sister missionary from both parental lineages to have chosen to serve the Lord in this way.

Last but certainly not least, the final hug carried heartache. I knew my twin sister's tears were not tears of joy, but tears of regret and sadness. She was the one who had always wanted to serve a mission, the one with the strong testimony. She was the perfect Mormon daughter who behaved the right way and believed the right way. This would be the longest amount of time that we would be separated, and breaking away from her hug was the most difficult of all. Once I did, I turned around and I kept on walking, putting one foot in front of the other and having faith that it would all work out.

I boarded the plane with Sister N and the six new elders, and together, we all flew to Detroit, Michigan. I was now a five-hour plane ride away from proving to everyone, especially to my girlfriends from high school, that I was not meant for a life of being sexually promiscuous or getting knocked up. I was meant to be a disciple of Jesus Christ by bringing people into his church, and I would try my damnedest to prove that I could do it, come hell or high water.

My dear rapist, I had one vision that began to form on the plane ride to Detroit, and I was able to maintain it for a straight eighteen months. This vision kept my feet planted on the streets of Detroit and it kept me from ripping the black nametag off my chest. It kept me knocking on doors, it kept me hiking through snowstorms, it kept me from running away from crazy companions, and it kept me from harming myself. It was the simple vision of walking off a plane in Salt Lake City after a year and a half and straight into the waiting arms of my father. I didn't want to walk into his arms as a quitter or as a sinner. I wanted to walk into his arms with honor.

Sadly, it was difficult to carry this same vision toward my father when you and I were together. I was so ashamed of who I had become and felt so unworthy of love, I could hardly look into my father's eyes, let alone envision myself wrapped safely in his arms. At times, I would try to convince myself that I would always be worthy of my father's love, no matter what. However, the doctrine of the church would constantly creep in and remind me that I was unworthy and that I needed to repent for my part in allowing your abuse to happen.

As a missionary, I thought of nothing more on the plane ride *to* Detroit, than the plane ride I would take home *from* Detroit. These were my only thoughts and they carried me into the arms of my new father, the Detroit mission president. In contrast, as your supposed girlfriend, I thought of nothing more than how I was going to free myself from your vice and find a way to walk into the arms of my father, as his alive and breathing daughter.

Never Yours,
Always My Father's

***

My Dear Rapist,

Waiting at the top of the escalator at the Detroit airport for their eight new children were President and Sister R. Outside of this new crew coming to them, they had roughly 200 additional missionaries to care for. President R was a short, tiny man in a nice suit, a surprisingly bald head and a large, gregarious smile. Sister R was a little taller than him, and adorned with blonde, grandma-styled hair, a cane in one hand, bright red lipstick, and a vibrantly colored dress.

In a sea of busy travelers, they were radiant and glowing. They stood out like white, heavenly angels in an abrupt new world of Black diversity. Even with my time in New York, DC, and Europe, I had never seen so much African American heterogeneity in one place.

I was a pompous and audacious white female,

believing I was superior to all of these nonwhite people walking by, simply because *I* had the one true gospel and they did not. I was illustrious because *I* had been saved thousands of years ago to come to earth at this time and save them, the people of Detroit.

Just a few years before this moment, I had been told in seminary that Black people did something wrong in the preexistence to deserve their dark skin in this life. I had also learned that blackness was a curse of Cain, marked dark to remind the human race what God does to people who disobediently turn against him.

I struggled to believe these racist teachings, but unabashedly admit now that a portion of me once embraced it. I am deeply ashamed and in this very instant, as my fingers move across the keyboard, I want to weep for my former years of holding such racist beliefs and attitudes. I would give anything to go back in time and beg my MTC instructors to teach me about my white privilege and what it meant to have a white savior complex.

My dear rapist, though I embraced the harmful racial doctrine as a young missionary, I was able to shed the bigotry prior to meeting you. When we were together, I never once thought our difference in skin color was a reason not to be together, in fact your Black heritage is one of the main reasons I was drawn to you.

I used to tell my friends and family that I hoped God called me to Detroit to find a Black man I could convert to Mormonism and then bring back to Utah to marry and have children with. In some ways, being with you made me feel connected to my time in Detroit and gave me a hope that

God had brought you to Utah since I had never found you in Detroit.

Back then, the Detroit airport was a major culture shock to my system. However, being dropped off in downtown Detroit and being told it was time to knock on doors was even more astonishing. Thank God that Sister N's skin color was brown, because as a white female, I did not feel safe in this foreign city. I had an acute onset of aphasia and refused to open my mouth as Sister N and I approached our first door.

We each held a little blue Book of Mormon in our hands and as she took the first spirited move to knock, we were a little stumped on how to actually be missionaries. The entire front door as well as the windows on either side of the door were covered in black metal bars. The stained, dirty home looked like a cross between an old, white house and a jail cell. For the first time, I took notice and looked up and down the street at every other house, realizing that all the windows and doors in the neighborhood were also covered in metal bars.

I suddenly found myself questioning our safety on the streets of Detroit. Just five minutes ago, Elder D, Assistant to the President, had told me I looked like Punky Brewster. In this moment of recognizing just how dangerous Detroit might be, I wanted to slide back into the '80s and be Soleil Moon Frye for a day. I wanted to be with my dog Brandon in my rainbow-painted bedroom. I wanted to climb into a wooden wheelbarrow bed and hear George, a grandfather foster dad, make dinner for me in the kitchen.

Yet, like the sudden change of a mushroom trip,

my spirit began screaming at me, convincing me that I was going to be safe. The spirit was reminding me that I had been set apart in a special prayer to have the mantle of a missionary, which meant extra protection and security. I had read the poems and had seen the cartoon drawings of unseen angels supporting and shielding young missionaries through unsafc and pcrilous times. I had heard the legends of ancient prophets appearing and standing in front of missionaries who were in harm's way. Surely those angels would make an appearance and protect me too.

Like a faithful sister missionary would do, I lifted my head high, kicked Punky Brewster's ass to the garbage-permeated street, and told the angels surrounding me that I would continue finding a way to knock on these oppressed prison doors. If it meant I had to knock on barbed wire to get the Mormon message heard, I would do it. After an hour of knocking on doors in my twisted knickers, Sister N and I were picked up by the elders with no success or hope of a baptism. Instead, we met up with the other six elders we had flown in with and went to the mission president's home. We had a beautiful, but exhausting, evening spending time with President R and his wife.

The couple were from Idaho, and we discussed the small personal connection that tied him to one of my aunts. President R had spent his career as an OB/GYN, and while my aunt was pregnant with her third child, her husband was tragically killed in a motorcycle accident. Left widowed and with no strong source of income, her situation came to President R's attention and he had made the generous decision to take care of her prenatal and birthing care, free of charge. This connection brought an immediate bond to the president and I. From that point on, I relished in his kind smile and altruistic hugs.

After spending some time getting to know one another, we all found our rooms, and once our heads hit the pillows, we crashed hard. Morning came way too fast and before we knew it, we were awake and packing our bags once again. It was time to meet our trainers and learn of our first area placement.

My first trainer turned out to be a tough, seasoned missionary with only six weeks left of her mission, and I was her greenie. She was assigned by the big man upstairs to teach me how to be Jesus's most fervent disciple. Sister F had the longest, most beautiful flowing red hair I had ever seen. Her semi-tan face was splattered with freckles, just like mine had been. She was a California skater girl through and through. Her raspy voice made her even more endearing, but also a bit intimidating.

We were heading to the Palmer Park area of Detroit, which was west of a big street called Woodward, and tucked between Six and Seven Mile. Sister F and I went back to our apartment to unload my suitcase and grab a bite to eat. The apartment building was an old, yellow-brick, V-shaped building with four floors, with our apartment being on the third level. It had an old, creaky gated elevator and a nice apartment manager named Dewey. Dewey was a gentle, older man who often checked in with us to make sure we were always doing okay.

It was my first official night alone as a missionary for the Church of Jesus Christ of Latter-Day Saints. Sister F did not have much time for play, and she wanted to get straight to work. Her first goal was to take me around Palmer Park and explain the area, so we hopped into the car and went for a drive. It was dark outside and the cars were moving fast in what she called the mystery lane. Sister F didn't seem phased by the heavy, inconsistent, and erratic traffic.

The driving in Detroit felt different than the crazy driving I had experienced in New York City. Detroit was like being in a constant *Fast and the Furious* film, but with 99 percent of the cars being more like beaters with heaters than the Chargers and the Camaros that Paul Walker and Vin Diesel drove.

The topless beach in Spain I had visited did nothing to prepare me for what existed between Six and Eight Mile. There seemed to be a strip club, a liquor store, and a crack house on every corner. Prostitutes were walking up and down the street with nothing on but crop tops and high heels. It was 1999, and for the first time in my life, I saw a drag queen with my own hazel eyes. I was just learning that Palmer Park was where a large portion of Detroit's LGBTQ+ community resided. Hookers approaching our blue Chevy Cavalier were just as common as drug dealers approaching us in our suits and dresses.

If anything stopped the drug dealers and hookers in their tracks, it would be seeing the black nametags pinned upon our chests. Once the tag came into view, the drug dealers practically became bodyguards for us missionaries. They knew we were there to preach Jesus' word and not looking for sex or drugs. Ultimately, they respected us enough to either turn around and go their separate ways or extend an invite to the elders to play a game of basketball in the streets.

Detroit was a dirty, dangerous, and downright scary place to be. The streets were a mixture of nice, maintained homes or partially burned down homes targeted by drug deals gone wrong. At this time, the city made no effort to demolish the scarcely standing, charred homes. It was not uncommon to walk down a street and find garbage on the curb.

The piles of trash included items such as shredded, stained mattresses, broken furniture, dysfunctional appliances, and soiled blankets or towels. Similar to the incinerated homes, the city completely ignored all the random piles of debris on the roads, and with the amount of junk spread throughout the city, I should not have been surprised with the abundance of roaches, maggots, and rodents we found ourselves often and cautiously saluting.

From the drug dealers, the hookers, and the alcoholic neighbor beating the shit out of his girlfriend every night, to the crack house next to our apartment, the attempted break-in by the homeless man curled up next to our building, and the cracked-out man who drove his car into the side of our apartment, I often wondered if I was going to make it out of Detroit alive.

But despite the culture shock and characteristics of this 1999 Detroit, I fell madly in love with the people. Their humility and generosity was something I had never seen before. Many had absolutely nothing to their name and barely had the means to put food on the table, yet they found a way to feed the missionaries a home-cooked meal of oxtail soup, grits, cornbread, and chicken wings.

Many of the converts in Detroit were African American women, leaving most of the responsibilities of running the church to the young male missionaries from Utah and Idaho. But since there was a rule in place that missionaries could not be alone with any member of the opposite sex, and owning a car was a luxury for most of the population we served, it was very challenging to get the older, single women to church.

It also made it a hassle to teach missionary lessons to those wanting to learn about Mormonism. Because there were more male missionaries than females, if the males found a single woman to teach, they either had to teach her outside, or invite the female missionaries to join them during the lessons.

This rigid rule, however, did not deter any of the women from getting their gospel-loving asses to church, or from investigating and learning about Mormon doctrine, despite the difficulty of getting there. Looking back, I wish I would've noticed our discrimination against these beloved, godly, women of Detroit. The church did nothing to educate us, or prepare us, on entering into the African American world.

I will never forget the first time I received a true wake-up call to our blatant racial ignorance. The same little black book I had passed around in the MTC, I passed around in Detroit. I made an exception in Detroit and allowed the members and investigators to sign my journal. I had dropped my journal off to a set of identical twins that I had met early on and had connected deeply with. They were both raised devout Catholic, and they were going to school to become school teachers. They both had a huge impact on me, and they were only about five years older than I was.

One of my companions, whom they had known and loved, wrote down the lyrics to a song that we would occasionally bust out singing: *"Picks and fros, hos and dos, that's what makes Detroit go 'round."* I'm not sure where the words even came from, I just remember we were two white girls, hysterically spitting them out without any thought to how racist they could be.

It was not until the twins came across them in my book, that I had discovered how hurtful they truly were. They returned my journal, pained and confused. They refused to sign my precious book and were no longer willing to meet with the missionaries. Tears burn in my eyes as I write these words and remember how senseless we were. This was but a pinprick into the discovery of self-righteousness, racial ignorance, and white privilege that lived within me.

My dear rapist, at the time, I could not see how we moved into their territory, forcing ourselves into their world, into their culture, and into their lives to change them. We tried to take away the unique traits and characteristics of their heritage, their music, and the way they practiced their religion, and turn them white like us. We were a group of young, gullible, white kids from a predominantly Utah and Idaho world. What made them unique and divine was simply not good enough.

We were more righteous and more valiant than they were, and in order to rescue them, we had to take Detroit out of them and pound white Utah Mormonism back in. Their salvation and their ancestors' salvation depended on us saving their souls. Ashamedly, while I tried to deliver them from their ancestral curse of Black skin, I was also making fun of them. In time, the twins found forgiveness and were willing to reconnect with me years later, and I will forever be gratcful for them for not holding me to a twenty-one-year-old version of myself.

Meeting you was a chance for me to redeem myself, a new start. I loved the idea of starting a life with a man of color. I knew my family would possibly struggle with it, but I wanted it, and I didn't care what they would think. I wanted to embrace everything about you and your heritage.

I started wrestling more and more with the church's reasons behind banning Black men from having the priesthood. No, my dear rapist, not wanting to be with you never had to do with the color of your skin. Fearing you, and a life together, had everything to do with your darkened soul. Honest to God, you were beautiful in my eyes, and I was giddy as a schoolgirl that you were willing to give me, a naive, Mormon white girl the time of day.

Never Yours,
A Repentant White Savior

✳✳✳

My Dear Rapist,

I spent the first three months of my mission in Palmer Park paired with a new companion every six weeks, and in this time, we taught and baptized one woman. Women do not have the priesthood, so the elders performed the baptism. At this time in my life, this did not faze me. I was more focused and excited on the fact that we had brought one soul unto Christ. As tough as Detroit was, I didn't want to leave. It was thrilling to be in one of the most dangerous cities in America.

I felt like an invincible superhero and believed God and his angels would protect me and the other missionaries at all costs. I wasn't ready to move on, but God told the mission president it was time for me to leave and relocate to Howell, Michigan. In a weird way, this move was also a form of culture shock.

I went from inner city Detroit, a city of almost four million people and hardly any white people, to a country town of 9,500 people with not a single Black person in sight. Howell, which is in Livingston County, is known to have been home to Robert Miles, former Klan Grand Dragon of the KKK. Miles had held cross-burnings and hate rallies on his farm in Cohoctah Township as late as 1986.

He died in 1992, just eight years prior to my arrival, and had left a haunting reputation on Howell as the KKK Capital of Michigan. Robert Miles had loved being center stage, and five years after I left Detroit, his ghost was back in the spotlight, which is something the townspeople had grown weary of. In 2005, Miles family members hired a local auctioneer and chose to auction off his collection of racialized possessions.

From my experience, the people of Howell were nothing like the Klan Grand Dragon. Most of the residents, when questioned about their town's racist history, yearned for the ghost of the evil man to go away. When my companion and I would go door to door, my mind would often wander, leaving me to speculate which farm and barn were a part of this ugly history.

Howell was beautiful, and it made me feel like I was close to home. The people were humble and down to earth. The Mormon church in Howell definitely felt more like a Utah ward, with a good mix of men and women, as well as a variety of young and old. I spent my longest time in this area, a total of seven months. I had two companions, and in this time we baptized five individuals.

I fell in love with the church members in Howell, the investigators, and my two companions. Twenty-five years later, I still have strong connections with many of these people who were a part of my life in Howell.

After seven months in Howell, God told the mission president to move me to Ann Arbor. My companion and I were assigned to work on the University of Michigan campus. This was definitely challenging for me. In Detroit I was mute, terrified of opening my mouth and educating the people on Mormonism. I had zero confidence when it came to giving the seven memorized missionary discussions.

While serving in Howell, I blossomed. Howell was a game changer for me, and I could not and would not shut up. I had zero fear in opening my mouth and my confidence levels soared. However, the University of Michigan campus was intimidating and it shut me right back up.

My companion and I were assigned to the singles ward, which placed us among men and women of our own age, and it left me completely tongue tied. In all honesty,

I was embarrassed to be a missionary among all of the students who were there for a secular education. We spent our days standing in the center of the Diag, an open space in the middle of the main campus, which contained many sidewalks running in diagonal directions. The U of M campus is recognized as a "Tree Campus," so with more than sixteen thousand trees and its green, green grass, the place felt like a magical forest. And like dogs pissing on trees, my companion and I marked the Diag as our territory and we preached repentance and salvation, putting Noah and Moses to shame.

I have three strong memories from the three months we spent proselytizing on this not-so-yellow-brick road. First, I experienced a tantalizing attraction to a hot, Black Marine who faked interest in Mormonism to get to me. The major guilt I felt for having such strong sexual urges as a disciple of Jesus forced me to call my mission president and share my lustful thoughts with him. I begged him not to move me out of the area and to give me another chance.

I ached to prove I was strong and capable of choosing Jesus over the Marine. The president agreed to let me remain on a condition—that we turn the Marine over to the elders. He quickly lost interest once he found out he would no longer be meeting with me, and I left the area with not a single baptism. I had come to believe that God was upset with me and my time in Ann Arbor was a complete failure, simply because I discovered I had a sex drive.

The second memory was of the sexual energy I saw and felt on campus. It was palpable, and I was starving for some innate need for affection. Everywhere I turned, I was drawn to couples having dry sex on the lawn, or couples pushed up against trees with their tongues thrust down each other's throats. The lesbian couple who later grabbed my ass assured me I was proselytizing in the land of Sodom and Gomorrah. Looking at, but not touching all of the fine, young, educated men made the newfound fire in my loins turn into a loin volcano.

I was undeniably and lasciviously horny. I was twenty-one years old and had been consumed 24/7 by Jesus and Mormonism for the last year. All I truly wanted was to find Mr. Marine and have him rip off my nametag, break it in two with his combat hands, and shove me up against one of the sixteen thousand trees in my midst.

The fantasy never lasted long, because I did what most good sister missionaries did—I replaced my foul and blackened thoughts with some good ole' fashioned primary hymns.

My final memory includes a tall, skinny, older gentleman, with tousled, curly hair who walked up to Sister D and I and spat in our faces. We were in the middle of a discussion with an individual showing interest in Joseph Smith and the man, who we later named Korihor after an Antichrist in the Book of Mormon, was livid about our presence.

Korihor's crazy, random rant emboldened us to testify to him of our beliefs in Joseph Smith and the Book of Mormon. The louder he got, the louder we got. He was getting flustered by our unwillingness to cower and go silent, so he decided it would be best to aggressively spit into both our faces. Without a flinch, my companion raised her right arm to the square and commanded him in the name of Jesus Christ to leave. Immediately, he stepped away from us and turned the other direction. His astonishingly abrupt departure, after demanding him to leave in Jesus's name, deepened both of our testimonies. We were undoubtedly modern-day Noahs, testifying on our Ark of the Diag, to a shit ton of erotic, sinful, University of Michigan students.

My dear rapist, I often think about the hot Marine on the University of Michigan campus. Similar to you, he faked interest in Mormonism to get to me, but he walked away when he discovered it would come between us. I wonder, did he see the same naivety in me that you did? Did he feel a need to conquer me and shock me, or did the black nametag stop him dead in his tracks?

Perhaps it was because I was more vocal about my love for Jesus and strived to be a modern-day Noah that he stopped the chase. Honestly, my dear rapist, I hate that I do this, this constant comparing and contrasting of you with others. But it is really difficult to not look at my life in two segments as a rape survivor and think of who I was before you and who I was after you. I truly hope for and look forward to the day that I no longer think this way.

Never Yours,
Horny on the Diag

***

My Dear Rapist,

After two companions, zero baptisms, and the birth of

my sex drive, I left the University of Michigan and spent the next two months in Mount Clemens, Michigan. My sexual discrepancies in Ann Arbor surprisingly did not warrant a missionary demotion to junior companion. Instead, I was given trainer status. I could not believe the mission president found me worthy of this calling. All feelings of regret and assumptions about God being upset with me melted away. I was going to be a trainer, and I made a promise that I would be the best damn trainer the church would ever know.

Out of respect for the missionary that I trained, I will not share details of our experience together. What I will share is that it is not uncommon for missionaries to show up to their assignment and within weeks, be diagnosed with a mental illness. The rigorous, demanding routine of the missionary schedule was very tough. We were expected to live with someone we had never met before and figure out how to get along, as contention was seen as a tool of the devil.

The stress and pressure of counting discussions, witnessing baptisms, and reporting our weekly successes was a very demanding numbers game. Every day was the same routine, day in and day out. We would wake up at 6:30 a.m., then have personal study time for an hour, and then eat our breakfast. After breakfast, we were required to do another hour of study time with our companion, and then pray together. We were obligated to leave our apartment by 10:00 a.m. and have every hour planned out on our devoted blue calendar.

Some days, we would make time for lunch, other times we would not. If appointments fell through, then we stopped what we were doing, prayed, and then quietly listened for inspiration on who to go visit, or what street God intended for us to knock on doors. Depending on the area we lived in, we may or may not have been fed dinner by the local members of the church.

If we were invited over for dinner, we were required to be in and out within an hour. After dinner, we went back to the streets, looking for more people to teach. We were required to be back inside our apartment by 9:00 p.m.. For the next hour, we planned the next day, offered companion prayers, expressed individual prayers, and then climbed into bed by 10:00 p.m.

Wake up, repeat. Wake up, repeat. Wake up, repeat. Wake up, repeat. We had no television, no movies, no worldly music, only church hymns. We could not call home, except on Christmas and on Mother's Day. One day a week, we had a preparation day, also called P-Day. On this day, we could spend our day playing basketball with the elders or go grocery shopping with the $140 monthly allowance we were given, or do our laundry. This one day a week, we were allowed to wear street clothes, but we had to wear the black nametag at all times. Our P-Day ended at 6:00 p.m., and then it was back to the missionary dress or suit, and back to the grind.

The strict life for a young missionary can break anyone. You could technically call it a Mormon boot camp, but it lasts much longer than a three-month army stint. This boot camp lasts anywhere from eighteen to twenty-four months, and if you do not perform perfectly, every single part of your soul can fill with shame. There was shame from other missionaries, shame from investigators, local members, the mission president, shame from family and friends, shame from God, shame from Jesus, and worst of all, a deeply driven, internalized shame that comes from your own heart. The most unfavorable thing you could do as a missionary was to either get sent home for bad behavior or give up.

Suicide idealization and depression is normal for those threatened with the possibility of going home without honor. The cultural and doctrinal pressure to serve an honorable and faithful mission creeps its way into every home, every heart, and every white envelope of those who choose to serve a mission. I should note, it is never an expectation or command for women to serve missions, but it has always been one for the men. Many young women refuse to marry a man if he did not serve a mission, making many young men in the church feel as if their worth is tied strictly to their status as a returned missionary.

With all of these pressures combined, my greenie was diagnosed with Bipolar disorder just a few weeks into her mission. Just as I did not understand racism and white privilege as a twenty-one-year-old female, I did not understand mental illness. If I could go back in time, I would give so much more love and care to my fragile and unassuming greenie. I would have curled up with her on the floor in a fetal position, rocked back and forth with my arms around her, and cried with her. I would have sat with her, breathed with her, and empathized with her during her panic attacks.

I would have yelled at her father and called him an unloving, uncaring bastard when he told her under no circumstances could she come home early. I would have done things so differently, but my self-righteousness and ignorance only made her mental health dissolve more rapidly.

My greenie defied her father's ugly sentiments and chose to end her mission early. When she left, my memories of Mount Clemens left with her. I do not recall any other memories, other than memories of her mental breakdowns. Fortunately, the mission president did not fault me for failing to get her to stay on her mission. While spending the evening in his home as we said goodbye to my greenie, I extended one minor request, which he granted. I had roughly six weeks left of my mission, and the strongest desire of my heart was to go back to Palmer Park. I was such a quiet, naïve, and insecure missionary when I first moved to Six Mile.

I wanted nothing more than to go back as a changed woman. I wanted to experience Detroit again with the confidence, boldness, and maturity I had developed over the last sixteen months. I wanted to be among the humble and beautiful sisters that I had fallen in love with. I wanted to feel like a superhero again, in a tough and terrifying city that I had not previously been prepared to live in.

Back in Detroit, with only forty-two days left, I was placed with my final companion. She was a loud and proud woman from Lubbock, Texas, and at first, she completely hated me. She had been with her trainer for only six weeks when I came into the picture. It is ideal that a trainer spend at least twelve weeks with their greenie, but unfortunately for her, she had to say goodbye to a trainer that she loved and adored and have me come into her life. I was exhausted by the end of my mission, and she was just getting started. She wanted to work hard, and I had to fight against my daily longing for rest. Over time, I won her Texas-sized heart and we had a blast together, creating many memories, and even seeing one baptism together.

I was ending my days in Detroit poised, joyful, utterly fatigued, and still ignorantly racist. In eighteen months, I got sick one time, but had never slept in, never taken a nap, and never missed a day where I didn't do my hair and my makeup. With all the walking and proselytizing we did, I burned holes in the bottom of my knee-high boots. I was one-hundred percent obedient by keeping all of the rules and making sure to live both the letter and the spirit of the law. I had fun. I busted my ass for the Lord, my companions, and for my father, and without any doubt, I knew I was going home with the love and support of my mission president.

With an abundance of admiration radiating deeply from his gentle eyes, his final words to me were from Matthew 25:21: "Well done, thou good and faithful servant. You have been faithful over a little; I will set you over much. Enter into the joy of your master."

My mission father loved me, he hugged me, and he treated me as one of his own daughters. I absolutely adored him and have never regretted it, even now as a nonbeliever. I made friendships that have and will continue to last a lifetime. As much as I was ready to go home and start a new life again, I did not want to say goodbye. I was scared of life outside this Mormon training camp. Ironically, I felt more safe to shut out the world and live inside the Detroit missionary bubble than I did thinking about going home and beginning the hunt for a husband.

But I did what any good Mormon missionary girl would do—I burned a few dresses, packed my two pieces of luggage, gave my tear-filled goodbyes, and boarded that plane to Salt Lake City, Utah. For 551 days, I had envisioned walking honorably into the arms of my father, and that moment was just hours away. Waiting for me at SLC International Airport were my parents, my grandparents, my brothers and their wives, a few girlfriends, and my twin sister with her new husband. The moment I saw my father, I melted. He is a man of very few words, but even without him speaking, I could see the emotion in his bright, blue eyes. My father was proud of me, and that was enough for me.

I was fortunate, my dear rapist, in having a remarkable missionary experience. I have no remorse other than wishing I had been better educated on mental illness, racism, and my white privilege. Detroit changed me—it brought me out of my shell, it gave me confidence, and it gave me the ability to learn to work well with other people who had differing backgrounds and different ways of thinking. It toughened me and it gave me an immense amount of gratitude for my wonderful, safe, and cherished upbringing.

I assisted in one of Joseph Smith's prophecies by erecting the Standard of Truth in Detroit. No unhallowed hand stopped my work from progressing. I helped infiltrate and plant seeds in Palmer Park, Howell, Ann Arbor, and Mount Clemens with God's eternal word. I believed that if Joseph Smith had been on the earth in 1999, he would have been proud of my missionary efforts. Once the priesthood leaders released me from the missionary mantle and I had removed my nametag, I took a long and much-needed nap.

It was my first nap in eighteen months. My body was screaming for rest, something that it had not been given since the day I first walked into the Missionary Training Center. Due to the neglect of my own physical body, Elder Epstein-Barr himself came knocking on my door. His presence made my post-mission fatigue much worse, making me so very grateful to be back in the home of my childhood—not as Sister McKnight, but once again as the dairyman's daughter. I could finally breathe again and be alone in my king-sized bed. I could go to the bathroom without my companion standing close by. I could wear normal clothes, listen to normal music, watch normal TV, and finally move about my day with no rigid routine.

The ability to relax would be but a brief moment in time. The next big thing to tackle would be to pull out the "Qualities in a Husband" checklist that I had created as a twelve-year-old girl in the Young Women's program. I was now on another mission: a mission to find my husband, my eternal companion.

The top three qualities I had listed for him were:
1. To be an active and believing Mormon;
2. To be an honorable returned missionary; and
3. To have a deep love of God.

As long as he fit these three descriptions, nothing else mattered. And I was convinced I was going to find him soon.

Never Yours,
A Good and Faithful Servant

CHAPTER 9

ADVENTURES IN LEVI-LOVING

"Too often, young people dismiss their petting with a shrug of their shoulders as a little indiscretion, while admitting that fornication is a base transgression. Too many of them are shocked, or feign to be, when told that what they have done in the name of petting was in reality [a form of] fornication."

(The Miracle of Forgiveness, Kimball, Spencer W., pp. 65-66)

My Dear Rapist,

Settling back into normal life was complex. I wanted to keep my worthiness status as a respectful, returned sister missionary, but I had a major complex about being labeled as weird. As I fought through a bout of mono and some slight depression, I entered into a hybrid medical assisting program through the local hospital. I didn't really want to do this, but I needed to do something to keep me busy and my mind off mission life.

The "look but do not touch" mantra of being around boys no longer existed, and so it was time to shop for a husband, get a ring on my finger, and get going with the hanky-panky process of making babies. While pursuing the six-month medical assisting certification, I did not work and needed to live at home with my parents. After being on my own in Michigan and being so social, it was difficult to live with my parents again. As much as I loved them, I needed more.

Rather than attend church with my parents each week, I made the thirty-mile drive into Logan on Sundays and attended a singles ward at Utah State University. Within two weeks, I found myself dating a cute returned missionary from the ward who had unexpectedly sent my libido soaring. He was tall and thin, with dark brown hair and dark brown eyes. We immediately started spending time together, and at the ripe age of twenty-three, I had my first ever makeout session with a boy I actually liked.

This was nothing like my first kiss, where I had only known the guy for a day. This particular guy also didn't kiss me to rip my lips off. He kissed me because he liked me. The sexual energy we felt wove us together stronger and faster than ten thousand pairs of Levi jeans. With such intense makeout sessions, we probably could have starred in a Levi-loving porn film, pushing Levi Strauss & Co. into the adult film industry. The Urban Dictionary describes Levi-loving as "the act, or motions of having sex, while fully clothed; i.c., bumping and grinding, and dry humping. Commonly used within Mormon culture." Yes, as you can see, Urban Dictionary specifically points out its relation to Mormonism.

The first time I Levi-loved with this cute new guy was an experience I will never forget. We were at his home, watching a movie with some friends, and after it ended, he invited me into his bedroom. He took me by the hand, and we slowly walked up the stairs and to his room. I knew this could be dangerous. I had just come out of my mission like a fennec fox in the Sahara Desert, thirsty for a pond of water.

Eventually, our makeout session ended up on his quilted bed, still fully clothed, hitting a bullseye with the Urban Dictionary's definition of Levi-loving. During these particular moments, a wet spot mysteriously formed upon his jeans, and something oddly familiar exploded inside of me.

It had been almost a decade since I had first experienced this internal explosion, and all of the lights suddenly turned on in my head. I had just experienced the "Big O," and it wasn't from riding a quarter horse in the fields near my home. It was from an actual human being.

My body that had just been filled with so much pleasure, though, was now being filled with deep, abysmal remorse. We had just copulated with our clothes on, and though I didn't completely understand all of the male mechanics of sex, I knew enough to know that he must have ejaculated. More than likely this meant he had experienced the Big O too. I kept trying to tell myself that God wouldn't be mad or thrust us to Hell because our private parts didn't touch skin to skin, but deep down, I knew I could not justify away our sin. I was nauseated and overcome with feelings that my soul was now stained red for allowing this to happen so soon after my mission.

By this time, I had still never masturbated. If I touched myself, it was solely to wash myself, wipe myself, or use a tampon. Remember, I was taught that masturbation led to murder, it led to unwanted pregnancies, it was dirty and filthy, and it would separate me from the love of God.

I had no idea that all those times I climbed swing-set poles when I was younger or rode off into the fields on a galloping horse when I was a teenager, that the amazing, internal explosion I felt was an orgasm. I did not know it was wrong, and I certainly did not know it was something to be considered sacred. I just knew it felt incredible. I never had some internal voice appear and tell me it was sinful or a reason to repent. I just knew that in my twelve-year-old brain, it felt natural.

It wasn't an addiction; in fact, I didn't think of it all that often, nor did I obsess over it or crave it either. I certainly never felt I needed to go talk to a bishop or a therapist. I just knew if I happened to saddle up Cocoa or Fresca or Brownie and I clicked my heels against their side, they would start running and I would be handsomely rewarded.

My dear rapist, I was twenty-three years old when

I grasped the correlation between the horses and my first desired makeout session. My body wanted it, loved it, and yet was so incredibly appalled by it that I didn't let the relationship last much longer. Like the cute missionary from Connecticut, this new guy mentioned marriage and I freaked the hell out.

My view of marriage at the time was nothing more than to have sex, make babies, cook, clean, and go to church. My mind and my heart were at odds with each other. My mind told me I should be getting married, and my heart told me to travel and see the world. I followed my heart, put aside my guilt-ridden brain, and told myself that this was not the right time, the right place, or the right guy to be experiencing the Big O with.

Never Yours,
Orgasmically Awakened

***

My Dear Rapist,

I dumped the guy, quit my job, and I moved to Jackson Hole, Wyoming. After a second summer adventure in Jackson, I moved back home and worked for the winter at the special needs center. After a winter of work, I wanted to spend another summer in a National Park, but this time I chose a much further distance from home. I landed a job as a waitress in Glacier Bay, Alaska. This particular place was an adventure of a lifetime, and I fell in love with Alaska quickly.

Glacier Bay Lodge is a fifty-room resort snuggled under hundreds of spruce trees in an area called Bartlett Cove. It is about a twenty-minute drive from Gustavus, and it is the only place on the island that offers hotel-style accommodations within the park. The restaurant, which is attached to the lodge, offers stunning views of the Fairweather Mountain Range. Home to more than 1,000 glaciers, most tourists come to Glacier Bay to experience the active, calving glaciers, specifically the Margerie Glacier. Margerie spans twenty miles in length and is the most active glacier in the area. It was common to see both black and brown bears, humpback whales, harbor seals, orcas, dolphins, sea otters, eagles, puffins, and sea lions.

In 2002, employees of Glacier Bay Lodge were offered free housing and free meals. Each dorm room had two bunk beds and a small bathroom. A separate building served as a cafeteria and a recreational room for employees to hang out when they were not on shift. To get a break from the lodge, you could do three things—hitch a ride into town to buy a limited offering of snacks from their single hardware store, you could hike, or check out a sea kayak and have the day cruise take you into the 3.3 million acres of park for some exploration.

I was fortunate to share a room with three other Mormon women. There was a small branch of Mormonism in the town of Gustavus, a town of only 500 year-round residents. Here, Mormons met each Sunday inside the home of the bishop, who happened to own the local hardware store at the time as well. Roughly twenty people would meet each week, and it was something I truly looked forward to.

Due to our connections with the local Mormon branch, we had plenty of free adventures on fishing charters and whale-watching excursions. By the end of the summer, I had over 200 pounds of halibut and salmon packaged and prepared to take home to my family.

One of my most favorite Alaskan memories was being surrounded by a pod of whales in the Icy Straits. Out with an older couple from the local Mormon branch who owned a private whale-watching business, we were nestled close to the timbered coastline of the Tongass National Forest not far from a popular halibut fishing hole.

The water around us swirled with bubbles, and we saw that the spiraling water contained hundreds and hundreds of tiny herring. One by one, a whale would arise out of the water with mouth agape and gulp down schools of the Clupeiformes. Once their feeding frenzy was over, the whales encircled our boat and teased us some more with their presence.

I was standing against the starboard side of the boat when I not only heard the spout of water from a blowhole, but I felt it. I turned around and witnessed a whale surfacing right next to me. She gracefully and purposefully arched her back, practically begging me to caress it. Like the slow-mo feature on a modern iPhone, time almost came to a complete halt as my hand moved gently along her backside. If that wasn't extraordinary enough, the captain of the boat had plugged two wires into his radio, and he then strung them outside and threw them overboard.

With the volume cranked up, we heard one of the most magical sounds ever—eight wild Alaskan humpback whales creating music with one another.

Though I was constantly enchanted by Alaska, I was not oblivious to the harsh side of the state. Once, on a two-day kayaking trip roughly forty miles north of Glacier Bay Lodge, my roommates and I came face-to-face with two massive grizzly bears at the first beach we scoped for camping. As we quickly reversed our kayaks away from shore, we were able to watch from a safe distance as they battled one another on their hind legs, biting, clawing, and growling to see who was going to get to mark the spot as their own enclave.

At the next beach we found to set up camp, all four of us slept soundly through the night, and thankfully with no disturbances. When morning arrived and we climbed out of our bags and unzipped the tent door, right in front of us was a large, steaming pile of bear shit. It was so fresh that we could feel its heat rising to our chilled faces.

Faster than obtaining a Big O on a horse, we tore down our camp, shoved our shit into our bags, loaded up the kayaks, and took off. We had not prepared ourselves with a firearm, bear spray, and had not left a map to the park rangers outlining our intended destinations. If something had happened to us, we would have had no way to communicate where we were, and it could have taken days, if not weeks, to find us if we went missing.

After paddling most of the second day, we finally arrived back at the pickup spot safe and sound. This iced-over world felt like heaven, with its abundance of unchartered territory and the purest of wildlife in their natural habitat.

My dear rapist, I was simpleminded in my outlook on the dangers of Alaska and I was careless in my trust of you. It feels like Mormonism instilled a level of innocence and assurance in me that has gone unmatched.

I placed an immeasurable amount of trust in God that he would protect me due to my level of faithfulness and in the way I honorably wore my garments and abstained from coffee, tea, and alcohol. I was taught that as long as I gave strict obedience to Mormonism's rules and teachings, I would be protected anywhere I went. Looking back, I can see that exercising faith in this way made me feel dangerously invincible too many times.

Never Yours,
Unguarded in Alaska

***

My Dear Rapist,

The Alaskan summer of 2002 would unknowingly play a big part in my future. Along with the many adventures, great friends, and a rewarding waitressing job, I did experience a small bout of summer lovin'. There were several employees that showed interest in me, but the one who caught my attention was Alex. Alex was visiting Gustavus for the summer to help his father and a family friend build a summer cabin. He noticed me long before I noticed him. He was connected to a Mormon friend of mine who was the captain of a fishing boat in town. Alex was a dreamy, twenty-two-year-old cowboy from Modesto,

California, and had the chivalry and civility of the romantic cowboys I would watch in the movies. He was roughly six feet tall with light brown hair, bronze skin, and light brown eyes.

His goal in life was to marry, have children, and pursue a career in the police force. He was lean but built, with just the right amount of muscle that made his Wrangler jeans fit deliciously around his sacrum and snuggle perfectly around his pelvic floor.

He was tantalizing eye candy, and he often left me drooling for more. My summer with a cowboy in Wrangler jeans was the icing on my glacial Alaskan cake. He was everything I ever dreamed of in a young man. He was handsome, he was romantic, he was thoughtful, and he was gentle. He was perfect in every single way except that he wasn't Mormon.

I did not let this prevent me from hot and heavy makeout sessions, but to his dismay, I never allowed things to go past first base. My rule was no skin-to-skin touching and no touching of the private parts. This was very difficult for him to accept. He never did push me to do more, but he once confided that he had slept with twenty-six women. To be with someone like me with such strict rules, but whom he also had powerful sexual chemistry with, was too much for him.

Unfortunately for me, due to his unwillingness to investigate the church, he could not be the right guy for me to make Mormon babies with. We finished our summer love affair on his worn-out Wrangler jeans and well wishes for each other's future. He headed home to Modesto to pursue the police academy, and I headed home to repent of my summer of Levi-loving fornication.

My dear rapist, as I reflect on the cowboy from Modesto and how many women he had been with, it leaves me to beg for a couple of answers from you.

What is it that makes one womanizer able to remain respectful to women and the other an abuser of women? Why was a twenty-two-year-old cowboy more capable of accepting my boundaries than a thirty-six-year-old Olympic athlete? Why was this California boy more adept at never disrespecting my innocence than you, an adult, a Hollywood actor, ever were?

Yes, I had some adventure in Levi-loving, but my fornication never went past the Levi or Wrangler jeans and it never seemed to be an issue, until I met you.

Never Yours,
A Levi-Loving Girl

CHAPTER 10

CELESTIAL PORN STAR

"The most important single thing that any Latter-day Saint ever does in this world is to marry the right person, in the right place, by the right authority."

(Elder Bruce R. McConkie, Mormon Apostle 1972-1985 New Era Magazine, January 1975, p.38)

My Dear Rapist,

I left Alaska with an overflowing cup of reverence and awe. Every single part of my being felt complete and happy. I moved back to Logan with a childhood friend and spent another winter working at the disability center. I had now been off my mission for almost two years, and after my wonderful dating experience with Alex, I was starting to feel ready for marriage.

My friend and I moved in with two new women we had never met before. Both girls were returned missionaries, and they were a blast to be around. I loved the singles ward we were assigned to, and the four of us roommates began creating memories together both inside and outside our apartment walls. There was an abundance of cute returned missionaries in our new ward, but none of them seemed interested in me.

After several months of no success, I started seriously praying and pleading with God to bring someone into my life whom I could marry and start my family with.

Hollie was a cute and brilliant blonde from Idaho, and she was one of my new roommates. Early into our friendship, she suggested that she would like to set me up with a friend of hers who was attending Brigham Young University. Max was also from Idaho, and he had dark brown hair and dark eyes, a combination I had always felt a weakness for. He was a shy pre-med student, a returned missionary, and he loved the outdoors.

These were three perfect attributes that any young Mormon woman would want in a potential Mormon husband, since what these attributes actually equated to was wealthy, religious, and adventurous. I was sold.

Max and I lived about three hours apart, forcing us to alternate our visits with each other every other weekend. Either he would travel to Utah State University in Logan, or I would travel to BYU in Provo. I had a former missionary companion living in Provo, so when it was my turn to make the 120-mile drive south, I would stay with her.

Brigham Young University is a private university established in 1875. Around 1940, BYU created a list of prohibitions that both students and faculty were required to honor. If a student breaks this honor code, the consequence could be expulsion from school. One established standard is that someone of the opposite sex cannot visit your bedroom or your bathroom. In addition, a midnight curfew during the week and a 1:30 a.m. curfew on Friday evenings is in place to prevent any heavy necking or petting, soaking, jump-humping, or unwanted pregnancies.

Soaking is a supposed loophole within the Mormon world that helps some teenagers and young adults feel justified in engaging in sex without feeling like they have actually had sex. It is assumed that when the penis enters the vagina and the couple becomes motionless, like a peculiar game of freeze tag, the penis is being soaked, not stroked. The lack of movement results in the preservation of both parties' virginity. Other terminology for soaking includes the Provo Float, marinating, and the "Dock and Talk."

And for some there is jump-humping, the Mormon young adult version of a threesome. A third-party member is invited to a soaking, but with a differing role. Their role is to pounce on the bed next to the couple or push up on the mattress from underneath the bed. This type of movement, because it is being generated from an outside source, also leads those involved to believe they are keeping their chastity pristine and whole.

It has been two decades since I was flirting with temptation on a BYU campus, and these terms did not exist while I was dating Max. The only thing I was aware of was Levi-loving, something Max and I actually never did. We kissed and held hands, but that was about it. In the beginning, we acted more like third graders with massive crushes—too scared to touch, or to do more than a ten-second kiss. Despite the immaturity of our relationship, Max and I quickly became serious. After two weeks of dating, we decided we did not want to date anyone else and we became exclusive.

It was a typical BYU Mormon dating experience: after two dates, we discussed marriage, after a month, we spent time ring shopping, and after two months, we began planning a wedding. Max and I had it all figured out. We would finish the school year, both travel to Alaska to work for the summer, and then we would have a wedding before he began fall semester at BYU. We were not even fazed by the honor code. We both fiercely wanted to be worthy of a temple marriage, and we did not want to take any risk of him getting kicked out of BYU.

About two months into the relationship, and after much discussion about getting married, we had a slight setback. It was my turn to spend the weekend in Provo, so after finishing work on Friday, I gathered my belongings for the next two days and made the drive south. We were feeling up for some adventure and decided to spend our Saturday visiting Goblin Valley State Park. Goblin Valley is a three-square-mile radius of hoodoos. Hoodoos are odd-shaped goblins, made of Entrada sandstone, which were deposited between 140 and 180 million years ago.

The four-hour drive to Goblin Valley from Provo gave Max and I a good amount of time to discuss our future plans together. I was happy and excited; I thought for sure that I had finally found my worthy Mormon companion. I was hoping Goblin Valley was where Max would propose to me, but he wanted to wait and pop the eternal question in Alaska. As much as I wanted that ring on my finger, Alaska would have been a much more magical place for him to bend down on one knee and slip a ring on my size six finger.

The next day, Sunday, was reserved for a three-hour block at church. We were sitting next to each other, holding hands and waiting for the sacrament to be passed when an unseen, peculiar voice entered my head. I had never heard voices in my head before, so this wasn't some schizophrenic voice that made its occasional appearance. It was a subtle voice that told me to ask Max a question that I did not fully comprehend. I cautiously turned my head toward him with uncertainty on how to ask the seven-word interrogative.

I questioned whether I should wait until after the bread and water had been served or until church was over. After weighing my options for a few moments, in flawless Ginger fashion, I blurted out, "Max, do you have a porn addiction?"

You would've thought I just flashed him my barely size A, unsullied boobs right as he was partaking of the sacrament bread. From zero to sixty, his eyes grew bigger than a pair of pepperoni-sized areolas and he whispered, "How did you know?"

Caught off guard by his answer, but naïve to what this actually meant, I asked him if we should go for a walk and have a discussion. He wanted to finish partaking of the sacrament, so as soon as it was finished, we made our way toward the exit. He was nervous and I was nervous, but we both felt this was an important part of moving forward with our relationship. We walked for a few minutes until we found a place to sit where we could be alone, and where we could be uninterrupted by others.

Within seconds of sitting down, Max started blurting out his history while looking at porn. I sat and listened to him share his story of how he began looking at naked women when he was as young as twelve years old. He had five brothers, all either already practicing physicians or on their way to becoming MDs. Apparently, all five brothers shared the addiction. None of their wives or girlfriends knew, but for some strange reason, Max felt compelled to be honest with me. I asked him what he meant by addiction, and he informed me that for him, it meant looking at porn three times a day. He shared a room with a good friend, they both had computers, and they both grappled with the need to lust after naked women.

He seemed relieved to have told me of his burden, yet as much as I tried not to act like it, his burden now became mine and I felt heavy with the news. I assumed that the porn he was looking at was something along the lines of a *Victoria's Secret* magazine, but it would take another few weeks before I realized what this actually meant.

We finished our Sunday by going for a drive, and I told him that I still loved him and that I wanted to be a supportive girlfriend and wife. I truly felt this was not going to have an impact on our relationship, especially because he promised me that his bishop knew of his struggles. The bishop had told him that as long as he was working on his addiction, he was okay to take the sacrament. Above all, he was also still able to go to the temple. Hearing this affirmation softened my nerves a bit, but I still knew there would be more heavy discussions in our future.

The following weekend, he came up to my place. Because we did not have the honor code at Utah State, nor did we engage in any Levi-loving, he felt safe crashing on my couch. This particular weekend, I did notice a slight change in his behavior. He began pointing out things about my physical appearance that he did not like. He was disappointed in my short nails, he did not like the fact that my stomach wasn't completely flat, and he hated the way I wore my hair.

Yet during our makeout session, I knew he was somewhat turned on by me because just as with the previous guy, a small wet circle appeared on his jeans. When that happened, he immediately pushed me away and told me we had to stop. I was a bit perplexed by his behavior, but I would never do something he wasn't comfortable doing. He ended up going back to BYU early and was deeply upset with me. He felt so guilty about the wet spot that he made an appointment to see his Bishop. He felt it was my fault that this had happened and told me we would need to be more careful in the future, stressing the importance of remaining temple-worthy. We did not discuss porn while he was at my place for the weekend, we only discussed his wet jeans.

The second weekend after finding out about his porn use, his behavior changed even more, and I became more and more concerned about our potential marriage. We were in Provo, on another drive, and this time he told me that he didn't just look at porn, but he masturbated. I don't know why, maybe because masturbation has been compared to murder, but this news devastated me.

I cried, and I could not hide it from him. This was a defilement on every level. His lusting after other women was one thing, but touching his penis damn near gave me a panic attack. If this wasn't bad enough, he proceeded to confide in me something even more frightening. A common habit of his was to go to class, pick out the prettiest girl in the room, and then sexually fantasize about her until he needed to go to a bathroom and jack off.

I didn't know whether to be flattered that he would be this honest with me or to run. For the time being, I chose neither. Instead, I told him I needed to go home and think about everything he had shared with me. Porn was one thing, but masturbating and thinking like a rapist was a whole new level of things to consider.

I cried the entire drive back to Logan, but decided against confiding in anyone about what I had learned. Max called to find out how I was holding up and, afraid to hurt his feelings, I lied and told him I still loved him and that we would work through this.

During the following week, I received an unexpected

phone call from Max's older brother in Texas. This brother had an established pediatric practice and was also serving in a high church position within his local area. According to Max, he was also a brother whose wife had no idea about her husband's sexual addiction. This brother felt it was his duty to fly me to Texas before our marriage and discuss with me the importance of a wife meeting the husband's sexual needs in marriage. I was so completely caught off guard by his candidness that all I could muster out was, "Okay, I will come."

Max was thrilled that I would be willing to do this. I am positive that my desire to prove I was prepared to do whatever it would take to please him gave him more courage to be more direct with me. While on one of our many drives, Max proposed several questions that he needed addressed before he was able to put a ring on my finger. He informed me that one day he would be a doctor, and that part of his job would require seeing women naked. According to him, when a man sees a woman naked, he has to "finish the job."

For every appointment that required him to see a disrobed female, he questioned my willingness to come to the office and take care of him, so he wouldn't have to commit sin and masturbate. Within the same breath of air, he then inquired of my submissiveness regarding sex after having a baby. He was worried about the six-week recovery period and needed to make sure I would take care of him in other ways if intercourse was not an option. The more he opened his mouth, the more I wanted to vomit. I wanted honesty, but this level of honesty was making my head spin and my vagina twitch with a dissipating libido.

It was spring break at BYU, and Max had decided to travel home to Idaho to visit his family. He figured it was perfect timing for me to finally meet his parents. I took some time off from work and made the five-hour drive in my red Pontiac Grand Prix, excited and nervous to meet my future in-laws.

Though I would be staying at my brother's home, I packed as if I would be with Max's family the entire time. This meant we would be going to church with his parents, which, to both of us, was the most important part of the visit. We spent Friday evening at my brother's home, and then Saturday, we spent the entire day in Boise. Though it was spring, the weather was chilly, and Max and I bundled up in coats and scarves and walked around an outdoor plaza with a movie theater, shopping outlets, and restaurants.

I had seen a Starbucks next to the theater and told Max that I would love to purchase one of their caramelized apple ciders to warm me up. He grabbed my hand tightly and warned me that we should "avoid the very appearance of evil." To say I was pissed was an understatement.

Like a frog in hot water, I was getting close to the boiling point and ready to hop out of this hypocritical, frightening relationship. But like a good Mormon girl would do, and not wanting to make things weird, I caved to his observation and chose not to appear evil with a cup of warm cider from Starbucks. I was about to meet my future mother-in-law, so I had to obey my porn-addicted, masturbating, returned missionary soon-to-be husband. After dinner and a movie, he drove to his parents' place and I went to my brother's home, wanting nothing but my bed. I lay awake all night, convincing myself that all of these red flags were not red flags, but maybe green flags with a bunch of little jitterbugs stuck to them. According to Max, his bishop had told him he was worthy to take the sacrament and go to the temple, so this must have meant God approved of him too. If his bishop and God found him worthy, then who was I to question him?

Sunday morning arrived, and I spent quite a while getting all dolled up and ready to meet the parents. I pulled on my floor-length denim skirt and my dainty, brown floral blouse. The top had full '70s-style sleeves and was high enough on my chest that you could not sneak a peek of my breasts if you wanted to. The skirt was super trendy, reaching my ankles with a frayed and dirty look, but it had not a single hole or tear. I thought I looked quite attractive and modest and was certain I was going to make a good impression. My light auburn hair was styled nicely with a Jennifer Aniston bob. I was feeling really, really good about myself.

I had about a thirty-minute drive to get to his parents' home. At that time, I thought about the excitement of going to Alaska together for the summer—the proposal that would happen while we were there, and our big wedding would be in August. I pulled up to the country home, feeling cheerful and grateful that I was finally on the path to marriage. Max opened the door, and right behind him was his mother and father.

They were cordial, but his mother immediately seemed apathetic and aloof. Our dinner lasted maybe an hour, with very surface questions about who I was and my Utah upbringing. As soon as dinner was over, we were out the door, saying our goodbyes. Perplexed about such a short visit, I knew something was off but had no idea what it was that I had done wrong. School started the next day for Max, and I had to get back to work. We each made the five-and-a-half-hour drive home, but in opposite cars and opposite directions. We did not have great cell phones in 2003, so our conversations existed mostly through email during the week while we were apart. We had determined the following weekend would be time for him to meet my family.

I was beginning to seriously question my desire to marry him, but continued moving forward like a naïve Mormon girl. We had decided that we would do a temple session together before driving thirty minutes north to meet my family. My parents were very excited, because in Mormon timing, at age twenty-four, I was beginning to be considered an old maid.

Prior to our temple date, Max had informed me why his mother was so upset. She was disgusted by my Levi skirt and told Max I looked like a slut. He told me if we were going to get married, I would need to throw the skirt away because his mother didn't approve. Not a minute later, he was describing his top sexual fantasy with me. As we drove to the temple, he shared his deep-seated desire to cut my clothes off me with a pair of scissors the first time we consummated our marriage. I felt no love in this descriptive mirage of his; if anything, the mere expression of his words felt like he was describing rape.

It took the denial of a caramelized apple cider from Starbucks, the disgust over a dirty denim skirt (that I never even Levi-loved in), and a sexual illusion with scissors to force me to see something was seriously off. Less than twenty minutes later, we were sitting inside of the temple and I could not take my eyes off Max. I peered into this priesthood holder, garbed in his holy temple clothing, and knew I could not go through with the marriage.

When the blinders slipped off, he looked dark, ugly, and disgusting. I thought back to all of the disturbing things he had told me and I concluded he was not my eternal soulmate. I had zero desire to take him home, zero desire to go to Alaska with him, zero desire to go to Texas and have his brother talk to me about sex, and zero desire to throw my denim skirt away. Damnit, I wanted an apple cider from Starbucks, and to hell with helping him jack off after he became a doctor and provided care to naked women.

Sitting in the temple, I realized that I did not love him; I loved the idea of being in love with him. We finished our temple session, got dressed into our street clothing, and walked out of the temple together without holding hands. On the drive back to my place, I told him I could not go through with our future plans together and informed him I was breaking up with him. After gathering his items, he climbed into his car and headed back to Provo as a single man. I never saw or spoke to him again.

I drove straight to my parents' home, walking into a full house of excited and happy family members. My face was covered in red, blotchy tears and I told my family it was over, and that there was not going to be a future marriage. I threw myself on my mother's bed and sobbed tears that contained months and months of revulsion I had been refusing to acknowledge. My sweet father walked into his bedroom and sat next to me, imploring me with questions. All I could do was spew out a jumbled mess of words. Somehow I even managed to blubber out that I no longer trusted him. This was the first time in my life that I questioned the integrity and attributes of my own father, and whether I could trust him. I had battles in my own head, fighting likc hcll to believe my father was not like Max and his brothers.

He seemed to treat my mother just fine in the public eye, but I began to seriously question how he treated her behind closed doors. I was desperate to believe my father was still a good man, but thanks to Max, I couldn't help but question who my father really was when no one was looking. I didn't just question my father's integrity, I doubted my brothers, uncles, and grandfather's treatment and views of women behind closed doors.

This experience with Max sent me reeling and pushed me onto a path of attracting nothing but porn-addicted Mormon men. I continued going to my own singles ward on Sundays but struggled. I could not look at a young man serving the sacrament, giving a talk, or saying a prayer without wondering if they had a secret, obsessive habit of wanking off.

Masturbating was the total antithesis of what we were taught to do as Mormon youth. I was told that Christ held God's power in his hands, and so did Mormon men. These powerful priesthood hands gave blessings of healing, performed saving ordinances in the temple, baptized others into the one and only true church on earth, and now my new reality told me they were capable of masturbating. Jolted by the knowledge that my male family members' hands were capable of using their priesthood power in such a self-pleasuring way, a large crack began to form in my testimony of the Mormon priesthood power.

My dear rapist, this experience placed a substantial drop of mold into my faith. I was suffocating from the rot and I wanted to run from my new, dilapidated view of Mormon men. I had considered going back to Alaska for the summer, or maybe even another National Park, but I wanted to get far away from Utah for longer than one season. It took several months to decide what to do, and after weighing my options, I chose to give the nanny gig another chance. I figured the East Coast would be close enough to fly home for visits but far enough away to learn to breathe again. Knowing the male-to-female ratio in the Connecticut singles ward and feeling a bit nauseated at the thought of dating, I requested a position in the New York City-New Jersey area.

My first real dating experience in Mormonism left me feeling like I was meant to be nothing more than a celestial porn star. My role was solidified: outside the bedroom I was to think like June Cleaver, inside the bedroom I was to act like Bathsheba the whore, and every second of every day I was to look like Kim Kardashian.

I packed my bags, boarded my plane, and left Zion. I was ready to take a long, deep break from thinking about marriage and enjoy a second experience living near New York City.

Never Yours,
A Not-So Celestial Porn Star

CHAPTER 11

A JERSEY ATHEIST

"As Americans – as members of the worldwide Christian community – we can defeat the godless, atheistic forces that threaten us. Yes, with the help of Almighty God we can – we must – win the war against the evil forces which seem almost to overwhelm us. The eternal verities revealed from God, through his inspired prophets, have not and will not change."

(General Conference and Ensign Articles, Godless Forces, 1969, Benson, Ezra T. Prophet)

My Dear Rapist,

The East Coast nanny agency I signed up with offered me several interviews in the Big Apple, but the most appealing position offered to me was in Franklin Lakes, New Jersey. The position required sole care for an eight-month-old infant boy, with both parents working outside the home and commuting to the city every day.

I would be paid five hundred dollars cash each Friday, all room and board covered, and would be given a Miata convertible to drive in my spare time. They offered a two-week paid vacation, extra time off during Christmas, but there was definitely no offer of a free summer experience in Europe. Vacationing with the family was not a perk I cared about this time; more important to me was the connection I felt with the mother and father. After my first experience in Connecticut, I now knew what to prioritize in selecting my next nanny position.

I was once again carrying the title of nanny, but this time the family had the courtesy to call me by name before explaining my title to their friends and family. The Bradfords were a white, upper-class family who were very kind and down to earth. Mrs. B was in her mid-30s and worked for a well-known insurance company. She was a beautiful blonde woman, very slim, and incredibly attractive. Mr. B was in his early 40s and worked in sales for a clothing department. He was also very handsome and in healthy shape, a possible Hugh Grant doppelganger.

They lived in a modest three-level home on just over an acre of property. They were very welcoming and made sure I knew that the 3,100-square-foot home was now my home too. Every once in a while, you could see the Empire State Building from their property, and the view pushed me to get into the city as much as possible. Learning from my mistakes in Connecticut, I wanted to create healthy boundaries with my new family. I was easygoing and tried to spend some time with them outside of my work hours, but also made a point to spend time alone, with friends, or living it up in the city.

There were no Mormon singles wards in the area, but there was a family ward. Within the family ward, there was a group of young single adults that would meet together after church on Sundays as well as during the week. Just as I had easily made lifelong friends in Connecticut, I made them again in New Jersey. There were about eight nannies and half a dozen young single men, including a set of Mormon missionaries. This was much more my style than the singles ward, and I had come to love many of the families in the Fardale Ward.

Some of my most favorite memories were of the group of us spending time in the city shopping, going to Broadway shows, and eating at trendy restaurants. The typical tourist destinations were not on our list. A few of us even signed up with a company called New York Cares, an organization that provides opportunities to volunteer in soup kitchens, at centers for people with disabilities, and with community events for homeless children, like trips to the Bronx Zoo and the circus at Madison Square Gardens. I decided not to go home for Christmas that year, and I instead signed up to work in a homeless shelter serving food. I really wanted to get to know the city on a more intimate level, and

I absolutely adored that I could do it with my friends and my cute fifteen-year-old cousin Brielle. My uncle and aunt lived in New Jersey, about an hour south of me, so it was nice to be able to spend time with them once in a while. Outside of spending time in the city, we spent a lot of our evenings hanging out at each other's homes or playing games and sports together at our church.

I must admit, my fondest memory of New Jersey was falling in love for the first time. My relationships with Max in Utah and Alex in Alaska never came close to what I had experienced with Jack, a Jersey atheist. Jack and I seemed to have connected spiritually, emotionally, mentally, and physically, forming a bond so deep that I considered walking away from Mormonism for him.

He was the first I considered this with, and you, my dear rapist, were the second. With him, the consideration was done out of love. With you it was considered out of desperation, fear, and shame. In my humble opinion, unexpectedly falling in love with Jack is a story that deserves to be shared.

My good friend Jodi and I received a random invite for a Sunday lunch from Brother and Sister Wayne from the Fardale Ward. The Waynes were an older couple who attended church with no indication they had children. They provided their address, and after printing directions from MapQuest, Jodi and I drove to the tiny old home, which had a gorgeous weeping willow tree impeccably placed at the end of a long driveway.

They invited us inside and led us to a petite kitchen with a round, wooden table. Though it was sunny outside, the lighting inside was dim. They showed us our seats and an older gentleman, Brother Wayne's father, and a teenager joined us for lunch. The teenager had long hippie hair, a five o'clock shadow, and a thick pair of bottle-lens glasses on. Hunched over in his tie-dye t-shirt, he was inhaling a bowl of cereal as the rest of us nibbled on sandwiches.

The conversation was lighthcartcd, a bit awkward, but overall genuine and met with the best of intentions. The Waynes were converts to the church, Grandpa had no interest in it, and the teenage boy seemed completely oblivious to our presence. At one point, the teen abruptly excused himself and disappeared.

Jodi and I continued eating our lunch and conversing with the Waynes. We inquired about their conversion to Mormonism, discussed both our missionary experiences with them, and mostly kept the conversation centered around the church. In some ways, it felt like I was on a mission again. It felt natural to attempt building trust and gaining respect with the local members of the church.

After twenty minutes of conversation, a very handsome young man walked into the room and said hello. He looked to be in his early 20s, with short brown hair, bright blue eyes, a clean-shaven face, and a simple t-shirt with jeans. It wasn't his hello that hatched a thousand butterflies into my stomach but his sparkling blue eyes and the dimples in his cheeks.

His smile caused a hasty surge of norepinephrine to fire off into my central nervous system.

The sister missionary in me instantly vanished, and a timid but very intrigued Ginger surfaced. I sat straight up, curious as hell at who just walked into the room. I instantly became nervous about my appearance and whether or not he would find me attractive. I wanted to make a good first impression, especially because he seemed to want to stay and talk with us. It wasn't long before he cut right to the chase and asked if we wanted to get out of there and find a place to play some pool. The two of us had never really played a game of pool before, but we were up for something new. Our handsome new friend had us climb into his white two-door, 1980s Ford Bronco.

He was surprisingly chivalrous and insisted on opening the door for both my friend and me. It was evident to Jodi that Jack and I had instant interest in each other, so she climbed into the back of the Bronco and allowed me to climb into the front seat. Jack's ability to be a gentleman was just one of his endearing qualities, and as the night wore on, the thousand hatched butterflies in my abdomen consistently fluttered inside of me. The way he looked at me continued to catch me off guard, leaving me with flushed cheeks and a desire to go find a horse to ride.

The guy wasn't simply looking at me, he was peering fiercely into my soul, and his charming, blue eyes would not stop scrutinizing my very existence. Even more impressive, he was multitasking by hanging onto every word that came out of my mouth. I had never experienced such intense inquisition into my heart, mind, and soul, and it left me feeling libidinously toward this riveting Jersey boy.

After several hours of playing sloppy pool, we called it a night and returned to Jack's home to get our vehicle and say our goodbyes. Before leaving, he asked for my phone number and said he would like to reach out to me in the near future. For the most part, there was no hesitancy in saying yes, as long as I promised myself that nothing more would come of this and we'd kept our new relationship in the friendship department.

At the time, I was talking frequently with a male friend in Utah whom I had served my mission with. We had always been really good friends, and I had been informed by other missionaries that he had a crush on me while we were in Detroit together. We once had a really good makeout session after I'd ended things with Max, and I had thought for sure he would try and date me after we swapped saliva.

I waited for him to take things to the next level, but he consistently dragged his feet. The truth was, he had a repetitive story in his head that he never felt good enough for me and I was way out of his league. I was patient and willing to continue our long-distance friendship while I was in Jersey with the hopes that one day he would wake up and ask me to move back to Utah to explore a relationship with him.

Jack brought out something different in me than my mission friend. Jack was a former Mormon turned atheist. In fact, before we left his home that first night, Jack let us know that the hippie devouring his bowl of cereal earlier in the day was none other than himself. I would later find out that he'd kept his head low and didn't communicate with us because he was embarrassed by his appearance. He was so taken by me that he instantly went to his bathroom to shave and clean himself up. To say I was flattered was an understatement. I was twenty-five years old, and for the first time in my life an attractive male was entirely and assiduously captivated by me.

It was almost midnight before I climbed into my comfortable bed to dream of this cute boy who we had just spent our evening with. My thoughts would not shut off, making it highly difficult to fall asleep. I could not help but contemplate the difference between Jack and the missionary friend back home. My friend was a returned missionary, he had a testimony of the church, he was attractive with brown hair and bright blue eyes, just like Jack, and I knew he would be safe to start a family with.

Jack was five years younger than me, making him a nineteen-year-old who was only one year out of high school. He was also an atheist who, even worse, rejected Mormonism. He already had three strikes against him: his age, his belief system, and, well, his belief system. How could a young atheist ever make a good husband, let alone have good morale? Eventually, the heavier questions were outweighed by the butterflies in my belly, and I eventually drifted into a deep, happy slumber.

The next morning, I awoke before my employers and got ready for the workday with an energizing smile on my face. The Bradfords had noticed my late arrival the night before, and Mrs. Bradford expressed her concern that I would be too tired to take care of the baby. I assured her I would be fine and not to worry about my lack of sleep. I was on an adrenaline high after meeting Jack and was in the best of moods all day.

It was springtime in New Jersey and absolutely beautiful. I was loving my job, loving my girlfriends, loving my involvement with the singles group, loving the family ward, loving being so close to New York City, and certainly loving my time with Jack. After that initial introduction and the evening of playing pool, we started seeing each other weekly. In the beginning, it was in a group setting, where he would join us playing volleyball at the church, or he would take Jodi and I on rides in his Bronco to get ice cream, or we would meet at a diner to get some grub.

Once he met my Australian girlfriend, a sassy petite blonde with a sexy accent, I worried he would drop his interest in me and start pursuing her. But he didn't. He never wavered, keeping his eyes solely on me.

Eventually the group dates were not enough, and he wanted alone time with me.

I was honest with him from the beginning and informed him that I had a friend back home waiting for me to finish my time in New Jersey. But according to him, until a ring was on my finger, I was fair game.

He wanted a chance to date me. I eventually told him that I would have to have a conversation with my missionary friend before I agreed to a single date with him.
My dear rapist, though I wasn't ready to admit it to myself, the moment Jack's cheerful blue eyes, endearing dimples, and joyful Jersey laughter converged together at the pool hall, I knew without a doubt that I was smitten. Something was different.

Something inside had hatched that had never been hatched before. I had no idea that saying yes to a simple game of pool and the blossoming of an atheist's love would lead to the testing of my Mormon devotion like it had never been tested before.

Never Yours,
Jonesing for Jack

***

My Dear Rapist,

Even though my mission friend dragged his feet, from time to time we would share the idea of the two of us getting married someday. The dynamics of our relationship were odd and, as before, I was beginning to feel desperate to start a family. I felt more and more like a Mormon spinster as the months continued to creep by.

It felt reasonable to marry a friend whom I had known for years, whom I found attractive, and who I meshed fairly well with. I had many heartfelt discussions with Missionary Friend about Max's porno habits and his alarming expressions of sexual concerns and inclinations. Missionary Friend had assured me that he had neither a masturbation habit nor a desire for porn.

He further shared details of his disgust at catching several missionary companions jacking off, and then beating the shit out of them for doing it when he was in close proximity to them. These tidbits of information actually made me feel safe with him and made me trust him more. Max had completely squashed my trust and safety in men, and I did not want to lose or let go of Missionary Friend for this very reason.

Given Jack's advances, I ultimately decided to give

Missionary Friend a call and tell him that I had someone pursuing me in Jersey. Deep down, I had plotted that by giving him this bit of information, it would push him to pick up his feet, request for me to come home, and move our friendship to the next level. It did the exact opposite. His insecurity button was touched, and my friend told me to go ahead and date him, but to prepare for less phone calls and less talks of getting married. He had no interest in asking for me to come home, and said he would rather just see what happened once I moved back to Utah.

This both angered and hurt me. It was as if Wreck-It Ralph had taken an oversized hammer and smashed my security to pieces. Missionary Friend's response made me feel like I wasn't worth fighting for and that I would never be worth fighting for in the eyes of Mormon men. I had never experienced a Mormon man fighting for me, or really chasing me, for that matter. In New Jersey, the ex-Mormon turned atheist chased me as hard as an African lion ready to mate with its lioness.

As soon as I got off the phone with Missionary Friend, I sent Jack a text message on my Verizon flip phone and told him I was ready for a date. The first date turned into two dates. Two dates turned into three dates. Three dates turned into being inseparable.

We could not get enough of each other, and we tried to spend as much time together as our schedules would allow. My days of nannying were spent watching the clock and counting down the minutes to hearing his old, beat-up Bronco pull into my driveway. I would run down the stairs, shout goodbye to my employers, run through the garage, and then compose myself in time to walk outside and climb into his passenger seat. Curiosity filled me to the brim as I wondered where our next makeout session would be.

But don't get me wrong, my dear rapist. As much as I loved our mutual burning desire for each other, it was the things Jack said and the things he did for me that kept my libido strong. Jack was a romantic and he knew, or at least consistently tried, to figure out how to connect with me on every level. If he wasn't burning CDs for me with an array of songs that made him think of me, he was coming up with different ways to catch fireflies in mason jars.

He was always surprising me by showing up to Mormon-themed events and activities. When he found out I was doing musical numbers in sacrament meeting, he made extra effort to plant his cute little ass in the church pew and come to hear me play. After witnessing my skills on the piano, he would often describe a picturesque dream of his.

He envisioned himself purchasing a piano and placing it beneath his father's weeping willow tree. He would then spread a blanket underneath the tree, lie down, and then watch and listen to me tickle the ivories to some of his favorite songs. Jack's vision was such a contrast to the imagery of Max wanting to cut my clothes off with a pair of scissors.

I could not believe the profound and unusual level of thought that Jersey boy put toward me. It felt like it had taken forever to find this, and in some ways, it saddened me that a Mormon boy never showed this echelon of care or interest. Jack's interest felt pure, fun, and honest, with respectful intentions. Yes, his reproductive organs were on fire, but so was everything else, most especially the beautiful organ beating inside his chest.

At the time, there was an important and historical Mormon event in New York that he requested he escort me to. This only deepened my reasons for falling hard for him. Mormon Prophet Gordon B. Hinckley was there to dedicate a new temple on Columbus Avenue that had been renovated from an old church building. This occasion required special permission and reserved tickets. I had told Jack I wanted to go and he said he would like to join me. Showing up to my piano playing at church was one thing, but this, this reached a whole new level.

A month later, Jack and I made our way into the city and went through the first, fifth, and sixth floors of the high-rise Manhattan temple. I spent weeks prior begging God to touch Jack's atheist heart and inspire him to return to Mormonism. I kept my eyes shyly upon him throughout the tour, grasping for any hint that he felt something metaphysical.

Though he no longer believed in Mormonism, I sensed he had a thriving affinity of his own for undefined feelings toward spirituality. His handsome smile was a permanent visual the entire time we were inside the Temple. He seemed to carry no fear toward the plethora of clean-cut authoritative Mormon leaders walking around in their polished shoes and sharp business suits and ties.

Once we were through with our tour, we decided to make our way toward Times Square and grab a bite to eat. After dinner, we began walking toward Penn Station to catch our train on the PATH back to New Jersey. We were just passing Madison Square Gardens when Jack pulled me by the hand and walked me to the side of the unique circular building. With the energy from attending a spiritual temple open house, a romantic dinner in Times Square, and the vibration of thousands of people walking its streets, the throbbing between Jack and I flew off the freaking charts. He pressed me up against the side of the building, and in the safety of the darkened sky, we kissed salaciously, frozen in time as the crowded city of Manhattan continued on around us.

The passionate kisses sent my brain into a tailspin, demanding God to intervene. I wanted my Father in Heaven to show up like a damn dove and rebaptize Jersey in the Hudson River, confirm him with the Holy Ghost on the subway heading north, and then marry us inside the soon-to-be dedicated Manhattan Temple. The pull to be one with him was not just physical, it was spiritual, and it was emotional. In that very moment, I snuggled up tight against his Levi-loving jeans and held back every desire to christen the world-famous building on 4 Penn Plaza.

Like a good Mormon girl, though, I pushed my sinful but oddly religious fantasy out of my mind and tossed it into the NYC urine-scented gutter. In a matter of seconds, I successfully reigned in my thunder down under and came up gasping for air. I was going bloody mad wondering what this nineteen-year-old kid was doing to me. Either my feelings were a thousand percent genuine and real, or Satan was tempting me to cave to my slutty porn-star name.

I lived for the weekends, I lived for my girlfriends, and I lived for Jack. My girlfriends and I spent time visiting the Jersey shore, Boston, and Cape Cod. Jack didn't do the short weekend getaways with us, but he did join us for dinners in the city.

A lasting memory, one that would leave me completely abashed for years to come, was the weekend we spent bar-hopping with Jack and several of my nanny girlfriends. We all met at my friend Michelle's house and she drove us to Hoboken to catch the train into the city. Unbeknownst to Jack, he would be getting a glimpse into the life of my great-great-grandfather Janus Hansen, a Mormon polygamist with four wives.

Jack led the way from bar to bar with six nannies hanging on to his handsome gentleman coattails. Out of the six of us, five of us were Mormon, and the other was Lutheran. Michelle, the Lutheran, was the only one who actually consumed alcohol with Jack. I didn't mind being around alcohol—it never scared me, nor did I ever feel compelled to drink it. I was of the mind that it was my duty to be an example of a good Mormon girl, even inside a bar with a bunch of drunks.

If anything, the belief that I was chosen stayed in the forefront of my mind, and I believed if I held onto this thought while the drinks were being passed around, my Mormon light would shine through and someone would be attracted to my righteous spirit. Of course, I wanted it to be Jack, so I stayed mostly by his side hoping that my Mormon influence would rub off on him. I did not anticipate that the more alcohol he consumed, the more endearing he would become. I had expected to be disgusted, but the repugnancy never arrived. However, the son of a bitch that did show up was the dangerous emotion called jealousy. Any attractive girl I perceived checking out Jack, I wanted to punch in the face with the fist that bore my CTR ring. It wasn't just the jealousy of other women that was bothersome, it was the envy that arose toward Jack that left me feeling discombobulated.

My dear rapist, I wanted Jack's freedom. I ached for the sovereignty he held as a nineteen-year-old Jersey boy. His ability to be nothing but himself, free of shifty religious eyes, in one of the most conspicuous cities in the entire world was downright alluring. In many ways, he displayed more maturity and senescence than I did as a woman five years his senior.

He appeared to be going through the normal stages of young adult life and living for himself; he was not living for Jesus, not for his parents, and certainly not for the patriarchy. This one and only time I went bar-hopping in New York added more fuel to the fire of my already growing list of perplexing perceptions and sentiments toward him and the church.

Not wanting to leave, but worried we would get stuck in the city, I needed to remind an inebriated Jack that it was time for us to make our way toward the green exit sign glowing above the bar doors. Our synthetic twenty-first-century polygamist group needed to be back to the PATH by 10:45 p.m. to catch the last train back to Hoboken. It was not difficult to persuade him to leave, and I admit, the walk back to 33rd Street was quite amusing. Alcohol really broadened the boy's smile and loosened his likable tongue. Thank God my girlfriends found him to be a delightful source of entertainment in the way he displayed his adoration of me and not a nuisance.

While we walked with some determination to get to the train before they closed their doors, Jack's footsteps had less resolve and a much more leisurely gait. I loved that he didn't seem to mind if we missed the last ride back to Jersey. His nonchalant vibe triggered my nether regions into thinking I needed to saddle up Cocoa and go for another ride. The guy made me crazy in every single way. I was horny for him, and I couldn't do a damn thing about it.

My garments were the perfect reminder of why these very thoughts were going to send me straight to hell. I did what any good Mormon girl would do—I thrust my filthy thoughts onto the metal train tracks and walked inside the train. Our group walked past a dozen other passengers and found our seats toward the back of the railcar. Jack, always the gentleman, chose to stand so the ladies could have a place to plant their sober nanny asses.

We had about a sixteen-minute commute, and as we sat down, it appeared as if the three-mile ride would be spent in silence. But then, in cool Jersey style, as the doors closed, my handsome blue-eyed boy stepped away from his spot and into the middle of the railcar. He had a mischievous, drunken grin on his face and with the excitement of a middle-school boy, he grasped his left hand onto the center pole and swung his right arm around to showcase me to the other passengers.

"This here is the most beautiful girl I have ever laid my eyes on. Would you not all agree?" he declared.

An angel named Flattered appeared on my left shoulder, brushed some pink powder on my cheeks, and whispered into my ear that this level of idolization was rare and I should hold it close. Then, an angel named Mortified emerged onto my right shoulder, glossed my cheeks in a deep red, and hissed into my ear that the man before me was nothing but a drunk.

He spewed the idea that it was the alcohol doing the talking, and that I should shrink and feel ashamed for falling for someone who liked the forbidden nectar of the gods. While Flattered and Mortified sat upon my shoulders and had a raging cat fight, Jack continued on, raving about his reasons for his attention. In the end, Flattered stood her ground and told Mortified to burn in hell.

I couldn't help it; I was falling in love and I wanted Jack all to myself. Alcohol talking or not, I knew the things he declared about me to my friends and to the dozen strangers in that railcar were real. Once we moved from the train to the car, I climbed in next to him, snuggled up close, rested my head on his shoulder and held onto him, with Flattered imploring me not to let him go. I had about three months left to finish out my nanny contract, live it up in NYC, and spend my time with Jack.

I didn't even want to think about how Mormonism would impact our relationship.

What I loved about him was that he showed me how to fully live in the present. We never discussed our past and we avoided discussing the future. As a result, surrendering to the moment gave me one of the happiest, most freeing times of my life. Every so often, when we were apart, I wrestled with the reality that Jack and Mormonism could not exist in the same space and would ultimately be forced to choose.

When thinking about Mormonism, I would tell myself that he was too young to settle down with. Even if he did come back to Mormonism, a kid his age could not possibly be ready for marriage.

It wasn't in my realm of possibility that if I was allowed to have sex without feeling shunned or disgraced, I could stay and explore our relationship without feeling pressure to get married. I carried the black and white worldview that this needed to lead to marriage or it was leading to nothing. There was no middle ground. I could not let go of the narrative that I needed to get married as soon as possible and start replenishing the world with Mormon babies.

Jack and I took advantage of spending as much time as possible together. Before summer officially started, he purchased a bullet bike, and he could not wait to take me on rides. I was very apprehensive, so in the beginning we began with slow rides around town. Eventually, they led to much faster rides on the highways.

One of our favorite places to ride was to a hidden duck pond near Franklin Lakes. The pond was nestled in a pine forest that shared its floor with some of New Jersey's most exotic tulip trees. Just to the side of the pond was a circular, flattened piece of ground that called to us, inviting us to take a rest. Our rest naturally led to passionate and heavy kissing.

Even with our clothing never coming off and our hands always away from each other's naughty bits, our longing for each other always remained robust. Adorned in his black leather jacket and a red bandana, I felt our level of

Levi-loving and canoodling was seriously badass and wild.

My dear rapist, as desirous as we were for each other, he never once crossed or questioned the boundaries that I had put into place. He never tried to touch my breasts, remove my top, unfasten my bra, unbutton my jeans, or put his hands down my pants. He never asked for sexual favors and he never begged for my virginity. He always, always let me take the lead and didn't once make me feel guilty or wrong for being a religious prude. He was a nineteen-year-old atheist who carried more respect in the dimple of a cheek than you did in a six-foot Olympic frame.

Never Yours,
Horny in Manhattan

***

My Dear Rapist,

My favorite memory with Jersey was the priceless gift he gave me about two weeks before I moved home. He was insistent that I keep my second to last Saturday free for him. He would not tell me what he had planned, all he would say is that I needed to be at his house by 6:00 in the morning and plan for a long day. I have always been good at being on time, even showing up early, and I did just that. He was still asleep when I arrived, so now it was my turn to surprise him. I slipped myself underneath his covers, wrapped my arms around him, and waited for him to awaken.

These moments I shared with him felt like pure heaven; I loved being in his Jersey arms. We had to force ourselves to climb out of the bed and take off for his mysteriously planned day.

From his home, the old white Bronco headed north and wove between towns I was not familiar with. After leaving New Jersey and crossing over to New York, I began to press Jack for information on where he was taking me. All he would do was shake his head, smile, and keep on driving. He was thoughtful enough to bring along snacks, some blankets, and some copies of the CDs that he had burned for me with his favorite songs.

It was pouring rain, and the more miles we drove, the more the rain came down. It was a good 150 miles before he finally released his secret into the air: he was taking me to Palmyra. Palmyra, freaking, New York. I was stunned—my atheist boyfriend was driving me to one of the most sacred places in Mormon history.

Palmyra is known to Mormons as the hometown of Joseph Smith, founder and prophet of the church.

According to church history, Joseph Smith's father and his brother Alvin purchased the one-hundred-acre farm located on Stafford Road around 1816. The land was covered in a forest of trees with nearly 110 trees per acre. It was estimated that the trees were anywhere between 200 and 300 years old, with many reaching as high as 125 feet and as wide as four to six feet at their base. Joseph's family cleared about sixty acres to develop their farm, as well as building a 1,000-square-foot log cabin. Roughly 1,500 maple trees had grown in the west grove, and it is believed that this is where Joseph Smith had his first vision in the spring of 1820, which would later become one of the church's most vital claims in the building of its foundation as the one true church.

It is taught that when Joseph Smith was fourteen-years old, he was confused by all of the different teachings of Christian religions. Joseph didn't know who or what to believe, and as a result he took the challenge from James in the Bible to ask God which church was teaching the truth. On a spring day, in 1820, Joseph wandered into the grove of trees, found a small area of cleared space, and knelt down and began a prayer.

According to Smith, God and Jesus appeared as two separate beings and told him that none of the churches were true, and that he should join none of them. This vision put Joseph Smith on a path to reestablish God's "one true church" on the earth.

Not far from the Sacred Grove is another historical site called the Hill Cumorah. This hill is where an angel told Joseph Smith he could find a set of golden plates. The golden plates were an ancient record of scripture, buried beneath the hill by an ancient prophet named Moroni. It is taught in the church that Joseph Smith translated the Golden Plates from reformed Egyptian into the English language. Once the translation was completed, Joseph Smith was commanded to return the plates to the Angel Moroni. Today, there is no evidence of the plate's existence other than the church's most prized book, The Book of Mormon.

Joseph Smith and his family were persecuted for sharing these things with the community and were eventually driven out. In 1830, a decade after Smith's first vision, the family moved away from the farm. Today, a forestry expert has identified that only six of the trees standing were alive in

1820. Of the 100 original acres that were forested, only 10 acres of forest still stands.

The farm went through several changes in ownership, as well as modifications in the way the land was utilized. The mainstream Mormon church purchased the land in 1907 and has made a commitment ever since to safeguard the forest and preserve it as sacred, hallowed ground. On April 6, 2000, the Palmyra New York Temple was dedicated. This date is significant for two reasons. April 6 is believed by Mormons to be the day that Christ was resurrected.

Also on April 6, 1830, the Mormon Church was formally organized. Constructed on an elevated ridge, the temple rests on the east end of the farm and was built in such a way so that those sitting in the waiting area could have a view of the consecrated farm, the Sacred Grove.

Jack sat in silence, giving me some time to process the word Palmyra. I had been telling him for months that if I could choose to do one thing before I left the East Coast, it would be to visit *Palmyra*. The fact that he had actually listened to me and took great care and effort to make it happen sent my brain into a frozen stupor.

In my twenty-four years, I had never had a single soul ever give me this kind of intimate, personal attention. This drive to Palmyra was not just a jaunt around the corner, it was a five-hour, 300-mile drive to a place that he did not even believe in. Nothing this kid ever did was for himself; it was always, always, for me.

Stunned and feeling breathless with the news, I sat in the passenger seat staring at him, not knowing how to communicate how much this surprise, and he, meant to me.

I am sure I showed some sort of excitement through my stupefied state of mind, but I was still trying to wrap my head around what he was gifting to me.

The remaining two-hour drive to Palmyra was chilly and cold. It poured rain the entire drive and the old Bronco's windows were difficult to keep defrosted due to the older engine. We held hands in silence and enjoyed the sound of the rain and the personalized list of songs quietly playing in the background. I kept a prayer in my heart, hoping to God that he would give us a break from the rain once we arrived at the historical site.

It was almost the end of August, so when we pulled up to the visitor's center, I took notice of the spiritualized, angelic trees. They were starting to show a shift in color, indicating that fall was in the air and about to knock on the forest door. The rain had changed to a small drizzle and the sun was trying to make an appearance, but the clouds were still too thick to let the light in. This didn't stop me from directly heading toward the grove of trees.

There were several geriatric missionaries at the log cabin, waiting to speak to us and educate us about Joseph Smith and his vision. I kindly smiled and informed them we were members of the church and asked if they would direct us to the entrance of the grove. Outwardly, I was patient with their directions, but inwardly I was ready to take off running before they finished. The minute they gave us the green light, I grabbed Jack by the hand and we took off for the woodlands.

I'm not sure why, but on this day, there was not a crowd of people rushing toward the special spot in the woods. We passed by a small group who were on their way out, but not a single person was following us in. The missionaries said there would be a bench in the forest, indicating the proposed site of where Jesus and God had appeared to Joseph Smith.

At this time in my life, I believed that the ground we were walking upon was as sacred as Gethsemane, or the garden tomb where Jesus was resurrected. Once we noticed the bench, I asked Jack if I could go ahead of him and have a little alone time. He was always great at respecting my wishes, so I was not surprised that he granted me this need. This was yet another indication, to me, that Jack wasn't a narcissistic asshole.

He could have easily been offended or gotten upset that I had asked for alone time, especially because he had put so much effort and money into surprising me by taking me to a place that he didn't even care about. The only reason he cared was because I cared.

Our intertwined fingers released their grip, and he slowed his feet while I continued toward the bench. I was roughly ten feet away when I put one knee to the sidewalk and unfastened my shoes. The boho tan wedge sandals had walked in too many worldly places, and the last thing I wanted to do was soil the forest floor with my unworthy Babylon slippers. I placed a sandal in each hand and reverently walked the remainder of the way in awe.

I had arrived. Time stood still. It wasn't out of fear, or anxiety. Like the creamy portion of an Oreo cookie, my body felt like it was smack dab in the middle of the parasympathetic and sympathetic nervous system. I didn't want to fight, I didn't want to run, I didn't want to rest, and I didn't want to digest. I just wanted to breathe in what I was seeing. Being perfectly in the middle felt like I was in heaven.

My heart and mind were busy trying to process a sight comparable to Bethlehem. Less than 200 years ago, Jesus had been here, God had been here, and now I was here. I was swimming in humility and gratitude with only the trees, the dirt, and questions.

Questions suddenly began filling my head, completely catching me off guard. I did not understand why I was second guessing Joseph Smith's claims. I had testified about this place a million times in Detroit, and God had answered me on my knees against my bunk bed in the Missionary Training Center.

My time in the Sacred Grove should have been instilling greater faith in me, not doubt. In Mormonism, there is one thing that goes hand in hand with doubt, and that is shame. Disgrace washed over me on the wooden bench, and instead of having my own Joseph Smith moment, I was waiting for God and Jesus to appear and strike me down for having such intrusive doubts.

Lost in questions, Jack appeared at my side and he tenderly took my hand. Like any good Mormon girl, I removed the doubts in my head and I placed them into the soles of my worldly sandals. I invited Jack to sit down next to me. Any sensual or provocative thoughts and feelings were pushed aside as I felt I had to share my testimony of Joseph Smith's First Vision with him.

For twenty minutes, I sat there and shared with him

the reasons why I believed it was all true and I spoke of my most cherished experience as a missionary, a story I rarely shared with anyone.

I was desperate for him to feel something here and ached for the Holy Ghost to touch him with his spirit. If there was any sort of happy memory or positive feeling that he'd had when he was a child in Mormonism, I yearned for it to appear now. He only sat there, taking in every word, never interrupting, never mocking, just listening. There was no fire from heaven, no beam of light, no appearance of Jesus, only my words and a hope that he would believe, because I believed.

During the expression of my testimony to him, the rain had completely stopped, the clouds had parted, and directly above us, the sun made its presence. It may not have been a stream of light, but the chances that the sun would make its appearance during the middle of my testimony seemed like a small sign to me. Jack may not have found significance in this, but it only added to my belief that God was paying attention.

We stood up and began our walk to exit the forest. After a few steps, I stopped and turned around. I asked him to come back with me and together we picked out roughly a dozen of the most beautiful, and largest maple leaves we could find. Some of the leaves were so massive, I thought they would be the perfect souvenir to take home. With the leaves in Jack's right hand, the sandals in my left hand, and our spare hands fused together, we began our walk out of the holiest place in Mormon America. I left my feet naked the entire walk out, refusing to ever put the boho sandals on again. They had touched down upon the very place in which God and Jesus had appeared to Joseph. Because of this, I now considered the sandals a purified enigma that I never wanted to tarnish again.

The moment we stepped through the trees, the sun decided to withdraw its presence, and like the closing act of a play, a curtain of clouds dropped to declare the ending of heaven's performance. We had just barely climbed into Jack's Bronco when the rain began to softly descend. It was evening as we pulled out onto the highway and headed home to New Jersey. The somber sky bade me to close my eyes and find some repose while I curled up inside a blanket and rested against the passenger side of the door.

My eyes had been closed for a microsecond when I started sensing the Bronco pulling off to the side of the road. I wondered if we were having car trouble, and I sat up to see what was going on. Jack angled the truck just right and pointed upward toward the sky. For no rhyme or reason, a firework show began to light up the horizon. I suppose since heaven didn't feel it appropriate to enthusiastically caress each other's lips in a grove of trees, heaven found it suitable to do so on some random highway in Palmyra. God himself seemed to have gifted us a personal, pyrotechnic sky while leaving his holy terrain.

The softly falling rain turned to a downpour, putting a halt to our incidental firework show and our celestial French kiss. As much as we loved it and did not want to stop, we had a four-hour drive home, putting our arrival time around midnight. It was an uneventful drive home, but with the lateness of the night, I decided to go ahead and sleep at his place. Ever the gentleman, he made his bed comfortable for me to sleep on, and he chose to sleep on the couch. I couldn't rest well knowing he was in the other room, so I invited him to just snuggle with me for the night. He joined me, and despite both our bodies being on fire for each other, like a good Mormon girl, I wouldn't let him touch me beyond wrapping his arms around me. And like a respectful atheist, he didn't even ask.

We awoke Sunday morning and I decided to skip church, since I was still on a high from the Sacred Grove visit and knew my time with Jack was limited. Instead, we went to a local diner for breakfast and I had the privilege of sitting there, admiring him drinking his black coffee while I basked in its yummy aroma. I was never tempted to actually drink it, but I would get a taste of it whenever I kissed his coffee-flavored lips.

After breakfast, we decided to go back to his place and spend some time taking care of the leaves we had picked out from the grove. He suggested I press them so I could preserve them. I had never done this before, so I let him take charge of educating me on the steps to do it correctly. I set up his ironing board and plugged in the iron. As he cut the wax paper and handed it to me, I started the pressing. He had spent a few minutes cutting up enough squares for the dozen or so leaves and after he finished, he came up behind to help.

I felt like Demi Moore sitting at her ceramic wheel in the movie Ghost, with Patrick Swayze's spirit capriciously making his appearance behind her.

Jack was now my Swayze. I could feel him behind me, but he was not touching me. He breathed quietly and slowly onto my neck, watching me iron the leaves from behind. Cautiously, as not to disturb the leaves, he slipped his arms underneath mine and held the iron with me. Back and forth, we gently glided the iron tenderly over the holy maple foliage.

If God was going to curse anyone in 2004 in New Jersey, I believed it was going to be me. I had no idea how it was possible for my body to feel spiritually and sexually on fire at the exact same moment in time. As we preserved the dozen or so of celestialized leaves, I not only felt the Holy Spirit, but I also felt a nice enormous boner, poking me in the back.

I immediately began cursing the stupid law of chastity in my head, desperate to believe that sex before marriage wasn't evil. It felt so unfair. I was twenty-four years old and yearned to feel all the feelings that were constantly swirling around me with Jack. I had never felt this much fire for a Mormon boy, for any boy. It felt so cruel that God would want me to deny myself of this, of being with someone like Jack, simply because he did not believe in a Mormon God!

I was being pulled in every direction, knowing what a good Mormon girl should do and wanting to do the complete opposite. My heart, my soul, my mind wanted to have him take me away from that damn ironing board and make love to me under the weeping willow tree that was five feet outside his door. I had been through the temple, I had served a mission, and caving to my sinful desire would mean excommunication from the church and even worse, offending God.

My dear rapist, Jack had never once pleaded to let him be my first sexual partner. The admiration he had for me, compared to what you had for me, is depressingly stark. He never hurt me—not with his words, not with his body, not with his breath. He was the one that treated me like a queen, not you. So like a good Mormon girl would do, I let that pretty little boner stay in his pants, and like the respectful man that he was, he did too. We did not do a damn thing other than kiss and Levi-love.

The day was coming to an end, and I needed to get back to my own place and get ready for my final week of work. I had sorting and packing to do, on top of wrapping up my time with my employers. I was dreading the idea of a life back in Utah, but I knew the chances of finding a worthy priesthood holder who could take me to the Temple were slim in New Jersey. As much as I loved Jack, he wasn't Mormon marriage material. He did not check off any of the three characteristics on my twelve-year-old list. I had no choice; I had to leave.

Jack asked if he could have the honor of driving me to the airport, and he arrived at my home early the next Saturday morning while I hugged my employers and the baby goodbye. We left early enough for him to take me to lunch, the both of us wanting to drag out our goodbye for as long as possible. It was only a forty-five-minute drive to the airport, so we spent a little extra time looking for a nice place to stop and eat.

We pulled into a dine-in sandwich shop near the airport, and he had me go ahead of him and grab us a table. The hostess walked me to a circular table with two chairs and handed me a menu. Jack seemed to be taking longer than expected, and after looking at the menu for a few moments, I looked up to see where he was. I didn't realize it, but he was already right next to me with his big, dimpled smile, and bright blue eyes. He was holding a large, wrapped package in his hands, giving me one final gift before I left him.

The wrapping did not hide the fact that whatever this was, it contained some sort of framed picture. Very tenderly, I removed the paper, not wanting to scratch or drop the massive square portrait in my lap. As I slowly stripped back the paper, I went through my head of all the possibilities of what he would choose to frame. Once the paper was completely off, I turned the frame over and took in a beautiful portrait of a large sunflower. Next to the sunflower was a poem, describing in poetic detail the essence of the flower and the quintessence of its meaning.

While I read the poem, he made sure to remind me that just as the sunflower pivots its face to follow the sun, something called heliotropism, that I too can follow my own internal circadian rhythm and grow when I follow the sun. As I sat there extracting my thoughts on the picture, the poem, his words, and how for the love of God I was going to get this gift on the plane, my feelings for him once again deepened.

Quietly, we climbed back into the Bronco and took off for the airport. I insisted that Jack just drop me off, but he was insistent to help me and be with me as much as time would allow. After offloading my luggage at the baggage drop-off, I had one carry on and my framed sunflower in my hands. At security, we embraced and did everything we could to not let go of each other.

God, I was a mess inside. My gut told me that I would never find this again, but my brain told me I would have to sacrifice this in order to find a worthy priesthood holder. In the grand scheme of things, Peter Priesthood was so much more important than an ex-Mormon atheist. Peter Priesthood could offer me eternity with God and Jesus, Ex-Mormon Atheist could promise me only outer darkness with coffee drinkers, gays, and lesbians.

Begrudgingly, and with one final salacious kiss goodbye, our lips parted and I began my stroll toward the ticket agent. I did not want him to see the tears forming in my eyes, and the further I walked down the terminal, the more they started to flow, giving me reason not to turn around and wave goodbye.

As I boarded the plane and got comfortable in my seat, I opened my phone. There was a two-word text message from Jack: "Don't go." Other passengers were still boarding the plane, so I decided to quickly call him.

"Don't go," he said, this time in his adorable Jersey voice. "I'm still inside the airport, just in case you change your mind and decide to get off the plane."

My dear rapist, it would have been so easy to stand up, grab my things, and run down the aisle of the plane toward the exit and toward him. I was fighting the pull to just give in and figure out how to start a new life on the East Coast with Jack.

He must have read my mind, because after a few moments of silence he interrupted my thoughts. "We will figure it out. Don't live a life of regrets, go where the sun is pulling you, Ginger!"

Damnit, he knew where it was pulling me. He knew it was pulling me to him, but deep down, I knew that if I got off that plane and followed my heart, we would end up having wild sex, I'd get knocked up, get excommunicated from the church, possibly even disowned from my parents, and then I'd forever be marked with a scarlet letter.

So I stayed on the plane. I kept my ass in the seat, told him I just couldn't do it, and that I needed to move back to Utah and start the next chapter of my life. I told him we could definitely stay in touch, but I also knew as much as I loved him, an atheist boy and a Mormon girl could not happily coexist. We were like oil and water. He was the oil: non-electrically charged because, well, atheists are dead inside.

I, with my self-righteous attitude, could be none other than the water, positively charged because I had God in my life. It was his fault that we couldn't be together. If he would only convert from oil to water, we could work, but he wouldn't—which left me once again an old maid at the ripe age of twenty-five.

My dear rapist, what Jack gave me, that Max took away, was trust. I had trust again that there were men in the world with good intentions, men who were capable of seeing women as more than a mere object, and men who knew how to be gentlemen. Jack also gave me hope and confidence, but above all, he brought back my spark.

In the end, I broke his heart. I chose religion over him. I chose my parents, my temple covenants, my holy underwear, my community, my friends, my church, my worldview, everything. I spent the next five hours on my flight to Utah persuading myself that I had made the right decision, that God was proud of me.

I gave up Jack for him. I coaxed my spiritual ego into believing that somewhere in Utah, I would meet a man just as amazing as Jack, if not better. It would be better because *he* would have the priesthood and *he* could take me to the Temple.

Never Yours,
An Optimistic Sunflower

CHAPTER 12

ZION'S HEARTBEAT

"Israel, Israel, God is calling, Calling thee from lands of woe. Babylon the great is falling; God shall all her tow'rs o'erthrow. Come to Zion, come to Zion Ere his floods of anger flow. Come to Zion, come to Zion Ere his floods of anger flow."

(Church of Jesus Christ of Latter Day Saints Hymn: Israel, Israel God is Calling, pg 7)

My Dear Rapist,

I left Babylon and trekked back to Zion—Salt Lake City, Utah, the heartbeat of Mormonism. Three of my girlfriends and I found an apartment together off State Street and 3900 South in Murray. (There was no way in hell I was moving to Provo and subjecting myself to another BYU Boy experience.) I wanted to try out medical assisting again, so I started applying to advertisements for receptionist and medical assisting positions.

One of the first interviews I had was for a private practice in the southern end of Salt Lake City. It was a beautiful, sunny day, and I walked into the surgeon's office dressed in pink slacks and a sheer white blouse, highlighting my Mormon underwear. Since I was back in Zion, I had every intention to wear my garments like a badge of honor.

The office was very clean and fancy, and the surgeon, along with his office manager, were there to greet me. It was a very pleasant, easygoing interview with a lot of personal and professional questions. I was quick to tout my service as a full-time missionary for the church, as well my many volunteer experiences in and out of the church. In Utah, the status of returned missionary carried a lot of weight.

The surgeon was pleased to hear this, as he was currently serving as a counselor in a bishopric. The office manager seemed indifferent to my bragging rights and appeared more concerned with my professional experience. If hired, I would not only be the main receptionist, but I would also assist with the billing and marketing. One day a week, I would drive to roughly twenty different physician offices in the greater Salt Lake and Provo area and kiss ass in the hopes they would send referrals to the surgeon I would be working for. New Jersey had given me quite a gregarious social personality, and I loved the idea of getting out of the office to meet new people. Two days later, I was offered the position.

My first day of work arrived, and prior to being trained on my office duties, I was taken on a tour of the office and introduced to two of the other assistants. The confidence I originally had slightly diminished when I walked into the break room to greet my new coworkers. They were two of the most beautiful blondes I had ever laid eyes on. With plump breasts, perfect symmetrical facial features, full lips, and fit figures, I felt I was greeting a couple of Barbie dolls.

These two young women were the complete opposite of me, as I never fit the Barbie doll mold and knew I never would. My confidence not only waned from taking in their flawless appearances, but it also diminished due to the instant smirk that appeared upon both their faces. Either they were laughing at me because I was flawed in every way, or they knew something that I did not.

I sensed they didn't like me from the start, which quickly caused me to withdraw and begin the wilting process. I had bloomed in New Jersey not only because of Jack, but because the cookie-cutter Barbie doll Mormon genre did not exist on the East Coast. I was very disappointed in myself. I had hoped that all the confidence I had gained in Jersey would last longer upon my return to Utah, but within two weeks of being back, it was quickly disappearing.

Despite this initial setback, I started losing myself into my new job during the day and began hunting for a husband on the evenings and weekends. I was developing friendships at the young single adults Millcreek Ward and soaking up the good-looking priesthood holders who I laid eyes on each Sunday. It was refreshing to sit among a school of Mormon men, swimming in the congregation with their sharp haircuts, white shirts, ties, and a hint of the holy garment.

I began to date, not much, but finding hope that maybe my lifelong partner was sitting in the church pews with me. Things were going very well in both my work life and my private life.

Jack and I were still talking, but my feelings for him were starting to change. I still adored him and was fond of our memories together, but my search for a Mormon man was beginning to overshadow all of the feelings I once had for him. I believe he may have sensed this, because a week before Thanksgiving, he surprised me with a ticket to Utah so he could spend the holiday with me.

My feelings were mixed on the news. I wanted to be excited, but the fact he was atheist and had turned away from Mormonism was still a reality I could not ignore. I knew there could only be two outcomes to his visit—either all of the feelings I'd had when we said goodbye would come flooding back or his visit would confirm we had no future together.

When I informed my parents that my quasi-boyfriend would be spending Thanksgiving with the family, they were not excited. The idea of their twenty-six-year-old daughter settling for a twenty-year-old ex-Mormon did not sit well. Of course, they had no desire to be rude and say he could not come. Instead, they told me he would not be allowed to bring coffee into their home and were adamant that I let him know of their strict rule. I relayed the information to Jack and, as always, he was true to form and expressed respect and understanding of their Mormon values.

Jack's flight touched down at Salt Lake International Airport early on Thanksgiving morning. The reunion inside the airport was a disappointment to both of us. He didn't have the clean cut, priesthood glow about him, and I didn't run into his arms all hot and bothered, ready to knock him over and slip him the tongue. This was Salt Lake City, where 90 percent of the population were most likely members of the church.

Showing public displays of affection within the epicenter of Mormonism would have brought on too many judgmental stares, finger pointing, and hushed voices of gossip. I especially did not want to risk seeing a Prophet or Apostle catching a flight or have my pornographic kiss turn on some young Mormon missionary returning home from serving the Lord. So, rather than giving him the welcome he rightly deserved, I kept the Holy Ghost between us, gave him an awkward hug and a pathetic, innocent peck on the cheek. Looking back, I feel so much sorrow for the way I treated him. He didn't deserve my embarrassment and internal scorn over the difference in our belief systems.

After a two-hour drive north, we arrived at my parents' home. This particular year, Thanksgiving dinner was a small gathering, including my parents, my Grandma Ella, my little brother, Jack, and me. It was painfully awkward, and I could not wait to get out of there and return to my apartment in Salt Lake City. Thankfully, we had zero plans of staying overnight with my parents, so we returned to my place to finish out our long weekend together. As much as I valued and appreciated his attempt to come and see me, I knew in the end that I was going to have to break his heart again. My devotion to the church and its ideals were just too strong, and as a result, my libido for him was not present.

The time finally arrived for him to go home, and after an unremarkable few days hanging out at my apartment, we collected his single bag and headed back toward the airport. I know he sensed that something was off with me, but I do not believe he was prepared for what I was about to tell him. I wanted to completely end things, including communication. I needed to stay focused on dating Mormon men.

He was hurt and I knew it. In fact, he was angry. Though I had always been upfront with him and told him I needed someone who could give me the Mormon life, I think he may have had an underlying hope I would have found a way to choose both him and Mormonism. He had every right to be angry—he had put his whole heart and soul into making me happy, and in the end, I squashed it. I stomped on his heart as if someone lit a brown paper bag full of shit on fire and put it on my doorstep.

I stomped, and I stomped, and I stomped, all for God, all for Jesus, and all for Mormonism.

Thanksgiving turned to Christmas, Christmas turned to Valentine's Day, and Valentine's Day turned into summer. Eight months had gone by and I was not any closer to getting a ring on my finger. I continued going on random dates, but I swear to God I had some invisible sign on my forehead that said "tell me about your porn or sex addiction." One particular guy I went on a first and only date with was the Elders Quorum president in my singles ward. We went out to dinner, and then he asked if we could go back to my place and watch a movie. My roommates were all gone, so it was an easy request to fulfill. I thought he was semi-attractive, but certainly not enough to get my sex drive working.

We were about twenty minutes into the movie, and out of the blue, he asked me if I had a flashlight. Curious, I inquired why. Without any hesitation he said, "I'd like to shine it down your pants and see if you shave your pussy." I was horrified, but shrugged it off and acted like it was no big deal. I had never been alone with the guy before, let alone had much conversation with him, so I was not sure if he would be easy to anger if I pissed him off.

I came up with some excuse as to why I wasn't going to unzip my pants for him, and as soon as the movie ended, I kicked him out and told him I had a headache. Later on, he would brag to me about his porn addiction and laugh, explaining how common, cool, and natural it was for men to jack off to porn.

This seemed to be the theme of my dating career within the church. None of these men wanted to catch fireflies in mason jars, take me for rides on their motorcycles, or express dreams of me playing the piano for them underneath a weeping willow tree. None of these men were New Jersey Jack, yet all of them wore holy underwear, were returned missionaries, and testified about the truth of the church and getting married in the Temple. I tried meeting men on LDSPlanet, a dating website specifically for Mormons, and that was a whole other level of shock. I began writing to one man in Florida who told me that he was looking for his "virgin by day and slutty sexpot by night, Mormon wife." He informed me that he "loved to beat his meat to my profile picture."

My roommates were on the same website, receiving dick pics from Mormon men, as well as pics of them ejaculating onto their own stomachs. What was ironic was that you could see the lining of their garments just underneath their open zipper, screaming they were temple-going men, but also capable of fulfilling every Mormon woman's fantasy.

One man I dated for several months, and whom I talked about possible marriage with, was a returned missionary going through a divorce. I was hesitant to date him until I knew his divorce was final, but he and the bishop assured me that as long as we didn't have sex, we would be okay. He tried doing other things, always ready to slip his hand down my shirt, or grab me between the legs, but he assured me that he was worthy to go to the temple.

I came to find out that he had been married less than a year when he got home from school one day to find his wife and her belongings gone. Left on the fridge was a small note simply stating, "I am done, please do not come looking for me." He had no idea where and why she left and sadly, I was the rebound. At this point, he seemed slightly disrespectful, but nothing compared to the other men I was dating.

It was General Conference weekend, and he had

invited me to make him breakfast before the Sunday morning session on TV. When I entered his apartment, he was sitting on the couch studying his scriptures. In a kind patriarchal tone, he requested I make breakfast and not disturb his reading before the prophet and Apostles made their televised appearance. Wanting to prove I could be a dutiful, obedient woman, I went to work in his kitchen. Grandma Ella had always made eggs with a dash of milk, and I felt inspired to prepare them as she had.

Not wanting to interrupt his quiet time, I tip-toed toward him and handed him his plate of hot food. I walked back toward the kitchen to clean up the mess, and just as I got to the sink, the plate of food came flying toward my head. He was livid. Apparently, they were the worst eggs he had ever tasted, and he demanded to know what I had done to screw them up.

Timidly, I told him that I had made them the way my grandmother had taught me, with a little bit of milk. He became completely repulsed and could not fathom why anyone would ever add milk to eggs. He demanded that I never prepare eggs like that for him again. Instead of standing up for myself, I cleaned up his kitchen in tears, while the Mormon Tabernacle Choir played softly in the background and he waited for the mouthpiece of the Lord to start speaking.

My dear rapist, for reasons I will never understand, I became a magnet for narcissistic, porn-addicted men. Most of my first dates never went past a first date. To no avail, every man would inquire why I was twenty-six and still single. No longer having a care in the world if I offended these men, I would tell them it was because I could not find a man that was not jonesing for porn. Most men would laugh and then proceed to tell me about their own sexual fetishes. It was like my dating life was a broken record: get asked out, go on first date, get asked why I was single, mention the word porn, hear the man's life story of why he looked at porn, then listen to a regurgitated testimony of Mormonism and his current calling at church.

I was becoming more and more confused about what it meant to flourish and live in Zion. Zion seemed to be nothing but a patriarchal society filled with porn-addicted, abusive, controlling men who liked to throw scrambled eggs and shine flashlights down girls' pants. My father had never treated my mother this way when we were around, yet the behavior of so many Mormon men made me start questioning again how he treated her behind closed doors.

These experiences were not just affecting me on a personal level, but they began spilling over into my job. Toward the end of the summer, I had started hearing firsthand stories about the sexual escapades of the surgeon I was working for. Remember, he was serving in the bishopric of his family ward. Specifically, he was a counselor, someone who helps the bishop preside over the ward with a responsibility to receive revelation for members and act in Jesus' name.

Part of being a counselor is also to be a role model to the young men and young women. This involves conducting worthiness interviews, alone and behind closed doors, with the youth and inquiring of them about their sexual purity.

I found out Mr. Surgeon was not only addicted to

porn, but he was having affairs with two of his assistants. One was a stripper on the evenings and weekends, and he would often go to the strip club where she worked. He would also stay late at work, sit in the patient recovery chairs, and masturbate while the assistants cleaned the instruments and talked dirty to him.

Things got so bad with Mr. Surgeon that he started shooting up his own medication while on the job. Upon learning all of this straight from the assistant's mouth, I was going through patient accounts and working on updating the billing. After a few weeks of investigation, I had personally discovered information that he owed patients and insurance companies well over $100,000. When I confronted the office manager about it, she blamed it on the surgeon. When I confronted the surgeon about it, he blamed it on the office manager.

My dear rapist, my head began spinning in circles. This was Zion. What in the actual hell was going on in the land of God's most righteous people? The common justification among the members was that the church is perfect but the people are not. This excuse for poor choices was not working for me. If anything, I wanted to run from Zion and spin my way back to Babylon. Instead of running to New Jersey, though, I chose to give Utah some more time and I looked for another place of employment.

Never Yours,
Aching for Babylon

✳✳✳

My Dear Rapist,

As it happened, the surgeon had an upcoming medical conference in Arizona and had paid for the entire office staff to join him. Out of the four of us employees that traveled with him, I was the only one that was single and active in the church. Most of our time was spent shopping during the day while he played golf. Very little time was actually spent at the medical conference. At night, we would all go to dinner together, but then he would go back to his hotel with his wife and we would go to bars or dance clubs.

Out at a dance club on our last night there, and in pure, religious, prude mode, I was appalled by my coworkers' abilities to attract and beguile a number of men on the dance floor. It was repulsive to my self-righteous Mormon spirit, and I moved myself to a corner and sulked, anxious to get back to the hotel and the safety of my bed.

While I watched them lure and seduce the drunken chaps, my repugnance, in all honesty, turned to resentment. They were the beautiful Utah Barbie dolls who had just removed their wedding rings before entering the club. I was the single Molly Mormon who couldn't get a single douche bag to look my way.

Without an ounce of alcohol in me, I hung my head in defeat as we made our way back to the hotel. My coworkers were happy and fulfilled by the men and booze from the night. I was the opposite, depressed and unfulfilled. I did not know how to have fun or attract normal men within the world of my religion. I yearned for what those three women had. They had sex appeal, they had freedom, they had beauty, they had husbands, and I? I had none of it.

They continued into the night with their drunken escapades, and I went straight to bed. I was desperate to get away from their worldly and adulterous behavior. If it had not been for the alcohol, I would have never found out why the surgeon hired me. Before I fell asleep, their loose, alcoholic tongues made it known I was hired mainly due to my returned missionary status. Mr. Surgeon wanted the Spirit in his office and had hoped that my righteousness would have a positive and lasting effect on his practice.

Humiliated and feeling like I had been the object of ridicule all year, I gave my notice to the office manager on the return flight home. I had felt so ethically and professionally degraded that I didn't even give a two-week notice. I was done, and the flight was feeling eerily similar to my flight home from Europe. After I quit, I heard that things began to unravel even more at the office. The surgeon's wife eventually found out about the affairs, something that she had been dealing with since his pre-med days at BYU, but oddly, she gave the two assistants an entire year to find new jobs.

Over time, I had actually become friends with the female stripper, and I was pleasantly surprised that she still had a desire to remain friends with me. She was not Mormon, but she did return to her own nondenominational church after leaving the surgeon's practice. Her pastor had encouraged her to go through a repentance process, and in so doing, was told she should inform the surgeon's church leaders of his behavior. She followed the pastor's suggestion and wrote a letter describing her actions with the surgeon while she was under his employment. When the surgeon was confronted by his church leaders about his behavior, he chalked it up to her being a bitter former employee who was only trying to ruin his reputation for getting fired. As usual, they believed him over her, and he continued in his service as a counselor in the bishopric for several more years to come.

This friend and I stayed in touch for many, many years and have nothing but good feelings toward one another. She is the one who connected me to my new place of employment, the job where I would ultimately end up meeting you.

It was October 2005, and having nothing put pure disgust for men in positions of authority, I wanted out of the medical world. After this experience with the surgeon, my experience with Max and his brothers, and the plethora of other men with porn addictions, my disdain and distrust of Mormon men was rapidly growing. My girlfriend told me about an available position at a troubled youth center, working in their travel department. This was a lockdown facility, a last resort before unruly and aggressive teenagers found themselves in prison.

Many of the kids were from out of state, some as far away as Alaska. Working in this department, I would have the opportunity to take the kids to doctor appointments, dentist appointments, and court hearings. At times, I would even get to chaperone the kids back to their home states if they did well enough to earn a visit home. Travel included day trips within the state as well as nearby states like Wyoming, Idaho, Arizona, and New Mexico. My boss would be a woman and I would have two male coworkers, totaling four of us in the travel department.

Before my first official day working in the travel department, I was required to go through an intensive two-week training, which was hard, and at times I had wondered if I was really mentally and physically strong enough to handle the responsibilities. In truth, after learning about some of the reasons why the kids ended up there, I was scared. Most of the kids had endured some level of sexual or physical abuse, and their acting out involved the use of weapons and harm, both to others and to themselves. I told myself that if I could survive Detroit, I could survive anything.

I was intimidated by the two males I worked with. Both were handsome, one was tall and built like a football player, the other was a bit shorter but clean-cut like a returned missionary. All three coworkers were married, everyone but me. Once again, here I was, the returned missionary, and the only one in the group that was not married.

Over time, the only real discussions to be had with my male coworkers were either about Sean Hannity's views on America or the size of a woman's tits. Again, I became painfully aware of how little my breasts were. If my self-esteem wasn't already low enough by living in the land of Mormon Mattel, waking up to the realization I had concaved knockers pushed my confidence further into the ground.

Everywhere I turned in this religious state, all I ever heard about was boobs, sex, and porn. I felt like I was standing in a snow globe, looking around for someone to start a life with and yet, the only thing happening was that I was being shaken. The snowflakes falling around me were nothing but sexualized words, demanding that I wake up and accept the fact that all I was meant for was to be a celestial porn star.

Cooking, cleaning, being a mom, being a wife, none of this really mattered. My eternal fate was figuring out how to be the virgin by day and the slutty sexpot by night. It no longer felt like love was the driving force in the temple marriage ceremony. From my experience, I was beginning to believe that the sealing factor was defined by how eternally sexually appealing I could be.

My dear rapist, I had been back in Zion for a year, and I had slipped further and further away from any Peter Priesthood putting a ring on my finger. I had noticed you in passing about one month into my new job at the youth center. Walking down the hallway, we caught each other's eyes. I was too shy to say anything, and all you ever offered was a simple hello.

Though I was timid, I recall always smiling first. You appeared to prefer to watch me cautiously rather than actually take time to talk to me. I found you very attractive, but also very mysterious. You were a striking man of color, with a very fit, athletic body. Because of how quiet you were, I could not tell if you were American or if you were from another country, and I wondered if you even spoke English.

Right around the time I started noticing you, I decided to try and give online dating another chance. I rejoined LDSPlanet and told myself I'd give it two weeks. In the two-week time frame, I began speaking with two men, exchanged numbers, and then closed the account. The first man was a BYU rugby player from Fiji, and we connected over Alaskan salmon. He was a huge flirt and I could see something serious with him, but the feelings were not mutual. He only seemed to care for my salmon dinners and our makeout sessions.

Levi-loving didn't happen with him, because he liked to wear khaki pants and athletic wear, material that was too thin for my liking. Yes, it is an odd justification, but Levi-loving felt less sinful due to the thickness of the jeans. In my uneducated mind, jeans were a much bigger barrier for a priesthood holder's seed to penetrate through. I did not want to get pregnant or get an STD from a little bit of khaki-loving.

The second man was Mr. Bill. Mr. Bill was very handsome and seemed, for the most part, respectful. He actually reached out to me first on the dating website. I recognized his last name, but was not sure if he was the person I was thinking of. The profile picture I had used was of me and a cute friend of mine with Down syndrome. Bill mentioned the boy in the picture and informed me that he had a brother with disabilities; this began our initial conversation with each other.

I had asked him what his brother's name was, and in a matter of seconds, I knew my hunches were right. I had worked with his brother during and after high school, and I knew his mother as well. The discovery of this connection was encouraging, and we continued to talk to each other for the next several weeks.

By the end of January 2006, I was feeling a little bit

better about myself. I had Mr. Fiji coming over in khakis to eat his fish, I had Mr. Bill texting me and showing interest, and I had you, the quiet African American man periodically checking me out at work. Then Mr. Bill invited me to join him for an in-person lunch. Due to the connection I had to his mother and disabled brother, I was pretty certain he was not a serial killer. For this reason, I agreed to a lunch date.

Two days before I was to meet him, I received a surprising phone call. You, the mysterious man from work, were driving home from Vegas with some friends and wanted to talk to me. I could hear loud music and laughter in the background as we talked, so I silently questioned your motives in calling me, certain you knew I was not like the Vegas girls you were leaving behind.

In a state with very few good-looking Black men, I was positive you were the type of man that could get any girl you wanted. After hanging up, though, I felt giddy that you were starting to show more interest in me and I went to bed excited, knowing that I would get to see you the next day.

Sometime during the night, while in a deep sleep, I suddenly awoke to an intense feeling of fear. I knew I had been dreaming but could not recall the specifics of the dream. A heightened feeling of fright washed over me, telling me that I should do everything I could to abscond from spending time with you. The formidable notion that I needed to avoid you at all costs kept me awake the remainder of the night.

I lay there in bed, tangled in disorderly thoughts and questions. You seemed so nice; I could not understand what could be so wrong with you. You had been required to pass a background check at the youth center, so surely if you were a rapist or serial killer, you would not have passed the screening. You seemed to be well-liked and respected by the other staff members, so of course you had to be normal.

I tossed and turned, annoyed that the unnerving feeling wouldn't disperse. I wanted it gone—I wanted to have a chance to get to know you, this enigmatic man I found so intriguing and who was clearly out of my league. Morning arrived, my alarm clock buzzed, and listlessly I climbed out of bed to get ready for work. While the small hand of the clock ticked by, the daunting feeling I had awoken to was starting to fade. By the time I had arrived at work, the fear had altogether disappeared, leaving my nervous system in a restful state.

For the first half of the day, work was like every other day, fairly normal and uneventful. Sometime after lunch, we crossed paths, and in doing so, you asked if I'd like to go on a date with you. For a brief moment, I reflected on my interrupted sleep and the warning that came with it. In the exact same space that my brain was telling me to run, my lips parted and said yes. I now had two dates back-to-back, one with you that evening, and a lunch date with Mr. Bill the next day.

I was at a crossroads. I have reflected many times over the years on my decision to ignore my internal voice that intentionally showed up with her warning. For many years, I believed I had outright ignored God and his concerted effort at keeping me safe from you. Other times, I have wondered if the warning came from a future version of myself, traveling back in time to remind me of the importance of listening to and following my inner voice. My brain knew something was off and I ignored it. The fearful feeling did not make any sense and, unfortunately, your charm was much more enticing than God's spirit or my internal voice. After all, I had been wrong before and was bamboozled by Max, the surgeon, and the egg thrower, so why pay attention to it now?

We both finished our day at work and had agreed to meet up at the movie theater near my place on State Street and 3300 South. I was still reeling with the notion that someone like you found someone like me attractive enough to pay attention too. I walked into the theater and there you stood—a charismatic, athletic god waiting in line to get our tickets. I had no idea that by meeting you on this night and ignoring the obvious omen to run, I would be making the most serious mistake of my life.

My dear rapist, you were the last thing I expected to discover in Zion. You were far from the husband check-off list I created in my youth. However, by the time I met you, I no longer knew how to define what a good and honorable priesthood holder truly meant. I had certainly reached old maid status in Mormonism, and being with you felt much better than being alone.

I was tired of my dating experiences and I had come to accept the fact that I was not marriage material among my own kind. Perhaps you would be another Jersey Atheist who would want me to play the piano under a weeping willow tree, or even more so, one who wouldn't give a damn about my inability to be a celestial porn star.

Hope had led me to Zion, and Zion had led me to

desperation. I thought I had nothing to lose by taking a chance on you, but I was wrong. I was absolutely fucking wrong.

Never Yours,
Desperate in Zion

CHAPTER 13

YOU

"Yea, and he leadeth them by the neck with a flaxen cord, until he bindeth them with his strong cords forever."

(Book of Mormon, 2 Nephi 26:22)

My Dear Rapist,

We ended up getting tickets for the movie *Annapolis*, starring actors James Franco and Tyrese Gibson. You portrayed yourself to be timid and slightly unsure of yourself. I found you incredibly attractive, and also kind and attentive. Your demeanor gave no indication that I should be running from you. In fact, your etiquette had the opposite effect on me. Your quiet, easygoing nature left me engrossed by your handsome, tight ass sitting next to me in the theater. The draw to figure you out was enough that I was willing to come up with an excuse to cancel my lunch date with Mr. Bill the next day. All I would need from you was an indication that this first date would turn into a second.

You were so damn mellow for the majority of the night that I didn't know quite what to think. It wasn't a behavior that left me insecure, but it was a type of presence that left me guessing. It was as if you were simply trying to watch me, read me, and study me. Though you had my brain flipping hypotheticals for two-hours straight, I never once felt a creep vibe.

The movie came to an end and we sat there in awkward silence as the credits rolled. Before we stood up to leave, you finally did it—you asked me if we could hang out again. There it was, the little morsel of a dog bone I needed to let Mr. Bill know that I wouldn't make it to our lunch date.

We parted ways after the movie, you in your sporty gray Audi and I in my ugly turquoise Chevy Cavalier. I went to bed that night feeling completely antithetical from the night before. I was elated, hopeful, and utterly captivated by your striking, baronial build. Right before I laid my head on the pillow, I sent Mr. Bill a message and informed him I would not make it to our lunch date the next day. And with that, my communication with Mr. Bill ceased.

Coincidently, you and I started crossing each other's paths more and more at work. Whether that was intentional on your part, I am not sure. For me, it was. I wanted to see you as often as I could. Your attitude at work upon seeing me was always calm and collected. You quietly watched me and often seemed to know the perfect timing in requesting we meet up after work.

Looking back, I can say that my behavior partially reflected yours. I figured it was none of my coworkers' business to know we were spending time together, so I also remained composed when I saw you. As unruffled as I tried to be, I had hoped you would catch me checking you out so that you would know I was still very interested.

In the beginning, we began meeting up either at my place or yours several times throughout the week. We started fairly slow, neither of us ready to give up our weekends for one another. I was still seeing the BYU rugby player, and I had a difficult time giving up our salmon dinners and a dessert filled with kissing.

I really liked the guy, but he never wanted a serious relationship with me. For a while, I alternated between seeing him and seeing you. It would take about a month or so for you and me to finally begin seeing each other on the weekends. Once we were spending four to five days together a week, I finally decided to let Fiji know that I could no longer see him.

February, March, and April were good months,

as I really didn't see any red flags. From time to time, you exhibited signs of depression and appeared a little despondent, but nothing was too alarming or frightening. Our time together was always behind closed doors, and if we did get something to eat, it was always from a fast food drive-through.

In the beginning it didn't bother me, but over time, I would wonder why you never cared to take me into public. I remember once wanting to go country dancing at the Westerner, the bar and dance hall not too far from your apartment. You had zero interest in going with me and told me I could go by myself. I took you up on that suggestion, got dressed, and started to head out the door.

You didn't like that I was going and leaving you home, so you put on some clothes and decided to join me. You actually appeared to be having fun, despite the fact you were constantly looking around as if you were embarrassed by me and did not want to be seen.

With all the time we spent together, I do not recall having deep conversations with you. The only discussions surrounding me related to Mormonism. The only discussions around you were your days competing in the Olympics and your time as an actor in Hollywood.

Your reputation was important to you, and you seemed to thrive on the connections you made within the acting community and with other athletes around the world. I continued to wonder why the hell you would want to spend time with someone like me; I knew I was nothing like the other women you had dated.

On occasion, you mentioned that you felt safe with

me and could trust me. Yet, the more time we spent together, the less I felt safe with you. By the end of March, you were beginning to express more suicidal thoughts and a desire to have sex. You hated the fact I was Mormon, and you wanted so badly to be my first. I was adamant I would never have sex before marriage, and like the other non-Mormons I had dated, I was not willing to throw away a temple marriage for anyone. I was not even willing to do it for an Olympic athlete-turned-actor.

After weeks of expressing suicidal tendencies, and my unwillingness to have sex with you, you started suggesting that we run away to Vegas and elope. You wanted me to give up Mormonism and walk away from everything and everyone I ever knew for you. You promised me a life full of adventure as we traveled the world together and I supported you in your Olympic career.

I cannot lie, the idea of moving to Hollywood with you and exploring the world together was very enticing. Getting back into the acting world was a goal of yours, and you would rattle off all the famous people you had connections to, hoping this would persuade me to pack my bags and start a new life with you in Los Angeles.

I should have picked up on the crimson-colored flags once your thoughts of suicide intertwined with your pleadings for sex. You would often remind me that your sex appeal was so strong, even men wanted to climb into bed with you. The bragging rights you carried regarding your ability to get any woman to take her panties off in your presence, yet your inability to get me to remove mine, drove you insane. In a passive-aggressive way, you gave me a new name. It wasn't a holy or revered name like the one I had received in the Mormon temple. You gave me the degrading new epithet of "SAV," which stood for "Stingy-Ass Vagina."

I do not recall having the big talk with you, indicating that we wouldn't date other people. However, due to your continual expressions of wanting me to give up my Mormon life and elope to Vegas with you, in my naïve mind, I had begun to believe we were a couple.

You started to present a narrative that we had some sort of tragic love story, going as far as comparing us to Romeo and Juliet. Due to my unwillingness to have sex and elope, as well as having Mormonism's hold over me, you began suggesting we should kill ourselves because we could not be together. At first, it seemed like a light-hearted tease, but the ongoing suggestions of killing me and then killing yourself stopped feeling like a joke, and I no longer found humor in your unconventional articulations of love.

Your infatuation with my sexual innocence seemed to become a focal point for you, and you loved to find alternative ways to sexually shock me. While hanging out at your place, at times you would walk out to greet me completely naked, just to astonish me and make me feel uneasy with seeing your penis bolstered straight into the air.

Prior to you, outside of assisting those in the special needs community with their toileting needs, I had never seen a penis, not even in a magazine. I had never beheld Alaska cowboy's, Max's, or Jack's schlong because, like a third grader, I believed it was wrong. Allowing you to see my privates or me taking a peek to admire your privates went against what it meant to be a good Mormon girl.

My dear rapist, I won't lie and say I didn't have sexual attraction to you. I found you irresistible. You loved to flaunt that Olympic body of yours, and I was almost twenty-eight years old. It was difficult not to take an extra second to look at what you were flinging around before I turned my head away in self-reproach. I had years of repressed sexual tension built up. My body was created to have sex, to find pleasure, and I was always so good at quelling my thirst to nothing but jean-on-jean action.

My garments, and you, were there to remind me of the importance of not caving and giving in to your seductive existence. However, you were always using reverse psychology on me. I wasn't stupid. In one breath you would beg me to allow you to free me from my virgin status, and in another breath, you were quick to remind me of my goal to save myself for my wedding night.

During the times you hurt me and began to chip away at my dignity, I still had sexual and emotional attraction to you. I explicitly remember the first time your attempt at displaying shock value went too far. I was in your tiny living room watching television while you were in the kitchen cleaning up.

I was on the far left end of the couch, waiting for you to be finished when, without any warning, you walked up behind me and smacked me in the face with your hardened dick. You didn't even give me time to respond before you walked away naked, smirking, and mumbling, "You stupid naïve Mormon girl."

Sitting there stunned, I sadly realized that this was my first experience getting up close and personal with a boyfriend's penis. This was the first time I felt the flesh of a penis not just anywhere on my body but stricken harshly across my face. I had waited twenty-seven long years, even passed up on deep intimacy with Jack, with the hopes that my first flesh-on-flesh experience would be magical.

It was far from wondrous; it was abusive and painful. You laughed at this like you were sitting in the audience of a comedy club and I, I kept my ass planted on your couch. All prior thoughts and experiences of dating Mormon men came flooding back and I concluded, yet again, all I was good for was for a man to express his sexual needs.

With you, it wasn't just mere words, it was action. You got a thrill by hitting me with your manhood. Whether you were a religious Utah man or an Olympic athlete and actor in Hollywood, it didn't matter. It was very clear to me that I was meant for sex and nothing more.

Never Yours,
A Stupid Naive Mormon Girl

***

My Dear Rapist,

After feeling the sharp sting of your phallus on my face, things really began to change. Your strange behavior became emboldened and more unorthodox, and at times inhumane. One particular memory, frozen in place, was a time we were joking around about something silly in my bedroom. Out of nowhere, you pushed me to the floor, pressed your left hand onto my forehead so I couldn't move, and with the rest of your body, you laid on top of me and held me down. You took your right hand and moved it toward your ass, and then notified me that you were going to shove your fingers up your anus and then force me to smell them.

I tried moving my head back and forth, begging you to not follow through with your disgusting proposal, but you wouldn't listen. While I was panicking, you were laughing hysterically. After a few minutes of your hands down your pants, you held true to your word and tried shoving your soiled fingers up my nose. After wrestling with you for a bit, and feeling wretched by what you did, I finally freed myself from your hold and walked away dry-heaving.

The timing of your fingers up your ass and forcing me to smell them prompted you to tell me of your fascination with European porn. The concept that porn varied from country to country was new to me. You, in another attempt to shock me, educated me on the difference. As ignorant as I was about sex and porn, it wasn't even in my realm to try and understand why you would get off on seeing a woman defecate or urinate on top of a man during sex.

Maybe you had some peculiar fetish with the scent of shit, and this is why you got off trying to force your foul fingers up my nose, but to this day, I have not looked up the different types of porn. Thanks to you, your description of European porn was enough to keep me away from it forever.

If this wasn't some unique way of inflicting abuse, then your attempts at suffocating me were. Without notice I would find myself pushed up against my bedroom wall. After placing one hand on my forehead and one hand on my neck, you would open your mouth and place it completely over my nose and mouth. After suctioning your lips to my face, you would blow as long and as hard as you could. Honestly, writing this brings tears to my eyes. I have no words to describe the terror I felt when you did this. I couldn't breathe, and while I struggled for air, you would snicker, take a breath, and repeat.

Prior to this, you had given me a colored drawing of the 2002 Olympics in Utah with your signed autograph. I had hung this 11x14 poster on the wall just to the right of my bedroom door. It was the wall next to this drawing, as well the wall next to my one and only bedroom window where you inflicted your innovative way to make one feel like they were going to suffocate.

By June, I was officially terrified. On the inside, I constantly questioned when you were going to kill me. On the outside, I portrayed everything was fine. The dialogue between us consisted of suicide, pleadings for my virginity, soliciting a trip to Vegas to elope, committing a murder-suicide, my Stingy-Ass Vagina, your hatred for Mormonism, your resentment of America and its ugly history toward your ancestors, your reputation, your connections to Hollywood, and your neverending game of sexual coercion.

With these varying discourses, your desire to never take me into public, and the physical and sexual abuse that was building, made me believe that my worth in the eyes of God and in the eyes of my religion was dead. By this time, you were repeatedly grabbing my vagina without my permission. Like I was a princess in despair, you acted like you were my prince who found a way to help me, as if I couldn't move on my own. You were quick to cup me between the legs, get your feel, and then push me up the stairs or out of the car. Your help was never gentle, but extended with force and in a way that established your power. Your muscular hands showed no such thing as a caress or sensual act of love. Your hold on my stingy-ass vagina was strong, like you were clutching a discus at a track and field competition.

We did have some good times, and that is why it was easy to justify staying with you. And I did allow things to go a little farther with you than I had with anyone else. You were already grabbing me between the legs without my consent, and it was tiring always having to ward off your requisitions for sex. I hoped that by giving in to some things, your degrading conduct would stop and the quest for my virginity wouldn't be so constant.

I was a fool. A good Mormon girl would have left the moment the waving red flags started rearing their silken threads into the air. But I was no longer a good Mormon girl. Remaining with you started to feel safe in a distorted and sickening way. The adage of "keep your friends close, but your enemies closer" rang routinely in my ear.

If I did cave and marry you, at least I knew what I was getting into, and I would not be bound to you through a temple ceremony. For all I knew, I could marry a Mormon man in the temple and be eternally bonded to an abusive porn junkie. I wrestled with both choices, to a point where I finally told my mother, "I'm either going to get a boob job or marry a man of color." I contemplated marrying you often, and it weighed heavily on me. My luck with dating Mormon men was shitty, and Jersey would never take me back after ending things the way I did. I was beginning to feel that the only two options for my future would be to marry you or be alone.

Either choice would ultimately leave me empty and alone. At the time I wasn't even worthy of fifth wife status for polygamist Kody Brown. Believing that my future was going to go from old maid to old cat lady, I did what many Mormon girls have done and I got a boob job. You came with me to one of the first appointments with the plastic surgeon, but I didn't allow you to persuade me in any of the decision making. I was doing this for me and no one else.

Silicone was not on the market at the time, so I was forced to go with saline. It only took three weeks for me to make the official decision and schedule my surgery. My mother drove down to Salt Lake to be with me during the entire surgical process. She also planned on staying overnight to take care of me for a few days while I recovered.

As the anesthesiologist was beginning to induce the medicine, he asked if I was single or married. I informed him I was single, and as I closed my eyes and went to sleep, the last words I heard him speak were, "Well, if you didn't get many dates before this, you will certainly get them now." One and a half hours later, my knockers went from a 32A to a 32D. I was one step closer to becoming a celestial porn star.

I woke up from surgery groggy but coherent enough to slide my hands slowly over my new, perky melons. I had done it, I actually went through with a breast augmentation, a much safer alternative than marrying a non-Mormon man of color. My mother drove me from the hospital and back to my apartment. On the way home, as we were waiting at a red light, I supposedly unzipped my hoodie, rolled down the window, turned to the car to my right, and yelled, "Look at me, I finally have boobs!" Unfortunately, the car of strangers beheld no new perky breasts   they only got a glimpse of the ugly white post-surgery bra wrapped in soft bandages.

We arrived back at my apartment and my mother helped me up the stairs. I was feeling really well and was surviving on Ibuprofen and Tylenol alone. I hated painkillers and had no interest in taking the Lortab or Percocet that the doctor tried to prescribe. The only thing that was difficult for me to do was to turn around to wipe myself while using the bathroom. Other than that, I was feeling amazing. After a few hours of being there to assist me, my mother saw me awake and painting my own toenails, so we agreed she could go home.

You had called to check on me and see how I was doing. After notifying you of my mother's departure, you proposed to come and stay with me through the night. My roommate was not working her graveyard shift and would be there, so we set up a place for me on the couch and you prepared a place by my side on the floor. By the time you arrived, I was feeling groggy again from the surgery. I fell asleep early, but before I did, you requested to see my new assets.

Though you supported me through the augmentation process, I still never granted you access to them. Even on the first night of you staying with me, I turned you down. I was a few hours into my first night of sleep as a newly-endowed woman when I was awakened by a painful throbbing in my head. I slowly pulled myself into a sitting position and started rubbing my temples profusely.

Like the subtle movement of an inchworm, I felt a pulse slowly creep along the side of my temple and up toward the center of my head. I had never felt this type of pain before, and it startled me. It was so prominent, I thought for sure I was about to die of an aneurysm. I fought against the urge to wake you, but gave in and asked you to help find some medicine. You seemed genuinely concerned and helped me through the pain until I fell back asleep.

You rarely gave me glimpses into a soft side of you, so when you did, it led me to believe that you actually cared about me. However, these moments were few and far between. You began to show your true colors again when you found ways to express that my new assets were not good enough for you. You hated my cellulite and were quick to point it out every time I wore pants that showed the cottage cheese on the back side of my thighs. No matter what I did to try and better my body, or my looks, it never seemed good enough.

This surgery, and the increase of your abuse, would officially begin a life of debilitating migraines. I am not sure if the augmentation is what turned things up a notch, but within the month, your talk of murder and suicide began to increase. I was becoming weary of your cries for sex, but also tedious with my own weaknesses and inability to say no to you in other areas. I allowed you to slip your hands down my pants and touch me, but swore I would never allow anything more. You had been grabbing me down there already, so what was the difference if I said yes if you were going to do it anyways?

You were dragging me down by your flaxen cord, and I didn't know how to loosen your grip. The suicide-killing monologues had me terrified. The fear, the shame, and God's desertion made me believe I had nowhere to go.

Remember the day when you were training on the outdoor track near your apartment? When I arrived, you were hunched over at the opposite end of the field. You noticed me and awkwardly started walking toward me. You believed you were having a heart attack and asked me to drive you to the hospital. You had become very quiet, and valid concern was written all over your sweaty face.

My memories of this day are jagged and sparse, but your speech while lying on the hospital bed etched itself into my mind like the ink of a tattoo pen upon my flesh. Worried you were near death, you whispered out loud the words, "I need to get right with God. I am not right in the head."

This sent me spiraling further into my trepidations because, pardon my language, I knew you were fucking right. I had known this, had seen it with my own eyes, and it sent a lightning bolt of terror down my spine. This was the one and only time in the ten months we were together that you vocalized to me you knew you were mentally unstable. These seven words kept a strong hold on me for the darker and scarier months ahead.

My dear rapist, I had stopped taking the sacrament, stopped going to the temple, and had stopped praying. God had abandoned me and I had abandoned him. I was swimming in abuse and temptation, and I believed it was solely my fault.

I deserved God's rejection simply because I had ignored his warning. His spiritual admonishment, I was certain, had more to do with knowing I would give in to carnal pleasure, than with the way you had abused me. I truly believed God cared more about my sexual transgressions than he did about your scurrility.

Never Yours,
Abandoned by God

***

My Dear Rapist,

By the end of June 2006, roughly two weeks after the breast augmentation and five months into our relationship, I was ready to give Mormon men another chance. I was traveling out of state for work, and during a layover in Phoenix I met a cute, returned missionary. We sat and talked for several hours while we both waited for the same flight to Salt Lake City.

He lived in a different part of Salt Lake than I did, but after finding out I lived there as well, he asked for my phone number and for a date. He was around 5'10, and had blonde hair and blue eyes. I was usually more attracted to men above 6 ft with brown hair and brown eyes, but found myself saying yes.

We ended up meeting up for dinner, and as cute as he was, I found him annoying and lost interest quickly. I didn't tell you about him right away because I didn't think it was that big of a deal. It never went anywhere, and as I mentioned before, you and I really never had a formal talk defining our relationship.

A few weeks later, sometime in July, we were spending time at my apartment. We were in my living room talking on my couch and I had let it slip out that I had gone on date with the blonde from my Phoenix layover. You were not happy, and in fact, you were so upset that you decided to go into my bedroom, shut the door, and give me the silent treatment.

You were in there for thirty minutes before I made the decision to knock on my own door and approach you. You called for me to come inside and I asked if we could talk. You were sitting shirtless on my bed and with your back against the wall. I stood in my doorway apologizing profusely for not telling you about the date.

You invited me over to the side of the bed, the side nearest to my bathroom, to talk. Before I knew it, you grabbed me and pushed me down onto my bed. I was on my back, weighed down by your body as your left hand held both of my hands over my head. Your right arm immediately began removing both of our clothing from the waist down. My pants and my Mormon underwear had been pulled down to my ankles and you shoved yourself right up against me.

While you rocked back and forth slowly, I tried to wiggle out of your grasp, pleading for you to get off me. Like a broken record, you repeated, "You know you want this. You know you want this. You know you want this." I was incessant that I did not want this and I was steady in my adjurations for you to get the fuck off. I was so completely caught up in waiting for the pain from the thrust of your penis tearing through me that I didn't look down to see how far inside you were. I couldn't look down; you had me pinned. I thought I felt your tip inside, but second-guessed myself. I never had a naked penis ever get this close to me. My focus wasn't your depth, my focus was on getting you to let me go and to climb off me.

Had I known what I know now, I would have had a measuring tape on my nightstand and asked you to pause your sexual assault so I could take measurements of the depth of your penetration. Time stood still. I knew you were angry that I went out with another guy and didn't tell you, but I didn't realize it would make you angry enough to do this. After what seemed like an eternity, you abruptly let go and climbed off. While I lay there frozen to my silken red sheets and having a difficult time trying to process what just happened, you turned off the lights and entered my closet.

My bedroom was pitch black, so I could not see you. With my pants and garments still around my ankles, you started barking. Yes, you started barking like fucking Cujo. Through your growls, you sneered, "I want to kill. I feel like killing. I want to kill you." You could have damn well cut my head open and seared those words into my brain with a branding iron. After hearing the word *kill*, my brain turned black.

A decade and a half later, I am still left with a darkened memory bank that is utterly void of what happened next. What I do know is that I never went to the police. With your constant need to keep a prominent reputation, I thought for sure you would kill me if I ruined it. In addition, how could I call it rape when you didn't fully penetrate and ejaculate? I had zero proof of what you had done, and it would be my word against yours. Why would you go this far and not finish the job? It would take years before I finally received that answer, an answer you identified in your self-published so-called inspirational book of egregious confessions.

You didn't have a condom, something you stressed the importance of in your God-awful, disgusting book. This is why you didn't fully penetrate. I know this with every fucking fiber of my being.

My dear rapist, for many years, I could not define your actions as rape. In my sexually illiterate world, rape meant complete penetration and the release of sperm. It would take your bragging rights of being halfway in, your declarations of being officially my first and that I was no longer a virgin, and your self-published book for me to realize that, indeed, what you did is legally defined as rape.

My sexual unsophistication as a twenty-eight-year-old Mormon girl would be the reason why I would never receive justice, and why you, my dear rapist, would later get to walk away and humorously be labeled as "Just A Good 'Ole Fuck Boy" by a Utah detective.

Never Yours,
Frozen in Fear

***

My Dear Rapist,

After you raped me, the one good thing I had going for me was that by then, I had quit my job at the youth center and had found a job working as a medical assistant for an ENT surgeon in downtown Salt Lake City. I had been feeling the pull to leave you for a while, but was not sure how to end things. I had enough sense to know that the first step would be to get another job so I would not have to see you during the day.

The day after the rape and your irrefutable barking threats, I went to work trying to act as if things were normal. My nerves felt like a 100-acre ant farm, with billions upon billions of microscopic ants running in every direction. I made it about halfway through the work day before I couldn't take it anymore and came up with an excuse to leave. I was a wreck, I could barely even function, and I feared you would come back over and finish the job.

I couldn't go home. I struggled with the thought of seeing my bed and my closet. I do not have much memory of what I did for the next several hours, but I killed some time before I was scheduled to drive north to meet my sister in Ogden for reasons I cannot remember. I tried hiding my distress from her as best as I could, determined to never speak of what had happened to anyone.

Nobody knows me better than my twin sister, and she could instantly tell something was wrong. Maybe it is due to our identical cellular makeup, but my twin and I were never good at keeping secrets from each other. Within a matter of minutes, I fell apart and shared tiny, broken fragments of what you did, and that I was scared for my life. I was adamant that if she told anyone, I would never speak to her again.

Rape wasn't in my vocabulary at this time. I had a difficult time reconciling your actions as such, because I believed in all the myths that our society attaches to rape. You didn't fully penetrate? Not rape. You didn't ejaculate? Not rape. You were someone I was dating, someone I considered marriage with, someone I thought I loved. Well, rape only happens by strangers in dark alleys, right?

Not rape.

Even though I could not formulate the word *rape* upon my tongue or confidently articulate it into a police report, my body and my mind knew the truth: I was now a statistic.

My dear rapist, lucky for you all these years later that neither my twin nor I are able to recall the details of what I shared. The only thing that we can both confirm is that it was enough to express fear for my life and that some sort of sexual assault had happened. The small portion I did share, combined with my determination that she never tell a soul, sent my sister into preterm labor. I placed a heavy, unfair burden of weight on my twin, and it was too much for her to carry on her own. Unbeknownst to me, she went home and opened up to her husband, then placed a call to my parents.

I drove home after seeing my sister, scared that I had opened my mouth to her, but also terrified at the thought of breaking up with you. I thought for sure that if I acted anything other than normal, you would become more psychotic, more angry, and go through with your earlier sentiments of taking my life. I don't recall seeing you that next night, and if I know myself, I am sure I told you I wasn't feeling well.

Forty-eight hours later, I attempted another normal day at work. Just as I had the day before, I made it through about half the work day before I needed to get the hell out. I couldn't breathe, and my sympathetic nervous system felt like it was on fire. I hopped into my car and started slowly driving south on State Street. I considered going to Fashion Place Mall to do some mindless shopping, anything to keep my mind off you and what you had done.

I was nearing 2100 South and State Street when I got a call from my sister. She asked me what I was doing, and I told her I had just left work and was contemplating some mindless shopping. She could sense I was still in a state of distress and begged me not to get upset with her. She had done exactly what I had asked her not to do, and she had called my parents.

At this point, she did not care if I stopped speaking to her, because deep down, she knew I needed help. She let me know that my mother, my aunt, and my uncle were on their way to my apartment to pick me up and take me home. They were twenty minutes away, and she pleaded with me to go back to my place and wait for them. Since it was summertime, my father was tied up in farm work and unable to join my mother in rescuing me.

Half angry and half relieved that my sister had broken her promise, I followed her advice and I drove back to my apartment. You had tried calling and texting me a few times, but I had ignored your calls. I wasn't sure if this would upset you, so I felt a sense of urgency to not stay long.

Sure enough, within twenty minutes, my family arrived at my door. The minute I saw my mother, I fell into her arms. I don't recall discussing much at this time with any of them, but I do remember the look on my aunt's soft, teary face, and my uncle's stern and indignant eyes.

While I gathered my toiletries, they filled my little turquoise car with as much clothing as they could. We were in and out of my place in thirty minutes. I didn't have to say much—they felt the gravity of the situation and knew, without question, the importance of getting the hell out. I was not in a condition to drive, so my mother took my car keys and climbed into the driver's seat of my car.

My back seat and passenger seat were maxed out with my belongings, so my poor mother was forced to drive the two hours back home alone. I climbed into the back seat of my aunt and uncle's car, curled up in a ball, and cried. I don't remember saying much, or even remember what I told them, but just as my sister knew something was wrong and that I feared for my life, so did they.

We arrived at my parents' home, unloaded my belongings, and I hugged my aunt and uncle goodbye. I was with my parents for about a week, not really speaking, but not really sure what to do or where to go.

I had left my roommates high and dry, without any explanation as to why I had up and left. I had turned my phone off, leaving you to send me frantic messages wondering where the hell I was. You were not happy that I was ignoring you or not letting you know of my whereabouts. I had opened up a little bit to my father, just enough for him to have felt something criminal had happened, and he encouraged me to file a police report.

My dear rapist, the time at my parents' house was mostly a blur. I do remember spending a lot of time in my bedroom, praying, fasting, and imploring God to help me get out alive from my relationship with you. I was so fearful of you that my mind spiraled into differing scenarios, leaving me to wonder if you had killed before, or if I was the start of a new, demented path for you.

After being with my parents for several days, I tried calling my roommate to let her know where I was. I intended to request that she not let you know of my whereabouts in case you came looking for me. I could not get a hold of her and tried calling my other roommate to see if she had seen her. Both of my roommates had boyfriends and they worked graveyard shifts at homes for adults with special needs.

They were rarely home in the evenings, and one of them would sleep at her boyfriend's house during the day. My other roommate had not seen her for a few days, and my mind went batshit crazy with contrasting scenarios on why I couldn't connect with her.

I had it in my head that you were so upset with me for leaving and not telling you where I was that you had gone to my apartment looking for me. When my roommate told you that she didn't know where I was, you didn't believe her.

As a result, I began to believe you had kidnapped her and were holding her hostage until I would come back to you. Of course, this didn't happen, but your actions sent me spiraling onto the edge of insanity.

Never Yours,

Now a Statistic

***

My Dear Rapist,

After a week of silence and prayer, I knew what I needed to do. It went against everything my parents had hoped I would say, but I made the decision to go back. Your level of crazy was something I needed to deal with on my own. My parents pushed for me to move to Boise and live with my brother for a while, but I couldn't do it. I knew two things were waiting for me in Salt Lake: finding a way to get away from you safely and finding my future husband.

Something deep inside my core told me that the only way I could safely cut ties with you was to end the relationship with you believing Mormonism would keep us apart. I had a keen awareness that if I were to bring up what you did on the bed or tell you how fucking psycho you were, things would not end well for me. My intuition was insistent that I blame things on Mormonism, never on you. Going back and knowing I would need to stroke your ego put me in a position to perform. By performing, I believed I would eventually get away from you, but I also believed that God had my eternal companion waiting for me somewhere in the heartbeat of Mormonism.

Against my parents' wishes, I loaded my car back up with my belongings, asked them to trust me that I knew what I was doing, and made my way back to you. I had a life in Salt Lake. I had a job, I had roommates, and I had friendships. Though I was terrified of you, I wasn't ready to walk away from the rest of it. It was a Sunday evening when

I returned back to my apartment and told everyone that I had attended to a family emergency. With the answers I had received from my fasting and prayer, I felt God was with me again, and that perhaps he was going to keep me safe. I tried to play it cool with you, but felt even more cautious and on edge than before.

Things were different and my hunches told me that you also felt a change. You still continued your games of weird behavior and talk of committing a murder-suicide. Pressure for sex seemed to decrease for a bit, but your need to brag about being "halfway in and my first" increased. Once in a while, I thought about filing a police report or filing a restraining order, but I knew enough to know that a piece of paper was worthless.

Whenever I started to think about getting the police involved, I'd pause and remember your obsession with your reputation. You were an Olympic athlete and an actor in Hollywood. If I fucked that up, I was dead.

We had a few weeks of calm. Yes, you weren't always a sadistic monster, and there were times I did enjoy your company. I started to believe that maybe the worst was behind us, and this meant we would have an easy breakup. Just as we never had an official "we are together" talk, we also never had an official "let's date other people" talk.

We attempted a day-fishing trip up Ogden Canyon and an overnight tent trip at Jordanelle Reservoir. It was during this time that you came up with one of your weird and disturbing mind games. Maybe it was the fishing at Porcupine Reservoir that gave you the idea, but regardless, this would be the start of you buying Styrofoam cups of fishing bait. It was not bait for us to go fishing with, but bait for you to play rancid games with.

When I wasn't looking, you would take the cups of worms and hide them in my car. It would take days of them decaying before their rotting smell would permeate around me. I would frantically search for the deceased bait in my car, fighting the urge to throw up all over the black asphalt underneath my feet. To this day, my olfactory sensory neurons easily recall their raunchy smell as they were scorched by the heat of Utah's summer sun. Maybe this prank alone would not have been very alarming, but mixing this with all the other crazy shit you did left me feeling continuously leery.

Your frequent petitions for sex did come back and, in some instances, you felt I owed it to you after how much time and patience you had extended toward me. You were also becoming miffed that you were by my side during the boob surgery, yet I was not giving you access to them like you felt you deserved. You even had the nerve to inform me that my new set of boobs belonged to you more than anyone else. Somehow you became the victim in our relationship because of my "Stingy-Ass Vagina."

About a month after your rape and barking, we were spending an evening at your place. It was a weekend, and we were up late, watching a movie in your bedroom. We had spent some time before the movie making out, and this time, things went too far. You had requested to give me oral sex and I wouldn't allow it. I don't know why, but at the time, I believed it would be less sinful to give you oral sex than to receive it. In an attempt to get you to shut up, I offered to make you happy. I had never done oral sex before, so I had no idea what the hell I was doing.

What I did know was that I was tired. I was a fucking discombobulated mess and no longer knew left from right or up from down. I thought I had gotten my answer to go back to Salt Lake, and in so doing, God would help me find a way to leave you, but I was undeniably entrenched in fear. At the time, I felt I only had three options. One, I could risk my life by leaving you and then be alone forever. Two, I could continue my hunt for a Mormon man and eternally seal myself to a porn addict. Three, I could stay with you and at least know the hell I would be living in as I fought daily with the imagery of you killing me. In reality, all three choices felt like death to me.

Every feeling a human could have for another human, I experienced with you. I won't lie, I know I had to love you to some degree. I am sure there were good parts about you that I fell for, and I don't remember them now, but there had to have been something good about you. You made me feel special, until you didn't. I never knew how to tell you to stop treating me so disparagingly, and for this reason, I thought I deserved your mistreatment and God's abandonment. I was now a piece of chewed bubblegum, a defiled and unworthy woman in the phallocentric world of Zion.

The dialog in my head when I was giving you oral sex could have indicated I had Dissociative Identity Disorder. The Mormon girl in me told me I was a dirty whore and that there would be no forgiveness for this. The sensible girl in me wondered how I would be willing to do this after you raped me and threatened to kill me. The scared girl in me told me if I didn't do it, you would continue to pester me for sex until you repeated what you did on my bed. The twenty-eight-year-old girl, who was so damn tired of being alone, told me that if I just went ahead and had sex, maybe you would knock me up and I would finally have a baby to love and take care of.

The returned missionary girl in me told me I was defiling my temple covenants and going against everything I had ever taught as a missionary. The old maid in me just wanted to know what it would be like to have sex without being held down, barked at, or threatened with death.

After a few minutes of going down on you and having this symposium in my head, I started to think maybe I should just do it—just give you what you had been begging for, for the last five months. I was close, so damn close to caving when a line from my patriarchal blessing popped into my head.

A voice reminded me, "Ginger, Satan can only tempt you as far as you will allow him." This internal message snapped me back to reality, and all of the other voices that were arguing inside my mind suddenly disappeared. The voice was right, I was caving into Satan's temptation. My good Mormon girl persona sprung back to life, forcing me to put a rapid halt to what we were doing and remind you, once again, of my goal to save myself for a Mormon marriage.

As much as you hated Mormonism, you were always willing to accept my Mormon excuses. Perhaps the inner voice I had heard at my parents' home in the days following your sociopathic debauchery was on to something. You were not upset that I had halted the oral action and were surprisingly content with just putting on a movie and cuddling on the mattress that was placed upon your floor. I don't recall which movie we selected, but whatever it was, you had an old-school VHS hooked up to your TV. I can back this up, because you and I would often go to the Blockbuster near my apartment to pick out movies. This was right around the time Redbox was starting to take traction and Netflix had announced their online streaming. You may be wondering why I am mentioning this, but it does carry weight into the next few terrifying moments of my life.

I had fallen asleep during the movie; I was on your left and we were cradled in a spooning position. You had your left arm underneath me, holding me, and I had curled up into a ball onto my left side. The movie had ended and it had played all the way through to the credits. I'm not sure how it got to the noisy, fuzzy, zig-zagged screen, but the black and white static that is pixelated at the end of a VHS tape came on so loudly that it woke me up.

I began to stretch myself out and roll over onto my back. The abrupt electromagnetic noise blasting through your TV made me believe you had also fallen asleep. After rolling onto my spine, and with your left arm still cradling my back, I opened my eyes. About eighteen inches away, but directly above me, was your right hand holding a knife. While the words "what the fuck are you doing?" rolled off my tongue, I attempted to squirm out of your arms. You were repeating, "I feel like killing you. I feel like killing. I want to kill."

Once again, the exact same phrases from my closet the month before were coming out of your mouth. I don't know how I did it, but I wrestled the knife out of your

Olympic hands and tossed it into the corner of your room. Similar to the night of your barking snares, I have lost all memory of what happened next.

My dear rapist, words will never convey the terror that comes from waking up to someone you think you love holding a knife above you and telling you they want to kill. This was the second time in four weeks where you had exhibited a physical desire to end me. A few moments with your knife would bring on sixteen years of a gruesome reoccurring nightmare.

In the dream, I would walk into a dark, tiled bathroom with only two things visible in the room: you and a white, porcelain toilet. You were always sitting at its base, looking dazed and confused. You were covered in blood, holding a knife, and your carnage was splattered all over the bathroom wall and floor.

Finding you in this state always made me question who you had killed and where you had hidden her body. Washed over with guilt, I told myself I could have prevented this if only I had filed a police report. I would wake up from these dreams panicked and always left to wonder if you had eventually snapped and killed another woman.

By mid-September, I was heavy-hearted and depressed. I was having occasional migraines and my immune system was not able to fight off some of the viruses that were coming at me. I was getting sick more than usual and also losing more and more weight.

Between the rape and the knife incident, I had dropped twenty-five pounds and had started to become very strict in my eating habits. I had read an article that

Cindy Crawford was able to keep her slim figure due to an 800-calorie-a-day diet. I was feeling out of control and my intake of food seemed to be the only thing I knew how to handle. As a result, I was wasting away and disappearing into myself.

I wanted you out of my life, but I was convinced that leaving you meant death. I didn't feel safe telling anyone of the things that were happening, not just out of fear of being killed, but because of shame. I constantly questioned how I had ever let things get this bad and why it was so hard for me to stand up for myself, especially because you rarely wanted to go out in public with me and seemed embarrassed by me.

You would tell me that if you ever took me home, your mother would hate me because of my skin color. You barely gifted me an ounce of love and the only thing you ever gave to me were cups of worms and a birthday card mocking my Stingy-Ass Vagina. Whenever we grabbed fast food, you never offered to pay for mine. I wasn't worth six pieces of chicken nuggets, an ice cream cone, or an item off the dollar menu.

I was sitting in church one Sunday, alone and feeling as worn and as tattered as the bottom of a worn out pair of two-year missionary shoes. I wanted to feel God's love again. I was desperate to go back to the temple and find refuge in the walls of his house, especially the serenity of the Celestial Room. I wanted forgiveness and redemption from ignoring God's warning.

My soul felt as dirty as your fingers up your ass, my mind as warped as the decomposed worms in my car, and my heart as heavy as a dozen Olympic bobsleds. Lost in thought, I had completely missed the first half of church. I was brought to the present with an interlude hymn being sung by the congregation. I was so entrenched into my own self-loathing that I neglected to hear the first three verses of the hymn "I Believe in Christ."

The words I suddenly attuned to caused me to tremble. It felt like God himself was standing behind me, shaking me by the shoulders, and imploring me to listen to the words of the fourth verse. In a subtle, loving voice, the following words were being whispered into my heart by something Divine.

> *I believe in Christ; he stands supreme.*
> *From him I'll gain my fondest dream.*
> *And while I strive through grief and pain,*
> *His voice is heard: "Ye shall obtain."*

(Church of Jesus Christ of Latter Day Saints Hymn, I Believe in Christ, pg. 134)

For the first time in seven months, I physically felt that God had returned and was alive within me. I knew it was time to make a choice, his presence told me so. It was time to leave you, even if that meant a life alone with God, or worse, you finishing me off with a knife. I no longer cared. I was so numb inside that I'd rather be dead than be with you.

I wasn't feeling physically well at this time, and I went home and had requested one of my male friends from church to come to my place and give me a blessing. You were there when they arrived and I, always wanting to be a missionary, I thought it would be good for you to see a good friend perform the blessing.

My friend, and another male from church, poured a drop of consecrated oil at the crown of my head, then placed their hands over the oil and started speaking. I was told the typical things that one would hear in a priesthood blessing, like *God loves you, he knows what you're going through*, etc. After some of the normal blessing verbiage, my friend took an unexpected detour. He proceeded to express concern over the mysterious darkness inside of me and the visibility of it bringing me down. He compared the darkness to a form of spiritual cancer and warned me that if I didn't do everything I could to start healing from it or turn away from it, it would destroy me.

This was my second witness in one day that God was paying attention to me and knew of the mess I had gotten myself into. After you heard this blessing, you flat-out told me that you felt you were the cancer he was referring too. You were so fucking confusing. At times, you would take your monster mask off and show me a contrite side of you, but that damn mask did not stay off for long.

After receiving two revelations, I made up my mind. I was ready to confess my fault in allowing the abuse to happen, abuse that had led me to cave and do the worst sexual sin I had ever done, oral sex. I did not want to confess my transgressions to my bishop in the Winder Ward, so I started shopping around on Sundays to different singles wards in the area until I found one I liked. Hoping to get a fresh start and ready to get all of the misgivings off my double D chest, I started attending a new ward for a few weeks. I decided I liked it enough to make an appointment with the bishop with one goal in mind: to confess my sins and make sure I was worthy to go to the temple.

Deep down, I had prayed that the new bishop would have the spirit of discernment with him and that God would tell him that I was in an unsafe, abusive relationship. If God told him, then they would know what to do, and they would know how to keep me safe from you.

It was a Sunday afternoon and church had ended. I sat outside the bishop's office and stared at the carpeted walls while I waited for my turn to go behind the heavy, closed door. Right on time, another young church member opened the door and walked out, and I was asked to enter.

The bishop greeted me by shaking my hand and beckoned for me to sit in the metal chair before his mahogany desk. He started asking me superficial questions, but I had no time for smalltalk. I cut to the chase and told him why I was there. I did not tell him of the things you had done to me, but I took full accountability for the things I allowed and had caved to.

I had asked the bishop how detailed he needed me to be. He said I could say as much as I wanted and, being the overly honest woman that I am, I told him everything. He was an older man, possibly in his sixties, and I thought it odd that he kept his hands hidden behind his desk. For a brief moment, I wondered if he was masturbating to the details of my fornications. I got so graphic with the oral sex and the fingering that I started to feel uncomfortable and believed I had gone too far in my sharing.

My dear rapist, I ached to hear the bishop tell me that

my sins were forgiven and that I would be approved to spend time in God's holy house. I was not surprised, though, when he denied me entrance into the temple. But adding insult to injury, he also cut off my ability to partake of the weekly sacrament. I had prepared myself for being banned from the castle on the hill; I had not prepared myself for losing access to the holy bread and water. Partaking of these two emblems on Sundays was a personal reminder that we could always utilize Jesus's atoning sacrifice and be forgiven.

Denying me access to Jesus in this way only left me feeling spiritually abused in addition to the abuse I was already experiencing.

I left the bishop's office mortified, not necessarily from hearing the word no and that I hadn't been forgiven, but dismayed that the Spirit did not tell him I was in a volatile relationship and needed help. Why didn't God show up here? Why didn't God inform him I was unsafe? Why did God allow him to sit and hear every little dirty detail of the things I did wrong? I had not ever given in and had sex, so why wasn't God blessing me for at least staying strong in that area?

I left the bishop's office more abashed for oversharing the nitty gritty of not being chaste than I was in not being forgiven. I never wanted to see his face again. I could not handle the idea of him possibly perseverating on the details of my confession when we crossed paths at church or when he saw me sitting in the pew.

In some ways, I left more traumatized and more confused after confession than I did before confession. I was stuck on God's absence during the meeting. His

Spirit showed up right before I was about to cave and have sex with you by whispering into my ear the line from my patriarchal blessing. So if God was available for that moment, why was God not available to whisper to the bishop that my life was in danger. I was going fucking crazy, no longer knowing who to trust, let alone how to trust myself.

Never Yours,
A Disoriented, Unworthy Whore

***

My Dear Rapist,

My twin sister knew I was trying to free myself from you and that I was open to dating other men. She had a connection to Mr. Bill and reminded me of our proposed lunch date the previous year. I knew things could not possibly get worse than the hell I was already living in, so I told my sister that if he was still interested, I'd love to give it a shot. Mr. Bill was perturbed about my no-show and informed my sister that if I wanted to go out with him, I'd be the one to have to call and make that happen. I was in the frame of mind that I really didn't give a fuck what any man thought of me, so I said, "What the hell, get me his number."

Finding a decent human being of the opposite gender to keep me distracted from you was of far more importance than actually giving a shit if the guy liked me. Mr. Bill was at least Mormon, from my hometown of Cache Valley, and I knew his mother and disabled brother. It would take a few weeks for me to work up the courage to message him, but

I continuously reminded myself that because of his brother and mother, I could feel safe.

Mr. Bill and I began communicating again, and after a few text exchanges, we decided to meet. He warned me beforehand that he was a volunteer for the Salt Lake County Search and Rescue. This would mean that if we were on a date and he received a call-out, he would have to cut our date short and take me home. I was a little nervous, but mostly indifferent.

I was finishing up my makeup when I got a knock at the door. After taking a few more seconds to finish brushing a bit of blush on my cheeks, I made my way toward the front door. After turning the knob and swinging it open, a handsome man in a black t-shirt and khaki pants stared back at me with a deadpan expression on his face.

Clearly not recognizing me from my profile picture he said, "I'm here for Ginger," in a bored, monotone voice. I did recognize him, but he was much more striking in person than in picture. He had nice olive skin, beautiful dark brown eyes, long gorgeous eyelashes, dark hair, and a nice athletic build. He was attractive, but God, his aura screamed nothing but asshole to me. I almost wanted to come up with an excuse for not being able to go out, but I had already ditched him once, so I wasn't about to do it again.

We had made plans to go up Millcreek Canyon, build a fire, eat dinner, and roast some marshmallows. I grabbed my jacket, a small blanket, and begrudgingly walked out the door with him. Things were awkward, and I was looking forward to the date ending before it had even begun. He was driving an old, blue, topless Bronco, and after opening the door for me, I softened just a little. At least he knew how to open a damn door for a lady. We only had about a fifteen-minute drive to the canyon, so we made our way east on 3900 South and attempted to engage in smalltalk. With the top of his Bronco off, it was difficult to speak, so we really didn't have much to say to each other.

We were about two miles into the mountains when his volunteer scanner went off. The person on the other end was describing a hiker in distress up Cottonwood Canyon, and Mr. Bill's help was needed. He turned to me, apologized for the short date, made a U-turn, and took me home. I was actually quite relieved and ready to be done with all men and told myself I did not need a man to make me happy. He pulled up in front of my apartment, allowed me to let myself out, and sped away. I was certain I wasn't going to hear from him again, and even if he was using the call-out as an excuse because he was not happy with what he saw in person, I was too tired to care.

I was taken aback when a few days went by and Mr. Bill contacted me again. I thought the guy had zero interest in me. I almost turned him down, but something in me told me to give him another chance. He actually apologized and had felt bad for dropping me off so quickly, but he wanted to take his Search and Rescue position seriously. I decided to follow that inner voice this time and give him another chance. We attempted another date up Millcreek Canyon, and this time it was a success. He was a quiet man, difficult to get to know, but he was kind. I learned a bit more about him as we talked about his brother with special needs, his mother, and his other three younger brothers. He was a mechanical design engineer and he worked for Black Diamond, a company that builds mountain sport equipment. He was a returned missionary, having served in Oklahoma, and had been previously married for three years but divorced for five. He lived on 3900 South and 3000 East and I lived on 3900 South and 300 East. He loved everything outdoors, including camping, river rafting, fishing, hiking, rock climbing, and ice climbing.

Mr. Bill was a man of few words and didn't smile much, but he had a very easygoing nature about him. Something inside of me consistently whispered a need for patience and that I needed to give this relationship time. There was no pressure, no rush, no feelings to impress, just an unusual calm that existed when we were together. He was an attractive, believing Mormon man that messaged me every few days to see if I wanted to hang out. There were times I said yes, and then a few hours before the date I would tell him that I was not doing well and would cancel the date. He was patient with me, told me he wasn't going anywhere, and suggested I take time to work through my shit.

I was still seeing you, my dear rapist, when I started dating Mr. Bill. The more I was around you, the more I wanted to be with him. My desire to spend time with you lessened and lessened, but once in a while, there was always some irrational draw back to you preventing me from completely cutting the cord. Even though Mr. Bill seemed interested, deep down I feared it wouldn't last long and that my only option for marriage would still be to elope with you.

It was October, and you were still trying to get me to leave everything behind and head to a Vegas chapel. At this time, you were also preparing for a trip to New York to do some Olympic training. I was having car trouble and you offered me your Audi to drive while you were away. You were once again exhibiting some depression and suicidal idealization in the days leading up to your departure. You had been gone for several days and I was having trouble getting a hold of you. During a lunch break at work, I decided to call your roommate, hoping he would either have heard from you or have answers as to why you were ignoring me. Your roommate answered the call right away. Apparently, you were not back East training for the Olympics but instead spending time with an ex-girlfriend. The phone call was short, but his final words before he hung up were the very thing I needed to hear, and I will forever be in his debt.

"Ginger," your roommate said, "you need to get as far away as possible. When you are not here with him, he has a different girl sleeping with him every night. When it comes to women, he walks with the Devil."

I sat in my car shivering, not from the cold, but from an intense, systemic sadness. Deep, cellular sorrow and rage creeped into and fired off all eleven of my body systems. My nervous system went into fight or flight. My respiratory system ceased taking in air. My excretory system began sweating. My muscular system contracted with tension. My endocrine system released cortisol. My integumentary system flushed the color of red. My digestive system dry-heaved air all over my steering wheel. My skeletal system wanted to break your jaw with my fist. My circulatory system sent my blood pressure through the roof. My lymphatic system swelled as it recognized the virus you truly were, and last but certainly not least, my reproductive system cried out for justice.

My dear rapist, you dragged me slowly down to Hell with your spiderweb-thin, cord weaving the belief that I was special. I finally understood why women like me could not leave men like you. You flipped me back and forth like a coin—heads, I was your abused toy, tails, I was your supposed queen. Feeling a despondency of emotions from the tidal wave of abusive memories and sexual degradations, I forcefully punched your number into my flip phone. I knew you wouldn't pick up, so I did what any good Mormon girl wouldn't do and I lied.

I left a message, detailing a fabricated dream that someone had informed me you were sleeping with other women. I expressed my sentiment of being done and never wanting to see you again. Your car would be parked at your house, I would not be available to pick you up at the airport, and you would need to find your own way home. For the first time in my life, it felt amazing to lie. I would have loved to share my true feelings and tell you that you were a monster, you were fucking crazy, and your own roommate had ratted you out. But I refrained and I chalked our breakup to a heavenly messenger from my dreams.

Within two minutes, you called me back, displaying your poor and ridiculous acting skills. I don't know why it was so difficult to see your shitty theatrics in person, but hearing it through the phone, 1,940 miles away, it was suddenly evident—you were a charlatan, a phony, a hoax, fraud, swindler, cheater, scammer, deceiver, imposter, abuser, and rapist.

"The reason I haven't returned your calls is because I am ready to kill myself. You won't marry me. I have been lying in the bathtub all day, ready to slit my wrists. If only you would marry me, then I wouldn't want to kill myself."

"Then kill yourself," I said. "I no longer care, I am done." I ended the call, and by doing so, slashed your flaxen cord from around my neck. After ten months of not recognizing your noose, I woke up and finally freed myself from your Satan-inspired hands.

Never Yours,
A Liberated Woman

CHAPTER 14

MY MORMON PRINCE

"Except a man and his wife enter into an everlasting covenant and be married for eternity, while in this probation, by the power and authority of the Holy Priesthood, they will cease to increase when they die; that is, they will not have any children after the resurrection. But those who are married by the power and authority of the priesthood in this life and continue without committing the sin against the Holy Ghost, will continue to increase and have children in the celestial glory."

(Joseph Smith, Teachings of the Prophet Joseph Smith, 300-301)

My Dear Rapist,

Your roommate saved me. Because of him, I was able to move on and cautiously consider opening my heart up again. Mr. Bill continued to reach out to me, and I had energy for no one other than him. I felt no desire or pressure to impress him. I was just me, broken into a million, tiny pieces. An inner voice, which I strangely trusted, continued to quietly nudge me into spending more and more time with him.

He was different. He presented himself to the world as an arrogant, inconsiderate asshole, seemingly always miffed at someone or something. Behind closed doors, he was a giant, gentle teddy bear. The stark difference between the two of you was something I caught on to within a few months of dating him. You, to the world and to me, were a charmer. You appeared confident and perfect, but in reality, there was a constant need for an accolade or ego stroke toward your empty and fucked up psyche. When nobody was looking and the curtains fell down, your mask fell off and you became the devil.

Mr. Bill never needed any of that. He didn't give a shit what the world thought of him. He needed no award, no spotlight, no recognition. He was just Bill, always there, never pressuring, never begging, just supporting. He found no need to be perfect or to pretend to be perfect, even often willing to admit his faults.

Mr. Bill's persona was the very thing I needed to help mend my shattered soul. While he quietly stood by, he was unknowingly rehabilitating me with his patience and "I don't give a damn what the world thinks" demeanor. For the first time in my dating career, I started to feel a safety net form beneath me. I had never before felt this sense of refuge in a man, let alone a Mormon man. He wasn't out catching fireflies with me, driving me long distances to historical church sites, or ironing sacred leaves on parchment paper. But he was beside me like a sturdy, old oak tree, waiting to hold me in his rugged limbs. He was the calm to my storm, always ready to listen to me and catch me when I spiraled from the effects of your abuse.

I knew we were getting closer, but I felt no urgency to move things along, and time was of no concern. We just kept moving forward like the flow of a soft, rippling stream. Things with Mr. Bill were going well, and in fact they were going so well that we shared our first kiss.

We were at his home one chilly evening, relaxing on his couch in front of a wooden fireplace. His dog, Dax, was lying on the floor next to us, all three of us feeling tired after a day of work. Mr. Bill was pressed against the backside of the couch, and I was on the open side, curled up next to him facing the fire. We were talking of nothing important, and without a single word, he invited me in for a kiss. I had been admiring his full, thick lips ever since I had first met him.

Touching lips with a man that I had zero desire to impress brought out a dreamy sweetness that I had no idea was possible. The ambience of a wooden fire behind us and the safety of his timbered arms added tremendously to the maturity and the expansiveness of the kiss. Like the gradual roasting of a toasted marshmallow, I slowly and nonchalantly melted into him. This wasn't just sexual, it was celestial, and he tasted amazing.

This moved our relationship a little closer to first base, but neither of us was quite ready to commit to the full game. I was seeking to follow my instincts and believed this may actually go somewhere, yet I didn't fully trust myself, or believe that I would keep his interest. It was almost Thanksgiving and I was yearning to get out of Utah and clear my head. I reached out to my uncle in New Jersey and inquired if I could spend the holiday with him and his family. I also needed to see Jack; it was essential to know if any of the spark we once had was still alive.

I booked my flight, reached out to Jack, and returned to Jersey once more. Jack picked me up from Newark airport, and together we made the drive to Morristown for our Thanksgiving dinner. As soon as I laid my eyes on Jack, I knew. I definitely felt a spark, but the spark was not for him—it was for Mr. Bill.

I was missing my space on his couch in his red-bricked house on 3900 South in Utah. I was longing for his thick lips, his big, beautiful brown eyes, his chiseled cheekbones, and his long-ass, dreamy eyelashes. I was especially missing the safety net he had weaved for me since walking away from you. Jack and I awkwardly talked, with me sharing a little about you and your treatment of me.

Of course, he noticed my new set of assets and mentioned they were unnecessary and I was fine just the way I was before the surgery. He was the same kind, wonderful Jack I remembered, but the kindle I suddenly longed for was the one I felt with Mr. Bill.

We shared dinner with my relatives, and after some light conversation, we said our goodbyes. I recall no other memories from this quick little East Coast jaunt other than that I received what I needed to receive—my answer about Jack and my answer about Mr. Bill.

I had zero patience for my return flight to Salt Lake; I wanted to be with my sturdy oak tree. Things started to shift more seriously between us and by Christmas, I was going home to meet his family. I had fond memories of Mr. Bill's mother and brother, so the reunion with her and our connections to the special needs world made me feel at home.

After dinner, we decided to go for a drive up Providence Canyon. Cache Valley had received a lot of snow this particular Christmas, so we had a starry, clear night mixed with the white, ethereal beauty. He was driving his 4x4 white Dodge truck, and when we got as far as we could, he pulled over. Faster than a rabbit in heat, I unfastened my seat belt, crawled over to the driver's seat, and straddled him.

Lordy, Lordy, my nether regions were on fire, providing us one of the best Levi-loving sessions I had ever had. I couldn't get enough of this guy, and it seemed he couldn't get enough of me. The feelings were so prurient, my soul wanted to climb right into his soul and be one with him. This feeling of oneness was the very thing that set him apart from everyone else I had dated.

Meeting his family and our romantic Christmas Eve makeout pushed us closer to second base of the Mormon dating game. He was dating one other girl and was trying to determine which of us he would take to an ice climbing festival in Ouray, Colorado. I do not recall why he chose me, but he did. A week after Christmas, Mr. Bill and I took off for the ice park that is known as the Switzerland of America. Ouray had gorgeous alpine vistas and over 150 ice and mixed route climbs. It is a man-made ice park stretching across two miles of the Uncompahgre Gorge. Traversing up the steep walls of the gorge gives climbers a chance to play on the world's largest public ice-climbing park.

I was flattered that Mr. Bill chose me to go. I expressed much excitement, but much apprehension. I had a strong fear of heights and I hated being cold. Since he had chosen me, though, for the first time since meeting him I had a desire to impress him. After making the ten-hour drive to Ouray, we found Mr. Bill's friend, grabbed our climbing gear, and headed to the gorge.

On the first day, we started at the base and did some practice runs, working our way up the mountain. For the entire first day, this was the focus. It was bitter cold, but I sucked it up and pushed through for him. The second day was different—we would start from the top, rappel down, and work our way back up. I got the hang of it early on as the climbing wasn't too high or completely vertical. There was a slight slant to the climb and the boys could see me and help guide my footing, as well as determine where I should place my ice ax.

On that second day, we started from the top, which meant putting full trust in the rope, the harness, and the person assigned to belay. That first step over the edge, with a 500-foot drop, was nothing short of terrifying. I watched Mr. Bill and his friend do it first, in the hopes it would lessen my rattled nerves. Watching them did nothing for my nerves, so when it came my turn, I was fighting a very strong urge to shit my pants. Dax, Bill's beautiful golden retriever, laid down just at the edge of the cliff, put his head on his paws, and told me with his eyes that he knew I was feeling scared. I started backing toward the edge of the cliff with my eyes on Mr. Bill, wondering if I could truly trust this man to keep me from falling to my death.

I put all my trust into Mr. Bill, who was belaying me, closed my eyes, and jumped. The instant free fall and rappelling down the side of that mountain was liberating. Mr. Bill was pushing my boundaries in a healthy way, encouraging me to explore uncharted areas within myself and proving I was capable of facing my fears.

My dear rapist, he wasn't instilling fear in me like you did, he was helping me overcome the paralyzing emotion. The realization of what he was giving back, not taking, assisted me in getting to the bottom of the mountain safely.

Once my feet were touching the ground, I looked around and discovered I was alone. I tried yelling upward, but nobody could hear me. For a moment, the fear came back as I realized I had to get back to the top alone, without anyone telling me where to put my feet or place my ax. I pulled on the rope to let them know I was ready to climb, knowing that the only communication they would be getting from me was through the tug of the rope.

I climbed about halfway up the mountain with no problem. There was an area that had a mixture of rock and ice, which brought me to a halt. I had no idea how to get around this hurdle, and I was still far enough down the face of the mountain nobody could hear me yelling. My right leg started shaking hard like it was having a seizure. I attempted to put my right foot up, but could not find any ice to shove my crampon into. I hung there for about ten minutes, contemplating what to do, as my leg continued to tremble uncontrollably, later described as the Elvis shake. I started to cry and panic, believing the search and rescue helicopter would have to save me. I tried screaming again for help, but it was useless. I decided I had two options: I could hang there until the boys figured out I needed rescuing, or I could find a way to make it to the top on my own. I did not want to have to deal with the shame of being a quitter, so I chose to get to the top on my own.

The only way to do this was to keep my eyes in front of me. I had to stop looking downward, to my left, to my right, and up the ridge of the mountain toward the sky. I stared straight ahead at the rock and ice, and putting my faith in God, I promised that if he helped me get to the top alive, I would never do an extracurricular activity on a Sunday again. I was breaking the Sabbath day and for a moment, believed I was caught in this predicament because I broke this rule. However, my biggest motivator to show up at the top alive was my refusal to die a twenty-eight-year-old virgin.

One shaky Elvis leg at a time, I found myself traversing my way up the mountain. As each ice ax pounded into the frozen mountain, I envisioned myself murdering your bragging right of being halfway inside me. Kicking my crampons against the ice, I found safety in my footing when I told myself I would never, ever accept you as my first. To this day, intrusive thoughts and memories of you show up in the most random places. My anger over my virgin status fueled me up the ice and rock like a fucking mountain goat.

As soon as I got to the edge of the cliff, I saw Mr. Bill, wearing his thin red beanie, looking down at me. If Jesus ever ice climbed, he would've looked like Mr. Bill in that moment. I swear I heard the heavens open and the angels sing when I saw his outstretched hand offering assistance to help me up and over the top.

My will to impress him had left me. At this point, all I cared about was that I was safe, alive, and no longer quaking like Elvis. I couldn't hold back the discombobulated sobs heaving from my augmented chest.

Tears of relief, joy, fear, and badassery flowed down my cheeks as if the sun was melting all the man-made ice in one day. I had just conquered a fear, all on my own, and in front of the one man that had brought a sense of safety back into my life. Once I caught my breath, I shared with him what had happened when I reached the halfway point. I would later learn that this is when Mr. Bill knew he was in love with me.

Had we been ex-Mormon, we would've ordered beers that night to celebrate being alive. Instead, we sat at the bar and ordered pizza, and I watched Mr. Bill check out the attractive bartender's tits. I was pissed as hell, not just because she had a nice, perky, size-B cup that she was showing off, but because my garments prevented me from showing off my perkier size D cup. Instead of shooting daggers at her all night, though, I turned into a quiet, submissive Mormon girl and gave Mr. Bill the silent treatment through the remainder of dinner.

Once we paid the bill and climbed into his truck, I unleashed my passive-aggressive outrage. How dare he check out another girl's chest while I just spent the day putting my life in danger for him? He knew he was in the doghouse and after getting back to our hotel room, he apologized. He invited me to cuddle up against him for the night, and all the anger I felt toward him vanished, as his presence once again reminded me I was safe.

Our time in Ouray was the final boost that pushed our relationship to third base. A few weeks after returning home, we were at my apartment and snuggling in my bedroom when Mr. Bill told me how he felt. My triumphant ice climb had made him realize that I was someone who would always fight to the end and never give up. This was the first time he outright told me he loved me, and as much as I wanted to say it back, I couldn't. I told him I had strong feelings for him, but I wasn't ready to say it back, and he understood. He was extremely patient and told me he had all the time in the world, that he knew I was still working through shit from you, and that he wasn't going anywhere. He told me he could see something in me that I wasn't capable of seeing, and he was okay with giving me time.

My dear rapist, two contrasting events happened on this bed with two very different men. One man told me he loved me, would be patient with me, and wouldn't force anything on me. The other? Well, I don't need to repeat it, do I? You know. You know what you did on this bed, and it was the complete opposite of Mr. Bill. A few more weeks went by as I pondered and contemplated the difference between the two of you, and I knew I was ready to repeat back to him what he had said to me.

Something had happened with Mr. Bill that had never happened with anyone else I had dated. When Mr. Bill and I were intimate with one another, I felt my reason for being alive; I felt an intense draw to create. A divine persuasion of familiarity pined for creating life, purpose, children, and a home with him. The impression of this was so overpowering that I could no longer imagine growing old without him. Being with him fulfilled the scripture I had heard my whole life of "meeting the measure of our creation." It was so much more than sex and physical attraction; he was the purpose of my creation.

Never Yours,
Loved by Mr. Bill

***

My Dear Rapist,

Once I opened up and shared with him that I loved him, we decided to cut ties with any other people we were dating. You and I were still messaging once in a while, but I had been proud of myself that I never gave in and spent time with you after your roommate helped me to see the light. After Mr. Bill and I were mutual in our expressions of love, I knew it was time to say goodbye to you for good.

We were still social media friends and my fear of you was still very real. I know it won't make sense to others, or maybe even you, but in my head, I had felt it was safer for me to let you stay in my life in small ways rather than to completely cut you off. I reached out to you and asked if we could meet in a public place for dinner, and we met at the Qdoba on 4500 South and State Street. We had a quick dinner and a quick goodbye. I informed you that Mr. Bill and I had become serious and things were looking like they could lead to marriage.

As I climbed into my car, you stood there staring at me, convinced that someday I would reach back out to you with the intent to cheat on Mr. Bill. Both of us had smirks on our faces. Your smirk was filled with disgusting arrogance, and mine was because I knew without any doubt that you were wrong.

Spring turned into summer, and Mr. Bill and I were seriously discussing marriage. We decided for my twenty-ninth birthday, we would go to Teton National Park. We planned to hike and camp while attempting to summit its largest peak, the Grand Teton. There are several different routes to get to the highest point, but due to my inexperience with hiking, we chose the Owen-Spalding route.

This route starts at the beautiful Lupine Meadows trailhead and switchbacks its way through to Garnet Canyon and then on to the Lower Saddle. Along the way, there are fields of wildflowers, creeks, and waterfalls. At mile four, the trail is no longer maintained by the park service and becomes more of a hiker's trail, leaving several boulder fields to cross over.

Around mile five, we hit the Morainal Camping Zone. Mr. Bill and I had spent a good portion of the day hiking our way to this segment. I had been terrified of bears the whole way up, and to the amusement of Mr. Bill,

I clicked my hiking sticks together like Vicky Robinson in the 1961 movie *The Parent Trap*. I was making it my duty to keep the bears far away from me and this man that I had unexpectedly fallen in love with.

Once we reached the Morainal, we pitched our tent and set up camp. We met a few other hikers and found out that just before we arrived, an older gentleman had to be taken out by helicopter due to altitude sickness. I had heard of this happening, but never really understood what it meant. Storm clouds had rolled in while we had been hiking, and not soon after setting up the tent, the rain came.

Mr. Bill and I spent most of the evening cuddling inside the tent as we prepared for the hardest part of the climb the next day. We fell asleep to the cool, summer rain, but while Mr. Bill slept through the night, I struggled to get any rest. Every little noise spooked me and left me prepared to punch a grizzly bear in his ready-to-eat-me face. As soon as the sun peeked its way over the mountain, we got up and primed ourselves to summit the 13,775-foot peak of the Grand Teton.

The first leg of our second day hiking was about a mile, and in that mile there was a snowfield that required a pair of crampons. Once through the snowfield, we came to a fixed rope that helped us through the Saddle's Headwall. After making it through this section, we were about a quarter of a mile away from the Lower Saddle, which is 11,600 feet in elevation. Just before arriving, I started feeling lightheaded and nauseous. Mr. Bill was a little bit ahead of me, but constantly checked on me to see how I was holding up. He could tell that I was struggling and decided to pause at some large boulders and wait for me.

After a few minutes, I caught up to him and quickly sat down. My vision started to blur and I felt a need to vomit. The longer I sat there, the dizzier I became. We were only 1,000 feet from the top, and I was determined to make it there with my hot boyfriend by my side. I stood up and began to move my feet again, but I almost fell over. I felt disoriented and ready to pass out.

Fearing that I was feeling symptoms of altitude sickness, I put my head in my hands and started to cry. My gut told me I needed to stop. It was important to Bill for us to make it to the top and I didn't want to let him down. He was next to me, patient, and requesting that I remove my hands from my face and look at him. I refused to open my eyes. I was ashamed that I was having these physical symptoms and preventing us from moving farther up the mountain.

Again, he continued urging me to open my eyes and take a look at him. After several more refusals and several more requests, I finally caved and let my eyes flutter open. Kneeling before me was Mr. Bill and in his outstretched hand was a ring. I alternated between staring at the ring between his fingertips and his beautiful brown eyes, completely missing that there were words coming from his mouth. It took several moments before I realized what was happening: Mr. Bill was asking me to marry him. This was a proposal. He was asking me to marry him.

"Yes. Yes, yes, yes, yes, yes. Yessssss!!!!"

The ring had been tied to a string that Mr. Bill had worn around his neck the entire duration of the hike. I never saw it, since it was hidden underneath his shirt, out of my sight and close to his heart. Together, we stood up, embraced, and kissed while several hikers below us had paused to watch the tender scene.

Believing that I was experiencing symptoms of altitude sickness, we never did summit the Grand Teton, but neither of us really cared. We both knew the best part of the adventure was coming off that mountain engaged.

The hike down went fast. We were both anxious to get to our hotel and get cleaned up, go out for a nice dinner, and then go back to our hotel and glorify our new commitment with a celebratory Levi-loving, tongue-heavy slob fest.

The next three months flew by, but planning the wedding was going to be a challenge. Mr. Bill was sealed in the temple to his first wife. Though they had been divorced for five years, and because neither had remarried, they were still considered eternally married in the eyes of God, the Church, their family, and their friends. We started meeting with our bishop and stake president, not just to let them know that we wanted to get married in the temple, but to also understand what steps would need to be taken for me to be sealed as Mr. Bill's second wife.

In Mormonism, temple divorces are taken very seriously and need to be approved by the prophet and apostles of the church. A temple divorce is to be avoided at all costs. The temple sealing is so sacred and so vital that Mr. Bill's ex-wife could not be granted a sealing cancellation until she remarried in the temple. It was considered far better for Mr. Bill to have two spiritual wives then for her to go without the blessings of the sealing covenant.

In order for Mr. Bill to take me to the Temple, he would need special permission from the Prophet and apostles. This meant that Mr. Bill and his ex-wife would have to both write letters to the prophet explaining their history and their perspectives on why or why not a second sealing should be granted. My eternal fate rested mostly on the ex-wife's story and her approval.

I knew Mr. Bill's side of the story. Like most Mormon men I had dated, he had looked at porn. Mr. Bill and I had had many tough conversations about pornography, and I was quite blunt with my experiences with Mormon men and the questions I had for him. Mr. Bill was the first guy I had dated that was actually capable of having a mature conversation about the erotic visuals so easily found on a Mormon man's computer screen.

Because of his raw authenticity and unwillingness to laugh at the pain that it had caused me, I felt I had more of a reason to trust him. He promised me that he would always talk with me about this and he also gave me permission to talk about it with anyone and everyone I felt I needed to. There were no reservations from him, nothing but full understanding and accountability, a rarity I had not found among other men in my church.

Five years after his divorce, Mr. Bill called up his ex-wife and informed her that he was getting remarried. I was sitting next to him when he made the call, and it was obvious she was not happy. She had zero patience for what he had to say and constantly cut him off, berated him, and shamed him for the times she had caught him looking at porn. She asked him if I knew of his sickness, and as he tried to inform her of my dating experiences and that I was well aware of his history, she again cut him off. She quickly expressed judgment over what kind of woman I was and wondered what was wrong with me as to always attract "those kinds of men." Through her ranting madness, he let her know that we were planning on going to the temple and he would need her to write a letter to the prophet of the church.

By September, we had met with the right priesthood leaders, filled out the needed paperwork, and sent in the request to the prophet for approval for Bill and I to marry in the temple. Our local leaders found us worthy and suggested we give the prophet three months to make a decision. They felt there was no reason why we would not get an approval, but the holidays were a busy time, thus the reason for a three-month wait. With this in mind, we set our wedding date for December 8, 2007.

My Dear Rapist, I went to work planning and preparing to finally make my Mormon dream come true. I would be twenty-nine-and-a-half years old, a spinster by Mormon standards, but I was finally going to have my temple wedding. All those years I had held out and didn't have sex, didn't drink coffee, didn't throw out my testimony, always paid tithing, didn't consummate my relationships with Alaska Cowboy or Jack, and didn't elope with you, were all finally paying off. I was 90 days away from obtaining the Mormon fantasy, a fantasy that I had been building in my pretty little head since I was an eight-year-old child. I was close, so very close.

Never Yours,

Mr. Bill's Fiancé

***

My Dear Rapist,

A month away from our wedding date, we still had no word from church headquarters. We had met with our bishop again to express our concerns, and he was pretty adamant that we had nothing to worry about. I was having anxiety attacks by this time—not over the wedding, but over you. At times, I found myself feeling so much fear that I would end up in Mr. Bill's arms, telling him I was scared that you were going to find me and kill me.

One day, we were working on the basement apartment in his house, and I was working on installing a set of kitchen cabinets. I was bent over on my knees, holding a sharp tool, and an overwhelming feeling of panic rushed over me. I was inconsolable, shaking profusely as I climbed into Mr. Bill's lap like a six-year-old girl. I told him that I knew you were going to find out where I lived and finish me with your knife. He just sat there holding me, not really knowing what to say other than, "You're safe, you're here with me, he won't find you."

Mr. Bill came with me to meet with my bishop regarding my anxiety over you. I didn't go into too much detail with him, but it was enough that he felt I needed to see a therapist. He sent a referral for me to LDS Social Services and I began therapy with a Mormon woman in downtown Salt Lake. This was in November 2007, one month out from becoming Mr. Bill's wife. Looking back, I can now see my therapist was not trauma-trained. Answers for my trauma included the Sunday school answers that we would write on the chalkboard at church. We were always taught that the answers to our trials, our suffering, and our mistakes were more prayer, more scripture reading, more repentance, and more church service.

"Forget yourselves and get to work" seemed to be the classic Mormon mantra for trauma.

I divulged the nitty-gritty details of your abuse to my therapist, and when it came time to discuss the rape, I shared with her my confusion as to why you never fully penetrated and ejaculated. Her answer was, "God was protecting you. You were wearing your garments; this is why he didn't fully rape you." Even as a fully believing member of the church, I thought her answer was absurd.

God had decided to protect me when my garments were around my ankles? Hmm, okay. If God was in this, why didn't he stop it from happening before you had even pushed me onto my bed? Why had God not stopped the barking in the closet and not stopped the threats of killing me?

This was complete nonsense, and my visits with her faded. I knew I could not continue therapy with a woman who believed this and who prescribed scriptures and prayer as treatment for abuse. Her answer, in fact, left me stunned for many years to come.

It was getting near the time we needed to print up the wedding announcements and invitations, and I was panicking. Our bishop told us that if for some reason the clearance to get married didn't come back, we could still get married in the temple for time, but it would not be possible for eternity. In other words, at one point, it was common for couples who could not get sealed to a second or third wife, but were found worthy, to get married in the temple "until death do us part." Our bishop informed us that we would have the same option if needed, because we were both found worthy to be there. With this knowledge, we went ahead and printed and mailed out our announcements and added that the marriage would be performed in the Logan, Utah Temple.

About two weeks before our wedding date, I was asking Mr. Bill every day if he had heard anything, and the answer was always the same: no. Five days before our wedding, he asked me if he could meet me at work during my lunch break. I knew for sure that he had finally gotten the clearance and he was coming to celebrate with me in person. I anxiously kept my eyes toward the office door, waiting for him to walk through with a relieved but excited face.

Instead, he walked through the door with a straight face, completely absent of any joy or elation. I thought maybe he was acting and doing this on purpose, especially when he asked if he could pull up a chair and sit next to me. He grabbed me by the hands, made me look him in the eye, and told me the news: we had been denied.

"You're joking, aren't you?" I said.

"No, I am not. We were denied, and here is the letter of proof."

There it was, a second white envelope from church headquarters declaring we were not allowed to be sealed in the temple. There was no reason, no indication as to why, other than four words: "this needs more time."

Mr. Bill was quiet, allowing me to sit in the moment

and process what this meant. My silence and confusion made him say, "We can call off the wedding, and I would understand if you don't want to marry me," he said. Rather than give him another second of self-doubt, I told him, "Hell no. At least the bishop said we can still get married in the temple for time."

Later that evening we met with the bishop, who had also received the letter. After making a few phone calls ,he informed us we would actually not be able to marry in the temple for time. He had not been aware of it, but the church was slowly doing away with this practice and allowing only a select few geriatric couples to do so. He had misinformed us.

The dream of a temple wedding crumbled before my eyes, and we were five days out from our scheduled date. My soon-to-be husband continued to give me a chance to back out, but I wouldn't do it. The only option I considered was figuring out how to plan a civil wedding in the next 120 hours. This meant I would have to find a venue and call all of our family and friends to inform them of the change.

The bigger issue at play wasn't just coming to grips with receiving a denial, but also the underlying shame that was instantly heaped upon me and my fiancé. Surely people would wonder, speculate, and gossip. I battled with the stress of others assuming something was wrong with Mr. Bill, or that the two of us hadn't been able to stop ourselves from having sex.

There is a pressure in Mormonism to keep engagements short, out of fear that Satan will work hard on the couple and prevent them from worthily achieving the "new and everlasting covenant of marriage." What consumes most couples prior to the temple ceremony is the realization that you are both about to have sex. Your whole life, the conversation around sex revolves around it being bad or it being sacred. Never can it be good, wonderful, and fun.

So when the clock is ticking and you're both about to lose your virginity, the only thing that really devours your mind is what happens after the reception ends. Some couples are so anxious to consummate the marriage, they do it in their car the minute the temple ordinance is complete.

How was I going to tell my parents that after years of waiting for a temple marriage, their daughter had been denied the holiest of ordinances by the prophet of the church himself? Mr. Bill suggested we put it off another year and go through the process again so I could have what I had yearned for for so long, but I wouldn't do it. I did not want to wait another year to start my life with him or to have sex.

We broke the news to our family, told them we would not be waiting a year and that we would be planning a civil wedding. I went to work getting things figured out, and fortunately, the notorious Old Rock Church in Providence was available.

While working through the formalities of it all, though, I panicked when no one was looking. What did this *really* mean? Did God know something about Mr. Bill that I didn't know? What if he was a monster like you, and this was another warning? I called you up during this time and proposed my fears of him being like you. You were confused by what I meant, but of course you would be—I had never confronted you about your abuse.

What if God wasn't upset with Mr. Bill after all? What if our denial stemmed from me ignoring God's warning about you? What if this was actually all my fault? My nerves were shot, not by the excitement in the days leading up to my marriage, but by shame and confusion.

I stayed with my sister the evening before the big day. I tossed and turned all night, second-guessing exchanging vows with Mr. Bill. Was I making the right decision or was the denial to the temple another warning? I got up and searched for some melatonin and downed more than the recommended dose so that I could get my mind to shut down. I climbed onto my knees in front of the couch I was sleeping on and poured my heart out to God, begging him to tell me if I was making a mistake. After falling asleep, I had a dream that gave me my answer.

In the dream, I was walking down the aisle toward a faceless man. After completing the wedding march, I turned and stood before the man, lifted my veil, and looked into the face of a complete stranger. I frantically looked around, searched for Mr. Bill, and could not find him anywhere. In my dream, I knew that the one I was supposed to spend my life with was Mr. Bill, not the faceless man. I woke up in complete relief, realizing the dream was not real and that I was hours away from marrying the one man that had always made me feel safe and grounded.

The morning of December 8, 2007, was snowy and cold. Cache Valley had a snowstorm during the night, and the roads were a mess. We arrived at the Old Rock Church early for a photo shoot, performed by my handsome gay friend Travis. My colors were a deep pink with hints of chocolate brown. While everyone gathered in their seats for the ceremony, I was upstairs getting ready. My dress was very modest and temple-worthy, so it covered my chest and my shoulders, but it had a beautiful lace-up backing. I could not get married in any other shoes than the white pleather hooker boots that I loved to wear. My hair was dark brown, almost black, and tied up on top of my head in curls with bobby pins. My flower girls were my two young nieces, Sarah and Brandy, and our ring bearer was Mr. Bill's cousin, Cody, who happened to have Down syndrome.

I was waiting at the top of the beautiful spiral staircase when the ever-famous "Pachelbel's Canon in D" came on, cueing me that it was time. I looked down the staircase and saw the bright blue eyes of my father staring up at me.

In that moment, before I took my first step down, I felt a mixture of joy and sadness. I felt joy that my father would actually get to walk me down the aisle, a tradition that does not take place in the temple, and sadness that I had let him down. They were two fierce but fleeting thoughts, and without much more thinking, my feet started moving. I was slowly walking down the grand staircase, terrified that I was going to trip and end up at the bottom with my ass and white hooker boots in the air.

After a successful walk down the steps, I connected my arm through my father's, and we finished our walk to Mr. Bill and the bishop. My father gave me a tight hug and a kiss on the cheek, and then let me go. He took his place just to the side of us to stand as a witness of our matrimony. I don't recall a single word the bishop said, as I could not take my eyes off Mr. Bill. He looked so damn handsome in his brown pin-striped suit and pink tie. His big, beautiful brown eyes peered back at me, and it would be one of the few times I would see tears glistening within them. He was happy and I was happy. In this moment, it was not some stranger's face from my dream that I was gazing into, it was the face of eternity.

Deep down, I knew we were both worthy to go to the temple, I knew we both wanted it, and in my heart, that's all that mattered. He was willing to take me there and he never shamed me or tried to get me to run from it, even at the cost of being denied an eternal marriage. He was so adamant to give me my dream that he had been willing to wait an entire year to give it to me. His eyes were telling me he was a man that was going to support me in anything and everything my heart could ever want.

This moment felt infinite and immortal, an accomplished feeling of amaranthine, and I knew no temple could ever take this away from me. I had finally married the right person, at the right time, and though it wasn't the right place in the eyes of my religion, my friends, or my family, it was the right place for me.

We exchanged rings, said our *I dos*, and transacted a G-rated but blissful French kiss. With roughly seventy-five people in attendance, we spent time receiving the typical congratulations and well-wishes, as well as more time posing for the cameraman. Our reception was not set until later in the evening, so we decided to have a luncheon at a nearby Mormon church. I had composed and written a song for Mr. Bill, and while our guests fed their bellies, I played and serenaded the audience.

I have never been gifted at singing and can admit I performed horribly. It was so bad that my father hugged me and told me never to sing in public again. He was half-kidding but also half-serious. He spoke the truth and I wasn't offended; he was right. Mr. Bill loved it, not just the wording, but the fact that I would even attempt to sing publicly was enough for him to appreciate the effort. This was my gift to him, and he recognized it as such.

I was not aware that he had prepared a gift to present to me as well. Months prior, we had picked out some beautiful logs in Park City with a friend, and Mr. Bill and the friend had spent months building a log bed for us. He transported the bed to the luncheon hall and set it up for everyone to see.

The reception later that night was lighthearted and fun. My Aunt Denise is a guitarist and lead singer in a band called The Rocky Mountain Express, and they gave us two and a half hours of entertainment and dancing. We kept refreshments light by offering a hot chocolate bar, brownies, and doughnuts. Many of my friends in the special needs community showed up to celebrate with us. It was truly a beautiful evening filled with rejoicing, music, and laughter.

After cutting and serving the cake, things started to wind down quickly. With most of our guests departing, it was time to leave the church and begin our honeymoon. I found my mother, father, and mother-in-law and gave them all big hugs, thanking them for all that they did to make this happen. I'm not sure the true feelings of my father on this day. However, I believe, for the most part, he was happy and content with the fact his youngest daughter had finally found a decent Mormon man to begin her life with.

I was adamant that even though we were denied a temple marriage, we wait until after the reception to consummate our marriage. I had waited almost thirty years for this. Losing my virginity inside of a car or quickly after the ceremony was not an option. I also wanted God to know that I was going to hold onto my virtue and honor Mormonism's rule about no sex before marriage.

I could have easily told Mr. Bill the moment we got that denial letter that I no longer cared, and to hell with it, let's go ahead and have sex. But I didn't. I was going to prove to God that I could still be a good and faithful Mormon girl, despite the rejection from his one true prophet on the earth.

Hand in hand, Mr. Bill and I climbed into our decorated car and made our way to the historic Anniversary Inn. I had a constant prayer in my heart that on the five-mile drive to the hotel that we wouldn't be killed in a tragic car accident. If this happened, my marriage would have been over before it had a chance to begin.

Without the sealing power from the temple uniting us, I would be eternally screwed and he would forever be sealed to his ex-wife. These thoughts would plague me for the coming year, but for that night, I tucked them into a small corner of my brain and had one hell of a night shedding my status as a twenty-nine-year-old virgin.

My dear rapist, flashbacks of the night on my bed, the barking in the closet, threats of killing me, and you bragging about being halfway in briefly entered my mind as

Bill and I began to make love. For a few moments, I felt I was in two places at once. I was trying to enjoy the nirvana I was experiencing with Mr. Bill, yet I was having dark memories of you.

I did not want to ruin my honeymoon with thoughts of you, and eventually found a way to push you out of my mind. With a final self-conviction, I told myself that you no longer mattered. Justice for your crimes was not of my concern in this life, I knew God would hold you accountable on judgment day. All that mattered was that I was safe in the arms of my husband, a man I deeply and unconditionally loved.

In the end, I finally gave to Mr. Bill what you took from me: I gave him me, I gave him all of me. I extended the invitation to enter and become one. There was no taking, no begging, and no demanding.

What existed between Mr. Bill and I was a connection so deep and so divine that our level of communication existed without ever having to say one word to each other. For one night, I allowed myself to forget that I did not achieve the sought-after temple marriage and instead gave my all to Mr. Bill and the half-dozen home runs we were hitting in the bedroom.

Never Yours,
A Telestial Wife

CHAPTER 15

I AM NO EVE

"The first commandment that God gave to Adam and Eve pertained to their potential for parenthood as husband and wife. We declare that God's commandment for His children to multiply and replenish the earth remains in force."

(The Family, A Proclamation to the World, par 4)

My Dear Rapist,

Mr. Bill and I got busy. Within a month of our marriage, I was pregnant. Mr. Bill was a blessed man marrying a pent-up virgin. We re-consummated our marriage at least two or three times a day for many months, mostly at my instigation.

The more memories I created with him, the more I was beginning to forget you. I was planting new seeds in my life and by doing so, you were being compacted deep into the farthest corners of my 120-pound frame.

Blissful and happy, Mr. Bill and I were modeling Adam and Eve, ready to multiply and replenish the earth. Mr. Bill continued working as an engineer and I either had my head in a toilet or got busy nesting and preparing for the impending arrival of baby number one.

We had decided to save our real honeymoon for the summer, so for our six-month anniversary, we booked a camping and kayaking trip to Seward, Alaska. We arrived in Anchorage and hopped onto the Alaskan Railroad, taking an exquisite coastal ride south.

The four hour and twenty-minute ride departed at 6:45 a.m. and took us through the scenic Turnagain Arm. This is one of the most magnificent places on earth, a place where the mountains and the trees meet the ocean. To the left, we were able to see Dall sheep standing on the steep rocky edges of the mountain cliffs. On the right, we watched for beluga whales moving with the incoming tide.

Once we left the Turnagain Arm, we entered into the wilderness of the Kenai Mountains. Just before reaching the alluring glacial silt waters of the turquoise Kenai Lake, we had the most pristine views of the Spencer and Bartlett Glaciers. Around 11:30 a.m., we pulled into Seward, a small city resting peacefully on a Kenai Fjord called Resurrection Bay. Mr. Bill and I grabbed our backpacks and walked through downtown Seward toward a two-mile dirt road that would take us to Miller's Landing. To the left was the salty ocean with random little sea otters floating on their backs, and off to the right was a steep mountainside with a massive, flowing waterfall.

Upward in the gray skies, we witnessed several bald eagles flying unchallenged and free.

Walking up to Miller's Landing made me feel like I was in Mother Nature's celestial room. We were surrounded by striking, snow-capped mountains and a forest of trees rising from the waters. We walked into a world so quiet that we could hear seagulls diving for fish and the reticent spout from a humpback whale. Mother Nature herself seemed to open her arms and say, "Welcome home. Here, you will find my God."

The check-in process took place within an older wooden, rectangular store that sold Alaska merch, coffee, and a small amount of café-style food. Outside, the building had a large, covered deck with several rocking chairs, old boat netting, and buoys hanging from the railing. The tide was in, so Mr. Bill and I took a moment to breathe in the glorious view of Resurrection Bay.

In the distance, we could see random fishing boats anchored down, waiting to catch their limit of salmon or cod for the day. A few fishing captains were lounging around, inhaling the same cool, misty air as Mr. Bill and I. Our arrival could not have been more perfect. In the middle of the bay, we had the privilege of watching a magnificent humpback whale put on a performance while he breached for us.

As we obtained the keys and directions to our tiny tree cabin, we were informed that a grizzly bear had been in the campground the day prior to our arrival. The realization that we were in bear country startled me. I had no idea bears would wander into an area like this. I ignorantly believed they stayed in more remote areas like Glacier Bay, not in an area filled with campers, kayakers, hikers, fishermen, and tourists.

I had no reason to impress Mr. Bill, so after arriving at our tree cabin and discovering we had no toilet, I asked him to go find a bucket. The nearest bathroom was thirty feet away, and I would not be taking any risks. The thought of a grizzly bear smelling my extra pheromones, due to the five-month-old fetus growing inside of me, forced me to relieve myself into a white five-gallon bucket throughout the duration of our honeymoon.

We stayed three nights in Seward, with our favorite adventure being an overnight kayaking experience in Kayaker's Cove. We were required to take a twelve-mile water taxi across Resurrection Bay to reach our cabin in a lovely, secluded wilderness haven. Mr. Bill and I spent the next two days exploring Alaska through a quiet, isolated sector of the bay.

From our tandem kayak, we got up close and personal with harbor seals, sea otters, and sea lions. It was just the two of us, Mother Earth, and our tiny little baby girl brewing inside my belly. A major benefit of this remote area was the communal outhouse we shared with the other guests. I received a two-day break from my bucket, a bucket my husband had so graciously emptied for me every day.

We ended our time in Seward on a Last Frontier honeymoon high. I knew my husband would fall in love with Alaska, and together, we discussed our desire to move back someday. On our train ride back to Anchorage, the Universe confirmed she had heard our discussion of moving and gently nudged me into a free-flowing conversation with a random woman sitting across the aisle.

Mr. Bill was standing on the outside balcony of the train, admiring the scenery surrounding us, when this strange woman and I began talking. She was a nurse in Anchorage and her family owned a commercial fishing business during the summer. Her husband also owned and operated an engineering firm in South Anchorage and, half joking, I inquired if they were hiring.

She mentioned that they were, and I asked her if we could pause the conversation so I could retrieve my husband. For the remainder of the ride, she and Mr. Bill spoke about the details of her husband's company and exchanged phone numbers, with a promise that they would both stay in touch.

The next three years are a blur in time. Mr. Bill spoke with the engineering firm in Alaska, but chose to accept a position in Grand Junction, Colorado. Within those next three years, we would have three children back to back and move four more times. The call to multiply and replenish the earth stirred deep within me. I was an old Mormon woman and had felt my eggs were on the verge of rot. I felt an urgency to get our spirit children to Earth as fast as possible.

Though my thoughts of you had receded, my negative coping mechanisms did not. The vices of trauma carried over into each one of my pregnancies, resulting in preterm labor and strict bed rest. These complications hit at thirty-two weeks with my first two babies and then at twenty weeks with my third baby.

Midway during my first pregnancy, I started having problems with my bowels and the experienced midwife suggested I take a natural laxative that would be a safe means for me to relieve myself from the pains of constipation. Though I had felt secure and unscathed by Mr. Bill, hearing the word safe from my midwife flipped an internal switch. This would begin my addiction to laxatives, another negative coping mechanism to add to my already two years of anorexia.

From January 2008 until November 2012, I was cultivating and nursing my babies while restricting and purging the food that was required to nourish them. I did not comprehend the damage this behavior could do to me or my newborns. I did not know that this need to control my input and output of food was a coping mechanism from your abuse. It would take years to realize that the reasons my body continued to go into preterm labor was a result of PTSD and my lack of nutrition. Your abuse did not just harm me, but it was harming the precious forms sprouting inside of me.

I was often in and out of postpartum depression and experiencing rough bouts of anxiety. I had no family members around to help and I felt profoundly alone. I wanted to support my husband and be with him where he needed to be for his career, but I struggled with being away from my family. I had not envisioned living six hours away with my first baby and not having grandparents, aunts, uncles, and cousins to love and spoil her. I felt disgruntled and resentful. I was certain my baby deserved and needed the same upbringing I had received. I ultimately resigned myself to believing that everything happened for a reason, and perhaps the meth-stained house that we were living in was exactly where the Lord needed us to be.

Three months after our baby girl was born in Colorado, we made the six-hour drive back to Utah and were sealed in the Logan Temple. I had just spent the last year living with intense consternation, believing that God was still mad at me for ignoring his warning about you.

I truly believed God wanted to punish me and would remove either Mr. Bill or my baby from this world, and withhold the blessings of an eternal sealing. Whenever Mr. Bill traveled for work, which was often, I would fall down on my knees and beg God to bring him home safely. Every hiccup, cough, or fever with my baby caused me to panic, believing that it was her time to die.

My dear rapist, I was often waiting for another lesson or punishment to remind me of God's damning consequences for rejecting him.

I was also on edge with my own life. If something happened to me and I ended up dying, according to Mormon doctrine, my baby would eternally belong to Mr. Bill and his ex-wife. The sealing practice of families can be a convoluted mess at times, and the general answer to put one at ease is, "Don't worry, God will figure it out in the next life." Perhaps for those who have never been in this predicament, this sentiment can be comforting. To the one who is living it, not so much. I consistently doubted if Mr. Bill would choose me in the next life. His ex-wife had not remarried, which meant the prospect of being his eternal second wife and sharing my babies with her was a realistic form of hell that could someday be my fate.

God ultimately had mercy on me. Mr. Bill finally received clearance from the prophet and apostles to take me and our baby girl to the temple. On January 27, 2009, we entered into the new and everlasting covenant of marriage, and I could now consider myself marked safe from losing Mr. Bill and my baby to his first wife. While I had finally found solitude that I had reached this goal, my spirit felt like it was being pulled into a riptide of shame. God, that damn shame always seemed to be lurking, hiding in every corner, ever ready to envelop me at every turn.

How many of my loved ones found it a coincidence that we were not just sealing ourselves to each other but to a three-month-old baby girl? Surely, I thought to myself, they all believed I fornicated with Mr. Bill and that it was unworthiness that had kept us from having an original temple marriage. I wanted to stand up and proclaim our innocence and brag that the temple denial did not sway us from staying pure until the exchange of our civil vows.

I wanted to weep, weep for joy that I had finally made it here, but weep in sorrow that, by all appearances, my baby was an indication I philandered away my pledge to remain chaste. Like any good Mormon girl would do, I packed the filthy shame away and I put my shoulder to

the wheel and pressed on. I was determined to prove them
all wrong with my faithfulness, and I became adamant in
not giving a fuck about the possible stories regarding my
virginity.

Never Yours,
A Spiritually Polygamous Wife

***

My Dear Rapist,

In the fall of 2010, we had returned to living in our
Holladay, Utah, home and Mr. Bill's employment was in
question. The recession was still affecting the oil industry
and knowing he may not have a future with his current
employer, as well as being tired of the travel requirement,
he began to consider other employment opportunities. As
if on cue, the Universe heard our discussion again. The
engineering firm in Alaska contacted Mr. Bill and inquired
if he would be interested in a position with them, and before
we knew it, he was flying off to Anchorage for an interview.

By November, Mr. Bill had given his notice, accepted
the engineering position in Alaska, and we had begun the
process of moving our family 3,000 miles away from home.
On December 28, 2010, we officially started our lives in
Alaska. Our oldest daughter had just turned two years old
and our son had just turned nine months old. We didn't know
a single person in our new homeland, but fortunately, we
found no need to stress due to our place in Mormonism. We
knew the area we would be moving into had a large Mormon

presence, and this would allow us to define the members as a sort of makeshift family. Moving to this cold, dark, frozen tundra began as a thrilling adventure. Mr. Bill and I were both very excited to return to the rugged frontier where I had pooped in a white plastic bucket while five months pregnant. As he busied himself with getting to know his new responsibilities as an Alaskan engineer, I began networking and making friends with our new church family.

Within the first three months of our move, I was called to the Relief Society Presidency at church. I was just a lowly secretary, but felt this was a huge gift to help get to know others and feel included. In the first meeting, the first counselor shared with me a horrific story that still haunts me thirteen years later. The subdivision in which she lived had over 900 private single-family homes on 250 acres.

The subdivision was set up by a strict HOA to ensure the residents preserved the natural beauty and the lighted trail system throughout its vast, wooded acreage. The paved trail system intrinsically lured in a plethora of brown bears, black bears, and moose that inhabited the area. When spring arrived, it was not uncommon for moose to calve their offspring right on the cemented pathways. The residents not only had to be on high alert for the aggressive mama moose protecting its young, but also for the bears that were chasing the baby moose for a tasty dinner.

The friendly woman decided to share with me the details of the National Geographic moment that had taken place in the middle of her driveway. One night, while she was asleep, she awoke to the sound of a blood curdling shriek. The wailing she heard was so loud and so piercing, she was certain a child was being murdered. She climbed out of bed and looked out her bedroom window to see if she could see the source of the pain-filled cry. Due to it being summer and living in the land of the midnight sun, she could clearly see the origin of the early morning squall that had brought her out of her sleep. Her discovery was not that of a child being murdered, but of a baby calf being eaten alive by a large brown bear.

As a young mother of two children, this was not only horrifying, but it was also paralyzing. This was not the story I needed to hear within my first few months of moving to Alaska. I was already in PTSD mode from you. Her story added another layer to a nervous system that had been living in fight or flight for more than four years.

Rather than get out and brave the neighborhood trail system or the ruggedness of the Chugach Mountain Range, I opted for more sex. More sex meant another pregnancy, and another pregnancy meant another preterm labor. Come May, I was twenty weeks pregnant and was placed on strict bed rest. 3,000 miles away from home and after only four months of living in a transient Mormon ward, I had no close friends to ask for daily help. The ward did the best they could to offer meals, but understandably, everyone was too busy to be a mother to my two children under the age of two.

October arrived and our third child made his appearance. He was healthy, happy, and showed up with a full head of hair. I was thirty-three years old, and in the three years since marrying Mr. Bill, I had given birth to our third child. A doctor informed us we should seriously consider ceasing our efforts at being Adam and Eve. More than likely, my body would reject future babies earlier and earlier, and with this last one wanting to be expelled at twenty weeks, the baby and I would be too high-risk. He also informed us that if a baby is born before twenty weeks in Alaska, the baby and the mother would be required to fly to Seattle. Neither of us would be able to leave the hospital until the baby was at least thirty-eight weeks old.

We would later learn this was not true, but with the fear of this happening, along with the medical expenses and the lack of help for our three children, we opted for Mr. Bill to get his spaghetti noodles snipped. Within three years of being married, and a month after the birth of our third child, our days of reproducing had come to an end.

While I was overwhelmed with mothering three children and no family around, deep down, I was devastated and jaded. Why did God not bless me with a healthier womb? I had been a devout, faithful Mormon girl. Was this just another punishment for ignoring him? Once again, my life was not turning out like it should for a Mormon girl.

First, I didn't get married as young as I had hoped, and now I wasn't getting the chance to have half a dozen kids like I had planned. I spent a short time mourning the loss of having more children, but was soon overridden with the stress of three kids under the age of three. I was becoming the Tasmanian Devil on steroids, spiraling out of control as a young mother.

It is often said that the sign of a mental breakdown for a woman is when she impulsively cuts off her hair. I had long, beautiful, thick black hair, and in one hour, the beautician made me look like the lovechild of Rod Stewart and Blanche from the *Golden Girls*. Rather than recognize my desperation for help, one particular woman from church decided to spread rumors that I was a lesbian. On several occasions, I had overheard her sharing that a male neighbor used to flirt with her, until he saw her with me. Assuming I was her lesbian lover, he decided he could no longer flirt with her.

This same woman also called Child Protective Services on Mr. Bill. She admitted to me once that she used to observe my husband at church and how involved he was as a father. It bothered her, in her eyes, and without ever speaking more than ten words to Mr. Bill, she believed he was controlling and abusive. She claimed that a man could not be this involved with his children without being a domineering, vituperative man.

The woman's husband was our home teacher, assigned to minister to us as a family in our home, and he did not have an active partner. Home teaching is a sort of check-in process for the church to see how families are doing and whether they need any help. Normally, home teachers minister in pairs, and instead of finding another priesthood leader to join him, he would bring along his wife.

They had been in our home less than three times, and with her already-formed bias, she did not like the way my husband joked about our potty-training techniques. Between her observations at church and his deadpan jests, she took it upon herself to call CPS. Thank God that Child Protective Services found the claims absurd and unwarranted. In fact, her claims were so fatuous, the investigation did not go past her phone call. We did not actually learn of this until several years later, after an intense international adoption. One phone call by this self-righteous, prissy bitch could have cost us the addition of our beloved fourth child.

To help cope with the stress, I lost myself into a world of painting and refinishing antique and vintage furniture. My self-esteem was founded in the likes, loves, and followers on my social media business page. My home décor and restoration business exploded. I survived off Dr. Pepper and saltine crackers while I sanded, painted, and stained furniture. The more beat up and rugged the furniture, the better.

I unconsciously resonated with each piece that moved into and out of my home. The nick here, the scratch there, the water-damaged top, the peeling veneer, all promulgated a story to me. The damage and the blemishes simply added character to the old wooden dressers, hutches, buffets, and dining sets that found their way into my isolated universe. Every piece breathed a desire to be restored and perfected to a state that only I, the master, could declare complete.

My thriving and growing furniture business, in many ways, saved me. It connected me to new friends and new social circles. As I struggled immensely with fitting into Mormonism, I found a new tribe and community that seemed to accept me and want me around. In my eight years of business, I focused on custom orders, furniture shows, and giveaways.

I loved giving a piece of myself to the furniture lovers of Alaska—at least someone in this world valued and appreciated my gifts. My local Mormon congregation seemed to be either indifferent to or annoyed by me. My kids were incapable of showing any form of appreciation for my poor attempts at mothering, and my eating disorder continued to brew underneath the chaos of my unbalanced, failing Mormon life. The one thing I had going for me was my artwork. My cravings to paint and sand were so profound, I once calculated that I completed over 800 projects while raising three young children. In retrospect, I wasn't really trying to restore and fix the furniture, I was attempting to upcycle and renovate myself.

The more I worked on furniture, the more I avoided the chaos of three children, and the more I compacted your trauma. I was seeking spirituality through prayer, church music, and scripture study. I was not finding connection within my church family. My testimony of the social aspect of Mormonism was deteriorating, and I started to avoid church gatherings during the week, only keeping myself in active status on Sundays.

I continued to have my one recurring nightmare of you, and after speaking with the bishop, he suggested I try counseling again. Others were still confiding in me or referring their girlfriends to me to converse about their loved ones with a porn addiction, and it was increasingly affecting my relationship and trust of Mr. Bill.

Though I was unconsciously compacting you down, my dreams were a constant reminder that there was a part of you still living inside of me. If I could have taken a laxative with your name on it, I would have. I did not know how to function, and would often express to Mr. Bill that something was wrong with me and that I had always been able to handle life before meeting you. Panic attacks became a norm, as well as trying different forms of antidepressants and anti-anxiety meds. The bishop sent me to see an LDS therapist in Anchorage. The single and only option was a retired social worker who was on a service mission for the church. I spent a solo session with the senescent counselor, giving him my history of dating porn-addicted Mormon men and a detailed history of your abuse.

I also confided how I had become an untrained therapist, always hearing stories of Mormon women and their betrayal trauma from their sex-addicted loved ones. After listening to my rambles for an hour, he finally spewed out seven words that quickly shut me up: "But men are wired differently than women." I promptly ended our session and left his office, giving up on therapy once again.

My heart began yearning for something more, something different. I was not sure what this meant, but I knew something was missing in our life and we needed a change. Moving back to Utah was not an option. Mr. Bill loved the career opportunities and experiences that he was gaining as an engineer in Alaska. I knew where I needed to be to get my answers. I believed the only place to get intimate revelation from God was inside his holy house.

I called up the Anchorage Temple and scheduled an appointment. I was anxious to push through the endowment of the temple experience and get my exhausted mom body into a chair inside the Celestial Room. This space is every Mormon mother's mecca for meditation. With no screaming kids around, no spaghetti sauce stains on the wall, no smell of a poopy diaper in the trash bin, and not a single toddler handprint on the window, this realm easily becomes a refuge from the chaos of motherhood. The Celestial Room is truly one of the only places on earth where a Mormon mother can find her tranquility.

My dear rapist, during one such mecca moment, I began pondering on my relationship with you. It had been seven long years since we had split, and I simply wanted to believe that God not only loved me, but could forgive me for my ignorance. I craved his approval. I entered the Anchorage Temple alone, more ready than ever to shed my crimson-stained spirit. I prayed for a sign, seeking validation that my sins from being complicit in your abuse would turn white. From the veil on my head to the silken slippers upon my feet, shame and guilt reared their ugly faces and completely washed over me and my holy robe. For several minutes I sat in it, embracing the heavy waves of my own spiritual filth.

Soon, the minutes gave way and, like the tide moving across the Alaskan ocean floor, the soiled waves began to recede. In its place, waves of purity and light enveloped me, cleansing me of your filth. An inner voice, something surely divine, told me I had been forgiven and that my cancerous soul was headed into a form of remission. The redeeming power of God's love overtook my loins, my sinews, and the very marrow of my bones. The longer I sat there, the more my spirit became weightless, white, and as pure as freshly fallen snow.

I left the 12,000-square-foot granite pantheon on Brayton Drive washed, anointed, and sanctified by the atoning blood of Jesus Christ. With redemption now flowing through my blood, thoughts of you became more sparse. The only time you made an appearance was within the ink of my pen as I filled out medical history forms. Checking off the *rape and abuse* box brought out brief memories of your athletic hands, but they dissolved when contemplating the need to check off the remaining twenty symptomatic boxes. My one reoccurring dream of you began to fade as dreams of an unknown child began to amplify.

I had come to believe that my days of multiplying and replenishing the earth were over. When Mr. Bill's noodles had been snipped, so were my dreams of having more children. However, when the dreams and visions of a strange child started to appear, I really began to wonder who this rediscovered God was.

My dear rapist, it is often said in Mormonism that "where much is given, much is required." With the unexpected gift of his forgiveness, it appeared God felt it was my turn to give back; I just needed a little nudge. In the same manner he spoke to me about you, he spoke to me about her. With you, he whispered fear into my soul, but with her it was a knowing.

With her, it was a deep, internal astuteness that Mr. Bill and I were about to embark on a divine and hallowed path to find our fourth child. The sweetened nectar of God's exoneration was a celestial potion. It aided the opening of my eyes to a variegated labyrinth of his divine hand. In the center of his palm was her, our fourth child, signifying that the command for us to propagate more children was not coming to an end after all.

Never Yours,
Never an Eve

CHAPTER 16

AN APOSTATE TRAITRESS

"Remember: when you see the bitter apostate, you do not see only an absence of light, you see also the presence of darkness. Do not spread disease germs... Save for those few who defect to perdition after having known a fullness, there is no habit, no addiction, no rebellion, no transgression, no offense exempted from the promise of complete forgiveness."

(Conference Talks and Ensign Articles, 1981 The Mantle is Far, Far Greater than the Intellect, 1995 The Brilliant Morning of Forgiveness, Packer, Boyd K.)

My Dear Rapist,

It was in the middle of the night, sometime in the fall, when I was driving down the vast, unlit, and empty road of Sutton, Alaska. I had been driving for some time when my headlights picked up on something ahead, lying in the middle of the road. Its form was oddly shaped, and it did not move. My instincts told me that it was not an injured animal, but that I should still proceed with caution to avoid hitting the mysterious object.

Struggling to identify the small mass in the road, I forced myself to leave the safety of my car to determine what it was. I opened my door, placed my feet on the asphalt, and moved myself to the side of the vehicle. With my beam lights on high, the bright rays landed upon an infant car seat. I rushed to the silent carrier and spun it around, expecting a baby to cry out in dismay. Lying inside the camel-colored plastic seat was a bundled-up, weightless blanket.

The moment my brain registered a missing infant, two vehicles were approaching from opposite directions. I grabbed the carrier and hurried back to my car. Just as I had locked the doors, several men came running from their trucks and proceeded to shout at me in Spanish. I did not understand the language, but the tone of voice and expressions on their faces said enough. I knew these men had the child, and if I did not act quickly, my chances of finding the missing infant would be slim. There was an exasperated insistence to their demeanor, and it alarmed me to the point that I woke up.

I could not make sense of the dream. Why an infant, and why was the dream in Spanish? This distinct vision appeared in the spring of 2014, and it was a catalyst to receiving months of strong thoughts and impressions that I could not shake off. I knew Mr. Bill and I were meant to add one more child to our family, but I did not know how to make it happen.

I began my research into Alaska's foster care program, believing this could be an easy and inexpensive route to adoption. After attending a foster care workshop and asking some really difficult questions, I felt this was not the path for us, at least not at this time. I would often find myself on my knees, asking God to lead us in the right direction, and placing the burden on him to present the much-needed signs on how to go about finding our child.

In the summer of 2014, our family spent some time in the charming town of Homer, Alaska. Resting on the shore of Kachemak Bay, this small coastal community on the Kenai Peninsula is known to be the halibut fishing capital of the world. One of its most remarkable features is the Homer Spit, a four-and-a-half-mile gravel bar that juts out into the ocean. Along the spit, you can find restaurants, tourist shops, and access to a boat harbor filled with fishing boats, ferries, cruise ships, and sailboats.

Off to the right is an old wooden boardwalk, and when the tide is out, you can climb onto a swing underneath the tattered wood and breathe in the salty air of the mystical ocean. Another favorite adventure, when the tide is out, is foraging through wet rocks to hunt for hermit crabs, octopus, mussels, and starfish. There is a good reason why Homer has earned the nickname of "the Cosmic Hamlet by the Sea." In addition to what I have described here, the clear view of

Grewingk Glacier, Mount Redoubt, and Mount Iliamna make Homer one of the most enchanting end-of-the road terrains you will ever step foot on.

My mother-in-law happened to be visiting this summer when we decided to make a trip and explore Homer. It was a beautiful, clear day with bright blue skies and vibrant long rays extending from the sun. Summers in Homer average fifty-six degrees Fahrenheit and always seems to have a constant breeze in the air. We decided to walk along the east side of the spit and enjoy the shopping in the handful of tourist shops. We drew close to a small, beloved alpaca sweater store, and I was anxious to take my mother-in-law inside and show her the eclectic, delicate wool attire that they had to offer.

I had been in the store a dozen times and had never noticed anything designed for a child. Hanging from the outdoor ceiling, right before the entrance into the main area, was a beautiful cream, pink, and blue dress. The moment I saw the dress, a glimpse of a little girl with dark skin and textured hair filled its flowing form. While staring at the dainty pinafore, I grabbed my mother-in-law's arm and muttered, "The child we are meant to find is a girl." I pulled the dress down from above, paid for it, and told myself that it would hang by my bedside until we found her.

From this moment on, God took our family on a miraculous, difficult, and divine journey to Colombia. For eighteen months, we prayed, we cried, and we fought to bring home our youngest child. This challenging odyssey instilled a deep reverence in us as we witnessed marvel after marvel of the Divine's hand in the process. We observed constant acts of love and support from family, friends, and church members as we raised the necessary funds for an international special-needs adoption. The Spanish-speaking men in my dream proved their appearance was not mere coincidence, as our adopted daughter is of Hispanic descent.

My dear rapist, I have pondered on how much detail I want to share, but the experiences we had in this journey are too sacred to share with you. It did take a long, grueling road to find her, and by the grace of God, we eventually brought her home. However, my purpose in bringing her to light is to accentuate my gratitude for the Divine and for instilling a conviction that there is an exquisite, higher power involved in each of our lives.

I often reflect on the serendipitous journey to our daughter and how the Divine made a constant and strong appearance just one year prior to the dissolution of my belief in the Mormon God. This conviction of a Divine power pulled me through the depths of despair when our Mormonism faith fell apart. Even more so, eventually it pushed me to pursue justice for your criminal behavior.

For now, I am *not* ready to share with you the depths of my spirituality and my views on Jesus and The Divine. I was taught in Mormonism to wear my spiritual and religious beliefs on my sleeve, to shout them to the world in the hopes of bringing others to Jesus and Mormonism. Culturally, it was also ingrained in members to hide our imperfections and humanity because the "natural man is an enemy to God."

After doing this for forty years, I am choosing to do the opposite for the last half of my life. I prefer to keep my spirituality and my feelings about Jesus and The Divine close to my heart. I am opting to wear my humanity and imperfections on my sleeve. In fact, I no longer believe my humanity is offensive to the Divine. I believe that God loves and honors my imperfections and is incredibly proud of my ability to be vulnerable and real.

When Jesus appeared to Doubting Thomas, he invited the beloved apostle to touch his wounds to discover that his existence was real. Jesus didn't ask him to behold his perfections, he invited him to observe the markings of his pain. In this way, I want to be more like Jesus. This is all you need to know about where I stand.

Never Yours,
Embraced by Jesus and the Divine

***

My Dear Rapist,

Because Mormonism played such a vital role in our relationship, I would like to share with you the details of my apostasy and the explosion of a forty-year belief system. The in-depth details of unpacking Mormonism, pursuing justice, and healing from you will be shared in a future compilation of letters. For now, I'd like to describe a portion of the agonizing, yet freeing process of leaving Mormonism.

For forty years, I lived and breathed in Mormonism without having a prominent reason to doubt its truth claims. I had no education and no aspiring career. All I had was a deep-seated desire to be a wife and a mother and to seek education solely from the wooden, patriarchal church pulpit. The idea of searching its history outside the church's correlated material never crossed my mind. My only real struggle with Mormonism as a forty-year-old woman was the social aspect of not fitting in and my distrust of porn-addicted priesthood leaders.

One year after taking our adopted daughter to the temple to have her sealed to us, I began wrestling with my underlying anxiety and depression. I was constantly looking for people and circumstances outside of myself to make me happy. I was obsessed with my weight and appearance, feeling a constant need to shrink and to hide. Stories of men in the church and their addictions continued to find their way into my untrained therapist's ears, and in return my relationship with Mr. Bill was being affected.

I was behaving more as Mr. Bill's mother, constantly nagging and distrusting his time alone rather than conducting myself as a supportive, patient wife. The number of women coming to me with more celestial porn star novels was becoming too overwhelming. It got so out of control, I informed Mr. Bill that if two more women came to me, I would need to see a therapist. Not only were the stories affecting how I viewed my husband, but they were starting to affect how I viewed God. Memories of you and stories of Mormon men collided with my questioning of God being an abusive sex-driven deity.

Within the month, two more women came to me, and as promised, I made an appointment with the bishop to receive a referral for therapy. I had misplaced my temple recommend and longed for nothing more than a meditative experience in the Celestial Room, so meeting with the

Bishop was not just about expressing my reasons for therapy but also to get a new recommend.

Prior to this meeting with the bishop, I had two back-to-back experiences in church that awakened me to just how bad my view of men had become. The first was listening to a Sunday School lesson on Abraham and Isaac. As the teacher described Abraham tying his son to an altar and God's intervention to stop the murder, memories of you holding a knife above me resurfaced.

I felt a panic attack come on as I suddenly found myself relating to Isaac and his fear of someone he loved wanting to kill him. While hyperventilating on this resonation, I questioned for the first time why God would demand Abraham to prove his love through murder. This story was no longer faith-promoting; it instantly became about abuse and manipulation.

In a matter of seconds, a new narrative formed in my head: the Old Testament God was a controlling psychopath whose insecurities needed to be stroked by murdering an innocent child. God was nothing but an invisible crime boss, asking Abraham to kill in order to be initiated into his gang.

One week later, I was attending Relief Society and we were all singing the closing hymn of "I Know that My Redeemer Lives." My eyes were locked on the painting of a resurrected Jesus at the tomb with his beloved Mary. Jesus was reaching toward her and while she was on her knees, she was looking up at him in an imploring and submissive manner. I could not unsee Mary bowing and groveling before her Master.

"Not Jesus, not him too," I thought to myself. Tears

exploded from my eyes as I tried to fight thoughts of Jesus, my Savior, allowing a woman to kneel below him. I tried to will imagery into the artwork that Mary would be invited to stand and be his equal, but it would not come. If Jesus is to understand all human experience, would he not understand how a woman would feel being in such a subordinate position?

I was horrified that I dare question if Jesus could be considering sexual favors from Mary. I do not admit this out of any disrespect toward my family members or those of the Christian faith. I share only to highlight the significance of what sexual trauma can do to the brain. Once I saw Jesus in this way, I knew I needed therapy and I needed it badly.

When I met with the bishop, I found him to be a lovely, kind man, around the same age as I. After spending an hour relating to him my dating experiences, my trauma with you, and the incessant, fifteen-year history of hearing stories of porn addicts, the bishop agreed that I needed therapy.

Not only did he concur, but he also spent time validating the rampant problems with porn in the church and tried to convince me that he was not a part of the problem. He understood my reasons for distrust and claimed I was not the only woman who had come to him with such concerns. When it was time to interview me for the recommend, I was able to answer all fifteen questions, except one.

Question number four asks if we, as members, sustain and uphold the prophet and leaders of the church. I began to confirm my ability to sustain the men in the church, but then paused. I asked the bishop if sustain meant the same as trust, and if he was asking me if I trusted the brethren, then I would have to say no. I reiterated that after everything I had just shared with him, asking me to trust the men was something I could not do at this time.

The bishop took a few moments to think about my answer and said, "I do believe it is the same. For this reason, I cannot give you a recommend. I think it would be best for you to spend several weeks thinking about this and then come back and reevaluate your answer."

I was stunned. After sharing an hour's worth of trauma, my reasons for therapy, and him validating my words and needs, he had denied me entrance into the most holy place in Mormonism. I was the perfect Mormon wife and mother. I was the ideal woman in the church, who served faithfully and who could answer fourteen out of the fifteen questions honorably.

I desperately needed to be in God's home and feel his love. Yet it was Mormon men who had made me feel like my worth lied solely in how I performed in the bedroom, and now it was Mormon men who were denying me entrance into God's presence simply over a lack of trust.

Three days after walking out of the bishop's office, a scandalous story hit the news in Utah. It was alleged that a former MTC Mission President had sexually assaulted and raped a sister missionary under his jurisdiction. Like a maggot on a four-day-old piece of bologna, I perseverated on the story and could not leave it alone.

I knew this kind of behavior happened on a local level, but for something like this to happen this high up the leadership echelon meant that something was terribly wrong.

I had been putting disturbing experiences and questions about the church on my proverbial shelf for years. However, it was the ignominy of this man and his sordid confessions that finally broke my heavy-laden shelf.

It was time. I could no longer go off my past experiences to make sense of Mormonism. I *needed* more, and I knew I needed to dive deep into Mormon history and rewrap my head around the evolution of the Mormon Priesthood power.

A friend who knew I was struggling reached out and asked if I had heard of a document called the *CES Letter*. This was an eighty-page document tackling the major truth claims found in Mormonism. He asked if he could send it to me and I granted him permission. He gave one caveat after he sent the document, and that was to not hate him after I read it.

I promptly downloaded the manuscript and began reading. In less than forty-eight hours, every single truth claim I had testified about as a Mormon missionary had been completely dismantled. The entire Plan of Salvation, Joseph Smith, the Book of Mormon, temple marriage, baptisms for the dead, eternal families, the belief in modern-day prophets and apostles rapidly eroded beneath my feet.

I felt like the Monarch of Fantasia, the childlike empress in the 1980s movie The NeverEnding Story. Like her, I stood quietly in a pile of rubble, wondering how my entire worldview could collapse so swiftly. Surrounded by my shattered beliefs, I looked around and found myself in an absolute state of darkness. I was in a black hole and struggled to catch my breath as I could not seem to find a source of light anywhere.

I attempted to move a piece of rubble titled "Joseph Smith," with the hope of finding a sliver of light glistening from underneath its granite surface. I desperately moved more and more of the crushed pieces of my testimony, but ultimately it was of no use. The light and my former beliefs were entirely gone.

As frightening as this experience was, though, I physically felt the forty-year-old shackles release from my brain. The rustic and heavily chained metal tumbled into the pile of rubble that was once my Mormon testimony.

It took two weeks to work up the courage to tell Mr. Bill that I no longer believed. Ridden with guilt and angst, I was prepared to give him permission to leave me and find a believing Mormon woman with whom he could continue on the covenant path. We had begun our marriage on the foundation of Mormonism, and I did not want to rip it out from underneath him or our children. After sitting down together and sharing the things I had discovered, I said the words that I thought I would never spit out.

"Mr. Bill, I cannot do it anymore. I am done with the church. I no longer believe in any of it," I cried. "You have my permission to leave me, to take the kids and raise them in the church, and I give you my word I will not put up a fight."

Mr. Bill sat in silence, registering the words I had just spoken. Slowly and softly, he exclaimed, "Ginger, if I am being honest, I don't think I have believed for a long time. I really only went along with it for you and the kids. I love you more than I love the church. If you are done, then I am done too."

My dear rapist, hearing Mr. Bill express this level of love was one of the most resplendent moments of my life. Many Mormon marriages fall apart when one spouse confesses a loss of belief. To hear my husband assert that his adulation for me was stronger than his belief system, I knew our road out of Mormonism was going to be slightly less challenging.

Never Yours,
A Mormon Dropout

***

My Dear Rapist,

Though I had expressed my intentions of walking away from the church, I was determined to prove the *CES Letter* wrong and to consider it as nothing more than anti-Mormon propaganda. I made a vow to the faltering God in my head that as I jumped down the Mormon rabbit hole of studying church history, I would continue to abstain from coffee, tea, alcohol, and illegal drugs.

I had no ambition to dress provocatively, no yearning to become a raging slut, and I had no desire to seek out a sordid, raunchy love affair. To my surprise, I still aspired to act Mormon. The one rebellious act I did ponder was the inclination I felt to remove my sacred underwear.

Roughly one week after sharing the news of apostasy with Mr. Bill, I decided to see how it would feel to go into public without donning my garments. I was nervous to run into friends or family that were part of the faith, so I chose to wear a pair of granny panties usually meant for my monthly cycle and a bra, underneath a pair of thick jeans and a large hooded sweatshirt. I found my way into the local Fred Meyer and nervously wandered into the lingerie section of the store. Every few minutes, I lifted my head and anxiously looked around, making sure nobody I knew was watching me pick out a few pairs of nicc, sexy thongs.

After thoughtfully picking out seven pairs, I walked toward the self-checkout stand. I was second in line, and my shifty eyes landed upon five of the last people I wanted to see. Two checkout stands away were Mr. Bill's brother, his wife, and their three children. I was mortified. Do I hide my face so that they could not detect my darkened countenance, or do I cover the whorish panties lying smack dab in the middle of my grocery cart?

I quickly lowered my head, paid for the contraband, and threw them into a brown paper bag. With a face more flushed than Sally Jessy Raphael's red lipstick, I waved to my in-laws from a distance and ran toward the door.

All the humiliation and apprehension I felt in the department store disintegrated as I pulled into my driveway, got out of my car, and walked excitedly into my bedroom.

Feeling a bit mischievous, I pulled down my granny panties and tried on the skimpy floral dental floss. Silent and alone, I stood before my mirror and alternated between feelings of intense libido and vast despondency. I did not recognize the body before me, as I had never visually examined it like this, nor had I ever felt safe to do so. I did not see a celestial porn star staring back at me—I saw a starved and malnourished body that had delivered three amazing children. I saw disgrace, I saw flaws, and I saw it as both a holy object meant to be incessantly clothed and concealed by the garment of the Lord and a body meant to sexually serve men.

Fighting through waves of sexual and spiritual emotion, I chose to remain in the sexual garb until Mr. Bill got home. Upon his arrival, I made sure the kids were entertained and asked my husband to have a conversation with me in the bedroom. Shutting the door, I brought Mr. Bill in for an embrace and assisted him in sliding his hands down the back of my pants.

For the first time in ten years, my husband copped a feel without touching the silken linen of my white, Mormon underwear. In the following three days, I *felt* like an apostate celestial porn star as we navigated a new world of skimpy, seductive thongs.

I'll never forget the first time I snuggled up to Mr. Bill, skin to skin, while falling asleep in each other's arms. Normally after having sex, members are instructed to put the garment immediately back on. Mr. Bill would often ask to admire my body and I rarely, if ever, allowed it. Outside of sexual activity, it felt wrong and shameful to stand naked before my own husband. As a result, the garment remained on until minutes before making love and when it was over, the garment promptly returned to my body again.

Being skin to skin with Mr. Bill reminded me of the times I had held my babies after giving birth to them. The skin-to-skin contact was an indescribable connection of love that reduced my stress, brought healing, and released levels of oxytocin that felt exceptionally therapeutic. While enjoying the transcendental bliss of my husband's naked physical form, I was suddenly struck with a greater light and knowledge—the garment had been much more than a symbol of my commitment to God, it was an incognizant reminder that the church had always come before Mr. Bill and I, even in our bed. In essence, my husband and I had just ended a decade-long threesome with the church.

After three days of feeling like an insurgent hussy, my religious scrupulosity kicked in and I began to feel unprotected and remorseful for removing my garments. I returned them to my body, shoved my new, sexy scanties into a drawer, and spent my time diving deep into the creation and history behind the hallowed, sacrosanct underwear. Once again, out of respect for my loved ones, I will not share the details of what I learned. However, I will not hesitate to say that due to its ties to polygamy, a practice that I do not align with, I knew I could remove them indefinitely and, in so doing, shed my shame and fear of being exposed.

As a forty-year-old woman, I spent the next six months working up the courage to dabble in coffee, tea, and alcohol. I finally got my tattoo, and I officially removed my records from the church. Within six months of my belief system collapsing, the church publicly excommunicated a man who was fighting to protect children from child sex abuse.

This man had fought loudly and boldly as he pleaded for the leaders of the church to wake up to the rampant sex abuse among its members. He did not make the church look good and, as a result, the church openly exiled him, making him a prime example as to why you do not speak out freely and negatively toward the church or its leaders.

With my negative bias and jadedness toward Mormon men, I was horrified the church would ostracize a man who was advocating to keep children safe. In unadulterated anger, I contacted a lawyer to receive help in resigning my membership.

Taking necessary steps to remove one's name from the church can be social suicide among believing family and friends, as it is viewed as a literal spiritual death. When one chooses this route, they are choosing to walk away from their baptismal covenants, temple covenants, marital covenants, and church community. Resignation and excommunication officially breaks the sealing power that ties you to your parents, siblings, grandparents, aunts, uncles, spouse, and children.

All the hard work and effort that my grandparents and parents had put into me, in raising a faithful young Latter-Day Saint, was completely severed in a five-minute online application. My hundred-plus-year religious ancestral bloodline was now butchered, and like Adam and Eve, I was forced to enter into the lone and dreary world.

This decision to resign would not just affect me in this life, but it would send me to Outer Darkness, a place even Hitler was given a chance to avoid through posthumous Mormon baptism.

My dear rapist, the Celestial, Terrestrial, and Telestial Kingdoms were now off the table for me. I had known the truth of Mormonism and denied it. It is taught in Mormon scripture that it would have been better if I had never been born than to deny the Mormon faith. Believing I was more evil than Hitler, my depression and anxiety sent me into an earthly form of Outer Darkness.

Never Yours,
A Daughter of Perdition

***

My Dear Rapist,

Though I had the support of Mr. Bill, in many ways he was not enough. Spiraling into a foreign world with an empty belief system, no community, and strained familial relationships, the only thing I could hold onto was the one thing that I *could* control—my input with food and my output with laxatives. These negative coping mechanisms of anorexia and laxative addiction that you first rendered me into, had now turned up a notch.

I tried my damndest to retain my belief in God and Jesus, but even they were slipping through my fingers. I was desperate for a new perspective and needed to get a break from my cold and isolated world in Alaska. Mr. Bill supported me in taking off for a few weeks to a place I had always dreamed of visiting. My brother, my cousin, my cousin's daughter, and I embarked on an incredible, two-week expedition to Africa. Our plan was to spend one week volunteering in special needs orphanages and schools, and then a final week on a Masai Mara Safari.

My dear rapist, as a privileged, American white girl, nothing could have prepared me for the level of impoverishment and scarcity we witnessed in Africa. One particular orphanage we spent time in was filled with thirty-eight children with cerebral palsy, one child with Down syndrome, and several others with autism.

In the main room, more than a dozen wheelchairs lined the walls, each filled with elementary-aged children and a handful of adults. Just off the main room were several bunk beds, also filled with children with cerebral palsy, but they were lying down on mattresses soaked in their own urine and feces. Cockroaches and bed bugs were visibly crawling all over the wooden bed frames. Down a haunting hallway extending from the main room was a single crib holding an adult woman. With mouth agape, she was covered in drool, crying and reaching for an unseen soul.

The children who were mobile slept on mattresses in the outside shed that also housed the chickens and the cows.Despite the jarring destitution we were witnessing, the children seemed happy. As we engaged with the children, a delightful boy with Down syndrome found a radio and requested we all dance. The children in wheelchairs smiled and clapped along, and those who were able stood up and twisted to the music. One particular teenage boy who was blind simply wanted to be held and loved by anyone who was willing to hold him.

One of my favorite children was a young girl with cerebral palsy who could walk but used limited sign language to communicate. She had clubbed feet and had a difficult time moving around, but she always had a permanent smile on her face. The activity that brought her the most joy was to kick around a flat beach ball in the front yard. I was struck by the ability these children had to find such delight and exultation in life when they had absolutely nothing.

When it came lunch time, the mother of the home inquired if we would help feed the children who were not capable of doing so themselves. I was sitting before a wheelchair-bound boy who could not have been more than ten years old. While waiting for the food to arrive, I pulled out a Tootsie Pop and held it toward his partially opened mouth.

It was apparent he was not aware of what I was holding, so I slowly rolled the sweet American sugar down his thick, protruding tongue. His chocolate brown eyes grew wider and wider as light spilled into his electrified pupils. The precious exhilaration on his beautiful, tender face, over a simple sucker almost broke me.

Ten minutes later, the orphanage mother walked into the room with the food on a medium-sized plate. We were asked to spoon-feed the kids a thick, pasty white porridge. I was not ready to move on from the adorable boy, so I chose to stay with him. Due to the child's tongue thrust, I needed to feed him slowly, as one small spoonful of porridge took at least thirty seconds for him to work through. A few of the other children began to cry as they noticed the porridge, but there were not enough hands to assist in getting the food into their starving bellies.

Believing I could multitask, I stood up from my chair and took one small step to my right, moving toward another boy waiting to be fed. In doing this, I ignorantly moved the plate of food away from the first boy. A swift but piercing shriek escaped his partially porridge-filled throat. I quickly turned my head back toward the boy, and the anguish in his alarmed and panicked eyes was undeniable. Without speaking a single word, the boy communicated to me his terror at the thought of his meal being taken away.

In this moment, the boy's shrill cry obliterated any remaining belief I had in the Mormon God. How could I be like Jesus and consider the lilies of the field, when God himself did not seem to be considering this helpless, orphaned boy with cerebral palsy?

These children were the most vulnerable of the most vulnerable. They had no parents, no birth certificate, no age, and no identity. They had no access to healthy food or clean water. They lived in their stained and soiled clothing while slumbering with bed bugs, fleas, cattle, and chickens. They could not speak and they could not walk. They were completely and utterly helpless. The one thing they could do was cry and scream when a sloppy plate of porridge moved away from their parched and empty stomachs. There was no God here. There was no God anywhere.

Holding my breath, I set the plate of food down and ran toward the door. Halfway between the house and the gray bricked fence, I paused and closed my eyes. Bent over, I freed the heavy, pent-up air from my chest, and with its release, sobs of despair and heartache bellowed out of my foggy, hazel eyes. God was gone. He had dissolved, vaporized, and altogether dissipated in a matter of three seconds.

I traveled to Africa to gain a fresh start and find a new perspective. Losing belief in the author and finisher of the Christian faith was the last thing I had expected in a Kenyan orphanage.

After taking several minutes to grieve and find my breath, I composed myself enough to walk back inside and finish feeding the boy. I sat and slowly fed him his porridge, but struggled to stay present.

Internally, I was crying out, recognizing my ignorance in believing that a white man in the sky would someday fix this level of poverty and inhumanity. Where was the justice and the relief for the boy in *this* life? Why would God answer the prayers for those looking for a lost set of keys in Utah but not ease the agony of a starving, disabled orphan boy in Africa?

Millions upon millions of questions began to fill the space in my head where God had just resided. Though my brain was becoming like the thick, mushy porridge that I was feeding to the boy, one illuminating thought continuously shone through the muck. I was beginning to see a harsh reality; my religion had kept me complacent in easing world suffering. Saying a prayer simply puts the burden on an unseen being in another world, another life.

I suddenly began feeling resolute in one thing: I needed to get off my white, ex-Mormon ass and start alleviating the oppressed and downtrodden in this life.

We left the orphanage changed. Saying goodbye to the children in this particular home was difficult beyond comprehension. While the kids exhibited a heightened level of joy to have a small group of American women love on them, we could not negate the profound level of impoverishment they were living in. The three of us held it together until we left the property. The moment we stepped foot onto the dirt road, we each systematically fell apart. Lost in our own world of vast despondency, we walked in silence while we waited for the arrival of our Matatu.

After a clean shower and a nice, cooked meal, I climbed into bed and was plagued with thoughts of why I, an Alaskan American girl, had been born with so much privilege. It didn't seem fair, and it bothered me to the point that I could not sleep. My new friend Diane was also vexed by the orphanage visit, so we lay awake talking about anything and everything that was troubling our hearts and minds. The conversation naturally flowed into her sharing experience with domestic abuse and I sharing my experience with you.

My dear rapist, for the first time in thirteen years, I opened up and described the full details of your torture with a woman I had only known for a week. Just as I questioned where justice was for the starving, wheelchair bound boy, I began to question for the first time where justice was for myself, the girl who was raped and abused by an Olympic athlete. Is it a coincidence that the day God evanesced from my life, I fully opened up about you? Or could it be that being 10,000 miles away from you, I finally felt safe and free to loosen my stifled tongue?

Perplexed by these questions, I eventually fell asleep with three ruminations on my mind. First, I thought of the poverty-stricken orphans. Second, there was my newfound and frightening atheism. Third, that the doctrine of one standing before the judgment of God someday was merely a myth.

Never Yours,
Agnostic in Africa

***

My Dear Rapist,

Morning came and it was time to prepare for our three-day safari to the Maasai Mara National Reserve. We had roughly 170 miles of travel in a specialized white safari van, and it would take approximately six hours to get there. I made sure to pack my white-lace temple skirt in my belongings, in the hopes that I could wear it while watching the sunrise over the Maasai Mara.

Holding the skirt in my hands, I reflected on the commitment I had made to myself after departing Mormonism. Out of respect to the faith, I had cut up my holy garments before disposing of them and had given the remaining temple attire to my sister. I chose to hold onto the temple skirt, and I was determined that I would adorn it around the world in places where *I* deemed heaven to be.

The first time I wore it outside the temple walls was in the Hawaiian ocean. A few months before traveling to Africa, Mr. Bill and I had taken the kids to Hawaii. With our feet planted in the soft, wet sand, I stood holding hands with my husband and four children. Looking out at the horizon, we had seen glorious iridescent colors of oranges, reds, and yellows.

With the music of the ocean moving across the ground, I felt a transcendental divine presence as I breathed in the elegance of our tropical surroundings. These ethereal moments with my family did not require a ten percent tithe or a command to abstain from coffee, tea, and alcohol. There was no necessity for an interview or a signed recommend from a pious Mormon man who scarcely knew me. Sacred handshakes, the veiling of my face, and not a single brick-and-mortar building was keeping me from having access to my family. *This* was Heaven. *This* was Sacred. *This* was Holy.

As I folded the skirt and placed it into my safari bag, my thoughts drifted from the Pacific Ocean and back to the helpless disabled boy who had stolen my heart. Had I known God would leave me less than twenty-four hours ago, I would have worn my consecrated piece of linen to the orphanage.

Though the home wasn't exactly what one would define as heaven, the children who belonged in it did generate a degree of sacredness and reverence that I had never felt before. In my new eyes, their home was a hallowed piece of ground, and it lit an inner awakening that I needed to be more like Jesus and devote my time to the marginalized and oppressed.

The long Maasai Mara road trip allowed for a significant amount of time to process past, present, and future perspectives. I could not stop thinking about you, and like the natural wonder of Kenya's Great Rift Valley, images of you escaping a mythical judgment day danced within my brain. My mind would not rest. Even as we passed by sheep and cattle herders in the small town of Narok and drove down rough dirt roads that led to traditional Maasai villages, thoughts constantly alternated between holding you accountable and my growing schism in agnosticism. Occasionally, herds of zebras and giraffes would bring me back to reality and I would take in the magnificent and awe-inspiring animals native to this part of Africa.

Before reaching our base camp, we stopped at a Maasai Mara village and experienced firsthand interaction with men and women of the tribe. Dressed in traditional red robes called the Shuka, the men led us on a tour of their circular, loaf-shaped homes. The huts were made up of cow dung, mud, sticks, and sand. After touring the homes, the women pulled out an abundance of their vibrant handmade beaded jewelry in the hopes we would purchase some of their ornamental work.

The men offered to sell the jewelry straight off their own bodies, which mainly consisted of beaded necklaces with a lion's tooth at the center. Once we were finished garnering jewelry for souvenirs, the men gathered together in a straight line and began to perform tribal songs and dance. This performance was one of the highlights of my entire African experience.

Spending time among the Maasai Mara village was the first time I had witnessed a patriarchal system outside of Mormonism. This was not National Geographic through my television, but indigenous history in real time. It was surreal to see the aboriginal elders of the tribe standing by, quiet and aloof, but still obviously in charge. I loved recognizing that the white man had not yet colonized this area and that the Maasai people still owned their own culture, heritage, and religious beliefs. Nonetheless, seeing polygamy as part of their system was very unsettling to me. I wanted to stay respectful and not cause drama, but I ached to pull the women aside and ask if they were safe or if abuse was rampant in their lives. I was just a white girl from the United States; was it even my place to consider this? Their practice of polygamy became even more startling when a Maasai man later entered our tent camp, requesting marriage from a member of our group.

The women of the Maasai Mara tribe unknowingly planted a seed of feminism in my heart. While I knew I could not shove my entitled, Westernized ideals down their throats, it was the first time I realized that women were being oppressed in other religions and countries around the world. I was incredibly disappointed in myself that it had taken forty years to wake up to the phallocentric world I was living in. Did the power of the penis really shape and guide the social constructs of all society?

What the hell was happening to me in Africa? Not only was I seeing the authority of the phallus running the human world, but now I was about to see it in the animal world. How did I miss the lessons in school and in the movie *The Lion King*, portraying patriarchy among magnificent beasts like Mufasa, Simba, and Nala? More and more questions were accumulating into the heretic corners of my psyche, including subjects that contradict religious faith: science and evolution.

The following morning, we were required to wake up early for our safari of searching after what early game hunters called the Big Five. Reverently, I pulled out my white skirt and carefully stepped into it. In the dimly lit tent, an old mirror hung next to the toilet. Behind me were four beds with white mosquito netting strung above them. The others in my group had already left for breakfast, giving me time to be with my thoughts regarding the sacred adventure we were about to embark on.

I had dreamed of Africa as a child and again as a young adult. I begged God to send me to Africa for my Mormon mission, but he had ignored my prayer. Just two weeks before departing for Africa, I had received official word that my resignation from the Mormon church had been approved. Is it possible that God knew if he had sent me to Africa as a twenty-one-year-old, I would have abandoned him then? Did I need to apostatize from Mormonism and then come to Africa to wake up to my white privilege and white savior complex?

My short time in the country was giving me major shifts in perspective. Yes, I wanted to discover new convictions, but God slipping out of my hands and waking up to a phallocentric world was not something I realized I would need.

Climbing into the safari van with my celestial skirt fitted around my waist, I was finally being forced to see that not only was I an agnostic apostate, but I was now becoming the type of woman that threatens Mormonism: a bitter, insurgent feminist. Entering into the national preserve, I rested quietly in the corner of the van until the orange sun began to hint of its coming presence. Standing up, we each placed the upper half of our bodies outside the roof of the van.

Grounding myself, I rubbed my hands up and down my laced skirt and watched the rousing desert sky turn to an array of purples, pinks, oranges, reds, and yellows. Off in the distance, the trees were shadowed in deep black, making this sunset one of the most heavenly sights my eyes had been privileged to see. In the Celestial room of the Temple, it is common to close one's eyes and seek inwardly for God. Yet in the wilds of Africa, my eyes were wide open, and divinity was making a visible appearance around me.

Confused, I began trying to make meaning of who or what the Divine was. As our safari tour moved forward, my curiosity became even more alive as we had a front row seat to herds of wild elephants, lions, leopards, cape buffalo, rhinoceros, hyenas, and cheetahs. One spectacular experience gave us the opportunity to see a lion chase after a lioness, grunting and pleading for her to mate with him.

The lioness wanted nothing to do with the bastard, but the piece of shit lion would not give up. Ultimately, the lioness gave in and allowed the lion to climb on top of her and do his thing. Obviously, its persistence made me think of you, dear rapist. I resonated with the lioness and her unheard signals, but also with her exasperation of not being able to get rid of her predator. Why the hell did I have to see you and your dominance in this moment? I came to Africa to get away from you, not be reminded of you.

While we watched the lion conquer his prey, the tour guide informed us that a lion would mate with fourteen different lionesses before going back to stay with its original mate. I was livid. Damn it to hell, why was I just learning that lions were polygamists and were also not capable of keeping their penises tucked away in their hides?

The themes of patriarchy and dominance continued

to thrust their ugly testicles into my face. I sat in the safari van, silently questioning the animal kingdom and the human world and why it was driven by patriarchy and sex. I wondered if this meant that the Mormon church could actually be right. Was eternity truly dominated by an omnipotent, phallocentric God who continued to generate spiritual offspring with billions of his wives? The chase and the conquer of this predatory lion, smashing his defeated lioness, gave me much angst as I realized that losing God in Africa had brought on too many tormented thoughts of you.

My dear rapist, I did not have these answers then, but I left Africa knowing one thing: I was a white-privileged, uneducated woman and I wanted nothing more than to shed my ignorance and pursue a secular education. After forty years of acquiring knowledge solely from antiquated scripture and Mormon men, it was time that I began to study from the most brilliant minds in human history.

Several significant things were left behind in Africa, and I have never had a desire to go back and retrieve them. First, I symbolically buried my vision of a Sean Connery-type Mormon God into the dirt at a special needs orphanage. This white, gray-haired, resurrected man with a thousand wives was now dead to me. God went extinct in the shrill cry of a helpless boy. The light in my eyes dimmed, not from sin, but from identifying God's absence in an orphanage filled with some of the world's most vulnerable, impoverished children.

Next, I buried the belief in the Maasai Mara that the power and perspective of the penis was the only way to manage the world. I was done adhering to the Old Testament belief that a woman's voice was second to a man's. I knew that I, along with all other women around the world, had every right to open my mouth and speak out. I didn't know how and I didn't know when, but I knew my days of remaining a quiet, subservient woman were coming to an end.

Finally, I allowed the belief of a futuristic judgment day with God to be swallowed up by the bloat of hippopotami in the Mara River. At the time, it did not register that the dissolution of this belief would eventually lead me to confronting you. However, what it did do was wake me up to the need to advocate for change in this life and not wait for a mythical day to resolve the injustices of our world.

I arrived home to Alaska ready to be with my children, ready to register for school, and ready to create new beginnings with Mr. Bill and our children. I applied to the University of Alaska and declared a Bachelor of Nursing major with the goal of becoming a forensic nurse. My intentions were to be a voice and a liaison for women and children who have endured abuse, sexual assault, and rape.

My dear rapist, little did I know that my pursuit of nursing was not going to be about nursing others back to health. On the contrary, the journey would be about nursing myself back to health and advocating for my own right for justice.

I did not fully comprehend how scary and debilitating the road would be. At times, pining for death felt so much easier than fighting for justice. But like the divine presence in the African safari sunrise, an unseen power full of love and grace delivered you right into my hands. Losing my former, ignorant view of God brought about a unique knowing, similar to the one I had felt with Mr. Bill and my youngest daughter. This knowledge of pursuing justice put the power back into my hands and with this power, a discovery of radical self-love and forgiveness rose like the magnificent African sun.

I am coming for you, and the end result may not be what the world deems worthy or inspiring, but this budding feminist spirit does not give two fucks. For all I care, the world can take their definition of worthy, just like an Old Testament virtuous ruby, and shove it up their asses. For me, the inspiration in my story is found in the simple fact that I am alive to tell it, and that one day, my children will have autographed copies of their mother's narrative of what it was like to confront her rapist.

With a secretly recorded phone call, you are mine.
An Empowered Survivor

AFTERWORD

As I finalize this first compilation of letters, I stand in awe at the frightful and challenging odyssey that led me back to *My Dear Rapist*. Reflecting on this, and the past thirteen years of living in Alaska, I cannot help but honor all that has been lost. When Mr. Bill accepted the opportunity to move here, I believed we were going to establish roots in the Last Frontier and have an adventure of a lifetime. It takes a tough woman to live in this vast, rugged wilderness, but I felt it especially daring to attempt a 3,000-mile move from a loving familial support system.

What I have come to realize is that I am a persistent and courageous woman, not from surviving a harsh world like Alaska. I am resilient because I finally faced my fears of confronting My Rapist. The exploration of uncharted territory was never meant for the Alaskan frontier, it was meant for the quest and conquer of my own apparitions.

Though Mr. Bill and I have built a beautiful life with four amazing children, it took losing a religion, an entire world view, God, community, health, and strained and lost relationships, to come face to face with my barren and vacated self. For some, perhaps losing everything means the loss of financial stability and wealth, but for me, losing everything meant losing what I have always held close to my heart: my religion and my relationships.

By being completely and utterly alone, this journey to *My Dear Rapist* gave me the ability to uncover answers on how to live a life on the other side of religion and trauma. These answers were not found in anyone or anything beyond me but were revealed deep within the walls of my broken and dilapidated soul.

Accessing the Divine on this journey has not required a tithe, rejecting certain foods, or permission to enter a holy building. I have discovered that this sacred power naturally dwells inside the heart, the mind, and the epicenter of the nucleus of every cell within our body. It does not matter what this power looks like, what gender it is, or which racial and social class it belongs too. What matters is that we live every day of our lives knowing that we *all* have access to it, simply because we exist.

The real journey for us all is to discover how to individually tap into its energy, as well as surrender to the belief that the word worthy has no place in the Divine's existence. Surely, at times we will be too deep into our traumas, negative coping mechanisms, sorrows, and shame to even recognize the Divine's energy within us.

However, it is not possible for it to ever depart us because it is tethered to our very essence. I have come to believe that the Divine is not so much about testing humanity but more about supporting and encouraging the individual innovations that we are capable of creating, from every experience that humanity thrusts upon us.

Justice does not always come in the form we envision and in which we long for. Most victims will never have the privilege of seeing their rapist or abuser behind bars, let alone be given the gift of confrontation. What victims can have hope for is the possibility of healing, empowerment, and peace. The quest for these rests solely upon the victim's timeline, and when it comes to forgiveness, no one, not even God, has the right to declare when and if forgiveness is available.

A victim should always have the right to fight for justice and accountability, even if the victim extends forgiveness toward the perpetrator. It is possible for one to hold space for forgiveness and a fight for justice.

The legal definition of rape is defined by the Office of Public Affairs as "the penetration, **no matter how slight**, of the vagina or anus with any body part or object, or oral penetration by a sex organ of another person, without the consent of the victim."

Criminal charges will more than likely never happen to My Dear Rapist because I did not pause the rape and measure his level of penetration. In the recorded confrontation, he admitted to joking about being halfway in but claimed it was a joke and nothing more, allowing him to walk away a free man. Though some may not believe me and claim he does not deserve the title of rapist, I will tell any critic to fuck off. He didn't just rape me physically; he raped me mentally, spiritually, and emotionally.

He raped my joy, my health, my laughter, and my innocence. Perhaps only a victim will understand this sentiment, but rape will always extend much deeper and broader than a vagina.

I am often asked why I went back to my rapist. As I have had time to reflect on this question I can offer

three main reasons: fear, desperation, and not trusting my
own inner voice. In Mormonism, women are, in some
ways, taught to *not* trust their own thoughts and feelings.
Confirmation for life's major choices generally come through
the hierarchy of our fathers, grandfathers, husbands, bishops,
stake presidents, the prophet and apostles, Jesus, and God.
As women in the church, we lean heavily on the intuition
and inspiration from those who hold the priesthood power.

This practice, though taught under doctrinal good
intentions, does nothing but harm women and halt their
process of learning to trust themselves. Women naturally
talk themselves out of emotional and stressful situations
because we tend to believe what society tells us: we are
crazy and irrational. Add on a patriarchal system that divine
and authoritative answers mainly come through men, and
this inability to trust ourselves deepens even more. Instead of
asking women why they react to abuse and rape in different
ways, maybe it is time we ask, why do men abuse and why
do men rape?

Ultimately, I did find a way to forgive my rapist,
but it did not come by laying the trauma at Jesus's feet or
through the hierarchy of a priesthood power. Thanks to the
Divine, the true gift came through laying the burdens of rape
and abuse at the feet of My Dear Rapist himself. By being
given the gift of confrontation, I have now placed the weight
of his actions at his athletic feet and I have now freed myself
from his sixteen-year oppression.

I look forward to chronicling my next set of letters.
These impending missives will provide an up close and
personal view into the Divine reuniting of an Olympic

athlete and an apostate Mormon traitress. These writings will expose a fight for life, a battle for health, and the achievement of peace and lasting freedom.

Freedom has been *this* survivor's form of justice. Completing this first book of letters finally closed the door on being a victim. I have now stepped over the rainbow and can see the world through the eyes of a survivor.

When all is said and done, I am certain of one thing: I will leave this world filled with peace, but My Dear Rapist will leave this world in fear.

Oh, how the tide has turned.
In all that has been lost, I have finally been found.

ACKNOWLEDGEMENTS

Writing this book has been incredibly heavy and emotionally taxing. This has not only affected me, but it has affected many of my family and friends. For these reasons, I want to first and foremost acknowledge my husband and his unyielding support and encouragement. From the first day I met Mr. Bill, he has been my sturdy, constant oak tree and that has never changed. He continues to push me to overcome my fears, and publishing this book has been one of those fears.

Second, my mother. My beautiful, Mormon mother has done nothing but reinforce the notion that as a woman, I have every right to share what is in my heart and to not let fear get in the way of speaking my truth.

I especially want to recognize the many loved ones, both professional and personal, who have taken the time to read and review *My Dear Rapist* prior to publication so that I could get these writings as perfectly polished as possible.

A ginormous thank you to my Alaskan editor and book coach, Joanne Haines, with Shelf Life Editorial. I especially appreciate Joanne's willingness to meet over coffee and for her enthusiasm in ensuring that my story gets published. Also, my editor, Ana Hansen with Sparks Editorial. Her gift of time and in-depth perspective was beyond generous and priceless. My Book Cover and Design

Artist, Juniper Hartmann with The Red Fox Creative. Junie's turnaround time and additional help with publishing has been phenomenal.

Last, but not least, a big thank you to my children, my friends, and my family who have encouraged and supported me through this entire process of learning how to transfer buried trauma to words and then onto paper. I am a blessed woman and I am beyond thankful for all of the love and support that has been extended my way.

AUTHOR BIO

Ginger Price is a stay-at-home mom who resonates with women from all walks of life who have survived gender- or religious-based violence and rape. For forty years she believed the only education she needed was from the patriarchal pulpit of her 200-year-old ancestral religion.

When her buried trauma came back to the surface after suppressing it for sixteen years, she was forced to confront the lasting effects of rape and abuse. Part of her healing started when she decided to write letters to her rapist. It is through these writings that she was able to discover her voice and her power that led to radical self-love.

With the unexpected dissolution of her Mormon faith, Ginger began pursuing an education and the dream of a career outside the home. She recently achieved an Associates of Arts degree through the University of Alaska and is now working toward a Bachelor of Communication, with a minor in Women and Gender Studies. She feels most fulfilled when she meets other survivors who have turned their trauma into advocacy and champion the safety of women and children.

Today she lives and writes from an Alaskan home tucked in snow-covered birch, spruce, and cottonwood trees. Her family includes four beautiful children, a twelve-pound Maltipoo, and a handsome, loving husband who has been supportive and encouraging of her recovery. She is working on a second manuscript in the same letter format as My Dear Rapist that highlights her journey through the legal system, the two-hour secret recorded phone call with her rapist, the quest for healing, and details on how Ginger was able to finally forgive her abuser.

THANK
YOU
FOR
READING

www.ingramcontent.com/pod-product-compliance
Lightning Source LLC
Chambersburg PA
CBHW021953130726
47903CB00014B/1276